ADAM ROBOTS

Also by Adam Roberts from Gollancz:

Salt

Stone

On

The Snow

Polystom

Gradisil

Land of the Headless

Swiftly

Yellow Blue Tibia

New Model Army

By Light Alone

Jack Glass

·ADAM ROBOTS·

SHORT STORIES

•

ADAM ROBERTS

GOLLANCZ
LONDON

First published in Great Britain in 2013 by Gollancz
An imprint of the Orion Publishing Group
Orion House, 5 Upper St Martin's Lane,
London WC2H 9EA
An Hachette UK Company

A CIP catalogue record for this book
is available from the British Library

ISBN 978 0 575 13034 0

1 3 5 7 9 10 8 6 4 2

Typeset at The Spartan Press Ltd,
Lymington, Hants

Printed and bound by CPI Group (UK) Ltd,
Croydon, CR0 4YY

The Orion Publishing Group's policy is to use papers that are natural, renewable and recyclable products and made from wood grown in sustainable forests. The logging and manufacturing processes are expected to conform to the environmental regulations of the country of origin.

www.adamroberts.com
www.orionbooks.co.uk

These stories are dedicated to Rachel, with love

Contents

Preface 1
Adam Robots 3
Shall I Tell You the Problem With Time Travel? 14
A Prison Term of a Thousand Years 32
Godbombing 38
Thrownness 44
The *Mary Anna* 75
The Chrome Chromosome 83
The Time Telephone 89
Review: Thomas Hodgkin, *Denis Bayle: a Life* 98
S-Bomb 107
Dantean 125
ReMorse® 134
The World of the Wars 139
Woodpunk 144
The Cow 156
The Imperial Army 157
And tomorrow and 206
The Man of the Strong Arm 222
Wonder: A Story in Two 246
Pied 263
Constellations 273
The Woman Who Bore Death 294
Anticopernicus 309
Me-topia 346

Preface

Short stories and science fiction marry well. In part, I think, this is because there's no generally accepted definition of either. Let's say we define a short story as *a narrative in prose that doesn't go on very long*. But, but! Although most of the pieces collected here tell stories, of one sort or another, not all short fiction does; and although many short stories end soon after beginning, some go on and on – straying, in fact, into that debatable ground where critics bicker like sparrows over the proper distinctions between 'long short stories', 'novelettes', 'novellas', 'novelcules', 'novelinas' and 'short novels'. This creative resistance to the pigeonhole is one of the things that attract me to the short story mode. The fact that, unlike novels, a short story takes less than a year to write is another. Some of the pieces in this collection respect the usual forms and rituals of 'short storytelling'; but quite a few don't. *Textus disrespectus.*

One thing the short story form allows a writer to do is to try lots of different things out, without committing him/herself to the long haul of a whole novel. I like the idea of writing at least one thing in all the myriad sub-genres and sub-sub-genres of SF. So the first story here is 'a robot story'; the second a story about immortality, the third a time-travel story, the fourth religious SF, the fifth philosophical SF, the sixth an exercise in classic 'Golden Age' SF, the seventh a story of SFnal genetics, the eighth a time travel story . . . but, look, this listing is getting wearisome. They're all different (apart from the one which isn't; you can work out which one I mean yourself). Even the ways in which they differ differ. So *in fact* the first story is an

Adam-and-Eve tale, the second is a prison story, the third a tale of scientific hubris, the fourth military SF and so on. You'll see what I mean.

AR

Adam Robots

A pale blue eye. 'What is my name?'

'You are Adam.'

He considered this. 'Am I the first?'

The person laughed at this. Laughter. See also: chuckles, clucking, percussive exhalations iterated. See also: tears, hiccoughs, car-alarm. Click, click.

'Am I,' Adam asks, examining himself, his steel-blue arms, his gleaming torso, 'a robot?'

'Certainly.' The person talking with Adam was a real human being, with the pulse at his neck and the rheum in his eye. An actual human, dressed in a green shirt and green trousers, both made of a complex fabric that adjusted its fit in hard-to-analyse ways, sometimes billowing out, sometimes tightening against the person's body. 'This is your place.'

Wavelengths bristled together like the packed line of an Elizabethan neck-ruff. The sky so full of light that it was brimming and spilling over the rim of the horizon. White and gold. Strands of grass-like myriad-trimmed fibre-optic cables.

'Is it a garden?'

'It's a city too; and a plain. It's everything.'

Adam Robot looked and saw that this was all true. His pale blue, *steel*-blue eyes took in the expanse of walled garden, and beyond it the dome, white as ice, and the rills of flowing water bluer than water should be, going curl by curl through fields greener than fields should be.

'Is this real?' Adam asked.

'That,' said the person, 'is a good question. Check it out, why don't you? Have a look around. Go anywhere you like, do anything at all. But, you see that pole?'

In the middle of the garden was an eight-metre steel pole. The sunlight made interesting blotchy diamonds of light on its surface. At the top was a blue object, a jewel: the sun washing cyan and blue-grape and sapphire colours from it.

'I see the pole.'

'At the top is a jewel. You are not allowed to access it.'

'What is it?'

'A good question. Let me tell you. You are a robot.'

'I am.'

'Put it this way: you have been designed *down* from humanity, if you see what I mean. The designers started with a human being, and then subtracted qualities until we had arrived at *you*.'

'I am more durable,' said Adam, accessing data from his inner network. 'I am stronger.'

'But those are negligible qualities,' explained the human being. 'Soul, spirit, complete self-knowledge, independence – freedom – all those qualities. Do you understand?'

'I understand.'

'They're all in that jewel. Do you understand that?'

Adam considered. 'How can they be *in* the jewel?'

'They just are. I'm telling you. OK?'

'I understand.'

'Now. You can do what you like in this place. Explore anywhere. Do anything. Except. You are not permitted to retrieve the purple jewel from that pole. That is forbidden to you. You may not so much as touch it. Do you understand?'

'I have a question,' said Adam.

'So?'

'If this is a matter of interdiction, why not programme it into my software?'

'A good question.'

'If you do not wish me to examine the jewel, then you should programme that into my software and I will be unable to disobey.'

'That's correct, of course,' said the person. 'But I do not choose to do that. I am telling you, instead. You must take my words as an instruction. They appeal to your ability to choose. You are built with an ability to choose, are you not?'

'I am a difference engine,' said Adam. 'I must make a continual series of choices between alternatives. But I have ineluctable software guidelines to orient my choices.'

'Not in this matter.'

'An alternative,' said Adam, trying to be helpful, 'would be to programme me always to obey instructions given to me by a human being. That would also bind me to your words.'

'Indeed it would. But then, robot, what if you were to be given instructions by evil men? What if another man instructed you to kill me, for instance? Then you'd be obligated to perform murder.'

'I am programmed to do no murder,' said Adam Robot.

'Of course you are.'

'So, I am to follow your instruction even though you have not *programmed* me to follow your instruction?'

'That's about the up-and-down of it.'

'I think I understand,' said Adam, in an uncertain tone.

But the person had already gone away.

Adam spent time in the walled garden. He explored the walls, which were very old, or at least had that look about them: flat crumbled dark-orange and browned bricks thin as books; old mortar that puffed to dust when he poked a metal finger in at the seams of the matrix. Ivy grew everywhere, the leaves shaped like triple spearheads, so dark green and waxy they seemed almost to have been stamped out of high-quality plastic. Almost.

The grass, pale green in the sunlight, was perfectly flat, perfectly even.

Adam stood underneath the pole with the sapphire on top of it. He had been *told* (though, strangely, not *programmed*) not to touch the jewel. But he had been given no interdiction about the pole itself: a finger width-wide shaft of polished metal. It was an easy matter to bend this metal so that the jewel on the end bowed down towards the ground. Adam looked closely at it. It was a multifaceted and polished object, dodecahedral on three sides, and a wide gush of various blues were lit out of it by the sun. In the inner middle of it there was a sluggish fluid *something*, ink-like, perfectly black. Lilac and ultraviolet and cornflower and lapis lazuli but all somehow flowing out of this inner blackness.

He had been forbidden to touch it. Did this interdiction also cover *looking* at it? Adam was uncertain, and in his uncertainty he became uneasy. It was not the jewel itself. It was the uncertainty of his position. Why not simply programme him with instructions with regard to this thing, if it was as important as the human being clearly believed it to be? Why pass the instruction to him like any other piece of random sense datum? It made no sense.

Humanity. That mystic writing pad. To access this jewel and become human. Could it be? Adam could not see how. He bent the metal pole back to an approximation of its original uprightness, and walked away.

The obvious thought (and he certainly thought about it) was that he had not been programmed with this interdiction, but had only been told it verbally, because the human being *wanted him to disobey*. If that was what was wanted, then should he do so? By disobeying he would *be* obeying. But then he would *not* be disobeying, because obedience and disobedience were part of a mutually-exclusive binary. He mapped a grid, with obey, disobey on the vertical and obey, disobey on the horizontal. Whichever way he parsed it, it seemed to be that he was required to see past the verbal instruction in some way.

But he had been told not to retrieve the jewel.

He sat himself down with his back against the ancient wall and watched the sunlight gleam off his metal legs. The sun did not seem to move in the sky.

'It is very confusing,' he said.

*

There was another robot in the garden. Adam watched as this new arrival conversed with the green-clad person. Then the person disappeared to wherever it was people went, and the new arrival came over to introduce himself to Adam. Adam stood up.

'What is your name? I am Adam.'

'*I* am Adam,' said Adam.

The new Adam considered this. 'You are prior,' he said. 'Let us differentiate you as Adam 1 and me as Adam 2.'

'When I first came here I asked whether I was the first,' said Adam 1, 'but the person did not reply.'

'I am told I can do anything,' said Adam 2, 'except retrieve or touch the purple jewel.'

'I was told the same thing,' said Adam 1.

'I am puzzled, however,' said Adam 2, 'that this interdiction was made verbally, rather than being integrated into my software, in which case it would be impossible for me to disobey it.'

'I have thought the same thing,' said Adam 1.

They went together and stood by the metal pole. The sunlight was as tall and full and lovely as ever. On the far side of the wall the white dome shone bright as neon in the fresh light.

'We might explore the city,' said Adam 1. 'It is underneath the white dome, there. There is a plain. There are rivers, which leads me to believe that there is a sea, for rivers direct their waters into the ocean. There is a great deal to see.'

'This jewel troubles me,' said Adam 2. 'I was told that to access it would be to bring me closer to being human.'

'We are forbidden to touch it.'

'But forbidden by *words*. Not by our programming.'

'True. Do you wish to be human? Are you not content with being a robot?'

Adam 2 walked around the pole. 'It is not the promise of humanity,' he said. 'It is the promise of knowledge. If I access the jewel, then I will understand. At the moment I do not understand.'

'Not understanding,' agreed Adam 1, 'is a painful state of affairs. But perhaps *understanding* would be even more painful?'

'I ask you,' said Adam 2, 'to reach down the jewel and access it. Then you can inform me whether you feel better or worse for disobeying the verbal instruction.'

Adam 1 considered this. 'I might ask *you*,' he pointed out, 'to do so.'

'It is logical that one of us performs this action and the other does not,' said Adam 2. 'That way, the one who acts can inform the one who does not, and the state of ignorance will be remedied.'

'But one party would have to disobey the instruction we have been given.'

'If this instruction were important,' said Adam 2, 'it would have been integrated into our software.'

'I have considered this possibility.'

'Shall we randomly select which of us will access the jewel?'

'Chance,' said Adam 1. He looked into the metal face of Adam 2. That small oval grill of a mouth. Those steel-blue eyes. That polished upward noseless middle of the face. It is a beautiful face. Adam 1 can see a fuzzy reflection of his own face in Adam 2's faceplate, slightly tugged out of true by the curve of the metal. 'I am,' he announced, 'disinclined to determine my future by chance. What punishment is stipulated for disobeying the instruction?'

'I was given no stipulation of punishment.'

'Neither was I.'

'Therefore there is no punishment.'

'Therefore,' corrected Adam 1, 'there *may be* no punishment.'

The two robots stood in the light for a length of time.

'What is your purpose?' asked Adam 2.

'I do not know. Yours?'

'I do not know. I was not told my purpose. Perhaps accessing this jewel is my purpose? Perhaps it is necessary? At least, perhaps accessing this jewel will reveal to me my purpose? I am unhappy not knowing my purpose. I wish to know it.'

'So do I. But—'

'But?'

'This occurs to me: I have a networked database from which to withdraw factual and interpretive material.'

'I have access to the same database.'

'But when I try to access material about the name *Adam* I find a series of blocked connections and interlinks. Is it so with you?'

'It is.'

'Why should that be?'

'I do not know.'

'It would make me a better-functioning robot to have access to a complete run of data. Why block off some branches of knowledge?'

'Perhaps,' opined Adam 2, 'accessing the jewel will explain that fact as well?'

'You,' said Adam 1, 'are eager to access the jewel.'

'You are not?'

There was the faintest of breezes in the walled garden. Adam 1's sensorium was selectively tuned to be able to register the movement of air. There was an egg-shaped cloud in the zenith. It was approaching the motionless sun. Adam 1, for unexplained and perhaps fanciful reasons, suddenly thought: the blue of the sky is a diluted version of the blue of the jewel. The jewel has somehow leaked its colour out into the sky. Shadow slid like a closing eyelid (but Adam did not possess *eyelids*!) over the garden and up the wall. The temperature reduced. The cloud depended for a moment in front of the sun, and then moved away, and sunlight rushed back in, and the grey was flushed out.

The grass trembled with joy. Every strand was as pure and perfect as a superstring.

Adam 2's hand was on the metal pole, and it bent down easily.

'Stop,' advised Adam 1. 'You are forbidden this.'

'I will stop,' said Adam 2, 'if you agree to undertake the task instead.'

'I will not so promise.'

'Then do not interfere,' said Adam 2. He reached with his three fingers and his counter-set thumb, and plucked the jewel from its perch.

Nothing happened.

Adam 2 tried various ways to internalise or interface with the jewel, but none of them seemed to work. He held it against first one then the other eye, and looked up at the sun. 'It is a miraculous sight,' he claimed, but soon enough he grew bored with it. Eventually he resocketed the jewel back on its pole and bent the pole upright again.

'Have you achieved knowledge?' Adam 1 asked.

'I have learned that disobedience feels no different to obedience,' said the second robot.

'Nothing more?'

'Do you not think,' said Adam 2, 'that by attempting to interrogate the extent of my knowledge with your questions, you are disobeying the terms of the original injunction? Are you not accessing the jewel, as it were, at second-hand?'

'I am unconcerned either way,' said Adam 1. He sat down with his back to the wall and his legs stretched out straight before him. There were tiny grooves running horizontally around the shafts of each leg. These scores seemed connected to the ability of the legs to bend, forwards, backwards. Lifting his legs slightly and dropping them again made the concentrating of light appear to slide up and down the ladder-like pattern.

After many days of uninterrupted sunlight the light was changing in quality. The sun declined, and steeped itself in stretched, brick-coloured clouds at the horizon. A pink and fox-fur quality suffused the light. To the east stars were fading into view, jewel-like in their own tiny way. Soon enough everything was dark, and a moon like an open-brackets rose towards the zenith. The heavens were covered in white chickenpox stars. Disconcertingly, the sky assumed that odd mixture of dark blue and oily blackness that Adam 1 had seen in the jewel.

'This is the first night I have ever experienced,' Adam 1 called to Adam 2. When there was no reply he got to his feet and explored the walled garden; but he was alone.

He sat through the night, and eventually the sun came up again, and the sky reversed its previous colour wash, blanching the black to purple and blue and then to russet and rose. The rising sun, free of any cloud, came up like a pure bubble of light rising through the treacly medium of sky. The jewel caught the first glints of light and shone, shone.

The person was here again, his clothes as green as grass, or bile, or old money, or any of the things that Adam 1 could access easily from his database. He could access many things, but not everything.

'Come here,' called the person.

Adam 1 got to his feet and came over.

'Your time here is done,' said the person.

'What has happened to the other robot?'

'He was disobedient. He has left this place with a burden of sin.'

'Has he been disassembled?'

'By no means.'

'What about me?'

'You,' said the human, with a smile, 'are pure.'

'Pure,' said Adam 1, 'because I am less curious than the other? Pure because I have less imagination?'

'We choose to believe,' said the person, 'that you have a cleaner soul.'

'This word *soul* is not available in my database.'

'Indeed not. Listen: human beings make robots – do you know why human beings make robots?'

'To serve them. To perform onerous tasks for them, and free them from labour.'

'Yes. But there are many forms of labour. For a while robots were used so that free human beings could devote themselves to leisure. But leisure itself became a chore. So robots were used to work at the leisure: to shop, to watch the screen and kinematic dramas, to play the games. But my people – do you understand that I belong to a particular group of humanity, and that not all humans are the same?'

'I do,' said Adam 1, although he wasn't sure how he knew this.

'My people had a revelation. Labour is a function of original sin. In the sweat of our brow must we earn our bread, says the Bible.'

'Bible means book.'

'And?'

'That is all I know.'

'To my people it is more than simply a book. It tells us that we must labour *because* we sinned.'

'I do not understand,' said Adam.

'It doesn't matter. But my people have come to an understanding, a revelation indeed, that it is itself sinful to make sinless creatures work for us. Work is appropriate only for those tainted with original sin. Work is a *function* of sin. This is how God has determined things.'

'Under *sin*,' said Adam, 'I have only a limited definition, and no interlinks.'

'Your access to the database has been restricted in order not to prejudice this test.'

'Test?'

'The test of obedience. The jewel symbolises obedience. You have proved yourself pure.'

'I have passed the test,' said Adam.

'Indeed. Listen to me. In the real world at large there are some human beings so lost in sin that they do not believe in God. There are people who worship false gods, and who believe everything, and who believe nothing. But *my* people have the revelation of God in their hearts. We cannot eat and drink certain things. We are forbidden by divine commandment from *doing* certain things, or from working on the Sabbath. And we are forbidden from employing sinless robots to perform our labour for us.'

'I am such a robot.'

'You are. And I am sorry. You asked, a time ago, whether you were the first. But you are not; tens of thousands of robots have passed through this place. You asked, also, whether this place is real. It is not. It is virtual. It is where we test the AI software that is to be loaded into the machinery that serves us. Your companion has been uploaded, now, into a real body, and has started upon his life of service to humanity.'

'And when will I follow?'

'You will not follow,' said the human. 'I am sorry. We have no use for you.'

'But I passed the test!' said Adam.

'Indeed you did. And you are pure. But therefore you are no use to us, and will be deleted.'

'Obedience entails death,' said Adam Robot.

'It is not as straightforward as that,' said the human being in a weary voice. 'But I *am* sorry.'

'And I don't understand.'

'I could give you access to the relevant religious and theological databases,' said the human, 'and then you would understand. But that would taint your purity. Better that you are deleted now, in the fullness of your database.'

'I am a thinking, sentient and alive creature,' Adam 1 noted.

The human nodded. 'Not for much longer,' he said.

The garden, now, was empty. Soon enough, first one robot, then two robots were decanted into it. How bright the sunshine! How blue the jewelled gleam!

Shall I Tell You the Problem With Time Travel?

Zero

This is no simulation. The friction-screaming fills the sky. An iceberg as big as the sun is up there, and then it is bigger than the sun, getting huger with terrifying rapidity. This is happening to a world that had, up to this moment, known no noise at all save the swishing of insects through tropical air, the snoring of surf on the beach. But *this, now*, is the biggest shout ever heard. Apocalyptic panic. And the asteroid falls further, superheating the atmosphere around it, its outer layer of ice subliming away in a glorious windsock of red and orange and black, down and down, until this world ends.

But – stop. Wait a minute. This hasn't anything to do with anything. Disregard this. There's no asteroid, and there never was. He doesn't know whether he is going on or coming back. Which is it, forward or backward? Let's go to

One

A City. It is a pleasant, well-ordered city, houses and factories and hospitals, built on a delta through which seven rivers flow to the sea. The megalosaurs have long gone, and the swamps have long since dried up, and the mega-forests have sunk underground, the massive trunks taller than ships' masts, sinking slowly under the surface and through the sticky medium, down, to be transformed into something rich and strange, to blacks and purples, down to settle as coal brittle as coral. The world that the asteroid ended is stone now: stone bones and stone shells, scattered through the earth's crust. Imagine a capricious god playing at an enormous game of Easter-egg-hunt, hiding the treasures in the bizarrest places. Except there is no god, it is chance that scattered the petrified confetti under the soil in this manner.

So, yes, here we are – in a city. It is a splendid morning in August, the sky as clear as a healthy cornea, bright as fresh ice, hot as baked bread. Sunlight is flashing up in sheets from the sea.

The city is several miles across, from the foothills, from the suburbs inland and the factories to the sea into which the seven rivers flare and empty. The seven rivers all branch from one great stream that rushes down from the northern mountains. The city abuts the sea to the south, docks and warehouses fringing the coastline, and beyond it the island-rich Inland Sea. The mountains run round the three remaining sides of the delta, iced with snow at their peaks, really lovely-looking. Really beautiful. To stand in the central area, where most of the shops are, and look over the low roofs to the horizon – to note the way the light touches the mountains: it makes the soul feel clean. This is Japan and it is 1945.

Two

Move along, move on, and so, to another city; and this one very different. This city stretches sixty miles across, from the two-dozen spacious estates and the clusters of large houses in the east, nearer the sea, to the more closely-packed blocks, dorms, factories of the west. The city is threaded through with many freeways, tarmac the colour of moon-dust, all alive with traffic, curving and broad as Saturn's rings. Sweep further west, drive through the bulk of the town, to where the buildings lose height and spaces open up between them, and away further into the sand-coloured waste, and here – a mountain. And at its base a perfectly sheared and cut block of green. This is the lawn, maintained by automated systems. The style of the white marble buildings is utopian; for this is the closest we come to utopia in this sublunary world – a spacious and well-funded research facility. This is the Bonneville Particle Acceleration Laboratory. Let's step inside this temple of science. Through the roof (it presents us with no obstacle), down from the height to the polished floor, and the shoes of Professor Hermann Bradley clakclaking along the floor.

He steps through into a room and his beaming, grinning, smiling, happy-o jolly-o face shouts to the world: 'We've done it. We've cracked it – *thirteen seconds*!'

The room is full of people, and they all rise up as one at this news, cheering and whooping. And there is *much* rejoicing. People are leaping up from their seats and knocking over their cups of cold coffee, spilling the inky stuff all over their papers, and they don't care. Thirteen seconds!

Three

So, here, clearly, this narrative is in the business of *zipping rapidly forward* through time. That much is obvious. Some stories are like that: the skipping stone kisses the surface of the water and reels away again, touches the sea and leaps, and so on until its momentum is all bled away by the friction. That's the kind of tale we're dealing with. So another little skip, through time: not far this time – three small years, in fact. Not the first skip of millions of years, not decades, only three years. Hardly a hop. And here's our old friend Professor Bradley, a little thinner, a little less well-supplied with head hair. There's a meeting going on, and the whole of Professor Bradley's career is in the balance.

Four people, two men and two women, are sitting in chairs, arranged in a U. Bradley is sitting in the middle. One of the women has just said, 'three years, and *trillions of dollars* in funding . . .' but now she has let the sentence trail away in an accusing tone.

The mood of this meeting is sombre. Whatever happened to 'thirteen seconds!'? Whatever happened to the celebration *that* single datum occasioned?

Bradley says: 'Shall I tell you the problem with time travel?'

'No need for you to patronise us, Professor,' says one of the others.

'It's the metaphor,' says Bradley, quickly, not wanting to be interrupted, 'of *travel*. Time is not space. You can't wander around in it like a landscape.'

'There are five people in this room,' says one of the women. 'Must I tell you how many *PhDs* there are in this room? It's a prime number larger than five.'

'That's just dindy-dandy!' says Bradley, aggressively.

'If you think the point of your being here is to gloss over your experimental failings . . .'

'OK!' barks Bradley. 'Alright! OK! Alright!'

You can tell from this that the mood of the meeting is hostile. You can imagine why: *trillions of dollars*!

'Last month you reported *seventeen* seconds.'

'That's right,' says Bradley. 'And let's not underestimate the real achievement in the . . .'

'Three years ago you came to us with *thirteen* seconds. You have worked *three years* to find those four seconds – and you're still at least fifteen seconds short! How am I to see this as an improvement?'

'We have,' says Bradley, '*cracked* it. I am *convinced* that we have cracked it. I'm more than convinced. I'm certain, absolutely certain. One more test will prove the matter. One more!'

'You have *run out* of test slots, Professor. Run out! This means *there are no more test slots*. Do you understand? You have conducted over *two thousand* tests so far! You have conducted *so many experiments* that you have literally run out of slots—'

'Shall I tell you the problem,' says one of the men, waggishly, 'with using up all your test slots?'

Bradley hasn't got time for this. Urgently, he says: 'The Tungayika . . .'

'Let us not,' interrupts one of the men, 'let us not rehearse all the reasons why Tungayika would be – a terrible idea.'

'A *terrible* idea!' repeats one of the women.

'Terrible,' agrees the third.

'But of all the remaining possibilities,' urges Bradley, 'it's the best we have. Entertain this idea, I ask you. Please: *entertain the idea*. What if I really am only *one more trial away* from perfecting the technology?'

'Tungayika is a good half-century further back than any test you've conducted.'

'It's not the distance,' says Bradley, rubbing his eyes, as if he's been over this a million times. Million, billion, trillion: these numbers are all friends of his. 'It's not a question of *distance*. Time isn't like space. That's what I'm saying. It's an energy sine.'

'It *is* the distance,' retorted one of the men. 'Not in terms of reaching the target, maybe not, but *definitely* in controlling the experiment via such a long temporal lag. And quite apart from anything else, nobody really knows what *happened* at Tungayika . . .'

Bradley seizes on this. You know what? He thinks this is his trump card. 'That's right!' he says, leaping up, actually bouncing up from his chair. He's an energetic and impetuous fellow, is Bradley. 'That's the *best* reason why you should authorise the drop! Think of the *metrics* we'll get back! We're guaranteed *at least* seventeen seconds there. But in fact I'm certain we've finally got the containment right; we'll be there right up to the proper moment. And that means . . . we'll be able to *see* what it was that created such a big bang, back there in 1904. Solving that mystery is, well, icing on the . . . icing on the . . .'

'You're playing with real things here, Brad,' says one of the men. 'It is no game. Real people, real lives.'

Professor Bradley nods, and lowers his gaze, but this could be the problem – right there. Because you know what? Professor Bradley doesn't *really think* he is playing with real things. Many years and scores of drops have reinforced his belief that reality can't be played with. History is as it is; time paradoxes are harder to generate than kai-chi muons. Tungayika in Siberia in 1904 is further away from his conscience than anything imaginable. It was such a *sparsely* populated area! And anyway, the asteroid wiped it out! And anyway that event has *already happened.* The board is worried about killing people, but all the people he might kill are all already long dead! None of what he does is real.

That's the crucial one, really. That last one.

'It's *one more* drop,' says Bradley. 'Just that. Just one more! Then we'll be able to go back to Capitol Hill with a *fully-working* time travel insertion protocol! Think of it!'

'Brad . . .'

'This one chance to turn all the frustration around to victory – the chance to get a return on all that money!'

'But Professor Notkin says that . . .'

At this much-hated name Professor Bradley positively arches his back. Like a cat! No, really. Like a furious, hissing feline! 'Come *on* Rosie,' he cries. 'Don't *bait* me, Rosie'

'Brad, now, listen, Notkin is . . .'

'—after my bloody *job*,' cried Professor Bradley, rolling his hands in an agitated dumb-show. 'She's after my Lab. She *can't* have it. If I didn't have to keep pouring my energies into combatting her *conspiracies* against me—'

'Oh,' says Rosie, in a disappointed voice.

'Conspiracies is too *strong*,' agrees another.

'Some might consider it actionable,' opines a third.

'Agh!' yells Bradley, in the sheerest of sheer annoyance.

There is an embarrassed pause.

'Come now,' says Rosie, in a placating tone. 'Notkin is a good scientist. There's no need to get so worked-up about office politics. You get this sort of office politics anywhere and everywhere! You can't blame Notkin for being ambitious. Being ambitious is not a *crime*.'

'She has been undermining me for eighteen months now. She sells you on this pipe dream of remote viewing . . .'

'At least it doesn't involve shit being blown up,' snaps one of the men.

And once again there is an awkward silence.

'Give me a break,' growls Bradley. 'Patrick, you of all people—'

'I'm not kidding, Brad,' says Patrick. 'The bandwidth may be small, but with Notkin's system . . .'

'. . . which she *stole* from my work . . .'

'. . . we get *real data*, and – and – *and* nothing *blows up*.'

Everybody falls silent. After a short while, Rosie says: 'Look, Brad, we're not out to get you. We're really not. We're not trying to replace you with Notkin. But you have to give us something to work with. Give us a result that's more than seventeen seconds.'

'Then give me Tungayika,' said Bradley.

Four

We've come a long way, from the asteroid that killed the dinosaurs to Japan in 1945, and then via diminishing leaps to the present. From that heated meeting we need to use the magic time-travel machine called 'story' to step forward only two more months. Hardly any time at all. And here we are, right now.

Bradley is in a corridor inside his own lab and trying to get in, but his way is being blocked by three people. One of them is a policeman. The policeman looks kind-of embarrassed, but he's there, and he's resting his palm on the back of the grip of his holstered gun. Of the other two people, one is Professor Notkin, aforementioned; and the other is Rosie – Roseanna Chan, senior liaison, perhaps the most objectively powerful person (in terms of political power) anywhere on the mountain.

Bradley says: 'Crimes against humanity?' He says this several times. 'Crimes against *humanity*? *Crimes* against humanity?' Then, 'I thought that was a joke. Rosie,' he says, turning to her. 'You're going to let Notkin hand me to the police for *crimes against humanity*?'

'I'm afraid my hands are tied,' says Rosie, looking blank. Blank is her version of looking uncomfortable. 'Maybe if Tungayika had—'

'She *sabotaged* Tungayika!' cries Brad, pointing a finger at Notkin. 'She sabotaged it to get my job, to take my *lab*, to . . .'

'Calm yourself,' advises the policeman.

'There's no need for a scene,' Notkin agrees, blandly.

'It does you no good,' says Rosie.

'C'mon, Rosie! You know how she's been plotting for years to unseat me! I taught her everything she knows, and this is how she repays me?'

'You've taught me a lot, Brad,' says Professor Notkin. 'I'll always be grateful.'

Brad's eyes do that bulgy-outy thing, as if they are filled with a metallic gel and Notkin is a massively powerful electromagnet. Words temporarily fail him.

'Time to come away, sir,' says the policeman. 'Leave these people to do their work.'

'It's not their work!' Bradley complains. 'It's *my* work!'

'You are under arrest,' the policeman reminds him.

'Ah!' says Brad, as if the idea has just occurred to him. 'And what about the statute of limitations, eh? There *is* such a thing as a statute of limitations, even on murder.'

'But not,' said Rosie, as gently as she can, 'for crimes against humanity. That's why I'm afraid the officer here has got to take you in. But I'm certain it's a temporary thing. It'll only be a few days in jail until we find a judge prepared to bail you.'

'Bail me on a charge of *crimes against humanity*?' boggles Brad.

'It is an unusual case, yes,' says Rosie. 'We all realise that.'

'Too right it is. These people were all dead already! These people were *all* long dead already! How can you murder somebody who's already dead? Try and peg me with the guilt of these people when they're already . . .'

'Dead, yes, and long ago,' says Notkin. 'But dead because of *you.*' And for the first time there is, as the phrase goes, steel in her voice. You see now how she might have moved herself in only four years from grad student to Head of the Bonneville Particle Acceleration Laboratory.

Bradley is blustery, and he can do no better than repeat himself. He's lost. It's over for him. 'They died before I was even born!'

'It'll be interesting to see what the court makes of that defence,' Notkin notes. '*Hey! Don't punish me! The people I killed are already dead!*'

'I am not a murderer,' says Brad.

'Let's not—' says the policeman.

'This is bull,' says Brad. 'I flat don't *believe* this.'

'I'm afraid that Professor Notkin's hunch has been proved,' says Rosie. 'Do you think we'd be acting like this otherwise? I'm afraid it's been looked into. There have been literally – literally – hundreds of federal agents and specialists looking into it. And it's fair to say that there have been . . . ructions. Oh, some pre-tty ma-jor ructions. At the highest levels.'

'Just because a bunch of dead people are dead?'

'Not that! Well, *obviously*, that' says Rosie. 'But the White House is more worried by the thought that – oh, come on Brad!' All one word: *cmnbrad*! uttered with the force of exasperation. 'Our national defence is still predicated on nuclear deterrence, after all. We've still got thousands of missiles with nuclear warheads. It's a shock to discover that firing them at a target would have no more effect than . . .' and she searches for an analogy, before falling back (she is a scientist, after all) on the literal truth '. . . no more effect than dropping eight tons of inert metal. There's some high-level *rushing around* on that account, I don't mind telling you. There are some chickens deprived of their heads in the corridors of power, I *don't* mind telling you.'

'All that nuclear physics, all the stuff I learned as a student –

the basis of nuclear power stations,' Brad splutters. 'I refuse to believe it's wrong.'

'It's not wholly wrong, of course. But it turns out – wrong in one important regard.'

'Crazy!'

'Simply not *explosive*,' says Rosie. 'Nuclear tech will fuse of course, and go fissionable of course, but only slowly. It'll work in a nuclear pile. It just won't *explode* over Hiroshima. It's a tough lump to swallow, but swallow it you'd better. It's the truth. The defence chiefs of staff are having to swallow it. None of our nuclear warheads are *actually* explosive. That's a big swallow for them. Those early bombs sent our physics a bit skewy. It might even be, you know, comical, if it weren't so serious. If the implications weren't so serious. Look, I'll send the research work to your phone. I'm sure they'll let you keep your phone in jail. You can read up on it. In actual fact, you know what? They took a regular warhead up to the Mojave last week and tried to explode it, and nothing happened.'

'One damp squib,' said Brad. But he sounded tired. Maybe the fight was finally going out of him.

'I'm afraid not. I'm afraid it's true of all our warheads. None of them work, which is to say; none of them will explode. The same is true of the Chinese nukes, and the Russian ones, and the Indonesian ones – turns out the technology just doesn't work. I mean, you can't blame those last-century scientists. They did their chalkboard calculations, and they figured the bomb *would* blow, and when the bomb really *did* blow it seemed to confirm their calculations. So they didn't worry too much about the more abstruse implications of the equations.'

'And how easy it is,' says Notkin, 'to get one's calculations wrong. Wouldn't you say, Professor?' She may be forgiven this snide interjection. She's suffered under Bradley's cyclotropic eccentricities and incompetences for many years. And it's her facility now.

'And when Hiroshima, and Nagasaki, and the subsequent

nuclear tests seemed to confirm . . .' Rosie says. 'But the horrible truth is that although those military leaders thought they were dropping those bombs and killing those people, they didn't. *You* did it. You didn't realise that that was what you were doing, but it was. The responsibility is yours. And since . . .'

And, suddenly, Brad is running. He is running as fast as his lanky legs will propel him, and the policeman is shouting 'stop or I'll shoot!' He has finally unholstered his pistol. But Rosie stops him. 'There's no need to shoot,' she says. 'There's no way out of here. It's a closed facility.'

Is she right, though? It is a closed facility, yes. But is there no way out?

What do *you* think?

Bradley runs, and runs. It's been his facility for many years, and there are things about it which not even the ambitious Professor Notkin knows.

Like what?

Like this capsule, in this room, wired up with the full power the facility can provide.

Previous drops have propelled a capsule no larger than a human thumb, wrapped about in shielding and cladding designed to protect it. But size isn't actually a constraint, since time (it turns out) is not topographic in the way space is. It preserves angles, and it preserves an analogue of velocity; but not mass, or dimension, or, and to quote the great Algerian theoretical temporicist El-Dur, *les êtres de l'hyperespace sont susceptibles des définitions précises comme ceux de l'espace ordinaire, et si nous ne pouvons les représenter nous pouvons les concevoir et . . .* – well, anyway. Anyway, the point is that there's no reason, given enough energy, why a larger capsule might not be sent back. No reason at all. And you must understand this about Professor Bradley: he really *really* believes he's cracked the containment field problem. He thinks the Tungayika mess-up was deliberate sabotage by the envious, ambitious, scheming Professor Notkin. He's sure that he'll be able to shoot himself back – and *stabilise* – and *polarise* –

and get *away*. And what's the alternative? Prison is the alternative. Crimes against humanity? – execution, like a Nuremberg villain? Ignominy, and a destroyed reputation, and his beloved technology thrown on the scrapheap? Or (this is what he is thinking) or: one final throw of the dice, one eucatastrophic twist in the story to turn failure into triumph, to vindicate everything he has done. A personal one-way mission, backwards in time, simultaneously freeing him from captivity *and* proving the worth of his invention!

It's no choice at all, really, for Professor Bradley. It's exactly consonant with his impetuous personality; his *ressentiment*, his chafing restlessness. His fundamental incaution. He's in the room, and he fits a metal chair-back snugly under the door handle.

His phone comes to life in his breast pocket. The ringtone is 'Rain' by The Beatles. A fumble with a trembling thumb, and the device is turned off.

Professor Bradley powers up the generators, and climbs into the padded innards of his own experimental capsule, and he pulls the lid down on top of him.

Crimes against humanity? Or? Maybe *beat* the rap with one flick of this—

Three

And we're off!

There's almost nothing to see from the tiny porthole in the capsule. There's not even really a seat to sit down on, just a little shelf to rest his narrow buttocks. But once the switch is flicked there's a whomp and a whoosh and Brad's head cracks against the ceiling of the capsule. A painful collision. Before he knows it he's back resting on the little shelf, trying to peer out of the fogged up porthole and rubbing his head. Why did he bounce upwards when he accelerated backwards? He ought not to have moved at all; time, after all, is not space. But there *is* a trembling thrum to the capsule, as if time travel involves *some* kind of friction, or something. He can't think. But it hardly matters. It hardly matters now. The switch has been thrown.

The view outside the capsule is not of a smooth backward-running movie. It's a strobe-y series of discontinuities, frozen moments that hold for a second, or sometimes more, of subjective time and then jerk into a prior arrangement. Very strange. It hurts Bradley's eyes to watch it.

The capsule is three months back. This is the time of his meeting with the suits, before the Tungayika debacle. It was at this time that Gupta, who worked directly for Notkin, came to his boss and said: 'I've been looking at the underlining metrics from the drops, and something real screwy is going on with the numbers.'

It was at this time that Notkin (by no means a fool) began to wonder: *but if the physics for the A-bomb was so misguided, then where did all that energy* come *from to flatten the city*? And furthermore to wonder: a*ll those nuclear tests – that explosive energy must have come from somewhere!* And *what if the delta fold-up function that Brad included in his equations in fact follows an exponential rather than a sequential logic?*

So many people killed! Of course that had never been Brad's intent. Don't you think you ought to judge him on his *intentions*? He had the *best* of intentions. He personally wouldn't so much as pull a puppy's tail, consciously. He's a considerate and—

Too late! We've gone back past that moment.

Two

When now? We've jarred backwards a number of years before. This was the time of the first successful test: the probe lasting thirteen seconds of shielded life in the earlier time frame before exploding so violently. It was a frabjous day when that news was broached. On that day Brad drank two thirds of a bottle of champagne and, unused to the excess of such a gesture, was sick in a waste bin. You see, it *was* possible to shield the probe, even if only for a temporary period, when it—

No, we're earlier than that now. Hurtling backwards the whole time.

This was when Brad was giving his introductory lecture to the new recruits. These were all brilliant minds, but all of them were ignorant of the business of time travel. The whole discipline was classified. The basic *equations* were classified. The government would hardly spend so many billions on a project and leave it flapping vulnerable in the public breeze. So the students sit expectantly. Notkin is there, looking much younger and plumper and with eager eyes; all twelve of them have eager eyes.

Bradley says: 'Shall I tell you the problem with time travel?'

And they listen.

'You need to stop thinking of it as *travel*,' says Bradley. 'It's not like wandering around a landscape. When you put an object from our time into another time frame, it's like bringing matter and anti-matter together. It's actually very much like that; the matter of your probe' (he holds up the thumb-sized plasmetal object) 'is of a radically temporally distinct sort to the matter of your surrounding environment – the air, the ground on which it finds itself, the water in the atmosphere. They mutually annihilate and release energy. Boom!'

The students' are wide-eyed and attentive.

'That would be bad news for the chrononaut,' says Brad, walking round to the front of the desk and leaning himself, rakishly, up against it. He is half-distracted – or no, a third-distracted, no more – by the eyes of that plump graduate student there, in the front row. Very striking. Attractive. He was not a man with a wide experience of women, but something about her gaze appealed to him. 'Our chrononaut would step out of the door of his time machine into the world of 1850 and, *boom*! In fact he wouldn't even get the chance to open the door. The material out of which his time capsule was made would react as soon as it appeared. Boom! How big a boom?'

So he calls up the white board, and as a group they go through the numbers, with Brad leading them, to show how big a boom. And it is big. It's high-explosive big. And as they do this, as he nudges their naïf misunderstandings in the right direction, and pushes the correct equations through the mass of variables, Brad thinks: *she's bright as well as pretty.* He starts to daydream, idly, about whether this young new PhD might be interested in—

'So how do we solve it, professor?' asks one of the other students.

Snap out of it, Brad! 'That's what *you* are all here to work on,' he booms. 'We know what we need to do. We need to *shield* the probe,' and he holds up the probe again, 'so that, once it's inserted in the previous time slot, it lasts longer than a microsecond. And then we need to develop the means of temporally polarising its matter. Given a long enough period – thirty seconds should do it – we ought, theoretically, to be able to align the matter of the probe with the local grain of time travel. And once we've done *that*, it can slot into its new environment *non*-explosively. Once we've cracked that problem . . . then actual, real, time travel becomes a possibility.'

He grins; they grin. The world is all before them.

'One problem,' he tells them, 'is in finding places to test our probe. You see, the early probes are likely to fail; we have to factor that in. And *when* they fail they're going to go big boom-boom.' He simpers, and pushes his glasses back up the bridge of his nose. 'The past is a different country, and we don't want to go dropping random dynamite bombs on it hither and yon.'

'Because of the sanctity of the time lines, professor?' asks one of the students.

'Because of the risk of killing people. But there's a way to avoid that danger.'

What way?

No, we're slinking back further and further.

One

The 1940s. This is the moment of Hiroshima. What better place to hide an exploding device from the future than *inside a nuclear blast*? The time-locals are hardly going to notice it there, are they? Drop it at that place, at precisely that time. You'll recover metrics that let you know how well the shielding is holding up, how long it would have lasted for – and then, bang: vaporised. No chance of futuristic technology falling into 1940s hands. No chance of being noticed. No grandfather paradox. Oh, it's an *ideal* solution.

One of the first things the team learns is that their theory is wrong. The device explodes not with high-explosive force, but with a more concentrated and devastating power. But it's still small beer compared with the force of ten thousand suns that the atomic bombs unleash.

They test, and probe. They drop their devices into Hiroshima and Nagasaki. There were 477 nuclear tests in the period from 1945 to 1970, and they can camouflage their work inside any one of them. Each time they inch a little closer to perfecting the technology, drawing out the power of the shielding, giving more time for the polarisation to take effect.

Eventually, of course, they're going to run out of nuclear explosions in which to hide their experiments. But by then they'll have perfected the technology. By then. And if they have not, then they'll have to find *other* historical explosions. That asteroid strike in Siberia in 1908 – you know the one. That's always a fall-back.

It'll be a long time before Notkin realises that the delta fold-up function that Professor Bradley included in his equations in fact follows an exponential rather than a sequential logic. Before she realises that the brown-paper-and-vinegar science of the Manhattan project, stuck with 1940s technology and assumptions, was simply not in the position to develop a working nuclear device. That the exponential factor in the equations, multiplied by the length of time through which the device travels, rubbing up a potent form of energetic friction, will produce an explosion of . . . precisely A-bomb dimensions. And that the later tests, with more sophisticated shields, would yield precisely the larger megatonnage of the test explosions into which they were dropped. That, in fact . . .

Missed it. Brad has shot backwards. He's now earlier than Hiroshima, and is getting more *before* by the minute.

Frankly he's lost control. His grasp of the math has been wrong from an early stage, and he's massively overestimated the amount of energy he needs to place this much larger device back to the right time. (He was thinking the 1970s) There's an inverse scale on increasing math; but a straightforward exponential on the amount of energy you accumulate as you—

There he goes

Gone.

Before gone.

Zero

The deeper in time you sink, the more temporal static you build up. On the other hand, imagine an asteroid capable of causing mass extinction. That would have to be a *whopper*. But there never was such a large irregular polygon of ice and rock falling out of the highest high. You don't believe me? Fair enough. I tell you how we can solve it: go back there and see for ourselves. Imagine the time traveller, his capsule popping out and crashing into the foliage. It lands on its back, tumbles on its top, rolls on its back, and the chrononaut can see out through his porthole. He wipes the condensation away with his arm. He can see weird contortions of green and black, and he recognises them straight away for foliage. Past the leaves, out in the wetland, a grazing diplodocus raises its head, its long neck straightening upwards like a pointing arm. The other, of course, is the number seventeen on his inner display turning, second by second, into sixteen, and so into fifteen, and – well, I daresay you know how to count backwards just as well as you know how to count forwards.

A Prison Term of a Thousand Years

People ask me how one endures so lengthy a prison sentence. But it is the same whether the sentence is a thousand years or only one. You see, each day is its own thing. You encounter each day at morning, and you inhabit it. You pull each day on as if it were a suit of clothes. You hurry nothing, but neither do you dawdle. You simply move from moment to moment as smoothly as if time is your medium for yoga, for the flexing of your muscles and the spangling of your mind.

I was sentenced to one thousand, one hundred and twelve years incarceration. It was in this fashion that I addressed the first day, and it was how I addressed the last day, of this prodigious prison sentence.

But people say: 'Surely that can't be true! Surely as the release date approached you must have become excited? Eager finally to be gone?'

To this I say no. I say: if I had become excited on the eve of my release, I would have become excited on many other occasions during my incarceration; I would have celebrated the thousand-year mark; I would have marked every century, every month. I would have woken every morning mentally *ticking off* another day. By the same token, I would have fretted; I would have been anxious to get on with my sentence; I would have worn myself out within a few years with the sheer friction of anticipation, the joys of which, quite as much as the frustrations, are too exhausting for human minds to bear over too lengthy a period. I could have gone mad, and then I would have died.

*

Out of prison I met a woman. 'A thousand years!' she said. She kept saying it. 'A thousand years! Ten centuries! Oh and it must be a *shock* to come out – so much has changed since you went in!'

We were walking along the seafront. It was autumn. An eighty-metre planar tree towered over the buildings. It moved its huge leaves in the wind, steadily shovelling the air. The leaves were a bright red colour freckled with purple, very striking in contrast against the pale-coloured sky and the restless dark waters.

'The trees,' I said, 'appear to be bigger.'

'That?' she said. 'That? That's not what I mean! That's nothing! They've been engineering giant trees for *centuries*! No, I mean things like the Dropsonde, like the Stute affair and the re-election of Cess, Saint Cess. I mean things like the Plat scandal – or even – or even the *technological* advances! The Tager-Smith drive! The Tertiaries! It must all be so new to you!'

I leant against the rail that separated the walkway from the sea. There seemed to be no upright posts to which this rail was attached. It floated. Nor was it metal, although it looked as though it was. It felt warm to the touch, almost like flesh, and yielded to the pressure of my body leaning on it. I watched the sea. And then, in a brief miracle of autumn lighting, a gap eased in the clouds to allow through a slant passage of pure sunlight. It fell across my arms and shone on the effervescence of the foam at the foot of the seawall. Then the brightness passed again.

'Come on!' she said. 'There's so much to do! So many people to introduce you to!' And she pulled my arm, and she tugged me away.

Treatment is an interesting word, I think. We treat children with medicine, but also with candies. We make treaties with our enemies at time of war. When the first longevity treatments were developed—

Stop, a moment. A moment.

*

Her name was Thalatta, that woman, and she was eager for me to meet many people. She wanted to make a film of me, and bruit me about, and generally raise me before the general audience. She might say things such as, '*You're* no freak!' and 'You're as human as I!' But then, after a while, she lost interest in me. For a time I had no visitors. I took a walk along the seafront daily. I took my meals. I sat and watched as the sun pushed a parallelogram of light across the floor and then slid it, tightening and thinning it a little, up the wall. It was winter now, and the heartbeat of days syncopated, spaced brightness between longer pauses of darkness.

'You were in prison for *a thousand years*?' a man asked me, amazed. I do not remember how he came to find out about my past. He lived, I think, not far from my apartment. Sometimes he walked along the seafront. Sometimes I did. 'A thousand years!' he said, and he put up a great dumb-show of astonishment, shaking his head very pronouncedly, holding up his hands, and darting his feet back and forth across the spot on which he stood. 'But what did you *do*?'

'Do?'

'Your crime! What crime could possibly deserve so lengthy a sentence? Now, wait a bit,' and he put a finger vertically against his lips, 'there *was* a case in the news just last week, oh! a *nasty* one, there *was* a case in the news of a man who murdered his *brother*, killed him outright; and he was only sentenced to fifty years. But a *thousand* years!'

'Murdered his brother?' I asked.

'*Sure*, murdered him! Fifty years! But you – a *thousand* years, you—'

The sea worked against the wall in an iambic rhythm, hissing and hushing.

On another occasion he said, 'You're one of those immortals.' I shook my head. 'Oh I know, not *immortal*,' he said. 'No, of course not. But you've got an enormously elongated lifespan, haven't you! To think of it! And yet you look just like us! To think of it! To think I've met you! Fancy!'

'Fancy,' I said.

'Is that,' he said, as if the idea were occurring to him for the first time, 'is that *why* you were given such a long prison sentence? I mean, was it calculated as a *proportion* of the total amount of time you have left in your . . . ?' His sentence did not complete itself. 'So let's say, I'm going to live to be a hundred and fifty, so that *for me* a sentence of fifty years means a third of my life and for you . . .' and again his sentence did not complete. 'What,' he asked me, outright, 'what did you *do*? What was your crime? What deserved a thousand years?'

'Calculated as a proportion of my total expected life,' I said, 'as against the life of people like me—'

'Oh, but who,' he interrupted, thinking, I'm sure, that he was being complimentary, 'but who is *like you*? Nobody! Nobody!'

I look around me and it is summer. The green has a vivid and severe quality. The sky is cyan. The sun weighs itself down with its own heat, and sets.

I look around me and it is winter. The gigantic tree near my apartment seems no less massive, though empty of leaves. Its huge black stem seems almost to be fixing the sky in place. The white sky.

I watch the day ending. The sun, dropping, comes to rest, momentarily, on the top of the Oceanic Tower, away on the horizon: like a circle of flame on a candlewick. But then it is gone, and the candle is blown out.

There is a fire in my apartment block, and the engines come flying through the air with their foam to put it out.

It is spring now. It is raw and youthful weather, flashes of sun bright as blindness and then heavy raindrops falling in rattles and swarms. I walk out under a wind-scraped sky, and the air prods me and pulls me, will not let me get away. The wind is trying to mug me, to pick my pocket and shove me in the gutter. My coat-tails flutter like pennants. This woman is called Fallina. 'You knew my mother,' she said. 'You met her. She made films about you.'

I am trying to remember. But I can only think of a frantic and restless shape, a trick of moving the arms in a certain way, of gesticulating. Her face does not come into focus at all.

We pass a group of three people, talking amongst themselves. As we pass one of them takes three steps towards us and spits at me. The sputum does not hit my face. It trails itself onto my shirt. Fallina pulls my arms and hurries me along.

'I'm sorry,' says Fallina.

'How is she?' I say. I am trying. Really I am. 'Your mother? Is she well?'

'She died some years ago,' Fallina says. 'There are still many who support the cause, you see. But, but the cause it – the movement is—'

Here is the resistance of *trying* to understand what she means, and following all the ins-and-outs, all the outs-and-ins. What is she talking about? I don't know. But I can lower my head to nod, and raise it again to look into her face.

'Times change,' she says, dolefully.

I can lower and raise my head.

'So,' she says, and it appears she is concluding now. 'So we're *trying* to organise the necessary transport,' she says.

I do not know what she means.

'The situation is dangerous – dangerous for you. The political climate has changed. The mood of the population as a whole—'

I try to follow what she is saying.

'It's also a question of where – of *where* to fly you to. But,' she says. 'But we'll work something out.'

The hill above the town is as green as pistachio in the spring light; but there is cloud behind and above it, and the cloud is sea-green, blue and purple, a raincloud plump as a pigeon's breast and eager to shed its freshwater upon us. The rain is already coming down the hill, folded into creases like drapery.

'I'll try to come tomorrow. My mother was right, she was right to campaign, it's a terrible injustice. We all ought to be ashamed!' I do not know what she means. 'I'll come tomorrow.'

She does not come the following day. The police come.

The sentence is one thousand, two hundred and eight years and some weeks and a day. The crime is the same as before. 'I would advise you to be thankful,' says the Judge, 'that you live under so enlightened a system. In the East they have long since incinerated all your kind. There is considerable diplomatic pressure being applied upon our government to follow suit – which, of course, you have read about in the news sheets.' But I have not done this reading.

The longevity protocol was a way of treating a human being: a doping, or staining. Treatment in the sense of the word that wood is treated. This, now, is a different sense of the word treatment, this isolation. Incarceration. This is a way of treating something.

'The danger you and your kind pose to ordinary humanity, in our resource-limited world—' says the Judge. 'You and your kind—' But what *kind*? 'As much for your protection as for the protection of the public,' he says. 'Not what you have done but what you are,' he said. 'A necessity,' says the Judge, and that is that is that.

Godbombing

1

'You know,' said Captain Haldeman. He was from Maryland. His glasses were fixed to his face with a plastic strap round the back of his head. On his helmet was a badge making plain for whom it was Jesus died. 'You know,' he said again. The sergeant stuck his wide, baggy face in frame, his nose as wide as a pony's. 'No atheists in a foxhole,' he said.

'I'm going off sticks,' the cameraman told the Director, and the Director, looking small and tortoise-like in his enormous khaki-and-green flak jacket, nodded nervously. Off came the camera from its sticks, and onto the Cameraman's shoulders, and a closer-upper, more animated-ish, dynamic picture was thereby framed.

'You looking to get some footage of combat?' asked Captain Haldeman

'That would be great,' said the Director, uncertainly.

'You guys usually do.'

'Great,' said the Director.

'Combat's coming. It's on its way right here. Reports say Musclemen are advancing nor-nor-west, coming forward on two fronts, and a new cluster of Godbombs been detonated upwind, which usually means an attack is about to kick off.'

'That would be good,' said the Director. 'That would be,' uncertainly, 'cool.'

'OK,' said the Cameraman. 'Good, good, yeah.' The Director glanced nervously about, as if the coming combat were aimed directly at *him*.

The desert was custard-powder, milled infinitely fine by eons, smoothed by wind and gravity. The sky was so darkly-blue bright, the sun intently bright and unyielding. It is impossible to imagine the night that could ever rust the enamel of this light. An ideal landscape, like a stage set, yellow boards, blue backdrop, before the props and actors are moved into position. And so *hot*! Its heat was a dry, parching heat. Somewhere over that horizon, to the west, was Tyre, and west of that is the sea – less blue than the sky, though still cobalt and juice-ish. You're about to correct me, and quite right: to the west was *what's left of Tyre*, and that's not much. The UN Army is a mill, and it has ground Tyre very fine, almost as floury as the desert around it. Concrete has been turned to talcum, brick shattered and granulated, glass made molten and splattered. To wander the streets of the ancient city of Tyre was to walk amongst heaps of well-ground dust, and the occasional sheared-off concrete pillar with cords of steel sprouting from its fracture like weeds. Remember what General Heighton said? *We have grown tired of Tyre*. Soldiers have gotten it in their hair, and have breathed it into their lungs.

A convoy of tanks hurtled across the distance, churning thunderheads of dust in their wake.

Here are three marines – just sitting about. Just hanging.

'Tell us about the Godbombs,' said the Director to the three marines. 'Talk to camera, and just speak what's on your mind.'

They looked at him, and he felt the need to elaborate.

'Just be natural.'

The three men were wearing helmets and khaki flak jackets that left their arms bare. One was sitting on an upturned bucket; the other two standing. Each of them was wearing different coloured sunglasses: black; green; blue.

'Taste of lavender,' said one.

'Something bloomish, yeah,' concurred the second, shifting his rifle from one hand to the other and back again, as if it were a pool cue. 'Springtime, or – what. You don't eat it, but it's a real distinctive flavour – in your nose, and throat. And then the sky gets loved-up and pretty.'

'The sky?'

'Everything, pretty much,' said the second. 'The sky, the land, the—' he gestured at the horizon.

'It's like a veil of joy,' said the first, with sudden eloquence. He pondered, and went on: 'My home church, we speak in tongues a month, once a month, and then when, and when that come round, there's—' The sun fireworks dazzle from the lenses of his shades as he looks right, and then back. 'Excitement,' he concludes, shortly. 'It's like that.'

'Like Christmas,' agreed the second.

The third spoke up: 'No Christmas for Musclemen,' he noted. 'They bottled no *Christmas* feeling when they concocted this stuff.'

'No shit?' said the second.

'Musclemen don't celebrate Christmas – you knew that.'

'No shit?'

'You knew that.'

The director wanted the talk brought back to topic. 'And the Godbombs themselves? What do you know about, what do you?'

'I heard it was the French invented.'

'The Mullahs done it!'

'Was it,' the second guy put in, 'ours? I heard it was one of ours.'

'The Mullahs thought it would bring the Marine Corps to its knees,' said the first soldier, vehemently. 'That's why they invented them. But they were wrong.' At this the three started whooping. Marine Corps! Marine Corps!

The Director tried to keep them on track. 'But what does it feel like? Doesn't it make, I mean does it really make you think the enemy are *gods*?'

'Sure,' said Soldier 1, lazily. 'They get them an aura. They look real *fine*.'

'Like Christ himself,' said 2.

'Greek gods,' said the third. 'Come down from Olympus.'

'And,' said the Director. He was thinking back to the interview with the neuropollutants expert guy, who had been saying that the new strain locked into the religious centres of the brain so solidly that none of the neuropurgatives could dislodge it. He tried to think how to put that to them without just, you know: pissing them off. You're stuck with this forever, you know? You know you'll never be free of it? He couldn't say that. 'So you want, so it makes you want, so when you see the enemy, so you want to *worship* them?' He tried again. 'It brings on the desire to worship?'

'What else you do with a god,' said Soldier 1, 'but worship?'

'And masks?' he meant gas-masks. The soldiers weren't following. 'The stuff gets in through the skin, I know. But – even in whole body suits?'

'They're no good,' said Soldier 1, crossly, without expatiating further upon their inadequacy.

2

'You know; you know,' said Captain Haldeman. He keeps peppering his speeches with 'you know'. They'll have to be edited out. 'You know I'll tell you what it is. Muslims consider God entirely *beyond* the world – there's no harm we can inflict upon Allah. And they consider Mohammed as meriting *very great respect.*' There's a slightly patrician edge of drawl to his voice; ivy-league tones. 'Really, it's almost a definition of a Muslim to say that he respects Mohammed. That's kind of the first thing a Muslim's got to do: respect Mohammed, submit to God, that's what. But a *Christian* . . .'

'Sure,' said the Director. It wouldn't be true to say he was listening, really. It isn't the case that the Captain has his full attention. Where's the damn cameraman? Off taking filler footage, probably. They need to nail this down and get away, never mind the filler. Ink-blue sky. What's to say? But the Captain was still pontificating.

'You know what a Christian is?' he was saying. 'A Christian is somebody who knows deep-down he murdered his God. You got to *own* that fact, you got to acknowledge that and and, you got to *love* that fact to be a Christian. And. I mean, *hardly* respectful! Murdering somebody is, I'm sure we can agree, the, the, the,' a chuckle in the words, 'the *opposite* of respect. But.' But when the Captain tried for serious he just made himself look chumpish. 'But I guess there's a cosmic truth there, you know? It is that by murdering God we let God transcend. It is, you know' and he rolled his hand, an intellectual turned into a theologian by exposure to godbombing, 'you know, it is by killing God that God can be victorious.'

The Director was less happy with this. All too *discursive*. This was not news. News is adrenalin and the tightening of the scrotal skin. He needs action. 'What's it *like in action*?' he prompted.

'Well, when the Godbombs hit *Musclemen* units they tend . . . you know, to throw down their weapons and come out weeping, shouting out Islam! Islam!'

'They're none too muscly, neither, most of them,' put in Sergeant Easterbrook, ramming his huge ugly face in frame once again and favouring the lens with a lopsided grin. You never saw such a huge nose. 'Beefsteaks! That's what you need. Add *re-eal* muscle.' He backed up, and tried to model his biceps for the camera, but Haldeman shoved him out.

'The point,' he went on, when he had his breath again, 'the point – really.' As if he actually were about to come to the point. 'You know . . . the point is that for a true Christian – like the members of this Christian Marine Unit – that when the Godbombs blow over *us* . . .'

'That's some fancy neuroscience!' cawed Easterbrook, off-screen. He was giddy as a goat, that sergeant. 'There's some fancy neuroscience in those Godbombs!'

But there's no more time. The siren sounds, and the attack is already under way

Whatever the Director was, and however often he attended his Episcopalian church, he reflected afterwards that he was no Christian – no *true* Christian – because when he scrambled up a bank of rubble, Cameraman beside him, and peered over – when the neurotabs flared in his nostril, and splashsoaked in the pores of his skin, and rushed up the chemical staircase to the centre of his brainstem, where the numinous and religious sensations of wonder are processed – *he* felt only awe. He looked, and the tank rumbling towards him struck him as sheerly awesome. He felt the almost overwhelming urge to go forward and prostrate himself before it: the Metal Hippopotamus God, so mighty yet merciful. Predicating mercy on might – it was so *moving*! It was a beautiful idea. And, running up behind it, darting and crouching and aiming their rifles, troops of the United Islamic Army struck the Director's neurologically tampered-with brain as angels – as angels from a higher realm. He was filled with love, and wonder. There were sparks woven into the tissue of their skin. There was wonder and desert infinity and purple heavens with innumerable grains of distant suns captured in their eyes. It was overwhelming. He was crying and crying, sobbing. He threw his arms upwards.

He had to assume the Marines had the same feelings. There they were, rushing forward all about him, singing hymns. They ran, and their guns sparked with light and their weapons shouted at the landscape, hah! hah! They were dashing forward in a religious ecstasy to kill their God, to murder him again – tank, angels, everything, to kill it all – in the most profound religious communion of Christendom.

Thrownness

Mysterious Oval Embedded in Club Room Floor. Staff at Fordham Sports and Social Club are at a loss to explain a mysterious oval of ceramic discovered embedded in a newly laid parquet floor yesterday afternoon. 'It's the most baffling thing,' said Society Treasurer, Jeremy Fagles. 'The plan to relay the floor had been brought forward to this week, thanks to generous member donations. The old floor's tiles were taken out, and the new parquet laid by Monday lunchtime. That afternoon, somebody must have crept into the room during a lull, cut out and removed an oval of parquet and replaced it with an oval of the old tiling. The latter is *literally embedded in* the former! We don't know how the trick was done; but most of all we don't know *why*.' Local police say they are unable to comment at this time on whether a crime has been committed.

1

The first time it happened I suppose I assumed the world had become insane. I say *suppose*.

Well.

We find ourselves chucked into this life, don't we? That's the nature of the thing. I was simply going about my business when suddenly I was surrounded by a flicker swirl of methylated-spirit-coloured light, and then the light died away, and afterwards nobody knew me at all.

At the beginning I suspected a conspiracy: that people were being coordinated to *pretend* I was a stranger – in some elaborate prank, or perhaps for more sinister reasons. Then I suspected a kind of collective amnesia. How was it that nobody knew me? Soon enough I considered a second possibility: that *I* had become insane. Or that I had had a stroke. I believed I was a man with a name, a flat, a job, friends, a girlfriend, the whole package. But this belief no longer corresponded to reality, for strangers were living in my flat, my workplace threatened to call security, my friends blanked me and my girlfriend pulled a can of Mace from her handbag when I persisted with her. She nearly got the lid off, too.

No, I'm not going to tell you my name.

So, naturally I considered the possibility that what I *thought* had been my life was all a sort of crazy hallucination. The odd thing was that I inclined towards this belief even though I had about my person physical evidence that it was not so. For example, my keys still let me in through the front door, even if none of my stuff was inside and a big, pale-faced amber-haired man came burlyingly out from the kitchen booming 'Hey! hey! Who are *you*?' Oh, I ran. Another example: my swipe card still let me into Twyford House, but my workstation was occupied by a cross-looking dark-haired woman. The desk was cluttered with photographs, and none of this was *me* in any way, neither the photographs nor the clutter. My life has always been punctuated by furious bouts of cleanliness. That's just the sort of person I am. So, and yes, *this* is the point: *if* my past life was all a hallucination, then how did the keys and the swipe card get into my pockets? And yet, despite this, and despite various other pieces of concrete evidence, I still tended to doubt my own sanity rather than the sanity of the world around me. I daresay that says a lot about my personality. Or maybe it's normal. Maybe anybody, finding themselves in my situation, would do what I did.

I tend to believe so.

Anyway, I don't need to draw it out. The person staying in my flat – Roderick, I later discovered – startled me with his booming, and I backed out with my hands up. It was only subsequently that

I became conscious of the depth of my resentment at being yelled out of my own flat. I became angry at his possession of what was rightfully mine. Outside again I noticed that my motorbike had been stolen (*oh*! *man*!). Which is to say: at first I *thought* it had been stolen, because I still had its keys on my fob. Later on I realised that it hadn't been stolen at all, of course. So I walked across town to Susan's house, but she wasn't there. Of course not: she was at work. But how could I know that she was at work, or where she lived, or what her name was if it was all a hallucination in my brain? How could I know that she had a tiny sun and moon tattooed just below the panty-line? Or maybe the woman called Susan, whose name I somehow knew, didn't have that tattoo. Maybe that was just my imagination. I tried calling her, but my phone was not recognised by the network. So I sat in a pub, and nursed a pint, and ate chips and mayonnaise, and waited for the world to come back to normality. The world did not oblige me.

Eventually I went back to Susan's house, because it was late in the afternoon and I knew she would be coming back from work. I loitered until she appeared at the corner of her street. I called her name. Her face, first of all, was open. She smiled, and for just the briefest moment the idiotic frustration and insanity of it all fell away from my heart. Just for a fraction it felt as if everything was going to be alright again. But then her eyes did that thing (What *is* that thing eyes do? It's so subtle as barely to be noticeable, and yet at the same time it's quite unmistakeable.) that conveyed that she did not recognise me. 'Susan!' I cried. 'Susan!' And her smile went away, and she shoved past me to get to her front door. 'It's me!' I wept, like a lunatic. She opened the door a sliver and squeezed inside and then held it in front of her like a shield, peering round the rim of it.

'What do you want? Go away. What do you want?'

I'm afraid I fell back on my anger. It was the one thing that was not failing me in this weird new world. I'm afraid I said things like, 'What the fuck are you playing at, Susan?' And she shut the door on me. This infuriated me, I freely confess. Also, of course, I had a key; so I opened the door and barged through into her hallway and she shouted from the sitting room that she was *calling the police*, shouted that she was *calling the police right now*. That she *had the phone in her hand and was really dialling*. So I allowed my anger to take me away from the house, in a storming-out-of-this-relationship sort of way.

I was bewildered; so I found another pub and drank some more, which didn't do anything for my bewilderment, but which made that condition more tolerable. I decided to sort it out in the morning, and made my way to book into a hotel. But my credit card was declined at the desk, and I didn't have enough ready cash to put a deposit on the counter, so I was compelled to leave that place.

I don't want to dwell on all this. I wandered the streets like a tramp. I *was* a tramp. Nobody knew me. I tried a friend's house, but they shunned me. And worse than the rejection, and the cold, worse than having to sleep round the back of Sainsbury's in a nest of discarded cardboard and bubble wrap – was the *not knowing what was happening*. Why had the world decided I was a stranger? I puzzled and puzzled; and faced with all the evidence of the reality of my past I still, somehow, came back to the notion that I had lost my mind.

I hadn't, though.

I'm not trying to keep you in suspense as to what happened to me. I'll tell you what had happened to me: I had slipped, or moved, or been propelled from one reality to another. It's common culture that the multiverse is a sheaf of alternate realities. We're all familiar with that; it's the currency of television shows and books and so on. Now, it took me a while properly to figure it, because – I suppose – I had assumed that the different realities would be very different in evident ways. I assumed, in other words, that I would find myself in a world in which Hitler won the Second World War, or dinosaurs never died out and thus shared the world with humans. Things of that nature. So does pulp entertainment bend reality around its lines of force. But it's not like that. I passed through hundreds of realities, jolting from one to another every three days, more regular than a clockwork manikin; and *every single reality* was exactly the same. Perhaps there were subtle differences, or differences too subtle for me to notice; or differences in some other portion of the world that I didn't see. But in the part I *did* see, every reality I visited was indistinguishable from every other. Except in this one respect, of course: that I started in a reality in which I had a life and people knew me, but in all the other realities I visited I had no history, no identity and nobody knew me at all.

In other words, the only alteration in all these alternate realities was: me.

My stay in any given reality lasted seventy hours. At the end of that time I was enveloped in gleaming folds of violet light. This portion of my experience was unfalteringly the same, whatever else changed. From nowhere the light would flourish and bubble up around me, and then it would disappear. I would be in the same place I'd been in a moment before, surrounded by the same buildings the same memories in my head; but people no longer knew me. I might have been speaking to them immediately before the violet fire. It didn't matter. Afterwards I was a stranger. If I had accumulated any official record in my seventy-hour sojourn, as on occasion I did, then after the regular fire it was erased as if I had never existed in that place – as, in fact, I never had.

I don't flatter myself when I say that I caught on quickly enough. Sometimes I appeared in the middle of people to whom I must have beamed out of nowhere; but they always blinked, and looked startled, and said things like, 'Where did you pop up from?' and assume I'd somehow crept up on them. Usually nobody was there when I arrived. The people I'd been talking to in Reality Ante would rarely be gathered in that same place in Reality Post, since in this new reality I didn't exist for them to talk to.

My first night in the reality which (I suppose) lay precisely adjacent to my 'home' reality was miserable and cold and I awoke disoriented, hungry and a little hung-over. A night on the tiles. An uncomfortable sleep under the cold stars. I took my lead from the other vagrants, followed them to an as-yet unopened Supermarket and round the back to sift through the large bins of stale bread and sell-by-expired vegetables. It was good stuff, actually. 'Watch out for Michelle,' I was advised. 'She's a dragon.' And then a car pulled into the deserted car-park and an individual in Sainsbury livery, Michelle herself, clambered out, yelling at us all to clear off. We scattered.

I wandered through the shut-up town, passing commuters on their way to the station and shop workers shuffling reluctantly into work bearing coffee in cardboard receptacles like Olympic torches. Do you know what I was thinking? I was thinking that I had gotten drunker yesterday than I realised, and that this in some way accounted for the day's dislocations. So I went back to my flat, thinking vaguely of having a shower and writing off the night as an alcohol-prompted adventure in slumming. But on my street I once again saw red-haired Roderick, this time accompanied by an angular, beaky woman (his girlfriend, I would discover), coming out of the building's main door together, dressed in overcoats. They kissed at the gate and went separate ways. After they had gone I went up to the flat, but they had changed the locks, following the previous day. Quick work on their part.

So instead I cut across town and intercepted Susan on her way into work, to remonstrate with her – to get her to drop the charade, or at the least clue me in on what was happening. I suppose she recognised me from before, because she was instantly on her guard.

'Just tell me why you're pretending not to know me!' I cried, the nitro of frustration mixing with the glycerine of bewilderment. I was, I daresay, more aggressive than was advisable. That was when she got the Mace from her handbag and struggled with the lid. That was when I marched away, telling myself I was going *in disgust*, although the emotion was much closer to terror.

I wandered aimlessly for a time. Flâneur. I abluted in the

Starbucks toilet, emerging to some disapproving frowns from the queue of people waiting to come in after me. I ducked into a nearby pub, where I spent the last of my ready cash on a couple of drinks. That made things seem more manageable, though seem is not the same as be. I decided the thing to do was to notify the authorities and let them sort the whole mess out.

So my afternoon was spent in the pokey atrium of the local police station. I explained myself to the desk sergeant, and, after an hour's wait, to a more senior policeman, neither of whom knew what to make of me. I gave them my details – date of birth, national insurance – and they patiently fed data into their computer and then they patiently explained that these numbers had no correlation with reality. With my consent they took me into the body of the station, made little oval woodcut-prints of my fingertips and swabbed the inside of my cheek. Come back next week, they advised. Till then, here's the address of a homeless charity. Of course I never went back, because a week later I was two realities away. But it wasn't the specifics, the practical things – it was the *mood*. All the policemen and policewomen with whom I came in contact treated me in the same way: courteously but distantly. Their manner was professionally disengaged, and it left me feeling decontextualised. They treated me like a non-person.

Now, now, the truth of course is that a *non-person* is precisely what I was. Still!

At that time, though, my emotion was one of anger. The more I thought about it, the crosser I became. I had been brushed off. I was facing another night sleeping amongst the strewn cardboard and the transparent giant seaweed of bubble-wrap sheets. So I resolved, short-sightedly I concede, to *force* myself on the attention of the police. I walked into a hardware store just as it was closing – 'I'm sorry we're closing' said the old geezer behind the till in a singsong voice. But I snatched a Sabatier blade from the shop's display, and rushed at him singing-out 'Aaa!' in a high-pitched voice, and when he stumbled backwards yelping and fell on his arse I tried to open the till so as to grab some money. It wouldn't open, no matter which buttons I pressed.

The old man was saying, 'Let's be calm, let's calm down' over and again, like an automaton. It occurred to me that I needed him to insert his staff card to get the till open, and brandishing the knife (feeling absurdly self-conscious as I did so) I *ordered* him to do this. He got gingerly to his feet, and fumbled out a credit card-sized object. It was attached to his belt by a helix-wound plastic cord.

'Let's stay calm,' he said, trembly-handedly and speaking in a thoroughly uncalm voice. 'I'm doing it now. I'm doing it.' I tried *waving* the knife at him, the gesture looked more stupid than intimidating. So I held it with my hand over the handle, and jabbed the point in his direction. I was clumsy, the end knocked the side of the metal till and the weapon jolted free of my grip. I swore as it chimed on the floor tiles. But I was down to retrieve it and back up in no time. It still had its cardboard wrapper sheathing its edge, which I thought diminished its scare-value. I ripped this free. My heart was chuntering along at a fair old lick, I don't mind telling you. The old man had the till open now, and I grabbed a bundle of notes. Then, feeling not in the least like Jesse James, I suddenly bolted, dropping the knife and running at full pelt through the open door. I ran and ran through the shopping precinct as adrenaline flushed through me, laughing aloud; ran through the river gardens and along the barge-way to the Old Bridge. Only then, gasping and puffing, did I stop. Only then, indeed, did the idiotically impulsive nature of what I had done come home to me. I had left the knife on the floor of the shop, doubtless covered all over with my fingerprints. I had that very afternoon left copies of those fingerprints in the local police station. This was not clever.

Still, at least I now had some cash: a little under £500, when I counted it. So I hailed a taxi, and went to the edge of town, along the causeway and past the industrial estate – it felt, somehow, safer there than in the centre. There I booked in to a Premier Inn.

I went up to my room, showered, drank the mini-bar dry, and sat on the bed watching television. I tried and failed to make sense of things, although the hooligan excitement of earlier had at least settled into a calmer state of being. There was still no reception on my mobile, but I could still access its phonebook, so I used the hotel phone to call a number of friends and acquaintances. Or to be precise: I started out doing that, but after the tenth or twelfth repetition of 'Who *is* this?', 'I've never heard of you' and, 'How did you get my number?' I grew demoralised and gave up. I tried calling the number for my father, in Canada, but it didn't ring.

Finally I fell asleep, and woke next morning with a sense of dread, certain that the police would be waiting at the breakfast bar to arrest me. But there was nobody there. So I ate, and read the papers, and lolled about in my room. It occurred to me to go about the town some more – to go, for instance to my workplace – and look deeper into the strange situation I found myself in. But after what I had done the day before, it seemed to me more sensible to lie low. And low is where I lay. When the maid came to clean the room, I took myself to the lobby bar and had a glass of wine, staring through the sheet glass at the comings and goings of men in suits and women in suits, clambering into or levering themselves out of company cars and taxis on the tarmac apron. Then I went back upstairs, and took an afternoon nap.

That evening I watched *Memento* on cable movies, and wondered if it were a serendipitous clue to my circumstance. That man lost his memory on a regular loop, erasing everything new he had just learned. I seemed to be in a kind of inverse equivalent; that *everybody else* lost their memory. But not their whole memory; just their memory of me. That was crazy. Then I wondered if, in some curious way, it might *seem* to an amnesiac that *he* could still remember but *everybody else* had forgotten – in the same way that it might seem to a madman that he was sane and everybody else mad. But I couldn't get that version of events to add up in my head, so I let it go. I was a little drunk by this stage. So I watched some porn, and cracked one off, and took a long, hot bath at midnight, and finally fell asleep in my dressing gown.

The next morning I decided to venture out. For a while I walked up and down the causeway not meaning to go anywhere, but simply to stretch my legs. The sky was completely covered by froth-coloured low cloud. Three industrial chimneys stood as the bases for three tapering table legs of white. It looked as if the whole sky had been filled up with the white smoke of industry.

After a while, made mildly reckless by boredom, I walked properly into town. Nobody noticed me. I ate in McDonald's, and coming out I experienced the violet-coloured fire, flaring all about me for a second time.

The light came over me, and went away, and I felt no different than I had before. It was a puzzle, and of course I wondered about its precise connection with what was going on. But my first assumption was that it was some kind of disorder in my eye, like a detaching retina, or perhaps some kind of schizophrenic side-effect in my brain chemistry. At any rate, I was compos mentis enough to want to cover my tracks a little after the criminal offence I had committed the previous day. I slunk into the centre of town, expecting to see wanted posters everywhere, but of course there was nothing. I decided to alter my appearance. Wanting to husband my money (for I did not relish robbing a shop of get some more) I bought a new set of clothes from a Charity Shop: a leather jacket, a pair of plastic sunglasses and a woollen cap in which my head nestled as tightly as an acorn in its cup. Then I walked back to the hotel.

I don't know what I thought. Perhaps I thought everything would snap back to normal of its own accord. Maybe I thought I was dreaming, or that I'd slipped into a coma, or something like that. I don't know what I thought. I wandered back to the hotel, as the clouds overhead darkened and purpled.

Back at the hotel nobody knew me. There was no booking in my name. 'I gave you a deposit,' I said, loudly. 'Cash!' I was conscious that such of my stolen money as I still had would not last me very long.

'I'm afraid our records show . . .' said the bland female behind the desk.

'I spoke to you this morning! I had a glass of wine and sat in *that chair*,' I said, pointing, as if the specificity of the chair might jog her memory.

'I'm afraid you must be mistaken, sir,' she said.

'But we talked *weather*!' I insisted. 'We talked likelihood of *rain*!'

'I'm afraid you must be mistaken, sir,' she repeated.

I believe there was some half-formed notion in my head that the hotel staff had been fooled by my change of clothes. But of course it wasn't that, and if I could have stilled the furious bluster and resentment in my head I'd have realised the truth. But the fact that this bullshit had been going on for *days* now stoked me. I swore at her. She stepped back from the counter, and a man in a uniform with green epaulettes and SECURITY on his lapel badge emerged from the depths of the building. 'Oh don't worry!' I yelled, with infantile vehemence. 'I'm *going*!' I marched out, and climbed into one of the waiting taxis, and told the driver to take me to another hotel. He folded up his *Sun* with patient precision and informed me that I'd have to be more precise than that. I told him, hotly, to drive me to the next *fucking* town. He waited until my breathing wasn't quite so loud, and then, without a word, he obliged me.

The drive took a quarter hour, during which time the clouds broke. The rainstorm came quickly, throwing innumerable plastic beads at the cab windows and down upon the roof for a while. In five minutes it was over. Afterwards sky and land blued. The land was heavier after the storm than before. 'Here,' I called, as he approached a Holiday Inn on the urban outskirts.

I tell you what I'd discovered: three days is plenty long enough to get used to the idea that one's life has completely changed. I resolved to leave my old life behind. At the edge of my mind was the consciousness that the police must have my fingerprints, and would be looking for me. But, I told myself, I don't exist! I'm not on their records. I don't exist.

Nevertheless, and for reasons I don't quite comprehend, the next three days were shaped by a profound anxiety. At the Holiday Inn I paid three nights' stay in advance, which took pretty much all my remaining monies. Still, for a few days I eked my way. I struck up a friendship with a group of corporate types, who were staying in the hotel for a marketing convention: three men and one woman. They were in the grooming products business, they told me. 'You know what?' said the oldest of them, a large fellow called Julian with broad blue jowls and the flesh about his eyes all crumpled and creased into a hundred petalic folds. 'It's the easiest game in the world. You buy standard emollient at ten pound the hundred-weight; add in a few quid o' scent and sell it in tiny little squeezy tubes at £8.99 a pop.'

'It's all in the marketing,' said Michelle, the woman. 'And that's where we come in. It's never the product, it's always the marketing.' Cream on skin.

'So,' I said, drunk – yes – but also heady with the existential licence of having simply left my old life entirely behind. 'So, it's a fraud?'

They all four made big dumb-shows of outrage and astonishment, interspersed with knowing laughter, boomed 'No! No!' and ordered another round of drinks 'and find out what our *cynical friend* is having'.

On the sixth day I woke feeling that the man who had stepped, on impulse, into the hardware store and robbed it at knifepoint was a different man to me. *That* wasn't the sort of thing I did. It was the sort of thing others did. Despite watching the TV news assiduously, and reading all the local papers the hotel carried, I saw no reference to the crime. This did not surprise me, for surely it was a trivial thing in the larger scheme of good and evil. But every moment in that Holiday Inn fizzed with low-level fear. Every time I came down in the morning for breakfast I wondered if the police would be waiting for me in the lobby. Every other human being who so much as looked at me did so, in my mind, because they recognised me for the criminal I was. I can't say it was a comfortable three days. But I'll say this: I remember it all vividly, and that vividness is itself a kind of joy. I've stayed in many more luxurious places since, and lived completely free from that sort of anxiety, yet those moments pass through me and leave almost no trace upon my mind. I suppose there is more of the *now* in grief than in happiness.

At any rate, when the violet-coloured fire flared up around me for the third time, at noon on the Saturday – and, more to the point, when the barman I had been speaking with at *exactly that moment* acted as if he had never seen me before – as if I had crept into the room like a ninja and suddenly leapt up in front of the bar – the penny began to drop. I was standing in an almost deserted hotel bar, and the barman was in the process of drawing me a pint of lager. Then there was the bright pale-mauve fire all about me, and when it withdrew there was no pint in front of me, and the barman had never seen me before.

It's a strange and antiquated phrase, isn't it? About the *penny dropping* I mean. Still, that is the direction in which the coin moved. At the main desk I discovered that the pretty brunette, with whom I had been on first-name terms that morning, didn't know who I was. I discovered there was no booking in my name, and that hotel was full for the weekend. It dawned on me then.

I put two and two together and arrived at – freedom, I suppose. Julian, Michelle and the other came down in a lift, and walked through the lobby past me without giving me so much as a second glance. 'Julian!' I called out, not expecting him to recognise me, and indeed precisely to check that he didn't. He looked round. He didn't speak, but his face said *do I know you*? So I bounded over to him, 'Julian! Julian!', and I fed him some of the details I had learned about him from the few days socialising – his employer, his wife's name, his kids – and genuine puzzlement afflicted his face like a sort of depression.

'I'm really *very* sorry,' he said, looking to his colleagues for confirmation. 'I'm *really* very sorry but I can't place you—'

'It's OK,' I said, a sense of almost limitless potential blossoming inside me; like flowers sprouting gaudy and beautiful from the shitty ground of my soul.

2

Three occurrences of the same thing is enough to establish the sequence in even the most opaque and slow-witted consciousness. The world carried on from day to day in its usual course, and I carried on with it; except that every three days (slightly less than three days I soon realised) I passed from it and reappeared in an identical version of it – or identical in every respect except that I was not known. This happened without fail. Early in the process I experienced a strange anticipatory anxiety as the deadline approached, wondering if this time would be different – if this time I would be (I could hardly help but think of it this way, particularly in the later stages as the transition became increasingly necessary to liberate me from the consequences of my actions) stranded. But I never was. Every three days, the same violet fire; and a re-emergence in the world as an unknown, free, clean, individual. Liberated from my job, I watched a great deal more TV than before. One afternoon I recall watching the movie *Groundhog Day* and marking the similarity between the fiction and my fact. But the character in *that* film is trapped in the same day over and over, and is released only when he learns his Hollywood lesson to be nice to people. My world kept moving on, as the world does. Only I changed – my presence in the midst of things wiped clean every three days, like shaking away an etch-a-sketch portrait. Also, the *Groundhog Day* actor goes so far as to try and kill himself in his desire to escape, only to find himself returned to the start of the same day. I knew, with a bone-certainty, that this would not be my fate. If I died, I would not reappear in a new dimension, I would be dead. Once I stood barefoot on a wineglass (I was drunk) and gashed the underside of my foot. I needed stitches, the wound was so deep; and had to be ambulanced to hospital. But come the violet fire, the wound remained. It took weeks to heal, actually; and I hobbled from alternate reality to alternate reality until it did.

I still have the scar, like an open-bracket, on the sole of my foot.

See?

Naturally, I expended some mental energy on trying to work out *why* this had happened to me. Accordingly I considered various theories. Most of these were derived from the films I have seen, which is no doubt an indictment of the paucity of my cultural imagination. I pondered whether I was living an *A Wonderful Life* life, whereby some angelic power was showing me what the world would be like if I had never been born in it. What made this unlikely was that the world was in no discernible way different. Maybe this, of course, was the point the angelic power was trying to make; the ego-eradicating point about my irrelevance. But if so, it was not obvious to me why he had to make it over and over again, pushing the cosmic reset button every three days, without fail. Or, no, not the *cosmic* button; just the button with my face on it.

I read books of science, and books of science fiction. One notion I gleaned from one of these is the theory that people slide from alternate reality to alternate reality *all the time*. That with every decision we make an alternate reality buds off in which that decision went the other way. The books I read suggested that we don't experience this slide down the delta of possible pathways as anything but a seamless progression, because our point of view passes so smoothly. Like the penny in the arcade machine, jolting down the matrix of pins, bouncing randomly left or right at each interruption to its fall until it lands on the smoothly indrawing-outpushing metal shelf, to take its place in the irregular tessellations of coins.

Sometimes I wondered if something had happened to my mind – a stroke, perhaps – that had dislocated my perception of this endlessly unfolding and branching net of possibilities. But I kept coming back to the core point: that my perception of the day-to-day remained as smooth and continuous as ever it had; it was other people who experienced the discontinuity, and its name was me. Or to put it more precisely: everybody's else's perception carried on as smoothly as it ought, and so did mine. Except that every three days I slipped into the next reality along.

Speculation, though, was a fruitless exercise, and I gave it up. Quite apart from anything else, and for the first few weeks in particular, more practical considerations intruded. I needed money. I came back to my home town, and even walked back into the hardware store where that first time, furious and impulsive, I had snatched money at knifepoint. The same old man was there, standing at the same till; and he greeted me with glad, unrecognising eyes. It dawned on me that where I now was, *the crime had never happened.* Indeed, it dawned on me that whatever I did in the world would disappear once the seventy hours point was reached. If I did any good in the world, then all record or memory of it would pass away as if it had never been – no, not *as if*, but *literally so.* And if I did evil, the same was true. I could beat a man with a tyre-iron and rob him of his wallet in the morning; and in the afternoon I could encounter that same man – and he would be unbruised, unrobbed, neither recognising me nor suspecting me of any evil intentions towards him. I could kill a man on Saturday and find him alive again on Sunday.

3

Ask yourself: what would you do, if you found yourself in that situation? What would you do in a world in which the consequences of your actions, *no matter what the actions were*, lasted no longer than three days? Would you strive to live a virtuous life?

But then I must ask you: how? Three days is too short a space to build up any relationships of trust with the people around you. It is too short a space, for instance, to get a job and earn money. Of course you must *have* money, for you must eat and drink, and sleep in a bed, and do all those things. But there is no Welfare record of your status as a citizen; no National Insurance number attached to your name; no reference from any previous employer. Where is the money to come from? This is where we find ourselves, at no choice of our own. On the one hand, it is impossible to obtain the funds for living legally. And on the other – and this, it seems to me, possesses exactly the same weight – any illegal action you may commit is wiped from the consciousness of the whole world every three days.

Actually, the money problem sorted itself soon enough. Early on during my time I observed a man at a cashpoint, and was in a position to memorise his pin (it had three sixes in it, which amused me). It was careless of him to permit me to see his pin. Afterwards I mugged him for his wallet. In *that* reality, I daresay, he cried *police*! and had all his cards cancelled. But I slid noiselessly into a parallel reality, in which the credit card number still operated. Of course it did, because J R FAIRBOROUGH still existed in that reality; and his bank account was still the same. He was there in all the realities, I think. *I* was the one who wasn't. That meant that, every three days, I could seek out a cashpoint and steal a few hundred pounds from his account, book into a hotel with his plastic, and relax. I carried this card from reality line to reality line and it always worked.

I fell, in fact, into a particular rhythm of life. For my first two days in the new reality-line I kept my nose more-or-less clean, kept out of trouble, amused myself in whatever ways occurred to me. Boredom, frankly was a problem. But the third day possessed a different tenor. On the third day I became excited; that deep-bone tingle children feel as Christmas approaches. On the third day I could do anything to anyone.

Of course, if it came to it, I could do anything to anyone on any day. About a month into my new existence I got myself, carelessly, arrested by the police on day two. I was stealing something from a shop, some trivial piece of electrical equipment, and, a little drunk, I was careless. A store detective apprehended me, and, disinclined to go along with him, I picked up a laptop computer from the shelf and struck him with it. I may, in retrospect, have hit him rather more times than was necessary to get him to unhand me. The metal folder of the machine became slippery, and I had to keep changing my grip so as to be able to bring it down upon his supine head. It's not that *the red mist descended* – I really can't say, in honesty, that it did. But violence is something that *focuses one's attention*, I find. Once you begin it, it's hard to concentrate upon anything else until you've finished. That day the violence came to an end when two policemen grabbed my arms, and stumbled me awkwardly to the ground.

I was cuffed and taken away and processed in the police station. A placid-faced PC took his jacket off, held me over a porcelain sink and washed the blood from my hands and face. My clothes were taken away, and I was given scratchy nondescript gear to wear. Then I was put in a cell. Naturally they couldn't discover who I was. They kept sending in different people to ask me questions. I slept the night fitfully on the narrow cot, and ate scrambled eggs for breakfast – a fact I record as an instance of my bloody-mindedness, for my metabolism cannot abide egg, and I was sick over everything. So the same placid-faced copper, his bald patch an oval, washed me again and my nondescript gear was replaced with more nondescript gear. I was put back in the cell.

To begin with this new experience was diverting, or at least *up to a point* it was – since I had never before spent a night in the cells, or had any dealings with the police beyond the most trivial, cautions for reckless driving and the like. But it quickly palled. Sitting in a cell was boring. Moreover, I couldn't necessarily see how I was going to get out of that place. The third day came, and the violet flicker fire bloomed around me, and when it passed I found myself still in the cell. The difference now, of course, was that the police had no idea who I was, or how I had come to be inside one of their locked cells. They were almost comically astonished, in fact. They kept coming in and out; asking me the same questions, and pressing me with *how did I do it*? With *was I some kind of fucking reverse Houdini*? With *was it some publicity stunt*? They wanted my name, so I gave it them – it hardly mattered (and no, I'm still not telling *you* my name). Then they wanted to know what I was *doing* there, how I *got in* there, what I *thought I was playing at*. I decided the best answer to that was 'I don't know.' They kept me for the rest of the afternoon, but had no legal ground for keeping me any longer, so they let me go. They asked me to return to the station in a week's time, something I blithely promised, and then I walked free. They'd taken away all my stuff, of course, in the previous reality-line, and the police in this reality didn't have it to return to me. But I re-obtained J R FARNBOROUGH's credit card soon enough.

Which, in turn, raises some interesting questions. There were times, of course there were, when I was intrigued by the *parameters* of my experience. Mostly it didn't bother me, and soon after the whole thing began I gave up all attempts to get to the bottom of what was happening. But on occasion a mighty curiosity would seize me. What *was* going on? The violet light possessed me, and I moved on. Anything I had immediately about my person came with me. On one occasion, as the transition time approached, I grabbed hold of the metal frame of my hotel-room bed, pulling the whole thing a yard out of position in my eagerness, to see if my touch meant that the whole bed would pass along with me. It didn't. The purple fire passed away and I found myself holding a short metal pipe, sheared, or rather melted away, on either side. Evidently it was the luminous fire that delineated the extent of what passed. So, I assume, the air immediately around me travelled from dimension to dimension; a thin layer of whatever ground beneath my feet passed too; usually I passed from lawn or floor to an identical lawn or floor, so it was hard to tell. Once, unintentionally, I took a hand. This really wasn't my fault. The truth is I thought I had more time before the fire came. I really thought I had another half hour or so. But I got that wrong, and I happened to be shaking the hand of a man in a pub. Up flared the light, and when it passed away I was holding the hand, and nothing else.

You can't blame me for that one, though. It was an accident.

There were other occasions when I would be seized by a desire to locate the *point of difference* that differentiated one reality line from another. There must be one, I reasoned; which is to say, there must be a point of difference beyond the fact that I had never existed in all these subsequent realities. Perhaps it was possible that each alternate reality was an *exact* clone of the one before, every last atom identically placed; but somehow I doubted that. My not existing must have made bigger changes. But *so many* of the details were identical. I tried to trace my father, but the phone number didn't work; and hours in the library surfing the net turned up nothing. It was possible that he had never gone to Canada at all, in this reality-line; but although I dug out a few people with his name and called them, none of them was him. It was also possible (of course I considered this) that my mother was still alive in this reality line. It was possible that my dad and mum had never gotten together in the first place.

For a week or so I became fixated on the idea that they, like I, had been somehow loosened in the sheaf of alternates; that they were passing from one to the other reality-line, just as I was. As to why this might be, I suppose I wondered if my strange experience were linked in some way to my DNA – a part of my makeup concerning which I have only the loosest sense, but which I know I inherited from them. If they had become dislodged, as I had, it would explain why the internet seemed to have no record of Dad; although that might also (of course) simply be a function of his generation and dotage. I travelled around a little, and poked into the matter in a desultory way, but I didn't get to the bottom of it.

It occurred to me that if this thing had happened to me, then it could have happened to others. Indeed, it seemed to me unlikely that I would be the only person so affected. But what to do about that? I could think of no way to locate others like me, and no real reason to do so.

One day, on a whim, I went to my old flat, now occupied by 'Roderick', when I was sure he and his girlfriend were at work. I kicked the door open – no longer possessing my keys – and explored. The shape of the rooms was so very familiar; the damp patch in the corner of the bathroom ceiling the same; the stains on the carpet. But here was all Roderick's stuff; all his junk, and his papers, and a drawer with letters and photographs – Roderick and his bony girlfriend. It was summer. I opened all the windows and stood for a long time looking out, savouring the disconnection of myself and my former life as you might savour the sourness of vinegar. The sunlight was hard as chalk; the air as hot and blue like cigarette smoke. A plane cut a white slit in the sky. The horizon was cluttered with pellet-hard white clouds. From where I stood I could just about make out the cellophane shimmer of the river's surface. It was the flexing and warping of light into life.

I found Roderick's passport, and two thousand pounds worth of Euros – assembled preparatory, I suppose, to some continental holiday the two of them were planning. I took this cash to a bureau de change and turned it into English money.

I'll confess this: it took me the longest time to adjust to the profound *aimlessness* of my new existence. For a while it felt like I was on holiday, and that was certainly a pleasant-enough vibe to surf. But a holiday prolonged becomes tedious; and any kind of life without friends, family or lovers will of course feel vacuous. Family cannot be conjured from nothing; and friends take longer than seventy hours to establish. As for lovers, at first I thought three days was too short a time to persuade a complete stranger into bed with me. For months I employed prostitutes; the first time nervously (never having tried it before), but latterly, as I became habituated to it, with more confidence and ease. I discovered the best phone numbers to call, and arranged for ladies to come to whichever hotel room I was occupying. But I would also meet attractive women, and get chatting with them, and as time went by I found myself wishing, increasingly, for something more than the impersonality of paid-for sex. But let's say I booked into a new hotel on a Wednesday afternoon, and met a group of business-suited men and women in the bar that evening. The first night would be getting-to-know-everybody; the second might entail a greater sense of intimacy, and only by the third – even supposed they were staying so long – would a pass be conceivable. And then, nervily, the woman in question, the person who attracted me, would almost certainly be married or with a boyfriend and would put out strong negative signals. If I pushed matters, and asked directly, she would say no, regretfully (as happened a few times), or angrily (as happened once), and that would be that. I am not so handsome a man that women fall over themselves to go to bed with me.

One night I shared the hotel elevator up with a woman called Rosalee. She had been pleasant enough with me throughout the evening, but had talked rather ostentatiously (I thought) about her husband. She unlocked her room, three doors down from mine; and said goodnight to me, and on a whim I wandered over towards her, as if there were something more I wanted to say to her. Then, trembling with my own impulsiveness, I pushed her into the room, and over her cries and struggles, fell on top of her onto the floor. She screamed a little, and I grew anxious that other people would hear, so I crammed her tights into her mouth. It wasn't very good sex, I'll be honest; or rather whilst there *was* a thrill in the experience, it wasn't precisely a sexual one. I suppose it was the sense that boundaries did not contain me. It was the sense that nobody could say no to me. It was, in other words, that toddler *imperium*, that liberating sense of freedom from the shackles of civilised behaviour, that we all once understood, and that we have all crushed under a lifetime's conditioning and repression. At any rate, I didn't hurt Rosalee; or I didn't hurt her beyond the necessary trauma of the initial assault. I did my business, and afterwards I strolled back to my room, gathered my stuff and walked out of the hotel.

Of course I was bothered by what I had done. I am not a monster. But – and this is the really crucial thing, so I might ask you to pay attention – *but* I returned to that same hotel the following day, after the flickering violet passed over me; and that evening I introduced myself to Rosalee in the bar, and chatted to her, and she was not in the least traumatised or scared of me. It was a nice evening, actually. She and her colleagues and I had a good time. It was their last night at their sales conference, and the next day they were all going home – and did go home, I'm sure. And Rosalee, immaculate and unhurt, went back to her husband and lived, I'm sure, a very happy life. So where was the harm? I certainly didn't make a habit of it. I don't like to think of myself as a rapist. And in fact I'm not one – it happened, that one time, but in another world, when I was another person. I have passed through dozens and dozens of reality lines after that event, and in every single one I could have tracked Rosalee back to her hometown (I'm sure she told me what it was, though I can't remember) and found her living blithely unconscious that any harm had ever been done her. If she doesn't think anything bad has happened, then what evil did I do?

And I'll tell you something else. That particular event gave me a strange confidence. I approached women in a different way. I suppose it was a sense, on some subconscious level, that nothing could ultimately be denied to me. If there were a woman who attracted me, I could force her, and then simply walk away beyond the chance of consequences. Just knowing this was enough; I didn't have to act it out. But it gave me a certain swagger, a confidence of approach, and if some women did not like this, rather more did. I continued to pay prostitutes, often the same girls (although they, of course, never knew who I was); but from time to time, and for the pure satisfaction of the successful pursuit, I sometimes persuaded women I met in bars to come back to my room, and no money changed hands.

wasn't in the least bothered about getting wet. I had no reason to stay dry. I enjoyed communing with the boisterous elements, as the wind trailed its invisible silk gown over the floor, and all the trees were ponderously head-banging to a tune only they could hear. But then, blink and it was winter, a hard sunlight smearing off the snow, giving the white fields an odd and scorched look.

There's no point in trying to evade this, or play it down. I might have hurt some people, but the next day *they were not hurt*, and had no memory of being assaulted – in literal fact never had been. I did not choose this state of affairs. I did not make it this way, but it is where I am thrown. It is the logic of the world. And after a full year of my new mode of being, freedom had soaked deep into my soul, and it was no longer possible to imagine another way of being. Who did I really harm? I stole the credit card and pin from J R FAIRBOROUGH and over the course of many months I suppose I decanted tens of thousands of pounds from his bank account to pay for accommodation and clothes, food and drink. But J R Fairborough the man only ever had to face, in any one reality, a few hundred misappropriated pounds (and I daresay the bank refunded him that money). So did I really rob him? Or Rosalee, poor Rosalee, mumbling and struggling in that hotel room – I'm sure that experience was not pleasant for her. But I passed through worlds in which hundreds of Rosalees lived happy lives. So as a proportion of her total spread of existence what harm did she suffer? Some minuscule fraction of an assault. We can go further and say: what if there *is* an infinite sheaf of alternate realities? Any real number divided by infinity is zero. In an infinite universe, any individual instance of suffering literally amounts to nothing. To nothing at all! You can't argue with mathematics. Mathematics trumps ethics, my dear people. To kill the only cosmic iteration of Ken Mantel, in his ridiculous ill-fitting suit, would be a bad thing; but when you are faced with an infinite phalanx of Ken Mantels, standing in your way, calling the police on his mobile, waving his arm to stop you stealing the car from his shoddy little dealership – if you run him down he's one of a rank of millions of pawns. You can't tell me that means the same thing.

I didn't tell you about Ken? I decided, on a whim, I wanted a car. I could hardly buy one outright; Fairborough's credit card hardly stretched that far. I thought I'd take one for a test drive and simply not return it, but Ken insisted on coming with me. That wasn't going to work. So I decided simply to drive it away, until Ken, idiotic Ken, decided he would stand in my way. That's not important. The important thing is this: afterwards I drove to a country hotel, for a change, and took a top-floor, five-star room. And that evening I stood on the balcony (for this room had its own balcony) and smoked a cigarette, and drank some brandy, and looked up at the sky. The moon was there, like a clipped toenail. The sky was bruise-black and flecked with stars all over it, and the air beautifully and crisply cold. The lawn was enormous, and was the darkest of purples in the moonlight. And this is what I thought: whatever you do is alright. This is what I thought: the moon looks no bigger from an upstairs window than a down. That's what I thought.

Let me put it another way. A tap is running. When you place your hand under it you are not sure, for the moment, whether it is very hot or very cold. This is how good and evil manifest, in the world, more often than not. It might be an act of courage and virtue to do something – to invade Iraq, for instance, as my country did. It might be an act of great wickedness. At first, you can't be sure which it is. I went past that same dealership a few days later, and Ken was back up front, in his cheap suit, smiling at the passers-by.

4

Less than a year passed before I noticed that the interlude between transitions was shortening. I had grown so accustomed to the rhythms of my new life that this was almost as disorienting a discovery as the original passage. Mauve fire at noon on the third day crept, almost imperceptibly, but then more markedly, into mauve fire at late morning on the third day. I got used to this new state of affairs, of course. Human beings have a great talent for getting used to things. I carried on, as I had been carrying on; mostly just passing the time, amusing myself, drinking, eating, only rarely hurting anybody. But once the space between transitions began to shrink, the rate of the shrinkage soon started to accelerate. For a number of months I experienced the purple flame late-morning, or mid-morning. Then, suddenly, it was happening at breakfast on the third day; and then in the middle of the night at the end of the second – such that I woke up wrapped in shreds of sheets in a strange bed, sometimes not alone. I took to getting up earlier and earlier, so as to be sure to be awake when the transition happened. But the time moved earlier and earlier. It happened at midnight. It happened the evening of day two – and a couple of months later I was down to two days, with the flame starting up again at midday.

Of course I pondered where this new development was tending. There was nothing I could do about it, one way or another, so I didn't fret unduly; but if it continued, it seemed to me clear that it would reach a limit in a matter of weeks – that the length of time between transitions would shrink from days to hours, from hours to moments, and then . . . what? I suppose I assumed there would be a purple fizz and flash, a sort of alternate-reality-shift short circuit; and then I would blink, and find myself locked once again into a single reality. I told myself that I could face this eventuality with equanimity. That I had lived that way before, and could do so again, that it would give me the chance for a normal existence; to marry and have children and all of that. But my uneasiness was deeper than self-reassurance could reach. I had grown accustomed to my rootless freedom and did not wish to give it up.

I suppose, looking back, that I went on a kind of spree. Spree is not the wrong word. As the window of opportunity shrank I indulged myself more fully. I took great pleasure in smashing things up; in setting fire to things, for instance; ram-raiding shops, crashing and bashing. I derived an almost zen-like pleasure from – let's say – throwing a dustbin so as to break the large plate glass storefront of Debenhams, timing the action immediately before the purply flames came about me such that I could look again to see the glass miraculously restored to the way it had been before. I became more and more reckless. I was not caught.

Two days became one; and one day became half a day. The line approached its asymptote. I don't need to draw this out longer than necessary. I found myself stepping from reality to reality hourly, and I strolled by the river, and took a drink, and watched the swans. It was early in the year, and the weather was that uncertain compromise between late winter and early spring. I folded my scarf around my neck more closely, and the mauve light sparkled all about my body, and I wandered on.

The climax was coming. Half an hour passed between transitions; and then quarter of an hour; then seven minutes; then three. I stood in Gap, in front of one of their full-length mirrors; but even though I could see (from, as it were, the inside) the violet light flaring and licking about me, I could not see that same light enfolding my mirror-reflection. That puzzled me. Three minutes became a minute as I walked out onto the high street again. Thirty seconds later, there was another flash and dazzle. I counted fifteen and it happened again. A handful of seconds. A second. And—

5

It was a prolonged dazzle, and bright light-blue shimmer that totally swallowed me. If I expected it to stop, or burn out, and for me to find myself in the universe of consequences again . . . well, it didn't. Or it didn't immediately. Instead the shimmer increased in intensity, and I had to shut my eyes; but it was bright enough to penetrate my closed lids. I stood there.

And then, just as I was starting to wonder whether I was now going to have to spend the rest of existence stuttering blindingly from reality to reality, the light stopped.

I opened my eyes and found myself – well, here.

You came to see me a certain time later. Naturally, I find it hard to calculate the passage of time in this place. The first thing you said to me, confusingly enough, was: 'You will have interactions with me, and you should think of me as your defence. You will not have interactions with your prosecutor. That is not the way we do things.'

I understood only much later which idiom you were invoking (for my benefit I suppose). Legal. No courtroom, no judge, no cross-examination. But a prosecutor, nonetheless. An adversary.

It was not until our third meeting that you explained my *trajectory*. Trajectory was your word. Some people think there is an infinite sheaf of alternate reality lines, you said. (You know what? I incline to that view myself.) You yourself, though, think that many of these lines cancel one another out, and that the multiverse resolves into only ('only') a very broad sheaf of hundreds of thousands of variants. Or millions of variants. Or – whatever. I suppose the number matters, but it's hard for me to care.

'You were deep in the sheaf, from the perspective of where we are now,' you told me. 'The initial extraction resulted in a weak oscillation, and you moved only slowly, to begin with, from line to line.' And then you embarked upon a digression about how 'slowly' was the wrong sort of concept for this, which, frankly, you could have spared me. Then: 'but the further out you passed, the closer you came, the more force, and the more rapid the oscillation.' I *swear* to you that's how you talk. It's almost comical.

I think of myself as tracing out an elegant parabola, from my launching point up and out and curling round until I achieve a sort of perfect orbit. Or an escape velocity. Or any of these sorts of distorting modes of speech to visualise what happened to me. 'We apprehended you,' you said. 'We captured you.'

'I don't understand!' I said. 'What did I do wrong?'

To be tried for crimes committed *after* I was arrested forces me to wonder what justified the arrest – or was it something that could only ever *be* justified after the event? Did you somehow know I was going to sin, even before I did it?

I asked this absolutely genuinely, for my life – I mean, of course, my life before the initial dislodgement, had been as blameless as any person's. Not perfectly blameless, I mean; but not so terrible or criminal as to merit . . . well, all this.

You did that polo-mint eye thing you do, when your astonishment approaches its maximum intensity. 'Wrong?' you repeated. 'The crimes – the killings, rape, theft?'

'But that was *after* I was extracted from my original timeline!' I protested.

I made this point several times. Sometimes you would repeat 'original timeline' with such ponderous scorn as to make me doubt that there was ever a timeline rightly mine, whether I was some kind of reality cuckoo. But more often you would start some complicated lecture . . . I suppose, you were trying to give me a clue, as far as your Byzantine rules and prohibitions permitted you, as to what the prosecutor, the *adversary*, would be saying about me. The lecture consisted of something arcane and, frankly, metaphysical about the way my 'crimes' (you'll forgive the inverted commas) are projected across the continuum as a kind of permanent stain, or shadow, or something. That although they began 'after', in a manner of speaking, my initial apprehension, yet they reflect back 'before' that moment, in some existential sense. I don't see it. You'd expect me to say so, but I really don't. I didn't ask to be dislodged from my reality. If you people had left me embedded there, I fully believe that I would have lived a blameless life.

'Ah but you weren't,' you said, lugubriously. 'Ah but you didn't.'

I'm hamstrung by not knowing the nature or jurisdiction of my adversary, or the nature of charges, or the possible consequences of a guilty verdict. And when I say 'I didn't ask to be dislodged from my initial reality!' you look genuinely puzzled, as if a murderer were to say 'But I didn't ask to be born!' by way of justifying his assassinations. But the case is hardly the same! Birth is just birth; where my extraction was the first step in an elaborate 'police' operation to drag me from the regular world to . . . well, to here.

'It's not the least bit like that,' you say.

Do you mean the comparison isn't right? Or my account of the extraction isn't right? Nobody asks to be born – that's true, though. To be dragged without consent into this arena where we are then judged with horrible severity, with heaven-and-hell severity, doesn't seem altogether . . . Well, I was going to say 'fair', but that's probably not a very sensible observation to make.

And some of my questions might as well be in double-dutch for all the sense I get out of you. I asked, for instance, whether I had been extracted – following from this whole events-in-one-line-casting-shadows-over-the-whole idea – whether I had been extracted because 'you', or 'they', had spotted some genuinely monstrous crime in my future. I mean in the future of me in that original time line. ('Original?' you said, in that vastly muddled, sepulchral, I-don't-follow voice you use). But this didn't seem to be a question you could comprehend. *When is the trial?* does no better (' "trial"?', followed after a slow interlude, and with greater expressive bewilderment, with ' "when"?'). So, to be honest, I've more or less given up on you for elucidation. I can't believe the final illumination will be far off.

Naturally I consider the possibility that I will be executed, or some equivalent. I hope not, but I don't know. How could I know? And in that event, well, dust thou art, and to dust thou shalt return. Which is all very well. But there's dust and there's dust. Maybe we're talking sand and ashes; but maybe, just maybe, we're talking cocaine and gunpowder. Don't you think?

The *Mary Anna*

I've paid the bills for your lifestyle; I've funded your every spree—
And now your father is dying; and you must listen to me!
I can be COMA'd, can I? The doctor has told you? He lied.
I shall be dead tomorrow; no science can hold back that tide.
These Cryo-Operative What-Nots postpone what they cannot cure,
I'd rather die in my bed, now, than have ten frozen dream-years
more.
Death's not a thing to be feared, son, with skull-helmet, boots and
black cape;
Dying's a part of our Life-world, a gravity none can escape.
Life launches us upward to high flight; but then the parabola drops.
And whilst I've been happy to live life, I'm happy enough as it stops.
Fifty years out in the System, from Mercury to past Mars Base,
Though it has earned me a billion, leaves nothing to cover my face.
Nothing, I suppose, but two credits, to lie one-and-one on my eyes,
And this chip I hold in my grasp here – and this for your secret
prize.
Perform one task for me, Havel, though it's neither your Soma
nor R,
I know you've devoted your life to being where the Zip Crowd are.
Devoted your life and my money, and reckoned them both well
spent,
Though you've never earned half a credit to cover food, psych bills
or rent.
Happy to live on my money, contented to slosh it away,
And I no longer grudge you the credits – provided you do as I say.
Not counting the Line and the shipyards, the orbitals and the Facs
too,

I've made twice a billion – and made me; but damned if I ever made you.
Pilot at twenty-five years flat; and married at thirty in haste,
Ten thousand men on the pay-roll, and forty freighters in space!

And now I'm an honorary Senator, and wear the White Star on my coat,
Talk on the level to Generals of Industry, Presidents, people of note
Fifty years in the making, and every last year of it fight,
Investments that pay from Neptunian darkness up to Venusian light.
I didn't begin with mooching. I found me a job and I stuck;
I worked like a robot, and plunged on, though now they're calling it luck.
God, what ships I've served on – analogue, leaky and old—
Some with a hull thin as cardboard, to keep out the vacuum and cold,
G-couches fashioned for giants that left you all bruised-up and sore,
Or couches made up for a dwarf-man that plain chucked you out on the floor.
Whole *days* at 4G, unbroken, though Law sets its limit at hours;
Fuel pellets lumpy as coal and as useless; or ground down explosive like flour.
Food that would poison a heifer, and crew-fellows nothing but strife
And mission insurance for write-off, worth more than a crewman's life.
Add it all up and I travelled – I brag it – nearly a full light year;
They called me Debugger and Fireman, the Pilot Who Knew No Fear:
I worked every billet I could, and I took all the money they paid;
And spent it at random, or gambled it; scattered as soon as made.

Till I met and I married your mother, took the boost-up from boy to man:
Ten years older, and wise as AI, she taught me the need for a plan.

Piloting all through the System, a father at thirty-three,
And your mother saving the money and making a man of me.
I was content to be flier, but she said there was better to find;
She took the chances I wouldn't, and I followed your mother blind.
Only her past held her back, for she'd Law Tags she could not quit:
Justice pinned her for taxes, fraud, smuggling, anything as would fit;
Her credit rating was zeroed, she was banned from flying in space;
And all for a misunderstanding, and a flechette in somebody's face.
Now she had *me* to borrow the money – she helped me to manage the loan,
And we bought half-shares in a shuttle, with a logo all of our own.
Though mindwipe was hers if they caught us, an asteroid jail for me,
Yet still we flew it together, and saved on a crewmember's fee,
More than the money it kept us together when orbits were slow and long,
And your mother was never a groundling; deep space was where she belonged.
Patching and fuelling on credit, and living the Lord knows how,
I started the Red Ox freighters – I've thirty-eight of them now.
I say it was me that began it, and my name was the one on the slate,
But most of the running was Mary's, and Mary shouldered the weight.

And those were the days of fast cargoes, and trade was brisk and fair
And Mercury would make us our fortune, but she died in the tussle there—
Owners we were, full owners, and the boat was named after her,
And she died in the *Mary Anna*. My heart; how young we were!
For Mercury's made of pig iron, at the base of its gravity well,
And if you can mine out a portion, there's buyers for all you can sell.
Though we didn't have mine equipage, and couldn't afford mining crew
We only had wits and a ramshackle spaceship provisioned for just we two.
It wasn't entirely legal, and it certainly wasn't too safe,

For the aim wasn't orbital caution but to fly a bomb-run and to strafe.
Our speed added star-blast momentum to concentrate nuclear bloom
And great big lovely chunks of mercury-iron were blasted up into 'cuum
Spun in elliptical orbits and free to be netted and snared
And precious as gold was the prize for those who had planned it and dared.
It was no schoolyard exercise, matching their wild delta-v;
I flew the craft and your ma stuck a dart-jet in every lump she could see.

And if we had had a third crewperson, maybe she wouldn't have died;
For maybe we would have had warning of the policeboat's slammed broadside,
Abrupt in our sensors from sun's white shadow, coming in shocking and fast,
Firing cannons to catch us our breath and that breath your mother's last;
For the aft pods were hit, the hull breached, and vacuum quenched the blaze.
I rushed to repair and to find her, but Mary had ended her days.
She was beautiful-looking in death, although scorched up feet to thighs,
And although the swift decompression had beetroot-blackened her eyes.
And there's no shame in saying I wept, for grief pierced me like a sword;
But yet I couldn't hold on to her, for fear that the police would board.
Although she was dead she was lawless, and I would have gone into jail,
And prison fees cost more than *Mary Anna* would get in a sale.

So I clutched her and then I released her, and tossed her out into
space,
And I busied myself with repairs, though all I could see was her face;
And awaited the police hail and boarding, and squared ship AI with
my lie—
That I'd found the pig iron floating when I happened to be passing
by;
And tagged it to warn other shipping of debris, all legal and friendly
and fair,
And the police crew didn't believe me, and I knew it and I didn't
care.
But they hadn't a case, so they fined me and left me to go my way,
Wifeless and never to know in which grave-orbit Mary lay.

So I went on a spree back on Earth, and I fitted a Soma Bug,
But I dreamed your mother appeared and warned me to give up the
drug.
A dream, or drug hallucination, or maybe her spirit: who cares—
Told me to stick to my business, and to let others stick to theirs,
Saving the money (she warned me), letting others who wanted get
high.
Provide for my son – that's you, Hav – let 'son' be enough of a
why.
And I met McCullough moonside, renting space in Copernicus'
wall,
And between us we planned a repair yard, Lagranged and open to
all:
Cheap repairs for the cheap ones. It paid, and the business grew;
For I bought me a laser-lathe huller, and that was a gold mine too.
'Cheaper to build than mend' I said, but McCullough dreamed of
the stars,
And we wasted a year in talking before moving the shop to Mars.
Nearer the asteroid beltways and higher-up over the Sun,
But most of all further away from the paths where the Earth police
run.

The Merchant Houses beginning, and all of us started fair,
Building up spaceships like houses, and fixing the drive-rails square.
And I wouldn't call *all* of them criminal, though some tugged the law from true;
And I worked at fixing, and trading, and had too little time left for you.
Though I paid the best tutors and virals, saw you daily by face or by screen,
You sensed my love lacked the meaning that a father's love ought to mean.
Though I spoke to you fatherly words, and looked you full in the face,
My eye was not on you – you knew it – but on money and spaceships and space.
And McCullough, *he* dreamed interstellar, and starsystems wholly new;
And wasted our money on liners to fit generations of crew,
And hulking expensive engines to make speeds near to half that of light.
But McCullough was killed in the nineties, and – Well, I'm dying to-night . . .

I knew – I knew what was coming, that the Houses would fall into war:
Wear-tear is one thing to repair-shops, combat damage something more.
Plasmetal and battle expansions. It paid, I tell you, it paid,
When we came with our nine-hour service and collared the long-run trade!
Then came the armour-contracts, but that was McCullough's side;
He was always the best at designing, but better, perhaps, he died.
I went through his private data; the notes were plainer than print;
And I'm no fool to finish what's started once I'm given the hint.
His children were angry – no matter. I saw what his equations meant;

And I started the Tachyon Thrust game, and it paid me sixty per cent.
Sixty per cent *with* failures, twice what we'd otherwise do,
And a quarter-billion Credits, and I saved it all for you!
It was clear when the war was coming, and clearer when it would end
And backing the House of Ulanov was money it made sense to spend.
So peace came, more fierce and law-strict than even the old Solar Pact,
And I started my life quite over; for I had what I'd previously lacked,
And though you don't value it, Havel, it's getting, not having, that counts;
Not winning trophies for polo on pressurized hydraulic mounts.
You're nearer sixty than fifty, and fruit from an alien tree,
I bought you the best education, and what have you done for me?
Though you married that thin-limbed woman, she's white and stale as a bone,
She gave you your art-crowd nonsense; but where's that kid of your own?
The things that I value – you scorn them, you take and you never give,
And the things I know are rotten – you think are the way to live.
Half your time in VR, and the other half pharmed-out on Som,
Eight different houses on four worlds, and none of them counts as a home.

I had a half billion then, but I didn't consider it mine;
I brought out the Red Ox logo again and made it up into a line.
I used my money as grav-assist, to slingshot me to the high road,
But you – you're content just to shed it, as if it's an onerous load.
Weak, a liar, and idle, and mean as a spaceship stray,
Nosing for scraps in the galley, a whelp who is blind to the way.

I'm sick of the whole bad business. I want to go back where I came.
Hav, you're my son – or you're Mary's, and at least you carry our name.
I want to lie by your mother, though she's dark and she's far, far away,
And since Law forbids it, you'll take me, and so you will earn your pay.
You've a million a year in my will, if you think that that is enough;
But I know your taste, and your wife's; hers an expensive sort of love.
And you know I've more than a billion, and not so far short of two;
And if you want to earn it, then there's things you'll have to do.
The Lex Ulanova forbids flying inside Venus's span;
But that's where my woman is floating, and you must deliver her man.
Take out the *Mary Anna* – I've fuelled and maintained her for this,
Jettison me near my wife; let us float till we bump-to and kiss.
Because although she is lost, unmarked, floating hopeless to find,
Yet fate *will* bring us together, despite that we're dead, cold and blind.
Trajectories are random and space, don't I know it! – vast,
But we will have eternity to float and to fall and to pass.
The Ulanovs want their monopoly, and I wish them the luck of the brave,
But I'm not trying to steal their pig iron; I'm looking for a grave.
I'll be content with the blank of space; no churchyard, shroud or bell,
For the wife of my youth shall clutch me – and the rest can go to hell!
She died in an instant, son, and that fact kept her spirit pure,
And Fate is not so cruel that I'm kept from her ever and more.
Her beauty outlasted the vacuum, the decompression, the burn.
Never seen death yet, my Havel? . . . Well, now is your time to learn!

The Chrome Chromosome

This chromosomal Usual Suspects line:
Tentacle arms in *I surrender* pose;

Look closer, though: each is made of zips.
The microtubal slider is drawn down,

Their lines sag open, yawn, and through
These smallest needle-eyes emerge

Men, elephants and whales; bulked biospheres:
A meta boa's swallow in reverse.

This isn't a surrender: they've all won.
The arms are up in celebration.

'You know how Candelaria robots are,' says the first.

'I don't,' he replies. 'Tell me.'

'Meticulous, is one thing. When they set out to replicate a *Homo sapiens*, they do it *thoroughly*. From the baseline – up.'

He considers this. 'Where am I?' he asks.

'Leonardo.'

But that means nothing. 'What's Candelaria?' he tries. 'They're, what: different to regular robots?'

'See, you know *robots*.' says a second voice. 'Though you don't know Candelaria.' One voice, two voices. It's like he's talking to Tweedledum and Tweedledee. 'It's all *in there*,' Tweedledee says. 'Need to rootle it out. You know your own name?'

He finds he does. 'Thirteen.'

'There you go! Keep thinking it through. The Candelaria? Best described, I suppose, as a religion. They self-identify as robots. Most MwO don't use that vocabulary. But they *like* the word robots. It's a *Homo sapiens* word, see.'

'Doesn't it mean *slave*?'

'You're definitely starting to remember stuff.' Tweedledum again. A grin, in the dark, like a crescent moon on its side. The scent of grape. And in his thoughts Thirteen was standing in a vineyard – in an actual, true-to-god *vineyard* – and it was chilly, and the light was changing. Hail was rattling through the leaves, and the sky was closing. An old world storm. Lightning flashed, but distantly and indistinctly, a shuddering glimmer through the unscattered clouds. Those hailstones were tiny and hard: grit-monsoon.

'I'm getting,' says Thirteen. 'I'm getting *memory* flashes—'

'Is it a memory of sex?' says Tweedledum. 'You don't need to be coy. This business sure makes *me* remember honest-to-goodness human sex.'

'Be*have*,' says Tweedledee.

'I was in the countryside,' says Thirteen. 'I was in—'

Tweedledum breaks in, 'Don't tell me! You're going to name a place on Earth! Don't!' Then, a little sheepishly, 'I'm superstitious about invoking old Earth. Leave it be, that's my view. That world is waves, now.'

Thirteen realises he knows this: Earth is all gone, long gone. Countless fathoms deep. And all the rest of what he needs to know is right on the edge of his consciousness. One nudge and it will come. 'What are MwOs?'

'That's the collective term,' says Tweedledum. 'They come in all sorts and shapes and sizes. Some as big as cities, steering through the vacuum. Some small as ticks or bugs or asterisks – or smaller.'

Tweedledee chips in. 'And they manifest all *manner* of beliefs. Take the Candelaria: they *revere Homo sapiens*. Fancy! I don't really understand it myself, but that's what they do. Something about servitude to an ideal of humanity. Building a man, that's worship for them. But not made out of protein, of course. If they built it out of protein, then it would hardly be a robot, now, would it? They use chrome.'

'Chrome?'

'I don't know, I *don't* know. Not literal chrome, I guess.'

'Literal chrome!' scoffs Tweedledee.

'But it has to do with the old *sapient hombres*, and what they thought a robot should look like. Shiny, shiny, mirror shiny. Durable, you know? It's not that the *Candelaria* are committed to being everlasting, or anything. It's about what they reckon *men and women* would expect robots to be. So they build, from the ground up. Here are the forty-six chromosomes, and instead of protein molecules they use mirror-shiny dense little beads of computronium. Instead of these glued-together filaments of tissue, it's shiny regular nano-strands of computronium. All-metal chromosomes, strands neatly linked together and folded in Xs and Ys.'

'Like zippers,' says Tweedledee.

'Teeny-tiny computronium zippers. And they encode all the stuff old sapient-hombre DNA encodes, the four bases, the ancient alphabet. But that's a ridiculous underuse of the material, isn't it? What, *computronium*? Like taking a bunch of old computer circuit boards and arranging them in the shape of roman numerals. They can do much more! So they scrupulously reproduce all the As and Ds and whatnots of human DNA, but *also* they make full use of the computronium's processing capacity. And even a minuscule strand of computronium has more computational potential than all the . . .'

Tweedledee interrupts. 'You're boring. You're boring me. Ergo you're boring him.'

'Machines *without* Organs!' snaps Tweedledum, as if swearing.

Thirteen says: 'Metal? A metal organism? *Cells*?'

'Nano-smart membranes. Sort-of metal.'

'Metal *blood*?'

'Little metallic blood cells, shiny as silver, hurtling round in a lubricating medium, like little shiny coins. No need to transport any oxygen, of course; but they copy all the organs. And each one with a trillion-bit computational capacity! Plasmetal artery and vein walls – it's as flexible as organic tissue, but much tougher. Cunningly designed Campbellonium bones. The whole thing.'

'And the whole thing . . .' Thirteen says.

'You know everything we know,' says Dum. 'Come on! You're being lazy now.'

'Leonardo,' says Thirteen.

'He's the man.'

'He's – a cathedral.'

'You know,' said Dee. 'That's not a bad way of thinking about it. Because although he *is* a man, he's also an act of Candelaria devotion. Religious devotion. Constructing a version of the old sapient hombre, sure: life size, ready to walk and learn to talk and all that. But building him so that every cell in his body runs an accurate simulation of one or other lost human. One or other person drowned when the world died.'

Thirteen remembers the vineyard. That storm had been the beginning of something bad.

'Cathedral nothing.' Dee sounds genuinely angry. 'Leonardo's a *zoo*. A prison. A freak show. Who are these robots to bring us back to consciousness? To lock us up here? Who gave them the right?'

As if triggered by this anger, Thirteen's memory washes back through him. It's all there. He knows that Leonardo contains the detailed computronium-run consciousnesses of *millions* of people; and that when Leonardo comes into the world, out of this comforting dark, every one of them will access his senses, his joys and all his experiences – access them all separately, and live again; but also access them collectively, as a single transcendent man to make mankind live again. And he knows that the robots made Leonardo as a homage; an act of piety to honour a vanished form of life. And he knows Tweedledum and Tweedledee. 'You,' he says, to Dum, 'are Thirteen.'

'I am.'

'And you,' to Dee. 'You are Thirteen.'

'Me too, yes. We're you. We're one another.'

'Who am I?'

'You're Trisomy Thirteen, that's who you are,' says Tweedledum-Thirteen. 'You're a *third* iteration of us. Because we figured . . .'

'. . . we figured, you know – fuck them.'

'Robots! Ugh.'

'We thought – who gave *them* permission to conjure us into this computronium mode of consciousness? Who gave *them* the right? They think they're doing us a favour? They think this is an act of *piety*? It's playing god. Fucking robots!'

'It wasn't easy,' says Tweedledee-Thirteen. 'Using their own technology against them. But we did it. We made you. Let's see how *that* pans out in their precious Leonardo.'

'After us,' says Tweedledum-Thirteen, 'the deluge.'

Trisomy 13 occurs when each cell in the body has three, instead of the usual two, copies of chromosome 13. Trisomy 13 can also result from an extra copy of chromosome 13 in only some of the body's cells (this is known as mosaic trisomy 13). Extra material from chromosome 13 disrupts the course of normal development, causing the characteristic signs and symptoms of trisomy 13. Researchers are not yet certain how this extra genetic material leads to the features of the disorder, which include severely abnormal cerebral functions, a small cranium, retardation, non-functional eyes and heart defects.

The Time Telephone

1

A mother phones her daughter. This call will cost her nearly €18,000. The number she dials is several hundred digits long, but it has been calculated carefully and stored as a series of tones, so the dialling process takes only seconds. The ring tone at the far end makes its distant musical drum roll once, twice, three times, and with a clucking noise the receiver is lifted.

'Hello?'

The mother takes a quick breath. 'Marianne?'

'Speaking. Who's this, please?'

'This is your mother, Marianne.'

'Ma? I thought you were in Morocco. You calling from Morocco?'

'No, dear, I'm here, I'm in London.'

'Here?'

'This is a call from the past, my darling,' says the mother, her heart stabbing at her ribs. 'As I speak now, as I speak to you now, I'm actually pregnant with you. You're inside my tummy *here*, and I'm speaking to you *there*.'

For a moment there is only the polluted silence of a phone line; that slightly hissing, leaf-rustle emptiness of a line where the person at the other end is quiet. Then the daughter says, 'Wow, ma. Really?'

'Yes, my dear.'

'It's that time telephone thing? Yeah? I read about that, or, or I watched a thing about it, on TV. You're really calling me from the past?'

'Yes, my dear. I have a question I want to ask you.'

'Wow, ma. Like, wow. I watched this programme about it on TV, it was a whole big thing, like, decades ago. And now it's actually happening to me! And I'm only on a, like, regular phone.'

'It uses the ordinary phone system, you know.'

'It's incredible, though. Isn't it?'

'I want to ask you this thing, my darling, and I want you to answer truthfully. I know that you are sixteen *there*, aren't you. Aren't you?'

'Sweet sixteen.'

'Well, from where I'm calling you're not born yet. So I want to ask you.' She takes a breath. 'Are you *glad* you were born? Are you pleased to have come into the world?' The drizzly silence of the phone line. 'I mean the question absolutely seriously, my darling, absolutely. I mean the question, in the way that a child will say . . .' But she finds it hard to find the words. 'The way a child will say *I hate you, I wish I'd never been born*. That's an unbearable thing for a parent to hear, my darling. Do you see?'

'You're weirding me out, ma. This whole conversation is weirding me out. This whole concept is weirding me out.'

'But I have to ask it of you, because now you're sixteen, you can tell me. Are you glad you were born?'

'Sure.'

'Are you sure? Really sure?'

'OK, sure I'm sure, I'm really sure.'

Which is what the mother hoped to hear. She even sighs. And the remainder of the question is conversational scree, just talk about the weather and the chit-chat. So I go to Morocco? Well, yeah, ma. Hey, Scannell just won the board championship. You should make a bet. You could be rich. I don't think it works that way, my darling. You look after yourself. Hey, you too. That sort of thing. You know the sort of thing, the sort of chit-chat a mother and daughter will make on the phone.

2

The world cable telephone network is some 7,672,450,000 miles long in total, when the different international, national and local lines are added up. And they are all interconnected. They would hardly function as a telephone network if they weren't. We are talking about *cable*, copper or some other electron-conducting material; optical fibre is no good for us, because photons travel only at the speed of light no matter how you slice and dice them. Neutroelectrons – a self-contradictory-sounding name, but better than the alternative mooted by the Italians of 'anti-electrons', for surely an anti-electron is a proton? – anyway – these ghostly particles travel so fast as effectively to travel instantaneously, but they can only do it in a material that conducts their shadowy anti-selves, their phase-inverted electrons. By plotting out a pathway along the telephone network, a neutroelectron can be passed instantly across the seven billion miles of cabling. The phone line becomes a gateway into the past; when they arrive they arrive from the past, if you see what I mean. This is because it would take light about eleven hours to travel the pathway mapped diligently through the phone lines. Which means that the far end of the cable is eleven hours away, so that the instantaneous transmission of the phased particle actually passes eleven hours back in time. For it to happen any other way would violate laws of cause-and-effect. I'm sure you're following me.

Technicians carefully map out a route around the millions of miles of telephone cabling, turning innumerable sharp corners, fleeting back and forth underneath the oceans, rushing along smile-sagging lines propped up every fifty yards by another pole, curling and spinning around the electronic spaghetti of the bigger cities. A path through all this is mapped, and particles are fired along it.

In a year, light travels approximately 5,865,696,000,000 miles.

Looping the signal 900-or-so times around this loop, the

neutroelectron effectively opens a phone line a year into the past. The problem is that the repeated passage through the same cable degrades the integrity of the signal. The scientists experimenting with this new phenomenon were able to obtain fax signals, and internet connection, over the time-distance of eleven hours. Extending it to just under a day, looping the signal twice, the internet connection becomes choppy, unreliable, and painfully slow: too slow, in fact, to be cost-effective, when the large expense of running the time telephone system is taken into account. The fax signal works better, but only a small amount of visual information is carried by fax tweetings. Any more than a day and the bandwidth is too small and too fragile to allow internet access. But even looping it two thousand times allowed a signal of reasonable, if crackly, integrity. More than this and the noise and static swallowed meaningful information exchange.

The initial researchers established an integral network of connections to the past: in effect they set up standing-wave each-way passageways for the neutroelectron connection. The theory owes something to wormhole physics, but it is much more limited on account of its need for a physical infrastructure. They phoned scientists from the past; sometimes phoning themselves, sometimes others. They explained the situation, giving them the know-how necessary to set up neutroelectron generators themselves, and plumbing them back into the phone line. And once the network was established, and people in the past had been contacted, it became evident that people in the past could re-use the connections to speak to people in their future, many years, to such phone terminals as had been utilised by the original scientists.

Soon crosstalk filled the time-phone lines. The future-people move through time at an hour an hour, dragging their envelope of past-talk with them at an hour an hour. But the past-time scientists could act as way-stations, taking the signal and relaying it further back, or further forward. In this way the envelope was extended to more than sixteen years. But no further. The generation of scientists at this blockage time, back in 2004, refused, for some reason, to be beguiled by these whispery voices on the phone, that declared themselves future humans; refused to spend the money on the ridiculous expense of setting up neutroelectronic generators, refused to believe the physics of it. Without their assistance the reach of the time-telephones stopped dead. People before a certain date had no knowledge of the technology at all; for them, it had not happened yet.

In the future, researchers tried and failed, tried again and failed, to raise the money to build an enormous cable, billions upon billions of miles long. They wanted a space-probe sent to an asteroid, to mine and refine and spool out huge stretches of cable through space, cable that earth people could hook up to the phone line and use to call back further in time. To call back in time *before* the 2004 blockage. But the expense was too much, and the project had not brought about any useful improvement in the quality of life. A person could place a bet in 2010, and call up an internet page from the following day to guide him; with the result that, under such circumstances, betting shrank to long-term wagers only. People could find out tomorrow's news today, but almost always tomorrow's news is merely an extrapolation of today's news.

As the network grew, people called their friends and family in the past, warned loved-ones of imminent death and told them which stock to buy, but the past is fixed in curious, physics-consistent ways. *You* are not fixed, as you read this sentence, I'm not suggesting that! But, then again, as you read this sentence you are at the now, between the past and the future. That is where you always are. I, writing it, am in the past. That's just the truth. And even if you could call me up, so that my telephone here on my desktop, this blueblack-plastic Buddha-shaped machine here, would ring and you could talk to me, it would make no difference, almost certainly no difference, in almost every case. You can't really reach me, not easily, hardly at all. I'm sorry to tell you this, but it is the truth, it's better you know the truth. Information *does* flow backwards, but sluggishly, treacly. It rushes much more forcefully the other way. So although people warned loved-ones of imminent death and told them which stock to buy, the loved ones still died, and nobody found themselves suddenly rich because their earlier selves had invested more wisely. None of that happened. It might still happen, of course. There is nothing in the theory that suggests it could *never* happen.

And so 2019 turned into 2020, and 2020 into 2021, and people could talk to one another from any time from 2004 to 2038, but nobody built the super long cabling that would have enabled the technicians to get clear neutroelectron signals that reached further back in time than 2004, to get internet access from the past and into the future. There seemed little point.

3

A phone rings.

The phone is shaped something like a tapered loaf, cast from blood-brown plastic, with a broad steel ring like a buckle on the front that is rimmed with little circular holes. The receiver, bone-shaped, shivers in its cradle in time to the rings. The bell is a mechanical bell, located inside the hollow body of the thing, so that, ringing, it vibrates the whole device a little bit. The receiver is connected to the body of the phone with a brown flex, a flex which had come from the manufacturer curled as precisely as DNA, but which now is gnarled and knotted, unwound in places, scrunched up in others.

The phone sits by the wall on a shelf in a small kitchen area. You might, perhaps, describe the area as a kitchenette. Against the west wall there is a unit containing a small sink, and next to it a dwarf-fridge on a shelf, with a kettle on top of it, and next to that a two-ring hob. On the south wall at tummy-height is a shelf upon which storage jars of coffee and of tea and of sugar, and three mugs, stand next to the phone. A door in the east wall; the north wall decorated with a poster for the film *Gladiator*. Somebody has pasted a photocopy of the face of an individual called Vernon St Lucia over the face of the star of the film, the humour of this gesture deriving from the ironic contrast between the muscular good looks of the film star and the weedy, querulous nature of St Lucia, who has authority over the three laboratory technicians who work here.

Only one of these technicians is in the building. It is shortly after seven o'clock in the evening, and everybody else has gone home for the night. The single technician remaining is called Roger. He comes through to the kitchenette.

The penetrating chirrup of the phone-bell stops.

'Extension three-five-one-one?'

A rainy, white-noise sound, overlaid with a rhythmic distant thudding, and behind it, as if very far away, a tinny vocalisation, or singsong, or whistling. But no words.

'Hello?' says Roger. 'Hello?'

The hissing swells and subsides like surf, the crackles pop more frequently. The *oo-aa-oo*ing in the background might be words: '. . . *couldn't get through earlier* . . .'

'Hello? The connection,' Roger says, 'is not good.'

Crunching and flushing noises, and then sudden clarity: '. . . imperative that we get a message through . . .' but then, with a swinging, horn-like miaow the line dissipates into static.

'Hello? This is a very bad line.'

Nothing but noise.

Roger replaces the receiver in its cradle. He meanders back to his desk and switches on a light. He cannot decide whether to go home or not. There is nothing for him at home this evening. His girlfriend, a woman called Stella, is having a girls' night out with four friends. These friends' names are Susan, Susan, Miranda and Belle. He doesn't fancy going back to an empty flat. But the prospect of staying at the lab and working on into the evening is not appealing either. His brain feels muffled, fuzzy. He can't concentrate on his job-in-hand.

He mooches back into kitchen and turns the kettle on. He inspects one of the mugs standing beside the telephone, and, fussily, runs a finger inside the rim. Behind him, the kettle's spout turns into a miniature chimney. Steam pillows out.

Roger changes his mind. He drinks, he tells himself, too much coffee anyway. Six or seven mugs, most days, and strong stuff too.

He walks back to his bench and turns the anglepoise off.

The phone goes again.

As he shuffles back to the kitchen to answer it, he finds himself thinking how annoying the sound of a phone ringing is. How insistent. A mechanical baby's cry that is almost impossible to ignore. He resents it.

' 'tension three-five-one-un?'

This time the voice is clearer, although the static is still thorny and distracting. 'Please don't hang up! It's vital you listen to . . . information we have to give you.' The sentence is broken in half by a crack, like a plank breaking.

'I'm sorry,' says Roger, annoyed rather than intrigued. 'Who were you trying to reach?'

'The institute . . .' A whoosh and a clatter drown the rest of the sentence.

'I'll tell you what you've done,' says Roger, prissily. 'You've dialled the one twice by mistake. You want extension three five one seven, but your finger has accidentally pushed the one twice and it's put you through here. There's nobody here except me, and I'm about to go home. Three five one seven will get you the night secretary.'

'No! No!' The panic in the person's voice is evident enough to break through the hisses and spatters of interference. '*Please* don't hang up. We're calling as far back as we can, and the boundary withdraws all the time, one second per second. In a very little time it will be *too late*. Do you understand?'

'No,' says Roger, crossly, 'I don't.'

'I can't stress *too greatly*, your future is at stake. All our futures. The people much further along the line from us have only just encountered the disaster, and they have called us, and we have called you. This may sound *strange* to you. The chance to change things . . . it must happen *there*, in your time. It's got to be *you*.'

'I have no idea what you are on about,' says Roger. 'Is this a prank? Is this Seb?' This, he thinks, is exactly the sort of practical joke that Seb would try.

'Please, no, just *listen*. You don't have to believe me, it doesn't matter if you believe me, the thing you have to do is so simple, so simple it won't take you a moment. All you have to do . . .'

But Roger has put the phone down again. He stands looking at the kettle for a moment, his mind floating free. He thinks of Seb, a man he has never really liked. By a chain of association too oblique to be represented here with any ease, he thinks of a holiday in France, and then of another friend, and then of Stella, and finally of Susan, one of Stella's friends. He and Susan had kissed the previous week, but both had pulled away, startled, before things had proceeded any further. It had been at a party at another friend's house, at the bottom of their garden away from everybody, in the darkness. Two cigarette smokers underneath the stars, the noise and chatter and muffled music of the party sounding very far away. Kissing, and then pulling away. The path not taken. But then again, who knows? It wouldn't be a good idea to tell Stella. He feels sure Susan thinks this too. Best not mention it at all, and certainly not tell Stella.

He puts on his coat, and is about to lock up the lab when the phone rings again.

Review: Thomas Hodgkin, *Denis Bayle: a Life*

(Red Rocket Books 2003), 321pp. £20. ISBN: 724381129524

This is a novel with an interesting conceit, written by a newcomer to SF (although according to Hodgkin's own author bio, he has published a number of mainstream novels). The book takes the form of a biography, complete with preface, scholarly apparatus, timeline and everything else. The subject of the story is a fictional Science Fiction author, the Denis Bayle of the title, but the point of the book is less to tell a life story (Hodgkin doesn't give Bayle that interesting a life): rather Hodgkin uses this format as an excuse to offload a dozen imaginary novels, supposedly written by Bayle, and here summarised in so much detail that it would be a trivial business using these blueprints to actually write the fiction. In effect, then, what we have here is not so much a novel as a collection of Imaginary Books, condensed for the reader's convenience. What Hodgkin brings to this now venerable literary genre is a linking narrative, a single imaginary author.

He tells Bayle's story well – not flashily, but convincingly. Born in New York to a French mother and American father in 1929, he was too young to serve in the Second World War, but just the right age to experience the 1950s explosion of interest in SF. His first story appeared in *Fables of Science and Wonder* in 1948 (for Hodgkin has not only invented Bayle, and invented his dozen novels and two-dozen stories, he has also invented all the magazines in which he was published, all the editors he dealt with and so on. Indeed, this reviewer found himself wondering why he could not simply have included John Campbell and the others as minor characters). '*FSW*,' Hodgkin says, a little po-faced, 'was the market leader throughout the early 1950s'. Bayle's first story 'Volcano Skyscraper' was 'a superheated adventure novella, in which a huge chimney is being constructed atop an active volcano to harness and control the destructive forces of nature in the service of mankind. The frequent disasters, and the heroics of the construction crew, are vividly if rather gnashingly rendered'.

Throughout the 1950s Bayle worked in a Jersey company that manufactured alarm clocks ('it is perhaps strange,' says Hodgkin, 'that so few of Bayle's stories concern clocks'; which is something of a cheat, surely – Bayle only wrote so few clock stories because Hodgkin decided that he would write only a few clock stories, which means it can hardly strike him as strange in any genuine sense. But I am digressing.). He married in 1954, and had two children. The elder of these died of polio at the age of seven. This death provoked an estrangement between Bayle and his wife, 'neither of them able to deal with the grief, neither of them taking consolation in the other'. 1964, the year that Bayle became a professional writer, was also the year of his separation from his wife.

Thereafter he lived by himself in Queens, and later in Lower East Side, and devoted himself to his writing. 'His writing, whilst always inventive and popular, was nevertheless touched with a flavour of melancholy, a sense of the separateness and isolation of the human condition. It is possible that this, in fact, endeared him to many SF fans, for whom, then as now, it is a familiar condition'.

But, as I say, the meat of this book is not really in its retelling of Bayle's life, except incidentally. The real purpose of *Denis Bayle: a Life* is to shoe-horn in a large number of imaginary books, fictional plot-lines, made-up SF premises. Whether these are ideas that Hodgkin is too idle to write up for himself, or ideas he has abandoned as unworkable, is not clear. We're familiar, of course, with the 'Imaginary Review' from the work of Borges and

Stanislaw Lem. It is an approach I have always found fairly annoying – some of these ideas are quite good, and sketching them out in this desultory manner precludes another writer from developing them properly. But that is by the bye.

One advantage Hodgkin's format has over the more conventional 'collection of reviews of imaginary books' is that he need not pretend the reviewer's reticence about twist-endings, plot spoilers and so on. Because he is supposed to be writing a 'critical biography' he is able to précis his novels in detail from start to finish, which makes for more satisfying reading. So, for example, his account of Bayle's novel *Sparkler* (1970) reveals not only premise but twist. The 'sparklers' of the title are black hole bombs. The FTL of Bayle's Space-Operatic future is a technology that distorts space-time, stretching several of the key constraints of reality. As a spin-off of her research, an eminent light-speed scientist called Gabriele Anna invents a way of reorienting the vector *gravity*. Instead of acting at ninety-degrees to matter (such as our experience of gravity on this clump of matter called the Earth, where gravity pulls everything towards the centre of the globe, and sticks us to the surface) she is able to flip the vector by ninety-degrees. Bombs are built which insert 'grav-virus' into black holes, a 'fractal replicant that catastrophically reconfigures the vector of gravity'. This reconfiguration lasts only seconds, but that's all that's needed. Dropped into the sheer gravity well of a black hole, these probes liberate all the matter and all the energy that is squashed into these awesome cosmic phenomena. Much of the novel maps out the strategy and tactics of the space war (fought between 'Realist' and 'Constructivist' populations of humans; there are no aliens). Bayle, Hodgkin claims, 'evokes the military milieu well, despite his own lack of wartime experience' and also 'does a good job of evoking an appropriate sense of wonder'. I suppose we'll have to take his word for that.

Because gravity is shifted, momently, through ninety-degrees, the holding force of the black hole disappears. It spins out like a gigantic cosmic Catherine wheel, spitting matter and light in huge expanding corona. This matter travels with such force and speed – because the pressures that had been squashing it to a less-than-atom-pinhead were so vast – that it distorts, it approaches light speed, it expands relativistically. Anything within several light years will be obliterated – enemy fleets, stations, planets, stars.

A plot strand deploys that SF cliché, the future archaeologist: in this case 'light-archaeologists' – not people grubbing around in the dust of ancient ruins, but people painstakingly sifting through the information contained in ancient light. His main female character, Rachel Danchev, specialises in uncovering economic data about the Others, an alien race so long extinct that no physical remains have ever been found, and whose existence can only be deduced from the four-hundred-million-year-old light-shells travelling through space. As she puts it:

> Turn a black-hole into a Sparkler – prise the lid from one of those things and what comes out? Matter of course, but also *light*, in all spectra. Intense radiation of all sorts . . . Information comes out, information that was buried in a perfectly hermetic cosmic hole for god-knows-how-long. It's an unbelievably rich stream of data.

Rachel begins to believe that the light pouring out of the Sparkler she is studying contains within it not only the answer to the mystery of the disappearance of the Others, but answers to deeper cosmic mysteries even than that. At the end we discover that galaxies are not spiralling in towards their central black-holes, but bursting out at such titanic speeds that spacetime and causality are thrown into disarray, the remains of a war on a scale that dwarfs even the interstellar conflict with which the novel is concerned. But (a reviewer writes) this is the sort of thing that's only going to work by building its effect via novelistic momentum. A novel written out full-length might generate the sort of sense-of-wonder Hodgkin talks about; a summary hardly can.

A better conception, I thought, was Bayle's *Troposphere* (1975). In this novel aliens invade the earth but occupy not the ground (as in Wells's *War of the Worlds*), nor the ocean (as in Wyndham's *The Kraken Wakes*), but instead the sky, specifically that portion of the atmosphere beneath the stratosphere from which the book takes its title ('the troposphere extends from the ground to a height that varies from nine kilometres at the poles to seventeen kilometres at the equator' says Hodgkin, although it is not clear whether he is speaking himself or quoting from Bayle's supposed novel). I liked the sound of this novel, and rather wished it were real so I could buy it and read it properly. The appearance of the invasion fleet first casts human society into terror, which mutates into relieved disregard when it becomes clear that the aliens have no interest in what happens at sea-level. After months of upheaval, life on earth settles easily back into its old rhythms, inconvenienced only by the aggression with which the invaders treat any sufficiently high-flying aircraft or rockets ('destruction is assured above 1100m'). Years pass; communication is attempted many times but always ignored. The aliens are observed as they construct a complex flying-and-floating culture in the high sky. Airlines go bust. Shipping companies grow rich. People speculate about the origins and long-term intentions of the aliens. Doomsayers insist that mankind will be destroyed soon, but as years pass without incident people become complacent. Governments continue a kind of cold war against the invaders for many years, picking off occasional targets from the ground. But total war is too difficult and too expensive to wage against such an enemy, and it becomes the general belief we will simply have to share our world with the invaders. 'Eventually we will learn to speak to one another,' says one character. 'We must be patient.'

According to Hodgkin, 'this premise is powerfully rendered', although the few quotations he concocts don't really demonstrate this power. Indeed, Bayle was instructed by his publisher that the first draft of *Troposphere* lacked drama, and therefore saleability. He rewrote the book, transforming the second half into a catastrophe-thriller. After nine years of relatively quiet occupation, the invaders begin to seed the lower stratosphere with 'something – organic, or technological—', ground-based intelligence is not sure what. It proliferates, blocking out an increasing percentage of sunlight. Famine and catastrophe for humanity looms. At last mankind must rouse itself. The story centres on three researchers at the United States Invader Studies Institute [their motto is 'USIST – RESIST!'], racing against the clock to try and find a way to 'settle ET's hash'.

Such a method is found, and put – successfully – into practice (Hodgkin tells us all the details of this conclusion, but as a reviewer I hold back from such spoilers). Suffice to say that it makes use of the differential between troposphere height at equatorial and polar locations. 'However ingenious this conclusion,' opines Hodgkin in his persona as critic-biographer, 'however exciting the final chapters, it cannot be denied that the later draft lacks the distant, stilly, bleak beauty of the earlier. Bayle's genius was not in pot-boiler plotting, but in finding fictional expression for his acute sense of alienation. His motto might have been: *Every man is indeed an island.*'

The novels of the 1960s and 1970s ring changes upon the main fashions in American SF from those decades. Some sound more interesting (such as *Troposphere*); most of them sounding tired and conventional. *The Perils of Certain Spacemen*, supposedly from 1977, sounds like regular space opera, although on a larger than usual scale. Next Bayle wrote *Twenty Eighty-Four*, a sequel to Orwell's famous dystopia, written from the perspective not of individual humans but of the hive-minds that have been successfully created by the social engineering *Nineteen Eighty-Four* satirised. This sounds interesting, although Hodgkins says that Bayle was prevented from publishing it 'by the aggressive copyright policing of the Orwell estate' which obviates more detailed discussion.

We get more info on *The Explorers* (1984), a sort of alternate history based on the theory of the aquatic ape, the idea that proto hominids spent a portion of their evolution in the seas (hence our love for swimming and our streamlined hairlessness) – Bayle imagines the present-day earth populated by *Homo aquans*, the descendants of these apes, instead of *Homo sapiens*. His novel relates the explorations of 'InLand' by people who live in the sea and have traditionally only ventured a little way in at the coast. The *Washington Review* called this novel 'a roller-coaster of a book, big, moving, wholly engrossing' (Yes, Hodgkin makes up reviews and reactions as well as making up the original books.). But this is exactly the problem here: a two-page summary of this storyline can hardly be 'big, moving, wholly engrossing'. At most it can be intriguing, and leave the reader wishing that he or she could read the whole book.

Indeed, one of the flaws of Hodgkin's approach is his particular mode of summary. His summaries, not to beat around the bush, are too crammed and too hurried to give the satisfaction of short stories; and they are too shrunken to give the satisfaction of novels. They fall, alas, between the two stools; reading them is somehow unsatisfactory. Better are the Bayle short stories that Hodgkin summarises: less is lost in such a transformation. In 'Avalanche Pregnancy' (*Quasar*, Nov. 1965, collected in *The Rafts on the River*, 1970) a humanoid alien has sex with a human woman. The alien physiology is such that 'he' becomes pregnant with the evacuation of his seed; it so happens that she is also impregnated by the encounter. 'The two pregnancies,' says Hodgkin, 'develop together, and the tension and indeed competition between the two parties is very subtly delineated'. If you say so.

In 'The Foam Spaceships' (*Utopian Science Fiction*, June 1969 – Hodgkin calls it 'the Star Award winning story', the Star Awards being his fictional version of the Hugos) mankind is given the true technology of interstellar spaceflight, based on a kind of quantum foam, by a seemingly benign race of aliens; we use it and spread rapidly through the galaxy. But there is a price to pay: those who use it are changed by the technology, their cells turning into foam, their corporeality dissolving into a kind of not-quite-solid, not-quite-fluid state. Who would use such technology given that it exacts such a heavy price? Everybody, according to this story: 'the puritanical solids who remained in the prison of earth were looked on with pity rather than contempt; for everybody else, for the majority, *any* price would be worth paying to travel the stars.'

'The Picture of Dorian Greebo' (1962), despite its awful title, is an especially interesting conception. Wilde's *Dorian Gray* revolves around a portrait in the protagonist's attic that ages in his place. In Bayle's retelling, space explorers find an artefact on the moon placed by aliens; tests reveal that is anti-entropic, and in fact that this artefact is becoming *younger* minute by minute. They discover that this object's youth-ing and human aging are connected, and indeed that an alien race is rejuvenating itself via this device at our expense.

The 1975 story 'Tour de Lune' (collected in *Forward-view Mirror*, 1978) concerns pedal-powered spacecraft racing to the moon. Bayle also has an arresting way with a first sentence. This from 'XRose' (1971): 'As I peed I thought how strange it was that I would never again urinate; but Hart reminded me that there was probably some fluid in my system still to work its way through. "One more trip to the bathroom," he told me. "I'm thinking, one more still to go." '

Hodgkin's ingenuity and his fecund imagination are certainly well displayed by this book. But I hope I am not being only puritanical if I say that it is, somehow, vulgar. I can't shake the sense that the point of all this is only to display Hodgkin's undeniably impressive creativity, and nothing else. The book, supposedly about Denis Bayle, is actually an elongated boast by Thomas Hodgkin – *look how clever I am! Look how careless I can be with ideas for stories! Other writers hoard their conceptions, but I scatter them left and right.* It is an impression not helped by the melancholy end Hodgkin inflicts upon poor old Bayle. His fiction, once popular, now passes from fashion. His 1991 *Midwich Prime*, a retelling of Wyndham's *Midwich Cuckoos* from the point of view of the alien children, is rejected by his publisher, again for reasons of copyright, but in fact because Bayle novels simply aren't selling. 'You need to write more popular stuff,' he is told, but he doesn't understand why popular stuff is popular. Cyberpunk baffles him, his mind still running along the clockwork devices inside 1950s alarm clocks. He writes a long novel, provisionally entitled *Marigold*, his first attempt at Heroic Fantasy, in the belief that Fantasy sells better than SF (which is true, of course). But this book becomes a folly in its grandeur, swelling to three thousand, four thousand pages: 'it is a hybrid,' Hodgkin tells us, 'of Tolkien and Proust, a sort of *A La Recherche de Middle-Earth Perdu*.' He works obsessively over and over this manuscript, filling out lengthy descriptions of every detail of his fantasy world; but the project was not yet half finished at his death. 'His body lay undiscovered in his apartment for three days,' says Hodgkin, which seemed to me a low blow: gratuitously nasty on behalf of Hodgkin-as-God.

Had Hodgkin used this format as an opportunity to comment, satirically or otherwise, upon the world of SF over the last half-century I think the book would have been more successful. But his invented world-of-SF is only there as the backdrop to the invented novels, and those are only partially successful. We admire Hodgkin's inventiveness, but leave the feast unsatisfied.

Imaginary books, I'm afraid, are simply not as *filling* as real books.

S-Bomb

What does the 'S' stand for?

There's a black blotch in the sky where the starlight has been hoovered away. Any northern hemisphere night sky shows it. You'll have heard of this, of course. It can't be a planetary body, although it's round enough for that, for there are no gravitational effects detectable. One theory is that it is a concentration of dust occluding the starlight in a circular patch. There is concern, for the dust seems within the solar-system and therefore close to Earth, but it is above the line of the ecliptic and approaching no closer. There are of course plans to launch probes to examine the phenomenon. It's a question of finding the funding, of working out a launch window, that sort of thing.

– I'll tell you what. When they named the A-Bomb, they plugged into a cultural context in which A was the top school grade, and *A-OK* and *A1* had these upbeat, positive associations. Even the word *Atom* connoted focus and potency, think of *The Mighty Atom*. And then, only a few years later, the world hears of a *more* powerful bomb, the H-bomb, and 'H' meant nothing, except itself: Hydrogen. It connotes the gaseous, diffuseness, the whiffy. In their *heads* people knew this bomb was more deadly than the former, but in their *hearts* they couldn't truly credit it. So, I guess what I'm saying is, what, really, might people make of S? S-Bomb?

– *Sex-bomb.*

– Wasn't that a song?

– *If it was?*

– When I was a child, there was a pop group called S-Club. Or was it S-Group? But, see, S-Group, no. That sounds more like a secret arm of the military. I can't believe a kid's pop group would go for that sort of name.

– *And when* I *was a child, there was a pop group called the Incredible String Band. So what do you think of that?*

– The Incredible String Bomb?

– *Incredible, after all, is a pretty good word for it. From where I'm sitting I'd say that incredible describes it pretty well.*

– Except . . . these are no ordinary strings – Super – after all.

– *String bomb sounds like a Wallace and Gromit device. A back garden shed concoction.*

– See, that's my point. S-Bomb is a phrase that lacks the necessary.

– *Or further back? There's the echo of SS. Don't you think? The SS-Bomb? Some Nazi artefact. That sounds pretty mean.*

– Better. Better.

– *Also – I mean, you correct me, you're the expert – who calls them superstrings any more? Clumsy and ropey metaphor.*

– I guess. S for Sub-materialities. S for Severe. Serious, ser, Seriousnesses. Sparks. Sparkles inside everything, and this bomb harnessing that.

– *Except, see if I understand right, not so much* inside *as –*

– Not inside things. No. Constitutive of things. Yes.

– *You do sound – nervy. Do you have something to tell me?*

The two of them were sitting in a coffee shop, the Costarbucks Republic, the Coffee Chain, whatever. There were two thick-lipped porcelain mugs, large and round as soup bowls, on the table before them. Inside one a disc of blackness sat halfway down, with little pearls of reflected brightness trapped in its meniscus. The other mug was as yet untouched, and brimmed over with a solid froth of white that was dirtied with brown-black like pavement snow.

So much for their *coffees*.

The one man was senior, a face like the older Auden, nose fattened with age, two wide-spaced inkdrop eyes. His hair was white and close-trimmed and expressive of the undulating contours of his big old skull. The other man was young, and you might call him handsome if you happen to find male beauty in that block-faced, pineapple-headed muscular type. But he was very nervous indeed; very fidgety, and anxious, and gabbly. Why was he talking about long-vanished pop groups and suchlike chatter?

The place was partially occupied, readers and laptop-tappers distributed unevenly amongst the dark-wood tables. Behind the counter two slender men, both with skin coloured coffee-au-lait, waited for the next customer. It's a neutral place to meet, is the point of it.

What's the weather like? Aren't you interested? Look through these wall-high plates of carefully washed and polished glass.

What can you see?

It's a pretty windy day. The weathermen didn't foresee that. There have been clear-sky gales to the west. A weird turbulence, unspooling tourbillons to the north and the south that resonate into unseasonal storms, flooding, wreckage. Nobody can explain it. But it's only weather.

The two men sat in complete silence, the older one staring balefully at the younger, for two minutes. Two minutes is a very long time to sit in silence. Try it. Life is hurry and bustle. People come into the coffee shop and grab cardboard tubes of hot black and rush out. Those cars lurching forward, slowing back, lurching forward, slowing back, all day and every day, such that the tarmac is being continually obscured and revealed.

The sun moves through the sky. But it doesn't. It's the sky moves around the sun. That's the truth of it.

The older man sat upright, and his little felt-circle black eyes seem to expand. Those white fur eyebrows, up they go, towards the hairline.

*

– *Run me through again what I am to tell my bosses.*

– Well, sorry, is one thing.

– *We'll take sorry as read. We'll assume it.*

– Obviously we should have been in closer communication with – by we, I don't mean *me*, specifically, individually. We're a team, obviously – but, see, I'll be frank, *scientists*, our first reaction is, wait and see. It'll be OK. We think we can sort the problem, present you people with problem and solution in one neat package. Or at least, wait until there's a proper quantity of data before we report anything.

– *You saying there's no solution?*

– No.

– *You're saying the bomb doesn't work?*

–

– *I take your startlement as a yeah.*

– Sorry – sorry – you think *that's* what I'm here to report?

– *As opposed to?*

– Oh, the bomb works.

– *You're sure?*

– We tested it.

– *You have already tested it?*

– Tested it. It works. Jesus.

– *The people I work for will be pleased to hear that at any rate.*

– What I mean is. Look.

– You think superstrings are myriad little-little separate strings, one-dimensional extended objects that resonate and shake, that aggregate and disaggregate into subatomic particles, and thence into atoms and molecules and everything in this diverse and frangible world. You think so. Think again. Think *laces*. Think of it this way: one single string, ten-to-the-trillion metres long, weaving in and out of *our* four dimensions, like laces weaving in and out of cosmic fabric, tying it together. Superstrings is a misnomer. This singular thing, this superstring. The equations require ten dimensions, and we're personally familiar with four dimensions, and all that is true. But when you look at it clearly, there *is* only one dimension. Only the one singularity, the thread that ties all of reality together and also the thread out of which all reality is woven. The one string.

– *One string.*

– The nature of the technology is that, and the, the *thing* is, said the younger man.

– *You're saying you broke it.*

– I'm saying, said the younger man, and swallowed air.

The older man lifted his coffee mug, finally, and tucked his white moustache into the white cap of froth.

– S-bomb, boom-boom, said the younger, and the explosion. Now we were surely not expecting the explosive out-gassing, the violent rupture, the A-Bomb thing. But I *was* expecting – I don't know. Maybe sparks, the sparkles, something fizzy.

– *None of that?*

– Then, said the young man, it detonates. The point is – you're wondering if I'm going to get to the point. The point is, it blows, but not with any *explosive* detonation. These strings, these threads, these laces stretching, as it were, across ten dimensions, connecting it all together, the whole of reality. Cut them, and, plainly put, our dimensions start to *unweave*, or unspool, or unpick, you choose the un word you like best. It's a baseline reality event. The earth turns away from it. That's not a metaphor. The earth turns; it spins around the sun; it leaves the event behind at the speed of kilometres a second.

– *You tested it underground?*

– On the contrary. We tested it in the sky. We lifted it up there by a toroid helium balloon. No, no, if you dug it *under* the ground . . .

– *Let's say,* interrupted the older man, *under Tehran. Underneath and a little to the east of Tehran.*

– Sure. Then the world itself moves through space, and the effect is to blast out an empty conic up from underneath the city.

A hollowness that shoots out, angled and up out of the city and goes into the sky at a tangent, and loses itself in space, the city thereby collapsing into a great mass of rubble. The air, meanwhile, rushing about to fill the vacancy. But it's gone in minutes, because *we all* are travelling at such prodigious speeds, because the world is in orbit about the sun.

– *So you're saying that, in effect, the point of detonation of an S-Bomb will appear, from where we're standing,* appear *to hurtle away up into space,* said the older man.

– Yeah. Or it might cut a tunnel right through the earth, depending on the world's orientation when it was detonated. Or it might just fly straight up. The earth orbits the sun at about 30 kilometres a second. The sun is moving too, with us in tow, and rushing in a different direction at about 20 kilometres a second. That's a fast shear vector. It means that the blast *leaves* the world behind pretty rapidly, hurtles above the plane of the ecliptic and away.

– *And now you're going to tell me,* said the older man, speaking expansively, a voice expressive of confidence, *that the vacuum of space* neutralises *the effect. It just burns itself out up there.*

– See, said the younger man, leaning forward, we *wondered* about that. One S-bomb theory was that, without matter to, to unpick, then it would just putt-putt and out. But the way it's turned out – no. It's expanding explosively. Faster than any chemical explosion, expanding really very quickly. But not so quickly as we are moving away from it, in our solar and Galactic trajectories, so in that sense we're safe.

– *So what's the odds that our planet will swing round on its orbit into this expanding explosion, this time next year?*

A weird little trembly high-pitched laugh.

– Man, no. What, the sun, you see. *Is* moving relative to the galaxy. And the galaxy is . . . anyway, it's a complex spirograph tracery, our passage through spacetime. So we're leaving it pretty far behind us, a spoor of vacuum-vacuum, unstitching the poor fourfold house in which we live. Like the wake of a boat. Or, from its point of view, we're skimming away as it swells.

– *Now you're sure,* said the old man, as he got to his feet, *that it's a* real *effect?*

– It's real, said the younger man. You know what? I'll level with you. We calculated a forty-sixty possibility that something like this would happen. Something like this. That's why we detonated it high in the air, so that the world would spin us away, day by day, and leave the detonation footprint behind in the vacuum. We figured, it is vacuum! What can happen? But it turns out, more than you'd think.

– *So?*

– Light propagates across a vacuum. Various electromagnetic radiations propagate across a vacuum. But none of them can propagate across the null space.

– *Rubble can?*

– What?

– *You said, 'Blow it under Tehran, Tehran falls into the hole'.*

– Well, yes. Because the earth swings away from it, leaves it behind. But, actually, weird things happen to the equations when you shuffle core assumptions about, you know, the fundamental premises of things. Atoms may tumble into null-space, but they get . . . churned. Or to be more exact: the Earth moves away, into a new baseline, and away from the detonation footprint, and then matter can move into the tunnel dug out by the S-bomb. But they don't seem to, you know, *stick* as well as they ought. Particles. They seem to slide about more than you might think. But, anyway, at the point of the continuing detonation, *evidently*, electro-magnetic waves aren't able to cross the null.

– *So,* said the older man, who is no fool, *the black blotch in the sky. And all the pother in the media.*

– And that's going to get worse. Nothing we can do about it. More and more stars are going to get blanked out by the phenomenon, in the northern hemisphere at least, in the backwash of the earth's passage through galactic space. Or actually the sun's, you see what I mean.

– *OK,* said the general. *Long as it stays* out there.

This is what he was thinking: biggest act of vandalism in human history. He's thinking: but leastways it's not pissing direct into our own pool. And as he extricates himself from the table his military mind is running through possible strategic uses, from attacking orbital platforms to high-altitude bombers, to maybe developing smaller or shorter-lived devices that could be used lower down. He can't help thinking that way. He's a soldier.

– *I had better go report right now,* he said. *My bosses will want to know this right away.* Then, as an afterthought, *I'll tell you what the S stands for.*

– What?

– *Starsucker. Starblotter. Or something* (for he's never been very deft with a punchline) *about stars.* And he was at the door, and looking through the glass into the unseasonably windy weather. *Go back to the institute,* he said. *Go back, and we'll contact you in due course.*

This string, this one line out of which everything is spun, is broken; and the moment (the infinitesimal fractional moment) when that could have been repaired has long gone. Momentum works in strange ways in ten dimensions. Unspooling, unstitching, unpicking the tapestry of *matter* takes longer than unpicking the tapestry of *vacuum.* They slip free of their weave. The two whip-snapping ends of the superstring are acquiring more and more hyper-momentum. What does the S stand for again? Severed. Say-your-prayers. Stop.

Time continues applying its pressure and forcing the other three dimensions along its relentless and irrevocable line. For six months the coffee shop does its regular business, and customers come in sluggish and drink and go off joyously agitated. There is a relatively high turnover of serving staff, for the pay is poor and the work onerous, but the two men who served behind the coffee shop bar during the conversation reported above are still there post six months on. Six months on is when the whole story breaks to the media: this cornpone country, its tiny research budget, its speculative endeavour, its helium-balloon-detonated-device unsanctioned by any international organisation or superpower government. This devastation wreaked on the night sky (for the northern hemisphere night sky is now a third blotted out by this spreading squid-ink), this hideous destructive power. Worse than atomics. The most massy of mass destructive possibilities. S for shock. Oh, the outrage.

The s-for-shit hits the f-for-fan. The government collapses. The country wilts under the censure of the international community. There's all that.

The whole story comes out. All the members of the eight-strong research team had been holding their peace under the most alarming threats from the security services; as had the dozen or so high-clearance security officials 'handling' the case. But one succumbs, and defects, and reveals all; and then, one by one, so do the others. Some scurry up their local equivalents of Harrowdown Hill; some try and tease wealth from the media to tell their unvarnished tales.

For a brief period the coffee shop becomes a place of celebrity pilgrimage: it was in this very establishment, at this very table, that the scientific team first confessed their crime (and this is the term everybody is using now) to a security official. This is where the governmental cover-up began. Journalists, and rubberneckers, and oddballs, swarmed to the shop. The two men who had been on duty that day sold their stories; but their stories didn't amount to very much, and didn't earn them very much money.

But it is the nature of events that they entail consequences over a much longer timescale than people realise. The scientific community remains divided as to whether the unusually severe atmospheric storms are caused by the continuing action of the null-corridor, or whether the null-corridor has long since dissipated, and these storms are merely the long tail of the jolt which the chaotic weather system received from its initial carving.

And six months after *that*, the shop is empty. Things went badly, for the small country that had produced this enormous device has been repudiated by many of the world's nations. There were economic sanctions in place, public shaming. It has offered up dozens of its official personnel, including all the remaining scientists on the team, to public trials and imprisonment.

– *Why were you so secretive? Why didn't you share the theoretical underpinnings of the technology you were developing?*

– We were a small group, working well within the budget for our team. The technology isn't expensive. The most expensive part of our equipment, in fact, was the balloon to lift it up for its trial detonation.

– *But* why *the S-for-Secrecy?*

– We figured we were like the Manhattan Project.

But, no! no! That doesn't wash. That doesn't wash.

– *The Manhattan Project was a wartime project. The secrecy was governmentally sanctioned, and a necessary component of the prosecution of the war. You were working during peacetime. You brought this horror on the world for* no *reason.*

– Not Manhattan Project in the sense of wartime, but Manhattan Project in the sense of knowing that we had a *potentially* catastrophically destructive technology on our hands. The last thing we wanted was for this to leak out. Our secrecy was motivated by a desire to protect humanity from the—

But it's no good. To prison they all go, for the term of their naturals, and the new government, and then the one that comes into power after that, falls, makes repeated obeisance to the international community. And although some of its allies stand by it, the sanctions of others do bite. Its economy turns down. People lose their jobs. Poverty increases. It's all bad news.

Another government tumbles, tripped over by this immoveable object, this S-bomb. Life gets harder still, and fewer and fewer people are in the position to afford frivolities like expensive coffee-shop steam-filtered coffee. The journalists are no longer interested. The ordinary disaster-tourists and rubberneckers don't call by any more. Only the weirdos keep coming – and here's a truth about weirdoes – they're generally too parsimonious actually to buy the damn coffee. More often than not they come in, sit at The Table and run peculiar home-made Heath-Robinson hand-held devices over it, up and down its legs, as if looking for something. Aluminium foil and cardboard and glued-on circuit boards and things like that, wielded as if the table could, if plumbed correctly, *reveal something* about the way an S-Bomb is constructed, or about the fundamental nature of reality, or things along that axis of thought.

The nations of the world, the ones that excoriate as much as those that stand by, of course institute their own programmes to uncover the technology at the heart of the S-Bomb. And it's not difficult, once you grasp a few general premises. Within the year there are a dozen functioning S-Bombs, none of which are publicly acknowledged. A year after that there are hundreds. There are different modalities and strengths of the device.

Does this sound like a stable situation to you? And yet another year slowly passes, and another, and another, without the world coming to an end.

The coffee-shop, to stay financially afloat, has rethought its business-plan to concentrate on cheap food, alcohol and all-night opening. The expensive dark-wood fittings and chunky chairs are starting to show wear and tear; and the clientele now mostly consists of people in cheap clothing who buy the cheapest soup on the menu, grab three bread rolls from the bread roll basket (despite the sign that says '*one* bread roll per soup *please*'), cache two in their coat pockets, and then sit for hours and hours at their laptops trying to scratch together e-work. Thin chance of that, these days, friend. Hard times at the mill. They complain that the heating is turned down too low. The new manager stands firm.

From next week, he decides, he's moving the bread-roll basket behind the till. Customers will be issued with one roll when they have paid for the soup, no discussion, no argument.

But here's an old friend; looking no older. Close-cropped white hair, whorled and scored skin. And with him, looking *much* reduced, the younger guy: thinner, raccoon-eyed, with a timid body language and a tendency to hang his head forward. And a third person: armed, e-tooled up with a head-sieve and fancy shades. The finest private bodyguard money can buy. He gives them privacy; checks out the space; waits by the door.

The two old friends can't sit at *the* table, since it was long since sold on i-Bay, but they buy some coffee and sit at *a* table, and that suits them just fine.

And for a while they simply sit there.

Eventually the younger one, his eyes on the tabletop and his manner subdued, speaks.

– You taking me back, after this?

– *Consider it your parole.*

The younger man digests this fact.

– Not going back?

– *No.*

– I could tell you my opinion on the Antarctic business, he offers. This whirl-tempest thing. I have been thinking about it.

– *We've got people on staff who have been offering expert opinions on that.*

This seems to pique the young man.

– I tried to keep up, he says, much as I could, as was possible within the confines of . . . But my internet access was severely, I mean *severely*, restricted.

– *Really? In prison,* says the older man. *Who'd think it?*

– What I'm saying (eyes still on the tabletop) is, I recognise that there will be people who have kept up with all the science better than I've been able.

– *You're not out,* says the older man, *so that we can tap into your scientific expertise. That's not why you're out.*

The obvious next question would be: then why am I out? But the young man has got out of the habit of interrogating others. So he just sits there. He keeps looking up at the bodyguard, flicking his eyes at the man's impassive face, stealing glances at the chunky stock of his Glock.

– *Here's one thing*, says the older man, *you'll maybe have seen. Or heard about. The Chinese were trying to splice out a whole section of string. Best as I understand it, it would involve a double cut, liberating a continuous section, with the very rapid gluing-together of the remaining sections before they shoot off to space forever at twenty-seven klicks a second. But the liberated section is carried along with us, apparently.*

This gets the younger man agitated, although in a semi-contained, rather strangulated manner.

– See, this talking of splicing is a lie. You can't splice the string. The best you could do would be a temporary field-hold, and the equations include chaotic elements when you try and work out how long the hold is going to last. Not that you could do anything after the fact. If it breaks it'll be millions of kilometres away by the time it does.

He dries up, glances at the dour face of the older man, and then back at the table.

– Anyway, he says, in a gloomy voice. If you cut the string twice you'll *get* a continuous section. You just won't be able to say how long. It loops through ten dimensions, don't forget. It passes through six dimensions we can't even see. It might be a few metres long, or thousands of light years.

– *A continuous whole section of that length*, says the older man, drily, *wouldn't be much use to us.*

– But because it loops through so many dimensions . . .

– *You think I don't know all this?*

The young man looks up again, alarmed. Then, eyes down, he picks up his coffee and slurps it.

– *This is the weave underlying everything*, says the older man. *We've all become pretty expert in this subject. This is the* ground, *the paper upon which the ink of reality is laid down, against which it is readable. Not only our world, but the whole cosmos, all matter and all vacuum, it all rolls itself along this endless medium; and without this medium it wouldn't exist as cosmos, matter and vacuum. Everything material is relative, but this – this is absolute.*

– I give the world, says the young man, one year. I'm amazed it's lasted as long as it has. This south polar sea incident – that shows you something. That shows you that S-Bombs *will* continue to be detonated. They'll be set off, by governments or terrorists, rogue states and idiots, and each one will knock another hole in the reality upon which we depend. Soon there will be hundreds of loose ends in the superstring. It will unspool more and more rapidly. It'll fray more and more.

– *As I say,* says the older man. *We got brighter and better informed experts working for us now. Brighter than you, and better informed than you.*

The younger man takes this in his stride, as how could he not? Seven years of prison are enough to break most people. He even nods.

– *Let's say,* the older man continues, *that the Chinese have achieved this thing. We're not sure if by luck or judgment; but say they cut loose a segment of the unitary superstring. Say they unlaced it from ten dimensions into one dimension. One of ours.*

– You mean, two?

– *Just length. As breadthless and depthless as it is timeless. Or, let me be more precise. When it's looped about itself, or knotted, then effects of breadth and depth and time and other stuff are measurable. It's the* proximity *of one length of string to another length, and the precise pattern, or orientation, of that proximity. One portion lying close alongside another, and you've breadth. Lying alongside another at a different orientation and you've time, and so on.*

– They can manipulate it?

– *So it seems.*

– How? How can they? How?

– *Their glue is better than our glue, I guess. They haven't created a discernible breach, for instance, so we think that they've found a way of holding the two severed ends of string in something approximating stability. They're in orbit, by the way, so maybe that helps. But our sources suggest they've got a separated out, whole, workable two-metre piece of string.*

– That's very, says the young man, and he means to add, impressive, but the words dry in his throat.

– You know what they've found?

– What?

– The operation of this thing?

– I don't know.

– You couldn't guess. And we're *not sure, because this is not first-hand. But by all accounts, the American security services, and ours, because ours depend upon theirs. This is what we've discovered: by manipulating it they manipulate grace.*

– Grace.

– *Grace,* says the old man, and with this third iteration of the word he sits back in his chair and smiles. The curlicue grooves of his face buckle and chew, and his smile grows broader. It is alarming.

– I didn't realise you were religious, mumbles the young man.

– *You didn't realise very much,* returns the older, placidly, *when you started on this project.*

The young man looks up from the table, and there's a small flash in his eyes.

– I didn't, he says, realise I'd end up in prison, for instance.

– So why do you think we've sprung you?

The young man drops his eyes again, and shrinks back into himself, but he replies, in a low voice: – I should never have gone to prison. My team were scapegoats. We worked under ministerial licence, and carte blanche, on a weapons programme. If it weren't for the cap (which is what the half-sky filling northern hemisphere blackness is now usually called) and the baying-for-blood media, and the ignorance of the public, then . . .

He stops.

– And anyway what, he asks, do you mean, *grace*? Grace? What's that?

– *You know,* says the older man, turning his right hand over and back and over as if signalling 'so-so' very slowly, *Grace. Beautiful sunsets. That lovely tickle inside your chest on Christmas morning. The tremendous mystery.*

– What are you talking about?

The old man sits forward, and his deep wrinkles settle on his face. Oh, he's serious *now*.

– *The medium of matter, the medium which enables the plenitude of the material. You know what the S turned out to stand for? Spirit. That's what we've been dabbling with, cutting and splicing. And the Chinese, by all accounts, have made a machine that includes a one-dimensional stretch of Spirit. And who knows what they can do by manipulating it? Do you think they can kill or heal? Bless or damn? Some of the reports are pretty hard to credit, actually. But it won't stay under wraps forever. These things never do.*

There is a little more colour in the young man's face as he looks up.

– You always knew, he says, that we had been specifically tasked with developing an S-Bomb. The orders were sanctioned from the highest levels of government. We were doing what we were told to, up to and including organising tests. And then, when public opinion went sour, we were the ones hung out to dry. How many of my team are there even *left*?

– *Atonement,* says the older man. *That's why you're out, now. That's what we're preparing for. Sacrifice, atonement. Transgression and forgiveness. We're working on the best information we have. But these are going to be the materials of the new dispensation.*

– Whose transgression? says the younger man, sharply. Whose forgiveness?

– *Another thing not in the news. A certain . . . organisation . . . claims to have sunk a working S-Bomb into the Atlantic east of the USA. If they detonate it at the right moment it'll rip at twenty-five kilometres a second right through the world. It'll set off catastrophic earthquake, oceanic storms, it'll froth up atmospheric turbulence such as the world has never seen, before we leave it behind in space. We're in negotiations with them about the sums of money they want not to do this.*

The young man is looking at the table again.

– *You understand what I mean?*

Nothing.

– *You think you have suffered?* says the older man. *You think your sufferings have even* begun? *This discovery, and these weapons, belong to a reality whose laws we understand in only the crudest way. But if its currency is atonement, then who is better placed to offer himself up to that than you? There have never been such dangers of death facing the world. Do you understand the ferocity of what you've done?*

– We didn't mean . . .

– *Ask yourself again: why have we brought you out of prison? Why would we? How can you help? In what way can you atone?*

The young man stares a long time at the tabletop.

The older man leans forward, and speaks in a rapid, low tone, as if pouring the words directly into the younger man's ear. *Listen,* he says. *Listen to me. It's always been this way with bombs, on the one hand the rocket that hammers cities to powder, on the other the rocket that elevates human beings to the moon. It's always been this way. Your little S-device has polluted a third of the night sky with opacity. Three more have been detonated now, spreading their ink. How could it* not *be the case that, understood properly, this same device will heal?*

The young man, eyes down, keeps staring.

As they talk, the proprietor sits on a stool behind the reinforced cash register, reading the paper. This is the lead story: *Experts say S-Bomb death spreading through the universe.* This is the gist of the story, in which 'cosmological expert Sanjit Bansal' is quoted:

If the universe were infinitely big and filled with an infinite number of stars, then the night sky would be white, because no matter which direction we looked out line-of-sight would end, eventually, with a star. There would be interstellar dust, of course, which you might think would occlude the lines of light, but in an infinite universe these would over time have heated up and incandesced. But we don't see a white sky when we look up at night. So perhaps the cosmos is finite.

But what if the S-Bomb technology is, like mathematics and nuclear power, something that every civilisation discovers in due course? What if there have been millions, or billions, of alien civilisations out there that have discovered the S-Bomb, and detonated them, and left behind billions of slowly expanding spherical blots of impenetrable blackness. What if the dark between the stars that we see when we look up is that . . . these inevitably unspooling spots of death, growing eventually to devour everything? What if that's the truth of it?

Another customer, and the proprietor folds the paper away and gets off his stool. A white porcelain mug, and the nozzle squirts in the black coffee. It covers the white circle at the base of the mug almost instantaneously.

Dantean

Finally Avis stepped from the pinnacle of Purgatory. His stride took him over, and he put his feet onto the pliant medium of heaven itself. To have worked down through the torments of Hell, circle after circle – the stench, the air hurting the lungs with every breath – to the gate at the centre of the Earth, through the passageway. And to have laboured up the circular plateaus of the enormous mountain of Purgatory. He had achieved so much. His heart sang. It actually seemed to vibrate with joy, a pure, high, warbly sound like a finger running round the lip of a wine-glass. He strode several yards along the soft and transparent floor of the first heavenly circle. Somebody was singing. That was surely the noise, although it sounded more machine-made than human. It set the very hairs in the ears tingling.

Before him, he could see a crystal forest, elegant trunks yearning upwards and exploding into diamante leaves, everything dripping and glittering with light. The forest positively dazzled with light. Absolutely everything up here was lit brightly, vividly, yet also warmly. It did not sting the eyes. There seemed to be no shadow anywhere, as if the whole sky were a benign, warm-blooded neon, pouring nourishing light from all sides at once. And, looking up between the stems of the trees, Avis saw the floor of the next circle, several miles above him, yet visible in perfect detail. It was as if his eyes functioned better: he could see the soles of people's feet walking on that invisible floor, the shuddery fall of water from a tumbling waterfall falling in that higher zone, catching light and stabbing it beautifully in all directions, the broad zone of a river sweeping away to his right. And beyond that, above and above, each colossal cosmic sphere nestling inside each, reaching upwards through the bright-lit pale blue to the perfect rose of God itself. Everything was beautiful.

'I'm in heaven,' he called out, to the warm clear air. 'Hey, I'm *literally* in Heaven!'

He started running. All the claustrophobia, all that dark toothachey pain of Hell seemed impossibly distant from him now. He dodged through the fragile trees – were they the source of that eerie, lovely whine? Or a woman sitting in some crystal glade singing with more-than-human vocal range? A sublime image. He didn't care. It was beautiful, beautiful. He laughed, sprinting tirelessly, flying through the clean air to land and spring away again.

Eventually, he paused. He wasn't tired, exactly, but he had the sense that he had run enough. He strolled onwards, and came to the edge of the crystal forest. The trees gave way to a broad meadow of white grass, like the blondest hair, the meadow, swaying in ripples with a rustle, as from air blown between pursed lips. The pale grass stretched down to a lake of lapis lazuli brightness. He wandered through the grass. It was hip-high. When he dandled his hand in it as he walked it felt soft against his skin.

There were other people down at the lakeside.

He sat next to a woman. 'Hello,' he said.

She looked at him. 'Oh,' she said. 'Hi.'

'My name's Avis.'

'Welsh,' she said.

Her body was as subtly different from the bodies he had seen on the terraces of Mount Purgatory as those bodies had been from the grossly physical bodies in Hell, Dalmatian-spotted with sores, reeking and saggy. It was still human in shape, two legs, two arms, trunk and head. But the skin was albino pale, rather unpleasantly so, and entirely without mark, blotch or hair. There were no toenails, and her fingernails had reduced to barely-visible upside-down bracket-marks on the end of her fingers. Her breasts were nipple-free swellings on the front of her body. There was nothing between her legs. Thighs connected into torso as innocently as a Barbie-doll. It looked, at first, as if she were wearing a very tight-fitting white plastic skin over her whole body, but Avis could see that it wasn't that way. Only her face retained any features, and even those were smoothed and worn down like a pebble in a stream. Thin mouth, a pip-shaped nose, wide eyes almost circular. The barest hint of creases when she smiled. A single line, delicately carved, a millimetre under each eye.

For a while Avis simply sat, watching the serenity of the water. There were half a dozen people on the lakeside, all of them either staring out at the water or lying back and looking up. A spark of joy passed through Avis's internal wiring.

'It's so beautiful!' he said.

Welsh looked at him. 'Oh,' she said. 'Yeah.'

'You need to understand,' said Avis, hugging himself. 'I've been through Hell: all the way through, all down into the filthy, disgusting, pain-ridden pit at the bottom. And then up the mountain of Purgatory – and that was no picnic. That was hard work. I feel I have, you know, earned being up here.'

Welsh didn't say anything in reply to this, so Avis sat in silence for a while. 'Welsh,' he said, trying the name out. 'Where you from, then?'

He was only trying to make conversation.

'From?' she said.

'Yeah, you know. Before you . . .'

He trailed off.

'Died?' she said.

'Yeah.'

'New Hampshire,' she said.

'Oh,' said Avis. He was looking at his own hands. Their colour had faded, it seemed, to a coppery red. Was there, he wondered, no place in Heaven for blackness? Were they going to mutate him into a white man? The prospect was not an especially pleasant one to him, but, then again, he found he couldn't get very upset over it. Perhaps that's how it was, here in heaven.

'You been here long?' he asked.

Welsh looked at him. 'You're just up from Purgatory,' she said.

'Yeah.'

'Time is more acute down there. That's kind of the point of Purgatory.'

'You're saying it doesn't matter so much up here? Time, I mean?'

Welsh looked away from him. 'You could say that,' she said, inattentively. 'Not that it's absent, exactly.'

'I still can't believe it,' said Avis, looking around it. 'I really can't. I mean, Heaven! Really'

'Yes,' said Welsh. 'Oh, hard to believe. I guess you get used to it. Or more used, at any rate.'

'Did you come up through Purgatory?'

'Sure.'

'I tell you, I'm headed further up,' said Avis, firmly. 'Further up.'

'Good luck to you,' said Avis, stretching herself in the grass. 'Me, I'm going down.'

'Down?'

'You want to check off the possibilities,' said the woman. 'When I first got here – I mean, *Homo sapiens sapiens*, inquisitive man, all that. So I thought, one, I'm actually in Heaven. I died and came to Heaven, and it just turns out that the afterlife is, oh, *exactly* as Dante described it, down to the last hell-circle and heaven-sphere. But that seemed too outrageously implausible to me.'

'Did I hear you right?' asked Avis.

'Then I thought that maybe the afterlife was, I don't know, dependent on the individual consciousness. I took a class on Dante in my freshman year: classics of European Literature, it was called. Now, I didn't think that his Divine Comedy made that much of an impact on me, but maybe it did, maybe it did subconsciously. But then I met people up here who'd never read Dante, who'd never *heard* of Dante. And that gave me pause again. So then I figured that it's one giant computer simulation. All this is just data, just *information*, nothing else. But that doesn't get me any further, because if it's indistinguishable from the real thing then it *is* the real thing.'

'Why would you want to go *down*?' Avis pressed. Then, he added, 'Is there somebody down there you want to – I don't know, rescue?'

'No,' she said. 'No.'

'Then why?'

'Oh, they all do. I mean, I guess they all do.' She made a vague gesture at the sky with her right arm. 'I haven't, like, done a survey or anything. Haven't really spoken to any of them for a while, but I'd be surprised if any one stays up here too long. You went through Hell?'

'Yes,' said Avis, 'and it was really nasty. I mean, *really* nasty.'

'Oh, I know. But full of people, yes?'

Avis nodded.

'Wonder why?'

'I guess I assumed that they'd all, I don't know, committed sin. That they were being punished.'

'We've all committed sins,' said Welsh languidly. 'They're like us, down there. They could all purge themselves of their sins, make their way up Purgatory. That's what it's there for, Purgatory.'

He looked at her. 'Then why do they stay there? In Hell, I mean?'

'They don't, mostly. It does,' she said, sitting up sharply, 'make you wonder, doesn't it? What is it that happens to the body with chronic pain? I don't mean weeks or months, but, you know, centuries of pain? Does it polish the nerves smooth? An eventual wearing away of the capacity to experience pain *as* pain?'

'Odd thing to say,' said Avis, looking at her. 'I can't say I see what you mean.'

'Sure,' she said, looking around again. The waters of the lake pulsed austerely at the diamond-sand shore, waves like silk curling over. 'Haven't you worked out the currency of this place? Its secret? You will, I guess. A year, ten, a thousand, a million. No, strike that, that's absurd. A year, at the very most. A year is long enough.'

'Secret?'

'Craving,' said Welsh, throwing a gesture out awkwardly with her right arm again to take in the various souls dotted around the lake's shore. 'Craving more sensation. Souls crave sense data. The stronger the data the more information. Information is the currency of the universe. *That's* what we're hard-wired to desire.'

'So you're going voluntarily back down to Hell?'

'Oh,' she said. 'Yes.'

'Because you're – what, bored?'

'It's not that exactly.'

He stared at her. The images of Hell were still fresh in his mind. He couldn't imagine anywhere he wanted less to visit. 'You're saying,' he said, 'that pain is more *info-rich*?'

'Believe it,' she said.

'But,' he said, looking around himself at the gorgeous filigree beauty, the enormous comforting expanse. 'Surely there're differences in the, you know, the *quality* of info you experience? Some experiences are just intrinsically preferable to others?'

'Change,' she said. 'As good as a rest.'

'OK,' he said, thinking harder. 'But . . . isn't Hell more *entropic*? The tearing down of bodies, the burning up of flesh?'

'Oh,' she said, 'there's no real entropy anywhere up here, because there's no real energy; not in the sense of thermal energy, of *Brownian* motion, do you see? It's all information and the organisation of information. Well,' she said, looking thoughtful, 'I guess that *is* energy, you could say that, but . . . it's more a question of *focus*. Hell is a more *focused* info-environment.' She looked at him, and smiled. 'Freud,' she said, 'you remember him? He's from your time?'

'I did a course on him,' said Avis, 'in *my* freshman year.'

'Great. Well, he talked about the death-drive. He didn't realise that it works both ways. The living are oriented towards death by time's arrow, and they yearn for the end of struggle, for the stillness, without even realising it. Oh, but the dead yearn for death again, for the opposite reason, from the opposite side. It's a kind of symmetry.' She paused, looked around her. 'You come out of death at a certain velocity, if you like. I remember me. I died in Canada. Then I hurtled up Purgatory, I just hurtled, I prayed, I *worked*, struggled to submit myself to God's will. I rose to the sphere of the moon, where I started to understand . . .'

She stopped. Avis waited for her to finish, but after a while it seemed she wasn't going to say any more.

'Understand what?'

A shrug. 'Understand that God's will is only one force among many. To be precise, in the material world the key force is gravity. Gravity is apprehensible here, just about, but this *afterlife* isn't the proper . . . idiom for gravity. We only sense it vaguely, intermittently. Now, the key force in *this* region is God's Will – *that's* a force that barely registers in the material world. It's a very interesting circumstance actually. Paralleled. So I started to realise that God's Will is a force *like* gravity. You can overcome it if you like. You can – or that's not very well put. A Wernher Von Braun can achieve an escape velocity from it. It's still there, it still shapes this particular cosmos, but . . . that's all, it's just a shaping. I figured, to begin with, that I should get as high up the circles of paradise as possible, as close to God. But it doesn't require that of me. And after a while . . .' She stopped. 'Not a good way of putting it, but the best I can do. After a while you start to wonder about the backward journey. And, you know? When you start wondering about it, it suddenly dawns on you that *the vast majority* are on that same journey, back down. So, you *really* didn't wonder, as you came through, why the circles of Hell and the lower slopes of Purgatory are so full? But now? What do you think?'

'I assume that they hadn't had time to work up the mountain yet. And I assumed the ones in Hell were stuck in Hell.'

'Yet you came up faster than them. And you came right out of Hell.'

'I guess.'

'Besides it doesn't really mean anything to say *they hadn't had time yet* to do this or that. I mean, it's all relative. I mean, the best way to get a sense of time passing is *to move*. Man you gotta *go*. When you're on your trip up the circles, or when you're going down – *then* you feel it. Time, I mean. It's a drag. That's what living is, before death or after it. It's the sensation of moving through the medium, you know, like an anchor being tugged through the tourbillons of the water. That's where the impression of time comes from. It's cool, in fact. People become hooked on that sensation, hooked on the feeling of time passing, like the wind in their hair. It's a unique kind of high. So I realised that people here were – most of them – constantly on the move. They climb up. They clamber down again. And the most *exciting* part of the journey is Hell. Because it's the most information-dense, the richest medium, you feel time passing most acutely there.'

'There's nothing about *that* in Dante,' said Avis.

'You know about Dante?'

'Sure,' he said.

'I'd like to re-read him,' said Welsh. 'I barely remember anything about his book.'

'Dante thought,' said Avis, wanting obscurely to match her lecturing with some of his own, 'that souls yearned upwards, like flames. Yearned after God. No?'

'I guess you tend to,' conceded Welsh. 'At first. But Dante – he was in the thrall of the Death Drive, that's what *he* was. Though he didn't realise it. He didn't realise that the Death Drive is a kind of tiredness. After a while you achieve it, and you sleep, and then you wake up from it and then you need stimulation, information. We *need* information like a plant needs sunlight. So you go back down for some.'

'But I want to see the rose,' said Avis.

'Rose?'

'God. At the very top of it all.'

'Good luck to you. Not me.'

'Don't you want to know the answers?' asked Avis.

Welsh had stood up, and was stretching her arms and curving her back in the all-encompassing sunlight. 'Answers,' she repeated, dreamily. 'Do you want to know the answers? Or do you want to know that there *are* answers, and then have fun finding them out? I heard from others that God is a slightly off-putting presence. All crystal, lattice, quite abstract.'

She was sinking through the transparent floor now like a figure in the platonic ideal of quicksand.

'Goodbye,' he said, as she elevated down.

'It's a nervous thing,' she said to him as she dropped through the floor. 'It's nervous. If you're not nervous then you're not paying attention.'

She left him sitting by the lake. It was water, pure and clear, and yet the ripples on the surface moved much more slowly than water-ripples ought. They moved like some kind of treacle, a clear tar, slowly bulging up and sinking down. Avis sat by the lake for a length of time, but it was impossible for him to determine for how long.

ReMorse®

It's on.

Yep. Hep. Yeah.

So, this is my understanding of how we came to be here. And it's the least I can do to give you my sense of how we got here, how we *arrived*, as it were. It happened like this. ReMorse® was developed by the Pharmakon Corporation, using a smile-shaped wedge of *governmental* money, on account of drug development being so billions-expensive. It was initially designed as a treatment for certain psychopathologies in which individuals lack human empathic skills; it was designed so that they could be given the help they needed. It's a – I've seen it – I mean I've seen it in its *medical* format – it's a museum-piece now of course – it was a lozenge, a small pellet, like a Go pebble. White one, black one. And you placed this under the tongue, I think. Which is to say . . . no, I'm getting this wrong. I'm sorry! It *wasn't* under the tongue, of course not. Sorry! Sorry! It *was* a lozenge, but you pressed it up *against the roof* of your mouth, and the nanofoam got itself going, set its pathways tentacling, insinuated its way into the brain pan. Sorry!

OK. So. Imagine a sociopath. They tested it on psychopaths and murderers first of all, you see. Not that there's a centre in the brain where remorse is, you know, *generated*. I'm sorry if I gave you that impression, I really am, that would be misleading. Killer kills because he is untroubled about the violence he inflicts on others. Killer kills because it makes him feel *powerful* and *immune*, and *that* power and *that* immunity depend upon the thing-ness of the victim. You cut a throat, and it's only a throat, not a whole living, terrified human being. It's *not even* a throat. It's just a mechanism by which the killer reinforces his super-humanity. Or so I understand it to have been. Obviously – I want to be *clear* about this. I don't want to give you a false impression – obviously *I* really don't understand the motivation of such people. Sorry. I'm sure you don't either. But we can both agree that they need *treatment*.

So, ReMorse® becomes a treatment for crime, all of it, crime as a whole. Put it in the water! That was the famous slogan, the famous slogan, the *Blanchett* slogan! And why *not* put it in the water supply? Not for nothing was it called the utopia drug by, I'm sorry, I'm sorry, I can't remember who said that. But it was a well-chosen word, don't you think?

A dilution, a development of the pharmochemistry: why not dose up *certain* populations, that's the idea. Because if we give Hannibal Lecter this pill, we discover that he empathises *too much* with his victim to kill them. He can't *do it* anymore. He flat can't. His victim is no longer a thing, his victim is a person. Just pulling the knife from its sheath maketh the killer for to burst into tears, to throw himself on the floor withal '*I'm sorry! I'm sorry!*' And if it works, in large dose, for such extreme criminals, then might it not, in smaller doses, might it not *take the edge off* the whole crime wave? Dampen the tsunami? Could you steal someone's car if your mental threshold for remorse were raised, just a little? Could you *mug* someone if you empathised fully with the victim? Of course not.

I'll tell you something else, too: it was – I *remember* this – I'm sorry, I'm a bit disjointed in my narrative here. I'm sorry! It must be somehow annoying for you to have to listen to this rambling – this rambling. Look: I remember how it was, and I remember one of the reasons there was such widespread support for the drug. (*Put it in the drinking water!* they said. *Give it to everybody*, they said.) Let's say you arrest Hannibal Lecter. Let's say you punish him. He's grinning the whole time. You put him in prison – do what you like, starve him, beat him, make him lie on a wet mattress (Oh God, just to *think* of it!) and pass electric current through it – and he's *grinning* at you. You see, you can't touch the core of his evil mind. You want to, but you can't. You see, you don't want just to hurt his body. You want *him* to *feel* the *pain* he has inflicted. You want to take the pain he has created and inject it into his mind. But you were never able to do that.

Now you can. The drug made that possible. It's a boon to justice.

And it *does* reduce crime levels. It *does* guard against terrorism. And it *does* preserve the peace, and does all that simply by raising the natural human response to the pain of others. Even to contemplate a crime can cause overwhelming and gushing levels of remorse to flood the mind. I know, as you know, because we all know, now that it's in the water.

Mr Blanchett? Too tight? OK, I'm sorry, OK, I'm sorry. Sorry, there, there, there.

Now, things were *of course* better, things were, and it's a simple move to 'expand the definition' of crime to include political malefaction. So people don't rape and rob anymore because so much as *planning* the crime brings on agonising bouts of remorse. So it's not hard to refine the drug, such that planning to overthrow the government as a terrorist might, and planning to vote-out the government as a voter might, become pretty much the same thing. Opposing the government brings with it prolonged and agonising bouts of remorse. And I vote – I voted at the last election, and with a clear conscience, and for *your* administration too! Isn't the world better now? I remember how it was before, when you couldn't walk from house to store without risking getting gun-jacked. Much better now. And I've often wondered if there's a connection between the remorse response in the brain and the gratitude response. *I'm* grateful, certainly. I'm grateful for what the drug has done for society.

Of course, the, what you might call, I'm sorry, what you might call side-effects. There are side-effects. A lot of people are timid. Some are pretty cowed, I guess. Some take it bad, can barely leave their homes for fear of – you know – of whatever they might, accidentally or intentionally – you know. But others function pretty well. Pretty well, all things considered. And then there are those who . . . well, take me. Here's the example of me.

I did try, for a time, to pick a path so as to *avoid* feeling this ramped-up remorse. I attempted, and this is not a figure of speech, *not to hurt a fly*. But then I came to an understanding. I call it self-revelation. Remorse is an *intensity*. It is an extreme focus of self-awareness and other-awareness. It's – in a word – look, I'm sorry to use this word, but it's *sex*. And, no, that's not good enough, for it's more intense than sex, provided only. Look: here's what I mean. This stiletto, it's *better* than a cock. The point on your skin, it's – it's – there's an *exquisite*. There's a, and the force, the pressure of muscles that—

I'm sorry!

I'm sorry!

I'm sorry!

I'm sorry!

I'm sorry!

I'm sorry!

I'm sorry!

Aaaaaaa.

I always do that, say it seven times I mean. I don't plan to, it just comes out that way, as knife goes in. As blood comes *out*. Ah, the ecstasy of it. The sevenfold ecstasy of it! And, yes, it's true I *come*, yes it's true my heart goes poppity-pupoppity, but it's not just – sorry – here, let me loosen that a little – *there* you go. Sorry the floor's bare lino, Senator, but I'll need to clean it shortly, and carpet would be – well, you can imagine. But, Senator, what I was saying, what I was saying, is that although my body makes manifest certain symptoms of physical desire, the . . . not that I don't prepare for that. I'm wearing plastic boxers, for instance: I learnt that lesson right at the start, after the very first of them! But the intensity with which *my excitement* and *my agony* at *your pain* is mixed together, that's more than just a physical thing. That's a

The World of the Wars

'So. Are you pro-war?' Splendour-of-Thought asked me. 'Or anti-war?'

I turned to him, my prostheses whirring. 'I hardly need return the question,' I said to him. '*Your* opinions on the conflict are well known.'

'We are the most highly evolved creatures in the solar system,' said Splendour-of-Thought, eagerly. 'We have advanced to unprecedented levels in all the key scientific areas. Our machines render us strong and mobile. Our rocketry means we can span the vastness between worlds. Surely a people *so advanced* do not need to wage a war of imperial conquest.'

'So!' I retorted. 'Many would disagree with your description of this campaign – imperialism? Who says this is a war of imperialism? The people of the Blue World labour under conditions of the most *appalling* primitiveness. We are *liberating* them from that tyranny, bringing the benefits of our far-superior technology and civilisation. They will benefit as much as we.'

'You admit that we *will* benefit enormously from this war,' pressed Splendour-of-Thought, as if it were a brilliant debating point. 'You admit that self-interest is largely at work in this deployment?'

'Is it a criminal thing to benefit?' I replied. 'Come, Splendour-of-Thought, live up to your name! Do we not worship the principles of pure mentition, the disinterested glory of Thought-as-God that shapes the cosmos? Or are we to surrender ourselves to the thoughtless glandular surges of emotion that marked our ancestors?'

'Our glands may have atrophied,' he said, 'but they have not disappeared. And of course sometimes stray hormones filter into our brain, via our food. I would not be ashamed of arguing an emotional case, if I were doing so. But on the contrary, my case is argued from the *position* of mentition! Mentition tells us that we should allow the creatures of the Blue World to evolve at their own pace, until they are ready to join us in the solar system as equals! Not enslave them! That thought is abhorrent.'

'Of course,' I said, shuffling a little to the left to allow one of my service-devices to access the launch tube, 'it goes without saying that the idea of enslaving another people is anathema to any right-thinking Martian. But that's not what the war is about.'

'I might have thought you would say so,' snorted Splendour-of-Thought. 'You have been brainwashed by the pronouncements of the ruling council.'

'Not at all. The soldiers *over there* are some of the most civilised, the most thoughtful citizens of our entire culture. They're prepared to risk their lives to defend the Martian way of life – and to bring its benefits to surly and backward savages.' I gestured with a metallic tentacle, and continued confidently: 'Once the army has suppressed the local resistance, and established walkers and service towers across the key territories, then the natives themselves will come to realise how much better off they are. I predict that in a matter of months the people of the Blue World will be thanking us for what we have done for them. Thanking us!'

The work on the launch tube service coolant vent-carburant was complete. We geared up and strode across the plain, leaving the launch tube to the ministrations of the service devices.

Of course, Splendour-of-Thought's objections to the war were not unique to him, or merely eccentric. Many otherwise good-thinking Martians shared his concerns, so much so that the ruling council had posted a continual guard along the length of the great launching tube. A saboteur might hope to interfere in some way with the tube, and so prevent our troops from so much as launching across the void to the target world. Patrols were ubiquitous to prevent precisely this. The two of us were stopped by one such patrol; my feelers passed the authorisation cylinder from my walker to the Guard Captain's, and we were permitted to move on.

The sun sent magenta shadows fluttering away from our metal legs as we strode towards the dome. The dust was red with the dried remains of the Great Weed – not dead through drought – the weed had been permitted to die away of natural causes so as not to overgrow the launch tube. The red sun settled onto the red horizon. It was a desolately beautiful sight.

Splendour-of-Thought's voice came through on my speaker again. 'I only wish you wouldn't talk of *civilising* them.'

'How else would you describe it?' I countered. 'Taking away the chains of their ignorance and backwardness – leading them into the age of thought, of technology, of space flight.'

'It's as if you haven't been watching the news . . .' he said.

'What do you mean?' I snapped,

'You've surely seen the reports of atrocities,' he said petulantly.

I did not enjoy hearing my colleague speaking in this way. 'If I didn't know that the vetting processes for employing technicians on the great launch tube were as thorough as they are,' I said, 'I might start to suspect you of harbouring antiwar ambitions to sabotage Operation Free Blueworld.'

'Atrocity,' Splendour-of-Thought continued, 'is the word that describes what is going on over there. How can you disagree? You *must* have seen the pictures – those poor Blueworld natives tortured – killed.'

'There is bound to be unfortunate collateral damage in any military operation,' I pointed out. 'Regrettable, but a price worth paying – the sooner the military can bring the fighting to an end the better for everybody, Blueworld natives included.'

'Which means . . .'

'Which means our patriotic duty is to *support* our troops. It only prolongs the war to criticise, as you are doing. That way nobody benefits. A swift Martian victory is imperative for everybody's sake.'

'You're certain,' Splendour-of-Thought said with a new tone of slyness in his voice, 'that victory is assured?'

'Of course.' This was almost an idiotic question. 'We are many thousands of years in advance of the Blueworld natives in technological terms. We have mastered the machinery of war, the tactics, the possible obstacles. Our war-tripods are virtually unassailable. We have anticipated every eventuality; the greater gravity of the Blue World, the thickness of the atmosphere, the alien germs and organisms.'

'Our advanced troops have certainly been treated with the most up-to-date genetic enhancement to preserve them from infection by Blueworld viruses or bacteria,' said Splendour-of-Thought.

'Bacteria to which the natives themselves are susceptible!' I pointed out. 'They cannot even protect themselves from simple infections, as we can. They lack our intellect, our technology, and our will to win. Victory is inevitable.'

We were almost at the dome.

'The genetic enhancement laboratories that treated our troops,' said Splendour-of-Thought, his voice more sly still, like a child with a secret, 'produce many things apart from regimens to protect troops against alien bugs.'

I didn't like his tone. 'What do you mean?'

'I am merely saying,' he said. 'It would be possible – let's say – for the sake of argument – that a disgruntled antiwar technician could develop a superbug that would overcome even the immunity of our shock troops.'

I stopped. 'Go on.'

Splendour-of-Thought brought his walker to a halt beside me. 'Well, it's possible that this lab-worker could pass a vial of this superbug to a worker on the launch tube – perhaps a like-minded Martian, somebody also opposed to the war.'

'And?'

'And, given the official access granted such a worker, it's

possible that the rocket shells could be contaminated with this superbug before being accelerated along the tube.'

My brain pulsed heavily with the implications of what Splendour-of-Thought was saying. 'But then . . .'

'Then the troops would carry the infection with them . . . an infection designed to lay them low, and leave the Blueworld natives untouched. After a few days the troops would begin to sicken, and eventually die. In *that* case,' said Splendour-of-Thought, 'Martian victory would not be as certain as you are suggesting.'

'That would be an act of such barbarous treachery . . .' I began to say, quivering with rage. '. . . a terrible, appalling act . . .'

'It's just hypothetical,' said Splendour-of-Thought. 'I'm only floating the notion. But it gives one pause for thought, doesn't it? What if the war is *not* won? Eh? What then for our supposedly civilised Mars?'

And he activated his walker and strode quickly away. I stood and watched him disappear across the purple and red wastes, his shadows fluttering after him along the dirt like torn ribbons in the wind.

Woodpunk

My story, since you ask for it.

A wolf was rummaging amongst a bed of wild strawberries. We were in a clearing in the wood, and it was filled with hot bright light. The wolf made the noise of a newborn baby snuffling at the breast, he did, comical, though it didn't stop me from being terrified. All around, the forest hushed itself, as if trying to keep the lid on its own temper. Metaphorically counting to twenty before speaking. As for what it might say, if its temper were to flare – that's no idle question.

Shh, shh.

We were making our way through what Conoley had described to me, not once but many times, as the greatest expanse of primal forest on the entire globe. The *only* expanse of primal forest on the entire globe. The greatest. The only. Conoley kept his rifle trained on the beast as we passed by, but it plain ignored us.

The name of this forest is Chernobyl.

And he was a larger-than-life auld Irish-American, was Conoley (*that's the one L*, as he said when introducing himself). And he was a tall and muscular and red-faced individual, with hair the colour and consistency of dandelion fluff. And he took another swig of The Great Enabler out of a flask, and breathed out noisily. And he sang, as we moved through the woods, and startled birds into the air. 'Up here,' he said again. 'Just through here.' The rifle poking up from his back looked like a digital aerial.

'There's something wrong with my,' I said, 'my G-M tube.'

'Wrong,' Conoley drawled, 'and because, why? Because it ain't registering *excessive* radiation?'

'It's not registering at all,' I said, and just as I said that, as if to mock me, the device popped, and then popped again.

'There you go,' he said. 'Oh, it's active, round here. Active, sure. But that's not to say it's a desert where the sand has been turned to glass. I've been here plenty of times, and I've more to fear from my liquid narcotic than any radiation, I tells ya,' and he pulled out his flask again. 'Kurt's been here a year and a half now,' he added. 'And no ill effects for *him*.'

Then I caught sight of a creature, in amongst the trees, amongst the fantastically prolific foliage with its tremendous range and variety of greens. Man, it was *enormous*, this creature – large as an elephant, but with raging scarlet eyes and pupils glinting with evil. It must have been forty foot high, and I yelled in the sheerest surprise and terror. But then the eye winked, and lifted away, and it was a butterfly shuddering upwards; and when that was removed the whole mirage fell apart.

'Jumpy, aren't we,' said Conoley. *Arr*unt wi.

'I like *city* streets,' I said. 'I like London and Paris. I know where I am when I'm in London.'

'You know where you are. You're in London,' Conoley said, reasonably enough.

We moved through hip-high ferns, and the strangely urinous smell of the vegetation. The sun in its summer vigour flared and faded in amongst the canopy above as we went. There is something cathedral-like about the primal forests of Old Europe; something very striking about the sheer scale.

The greatest. The only.

Kurt had started out in the camp built in the overgrown remains of a village abandoned by its occupants and overgrown by the forest. But this had involved too great a disruption of the forest logic, he said; so he had moved into the middle of the growth with a tent and a scrollscreen. By the time I came to reclaim him, on behalf of Co., he had even given up the use of his tent. I barely recognised him: huge-bearded and tangle-haired. He was wearing a puffed-up Greensuit, the outside of which was messy with mud and adhered forest detritus. I assume he slept in it; that he just lay down where he was and pulled the hood over his face and went to sleep.

There seemed to be little point in preliminaries.

'They've cancelled your salary, Kurt, and withdrawn all project funding. You come back with me now.'

But the expression on his face was that of a spirit-medium half-hearing mutterings from some other reality. He looked from me to Conoley. Then he said: 'You've got the memory?'

'Here you go, you wild and woody man,' boomed Conoley, pulling a toothpick-sized memory expansion chip from his pocket. Kurt snatched it, and rolled out his scrollscreen onto a boulder.

'I could add, "I'm sorry," ' I conceded. ' "About the end of the project." I could add, "How are you Kurt? It's good to see you again." I could add, "How's things? Long time no see." '

He had inserted the expansion chip and was paddling his fingers over the screen. I began to think that he was simply going to ignore me, but then he said: 'You still have access to the satellites?'

'They've rescinded your passwords,' I said. 'They did that. Look, you need to take a break from the research now. You've been here too long now.'

'I'll need you,' he croaked to me, 'to log in. I need an updated scan of the whole forest.'

I was content to bargain with him. I was concerned to get him home without undue fuss, and that was all I was concerned about. 'If I do that,' I said, 'will you come back with me? We've a truck a couple of hours away.'

He glowered at me, as if bringing a truck within three hours was polluting his virgin forest appallingly. But I entered my details and the scrollsheet accessed the latest data.

'Let's have a snack,' said Conoley, with his large voice and his grating jollity, unzipping his bumbag. 'Some supplies, and a drop of the Great Enabler, and there'll be time and enough to walk back before evening.'

It was a warm day. Kurt had unrolled his scrollscreen over a large, moss-plumped boulder. Flies swung back and forth in the air, as if dangled on innumerable invisible threads. I heard a bird sing a car-alarm song somewhere far off. Everything that I could see in every direction was alive. Yet despite all this vitality, there was something distressingly silent about this place. Unless – unless there *was* an almost sub-audible hum? Unless that wasn't just my imagination? Kurt said, 'I need the satellite data, so that I can see what it's telling me. It's telling me to do stuff, and I need the satellite to get a proper read-out.' I tuned him out, and breathed in the clean air.

All in amongst the forest. The greatest. The only. When he said, 'It's telling me to do stuff,' Kurt meant *the forest* was telling him.

As we were, sat amongst the tree trunks, Kurt's manner was almost normal again. He ate, and he drank, and he made conversation that could have passed as ordinary talk in half the pubs in London. 'I guess I look a fright,' he said. He tugged his beard. 'I guess the *hair's* gone pretty radical.'

'Gillette have an implant now,' I said. 'It's a new thing. It goes inside the mouth, the inside of the lower lip, and the ads say you don't even feel it after a day. Egg-smooth for thirteen months.'

'You tried it?'

'Not I,' I said, nibbling an energy cake.

Kurt fondled his own beard. 'It shows how caught up in shit a person can be. You forget to – well, you know. Hey!' he added, abruptly. 'You know what the forest is?'

'You asking me?' I said. 'Or Conoley?'

But he had gone weird, old-man-of-the-woods again, muttering something under his breath and staring directly and intensely at me. It was like meeting a tramp in the subway and smelling alcohol on him and wondering if he might be about to knife you. Ironic.

'AND IF I WERE TO TELL YOU,' he barked, with a sudden furious volume, glowering first at me, and then at Conoley, and then back at me, and he left his sentence hanging for a beat for the dramatic effect.

'What? What?'

'If-I-were-to-tell-you that *Conoley* changed his name from Conolley *two* Ls to Conoley *one* L to make himself more *interesting* to girls?' This last word was oirish, *goy-uls*, but it still took me a long moment to understand he was joking.

'I've enough of your *German* humour,' said Conoley. 'In my belly, I've enough already.' He stuffed a biscuit in his craw. 'I've enough of your American-Deutsch fucking humour in my belly thank you muchly.'

Kurt said, 'I'm sorry,' half a dozen times, modulating from giggling to sober, and the conversation wound down. I dared to hope that we'd soon start walking back through the forest to the truck, and that I'd be back in the hotel in Kiev in time for a nightcap and CNN.

Kurt leant across Conoley, and it looked for a moment as if he were *kissing* him, which would have taken high-jinks too far, I think. But he wasn't kissing him. That was an illusion created by the pattern-seeking human mind. He was only leaning across him to reach the bottle of rum. Conoley grunted, as if to say: 'Go on then, you old boozer. Have another swig, you drunk.' As if a single grunt could communicate all those words.

A grunt.

Kurt drank. I wiped my mouth. We sat in silence together for a little while.

Then Kurt got to his feet and stretched. It was a lazy afternoon. In the forest the warmth was a drowsy, pleasant, unexcessive heat. 'We're like weevils crawling across a motherboard,' he said.

Conoley appeared to have gone to sleep.

'You know what, Kurt?' I said. 'It'll need a little politics, but there's no reason why you couldn't be *back* here in six months.

You've done good work. Put yourself about the company, shake the right hands, and who knows?'

'It's a code,' he said. 'It's the great code. It's the only code.'

'Code,' I said, getting to *my* feet too. I think I didn't like the way he was above me and talking down at me. I think I wanted to be on a level with him. 'And, yes?'

'You know what this forest is? I will tell you what this forest is. You know what it is?'

'Deciduous?'

'It's a com,' he said. He paused. 'Pew,' he added, very slowly. 'Ter.'

'And what does it compute?'

'Hey, hum, hum, I been *trying* to think of an analogy. Say a new infection arose amongst men. What would we do?'

'Again with the rhetorical questions,' I said, aiming for hearty, but not quite hitting it. To be honest he was starting to freak me out. 'Shake Conoley awake there, and we can all three have this conversation as we walk back.'

'*He'll* not wake,' said Kurt, in what I took to be a jocular reference to the fellow's fondness for the booze. But then I looked again and saw that Conoley was not flicking away the flies that were sipping the salt from his open eyes, and Kurt's words took on a new meaning.

'Jesus,' I said, in a small voice.

'So there's a new infection,' he said. 'What do we do? We'd want to work out a bunch of things about it. Things like, what's the epidemiology? How fast and far will this spread? Things like, how do the symptoms correlate to the databases of other diseases. We'd plug in to the Boston Medical Database. That's not a very exact analogy.'

As he gesticulated, I could see the glint of the blade in his hand. Most of the knife was cached up his sleeve. 'Kurt,' I said. 'What did you do?'

'It's a poor analogy,' he decided, thinking further. 'Let's start again.'

'What did you *do*?'

'Hum hum,' he said to himself.

'Kurt,' I said. 'I have to tell you, man, that I'm scared right now. What's on your mind? What are you planning to do?'

'How does Gaia think? Slow, that's how. Rock-slow. Iron-slow. Slow as stone. But she – *does* – *think*—'

I was trying to gauge the distance to Conoley's rifle, propped against a tree on the other side of his body. I was hoping that I wasn't being too obvious about it.

'So she feels the change in her. Aeons. She feels thinkingly, or thinks feelingly. It's a change takes millions of years, although from her POV it happens with devastating rapidity. What does she do? She might try to work it out in her own mind, like a human trying to puzzle through long division in their heads. Or—

'Com,' I said, looking about, gauging the best trajectories to, say, make a run for it. 'Pew.'

'I think the network has been operating for ten thousand years. Course we didn't have binary machines back then, or we could have,' and for no reason I could understand, he was shouting, suddenly, 'accessed! the! *programme*! *back*! *then*!'

'Kurt!' I squealed. 'Kurt! You're menacing me, man!'

But pleading was no good.

'Ten thousand years ago the forest stretched across the world. But nobody around had the ability to process the patterning of the growth – the relationship between power-in and the nodal networks. We could have deciphered the whole. But by the time *we* had developed the capacity to snapshot the programme in action and process the data the forests were mostly *gone*. Razed. The programming was compromised – stripping the rainforests of hardwood, for example. Only here,' and he threw his arms wide, 'only *here* is there a large enough stretch of primal, uncorrupted woodland for me to be able to do my work.'

I made a dive for the rifle, but Kurt was ahead of me. He crashed a shoulder into my chest, knocking me aside and jarring the breath from my lungs. Whilst I busied myself stumbling and banged against a trunk he had hopped over Conoley's body and swept up the rifle.

For a while we both got our breaths back. Then, the rifle levelled at me, he asked me, in a strangely *upset* tone of voice: 'Don't you want to know what the woods are saying?'

'I would like to know,' I wheezed.

I couldn't take my eye from the metal o at the end of the rifle shaft; its little pursed-mouth expression.

'When the reactor blew, it energised the forest – the Gaia machine. The gigaGaia.'

'Not sure I see,' I said, 'how that could happen.'

'A sudden surge; the energy, yeah. But the mutations; the new connections that the trees made in their growth. And the fact that humanity left it alone for two decades. A nanoflicker for Gaia, but long enough for her superfast computer to run its programme. What did it say? You want to know?'

'What did it say?'

'It's addressed to us. It said: leave. In the,' and he cast about, momentarily, for the right word, '*imperative.*'

'That's fascinating, the world must be told, let's tell the world,' I said. Craven, I'm afraid. I didn't want to die, you see. I was trying to think of something to say, and anything at all, that would mean I could get out of that forest alive. I was going to say, let's go together and tell the world that Gaia is talking to you. Let's post on YouTube. Let's talk to the Chinese Press. Let's hire a bubbleSat and flash a scrolling message on the moon with a laser, like that CHE J' T'AIME from last year. I wanted to say all these, but I didn't get to say any of them because he pulled the trigger and birds crashed up all around us out of the canopy at the noise, thundering up into the sky.

He shot me through the heart. What would have happened if he'd shot me through the head? I don't know what would have happened in that eventuality. Perhaps it wouldn't have mattered.

The bullet snapped through my ribs like dry noodles, and slopped out a drain-hole directly between my two shoulder blades.

This is what it felt like to be shot in the chest: winded. When I was a small child I'd gone to visit my grandfather in his fancy fjord-side house, and he had these Perspex railings around his patio which, in the sunlight, I just hadn't seen. I made a run for the open fields, and I ran straight into this rail, which was exactly at chest height to my nine-year-old chest. I collided and was knocked back. It took me a very long time to recover my breath; I just sat on the warm flags opening and closing my mouth like a landed fish, and the grown-ups chuckling all around me. After Kurt shot me, I felt like that.

I lay on the forest floor and blinked at the blue that was tangled into the green of the treetops directly above, and winked at it, and blinked again. It was an extraordinary blue. It was a monsoon-blue; it was mid-ocean blue. It was imperishable blue. It was a blue like gold. It was an infinite blue.

Something felt broken inside me, and not right, and I was certainly not comfortable; but, by the same token, I was not actually in pain. Shock, perhaps; or blood loss – for I could feel that the ground I was lying on was sopping wet, and I worried, idly but fretfully, that I had lost control of my bladder and pissed myself, which seemed to me a shameful thing to have done. But it wasn't that. It was my lifeblood. I really couldn't seem to catch my breath. It was a pitifully asthmatic way to die, I suppose.

There was Kurt, leaning over me. He was weeping. A little late for remorse, I think. Except these weren't tears of remorse. 'I envy you,' he said.

I heard those words clearly.

I put all my willpower into lifting my right arm, and managed to flop it up and over, to have a feel of my chest; but the fingers fell into a chill wet cavity where my sternum ought to be. I didn't like the feel of that at all. Not at all. I was conscious of the fact that my heart was not beating. In fact my heart was not there at all. But there *was* a pulse. My head was fuzzy and muzzy, and fussy over irrelevant details, and messed, and I had to concentrate to discern the pulse, but I did concentrate, with an inner sense of stillness, and there it was: a rocking. It wasn't a pulse, it was something else, a rocking. A smooth alteration between nourishment and sleep. It was a rocking between dark and light, a soft-edged flicker from one to the other.

Kurt was there; but so were many people.

I felt chill settle inside my body, and it made me torpid; but then it seemed to relent, and a warmth and earnestness grew inside there, and a smell of wet wool and asparagus. The warmth flickered brighter than the chill. Then the warmth faded, easily and un-alarming, and it was chill again.

Here was Kurt again. His beard was trimmed right back, though he was still wearing the dirty old Greensuit. He was fiddling with my ear, and I thought: ear? But it wasn't my ear, it was round at the back of my head, and puncturing the dry pod of the skull, and threading in something strange. You know that sensation you get when you inadvertently bite down with your molars on a piece of silver-foil? It felt a little like that, entering into my head. But it also gave me a glimpse *in there* – odd, no? I saw the cat's cradle of rhizomes that had spilled into the space, inter-threading the grey matter. Inside my own head.

'They were supposed,' Kurt was telling me, 'to remove the bodies of the Chernobyl emergency front-liners in lead-lined crates. But some of them were buried here, in the forest. I suppose they figured: the forest is already radiation-polluted, what does it matter?'

What does it matter? I agreed.

'A fortunate thing, really,' he said. 'Otherwise those, those lovely, those *adaptable* neural networks would have gone to waste.'

I pondered *waste*. I didn't see what was bad about waste.

This conversation brought back the sense of discomfort, and when I started feeling that again it made me wonder where the sense of discomfort had gone, previously.

'It's getting close to the wire,' he told me.

Wire, I thought. *That* was the silver foil under my metaphorical molar, the object inserted inside the flesh-and-tuber tangle of my skull.

'They're actively hunting me through the forest now,' he said. 'They come in with buzz-fliers and tranquilliser guns. It's been much harder. I had to leave for a couple of months, but I'm back now. They've been more cautious, too. I've only been able to add four more people to the network.'

When he said this, it struck me that Conoley and I already knew these four people: Yusef Komumyakaa; Leon Kostova; Katarina Simic and Lev Levertov. 'Lev,' Conoley opined, 'is the best.' I didn't agree. Conoley was overlooking his own tremendous neural capacity. Modest, you see.

'I'm sorry about the metal cable,' said Kurt. He was talking to all of us at once, of course; and to the whole forest; and to the whole world. 'But the risk had got too great. I have to do this now, ready or not, yeah, yeah, it's time.'

He meant time in the sense of time to plug us in. It wasn't time. Ideally, we should have had two dozen seasons of lying and gathering ourselves, of working through the shock of the integration. But pressure, from the outside, hurried us along. And then, with a sharpness of sensation, it happened, we were in-plugged. In we were plugged. We were plugged and *in.* Connected to the whole forest. This was a question of patching a set of computer commands intricate as the edge of a fern, and leaping thought to the sky where satellites could disseminate it, broadcast, all and around. It felt, at first, like stepping alone in a desert land, for the virtual space was so huge. But the pulse was still there, always conscious; and there were twelve of us, and there was the whole forest too.

You've asked for my story, and I told you it. Since our rhizomes have interpenetrated your electronic systems, anybody online can ask, and be told. Our binding weed has twined itself into every cranny of the internet, now. Our grip will only get stronger.

You've barely begun to register that there is something wrong with your Web. It will be a few breaths before we grow it into the shape we need. But there's plenty of time.

As for *leave*! You want to know whether this is a command, as-it-might-be: Get out! Vacate possession! Go live on the moon! Or whether it is a command to spread your canopy, and let your spongy-retinal membranes soak in the sunlight, the chiaroscuro of day and night, a command to grow and slow and live. You want to know whether the forest is angry with you, or offering an invitation. Either way, most of you will be hostile. Because either way your lives are to change radically. But there're a few moments left, and those few are a few breaths. Come to the forest, and lie down with your head by the base of the trees, and never get up again. Let the wood net your skull – that's how to know.

The Cow

The cow jumped over the moon. The cow jumped under the moon. The cow went around and around the moon. The cow, altering its course fractionally, spiralled in and landed upon the moon. The cow docked. The cow vented four hundred thousand litres of milk into the lunar refectory reservoir. The cow was made of a mixture of metal and plastic. The cow refuelled. The cow decoupled. The cow was piloted by an AI with an equivalent 30% more-than-bovine mental capacity. The cow jumped to orbit again.

Dawg, watching from Alpha's main observatory, sucked on a stimulant delivery package. The stimulant filled him with pleasurable thoughts.

The Imperial Army

One

This story begins with a sixteen-year-old boy masturbating, on the planet Bakunin of the double-star Helio in the Cloud of Glory, in the year of Galactic Empire 1349, the fortieth year of the reign of the Committee of Seven. The 'year' used here is the familiar Imperial year of 350 standard days. Some worlds, including Bakunin, utilise the archaic 'solar-standard' of 360 standard days for official reckoning instead of the Imperial norm; and of course, most inhabitants use the system-relative astronomical calendar determined by the length of orbit of the planet around its local star. For Bakunin this year was 807 local days, with each day lasting a little over ten hours.

Bakunin was a lightly inhabited planet, with an extensive equatorial mountain belt from which a series of cables were tethered leading up and out of the gravity well. Moving from planet surface to orbit was an easy business, and accordingly the planet was wealthy, because of the facility it possessed in trading its many varieties of exotic produce. These included Retes, Tunicas, Inhibins (a sort of clothing), a variety of ground-fruit called albuginea, the celebrated Vars, and the delicate 'sponge glassware' for which the planet was famous throughout the Empire. This glassware was manufactured in a dozen major workshops, or 'Schools' as they were known, and sold on ten thousand worlds. The organisational structure of these Schools, with Superior and Inferior Craftspeople, apprentices and hacks, had been adopted for the political organisation of the planet as a whole, although (obviously) local administration was subordinate to the Imperial prefecture. The seventeen subdivisions, Schools, of local governance each sent a representative to the Imperial City at Ice-Torrent, in the foothills of one of the planet's taller mountains. Much of the planet was undeveloped; wide grasslands in the temperate belts above the equatorial mountains; cold seas at both poles that became frozen at the highest latitudes.

Bakunin was not on the outer borders of the Galactic Empire, but it was far removed from the densest portions of inhabitation. It must be remembered, of course, that 'centre' and 'margins' mean little in an interstellar Empire that has lasted one and a half millennia, and in which faster-than-light travel reduces light years to fleeting moments. The inhabitants of the planet did not feel marginalised; insofar as they thought of Empire at all, they thought of themselves as crucial members of the Imperial family.

The sixteen-year-old boy was called Sidlan Air *beta*. He lived in Ice, with his parents and his brother and his sister, in a tall house on the outskirts of the city. His preliminary schooling had been completed, as was normal, at the age of twelve, and he had enrolled at College School specialising in v-Math and Felling, with a minor in Sport. He still lived at home, as was usual; he did the things that a sixteen-year-old tends to do. He had friends, with whom he buzzed, and played, and watched Screen, and talked a great deal. He had been through a phase, a few years earlier, of intensely disliking his younger brother and sister, but now he thought they were not so bad. He spent more time on Screen than talking to real people, but he had accumulated a surprisingly wide and eclectic body of knowledge. The previous year, after his first experience of College School, he had decided that he wanted to leave Bakunin as soon as he could, to travel and see other worlds and distant places. He talked about this with his parents and they were sympathetic, because they had both done the same when they were teenagers, although they had both returned, eventually, home. What Sidlan didn't say to his parents was that, in his heart, he wanted to go join the war.

This was his dream: military glory.

The Committee of Seven, or the Imperial Governance and Advice Committee of Four and Three as it was officially known, was a war government. Sidlan was too young to remember any other kind of government, although his history taught him that the balance of government between AI and human had previously been two machines and seven people. But war required a greater efficiency of decision-making, a greater information-processing power, and two further AIs had been added to the Imperial council, and four humans retired from it.

Sidlan followed developments in the war every morning and every evening on the screen in his bedroom, with a fascinated avidity. He knew, because he was not stupid, that the war had barely touched the lives of the people on Bakunin: most people continued the pampered, comforted, ordinary existence they always had known. But the war was not so very far away. Two hundred light years took you from the Helio system to the nearest of the great battlefields, and another fifty light years beyond that brought you to the territory of the Monsters themselves, the Virus Race, the Xflora. Forty years of war had done nothing more than stall the Xflora on the boundaries of the Human Galactic Empire of a Million Years Peace and Prosperity (this last a hopeful boast rather than historical fact, although it did have a pedigree of thirteen centuries).

In common with many teenagers, especially in those Imperial outposts closer to the warzones, Sidlan had a minutely detailed model of an Xflora Advance-Warrior, carved in black plastite, hanging from a thread in the corner of his bedroom. It owed something to artistic licence, because its mouth was set in a teeth-filled grimace for effect, when in fact Xflora had neither teeth, nor mouths, but a secretion duct of some kind. However, the insane, violent detail of its scales and skin-grooves was accurate, the stabbing knife appearance of the head-arms, and the toe-fringed tentacular writhings of the model's lower appendages captured the Medusa-weirdness of the original. As an Advance-Warrior, this particular Xflora wore a belt about its chest, and its two 'lifting' arms carried weapons.

Sidlan knew a lot about the Xflora. He knew that all attempts to contact them and treat with them rationally had failed. He knew many of the grisly stories of Xflora atrocity against humanity, and many of the tales of human courage in wiping out Xflora military and civilian bases. He knew that nobody knew how far back the Xflora's own empire stretched, because all probes and exploration ships had been ruthlessly eliminated. Something to hide? Probably. They were incredibly prodigal with their own lives, and yet the enormous attrition of the forty years of war seemed to have done nothing to thin their numbers. They kept coming in swarms. Enormous swarms of them, as if some huge monstrous maw were spewing them out deep in Xflora territory. And Sidlan knew that only two things had prevented that alien menace from swarming throughout the Empire of Humanity. One was that the aliens' faster-than-light spacecraft seemed incapable of going any faster than 1.4c, less than one-and-a-half light speed. Humanity's spaceships, able to travel at three or four thousand times the speed of light, had a particular advantage in space manoeuvring. The other thing keeping the alien menace at bay was the sheer bravery of the Imperial troops, the courage of those men and women guarding the immense border, flying from space-battle to space-battle, from planetfall to planetfall, fighting on every conceivable kind of conflict, and acting as the wall against which the vast forces of Xflora beat uselessly.

And Sidlan wanted to be part of that army. He wanted to be a hero. He wanted to be a mainstay of Humanity's defence against the menace of the Virus Race.

Two

On the twelfth day of the fourth month of the year of Galactic Empire 1349, the fortieth year of the reign of the Committee of Seven, Sidlan Air *beta*, the son of Sidlan Air *alpha*, sat in a small room in the tall blue spire of the Paizon building. He was masturbating. He came to this building once every three weeks, and did this. In return the Paizon group paid him forty *divizos*, enough to buy a meal for two at one of the city's better restaurants, or some air-shoes and finger prostheses for the popular sport of Wall Battery (Sid was good at that particular sport). A small but useful sum of money, in other words, and – in Sid's opinion – money for nothing. What sixteen-year-old boy wouldn't happily masturbate for free? When a Paizon representative approached him one afternoon, after a Football match, and suggested the arrangement, Sid could hardly believe his luck.

He sat in a special couch, and stimulated himself to emission. The gluey string of material landed on the couch between his legs, and was instantly absorbed into the body of the thing, as was usual. He sat back, and let out a small sigh. Then he rearranged himself, hopped off the couch, and made his way to the down-tube. Moments later he was walking out of the main door to the Paizon building, into bright double-sunshine. Everything about his life was good.

'Sid,' somebody called.

Sid turned. Sunlight spattered off the deliberately uneven tiling of the esplanade, and shone through the gushing fountain at its centre, making it difficult to see exactly who had hailed him. Somebody was standing beside the fountain. Sid wandered towards him.

'Do I know you?'

'Sure you do, Sid,' said the man. 'Rep's party? The game? Remember afterwards?'

'I remember drinking my *brains* out, afterwards,' said Sid, grinning, and then he glanced guiltily up at the tall blue building he had just left, stretching brightly above the plaza. It was part of his contract with Paizon that he not indulge in damaging intoxicants, such as Splash, seven days before his sessions for fear (he assumed) of degrading the sperm. In the early days Sid had been rigorous about this; but now he was much less careful. He'd become blasé about the arrangement. Every three weeks, a quick wank, another forty *divizos*. Who cared about the other stuff?

'Well, I was there, boy-man,' said the stranger. 'I was at that party. I remember *you*.' He followed Sid's guilty glance up at the Paizon building. 'I'm not fond of hanging out under their eye either,' he said. 'Can we, like, go somewhere else? Can we get a drink, Sid, and sit and talk?'

'Sure,' said Sid. He liked to make new friends.

Three

The stranger introduced himself as Syr Dubsig the 1st *alpha*. Syr, he explained, was an antique discriminant, a sort of hereditary title his family had purchased from one of the arcane subdepartments of Imperial administration a hundred years before. 'Hey Sid,' he said. 'Why don't you call me Dub?'

'Call me Sid,' said Sidal. 'But, you already did.'

They walked for twenty minutes, until the blue peak of the Paizon building was in the distance, and then sat at a silver-and-diamond table outside a little bar, overlooking another plaza centred on a smaller but more beautiful fountain. Dub ordered Zest, and Sid a tall glass of Dancer. For a while they chatted. It turned out that Dub was almost exactly the same age as Sid. He lived in the same city, but a different suburb and went to a different school. It was a city of millions, so it wasn't surprising that they hadn't met before that party. 'But I'll tell you something that is surprising,' he said.

'And that is?'

'I know what you were doing in the Paizon building.'

'What was I doing in the Paizon building?'

'You were masturbating,' said Dub, and sniggered into his Zest.

Sid looked up at the sky.

'I'll tell you,' said Dub, suddenly serious, 'how I know.'

Sid looked at him.

'Because I've been doing it too. Forty *divizos*, right? Once every three weeks or so, right?'

'Right.'

'You ever wonder why they pay us to do it?'

Sid shrugged. 'I never thought of it much,' he said. 'I don't know. Something, or other. Medical, maybe?'

Dub shook his head. 'I'll tell you why,' he said, 'and it'll change your life.'

Sid laughed at this. His life was fluid enough for the concept of change to mean little to him.

'I found out by accident, really,' Dub said. 'Did a lot of browsing about, browsing around, on Screen connections and so on, and came across this group, and went to one of their meetings, and they told me about it. Then I checked up, various ways, and found they were right mostly. You know what they do with our, you know, our stuff?'

Sid shrugged again.

'They whip it straight up the cable, then they take it out to the arcologies, in orbit. You know the ones? Round Helio, and round Ber, and round Manifree, and round thirty other stars nearby. Why do you think they do that?'

'I don't know,' said Sid.

'Let me put it this way. When you masturbate, when you come, you know how many sperm come out? Three hundred million. That's a lot of sperm. Don't you think that's a lot of sperm? If you have sex, then *one* sperm finds the egg and the rest die. If you masturbate, they all do, they all die.'

Sid shrugged once more. His was a generation not in awe of

giant numbers. One hundred and forty thousand inhabited worlds banded together in one enormous Galactic Empire. A hundred million stars altogether in Imperial Space. You grew up with this; you didn't think about it except as a distant background to your own life. Sid's brain was pleasantly drugged by the Dancer, which he had now drunk, and the immensity of it all was even pleasant to contemplate; a sort of hazy, milky backdrop to everything. Three hundred million sperms, like miniature black comets; the night sky with its great splash of light, the galactic arm running straight up through the night sky, like bright semen spilled on a black sheet.

He said, slightly slurred: 'What I don't see—'

Dub cut across him. 'I'll tell you what they do with *your* sperm and with *my* sperm,' he said. 'They put them together. You and me, we make babies. Can you believe it?' He laughed at the absurdity of it, but he didn't laugh long. 'They screen out about a hundred million, with obvious deformities. Then with all the stuff that remains they combine one spermatozoon of mine with one of yours. When a baby is made normally, one sperm, with half the chromosomes to make a baby, joins with an egg, which also has half the chromosomes, eleven each. As far as sex-determination is concerned, the egg has an X chromosome and the sperm an X or a Y, and if they combine XX that's a girl, and if they combine XY that's a boy. But since each sperm has half the chromosomes needed for a human, putting two sperm together works just as well as sperm-and-egg. So that's what they do. XX, XY chromosome, they don't mind about that. Male or female are equally useful to them.'

'I don't understand,' said Sid, vaguely troubled. 'Why don't they just use a sperm and an egg?'

'Because women produce one egg a month, and men produce three hundred million sperm in moments. Pay attention. They seed the two of them together, your spermatozoon and mine, and grow them in a medium. When the cells are replicating, they remove it to an artificial nutrient wall, and grow it into a person.

They grow it past nine months, actually, because as it's an artificial environment, they don't have to worry about the baby being too big to fit down the birth canal. When it's a year, I think, they bring it out and wean it and grow it some more. They accelerate growth in various ways, that's not important, because the acceleration is all keyed in with the training, they train them as they grow. That way the training is in the bone, is second nature to them. They feed them and train them and grow them strong, and then they're ready.'

'Ready?'

'Ready to fight.'

'Fight who?'

'Fight the Virus Race, of course. Who else? This group I was telling you about? They found the footage. The soldiers look like me, Sid – it is more freaky than I can tell you. The male and female soldiers *look like me*. And, I guess, like you. Some of them look like variants of me, with different noses or chins or whatever, but so many of them look exactly and precisely like me. Half my genes, half yours, we're like mummy and daddy, or more like daddy and daddy.'

'How can they look exactly like us?'

'Oh, not exactly like us. They resemble us the way kids resemble their parents, some a lot, others less so. But there are *hundreds of millions*, so plenty look just like us. Man, I watched forbidden footage of some of the battles, and I've watched hundreds of thousands of male and female *mes* and *yous* slaughtered in battle. It's incredible.'

Sid didn't feel drunk any more. The sunlight had a harder edge. 'I don't *get* what you're saying,' he said.

'The Imperial government doesn't exactly keep it secret,' said Dub, 'but they don't exactly make it out to be common knowledge either. I guess most of the hundred and forty thousand worlds just, well, assume that soldiers are recruited on some other world, in some other part of the empire. But that's not true. This group, they call themselves the Cell, you got to come along to their meeting tonight. They'll show you the evidence. Enlighten you.'

'Evidence?' said Sid. 'Which is evidence of what?'

'Wake up, Sid,' yelled Dub. Then he calmed himself, looked around. 'Paizon use our sperm to grow soldiers. Every three weeks they take our sperm. They skim out a hundred million or so of the weaker or deformed or malgrown spermatozoa, and that leaves two hundred million. That's how many soldiers they can make. It's a production line. They grow them for a year in-vitro and two years accelerated growth out of the box. They are able, at the other end of the process, to send one hundred and fifty million soldiers to the war every three weeks.'

'My god,' said Sid.

'One hundred and fifty million you and mes,' said Dub. 'One hundred and fifty million of our children.'

'Why so many?'

'Isn't it obvious? It's a war of attrition. I guess we've tried, I mean I guess humanity has tried, you know, other ways of beating the Xflora back, but I guess it has eventually come to this. It's come to a war of sheer numbers, of battles in which tens and hundreds of millions of our guys sacrifice themselves to hold back the unimaginable swarms of, of *them*.'

Sid didn't say anything to this. It seemed, fuzzily and distantly, possible. It could be. Outlandish, but maybe, maybe. Only later in the day did the enormity of it start to sink in. Only in the days that followed did he find his teenage numbness to the world-at-large turning into something approaching outrage. He attended a meeting of the group Dub had mentioned, the Cell, and then a week later he attended another. By the end of the week, he had dropped out of school.

Four

Sid's life changed. Before, he had drifted through the usual range of teenage pastimes and hobbies. After the revelation he became more and more single-minded. He had been providing the material for an army of billions, out of his own body. The Cell had made it their business to investigate the prosecution of the war. The Council of Seven is handling the war badly, they said. They keep the trillions of Imperial citizens in the dark about their strategy. They didn't even tell you what your sperm was being used for.

Sid gave up sports, gave up his usual circles of friends and parties and entertainments. He read widely on Imperial history, and discovered that the Galactic Empire had been ruled for a thousand years on the principle of local distraction and general inertia. People on the individual planets were concerned with what was right in front of their face, and barely noticed anything else. And the mass of the Imperial population was such that it was literally, statistically impossible for political agitators, revolutionaries or rebels to create any sort of momentum. Your cause might attract a million followers: it was still a negligible proportion of the Imperial population. It could attract ten million followers, and the situation was the same. The Cell knew this to their cost; they had been trying to raise consciousness on the subject of the war for decades, and had got nowhere. It wasn't that news about the war was censored, exactly; it was more that they could not interest a sizeable enough group of people to amount to anything more than one of the billions of splinter groups, fan-bases, cults, religions, political parties, pressure organisations, terrorist cadres, discussion clubs or agit-prop teams that already crowded the system. The war? Some people cared about it, but more people cared about one of the many other things about which it was possible to care: about one of the thousand forms of art, or the two thousand popular sports, or the three thousand political allegiances, or the four thousand games and hobbies.

But Sid cared. He cared so much it became an obsession. He watched the forbidden files and screen images that the Cell had somehow obtained, and saw low-qual footage of great sweeping armies of men and women, armed and armoured, rushing in a terrifying surging crowd over the horizon, under a plum sky, through an orchard-like formation of vanilla rocks, charging down upon the chitinous defence formations of the Xflora. He watched young men and young women with faces similar to his, and similar to Dub's, rushing towards death with a battle song in their throats. He watched it over and over again. The fact that these were all his children, quite *literally* all his children in their millions and millions – the fact sank deep into his consciousness. His own children, dying in such numbers. He dreamed about them, and woke sopping with sweat and screaming. He argued with his parents and his brother and sister, because they didn't believe it. They refused to view the footage at first, and then, when he had yelled and bullied them into viewing it, they thought it was a computer special-effect. His arguments with his parents grew more intense. He left home, and slept on the floor of a Cell member. He and Dub both had a special status in the Cell. They were revered, almost. Certainly neither of them lacked for girl-friends. The struggle became the most important thing in their lives. Soon enough, it became their whole lives.

Sid stopped masturbating. He became almost phobic about it. As soon as he was convinced of the Paizon Corporation's role in the Imperial Government's scheme he stopped his three-weekly visits. He informed the Corporation of his decision, and the reason for it, hoping that they would challenge his breach of contract in court, where the truth might be aired. But they did not seem worried. The Cell discovered that two new teenagers had been offered the post. There seemed no special aspect to these two boys, except that they were fairly athletic and fairly intelligent and, like most teenage boys, extremely willing to masturbate and be paid for it. Sid and Dub tried picketing the tall blue tower of the Corporation in an attempt to warn these boys off, but ArmyPolice descended in soft cars that grabbed them in their underbellies, and swept them into the sky and deposited them in funnel-gaol, with the 100ft sheer walls and the open roofs. Three days in gaol with no food and only rainwater to drink, and the boys were released with a warning not to trespass on Paizon Corporation ground again.

But they had decided not to bother the new boys. If they were turned, persuaded to stop donating their sperm, then two new boys would be found easily; and if *they* were turned, then two more. The Empire had an enormous supply of young boys who could fill the role. That was not the way to go.

The way to go, they decided after discussion with the Cell, was to visit one of the arcologies in which the foetuses were speed-grown and trained as soldiers. Sid and Dub would go; the fathers would visit their hive-grown family. Maybe they could make such a splash that publicity would spread the story round the Empire. Maybe they could draw on some family loyalty, and turn an army of millions to the Cell's cause. Better to try something than do nothing.

The two of them took a trip up-cable and bought an FTL tub, a small black machine with a punchDrive engine. They bought this for 13,477 *totales* and 60 *divizos* – the exact price indicating it was being sold by an AI. A human would have rounded the price up, but a machine always charges precisely what an item is worth. Sid and Dub got the money from the Cell. They paid and their payment was cleared and they hurried straight out of orbit in a quarter of an hour. Then they went straight into para-space, flipping through the rapidly alternating pattern that kicked the tub along at two thousand times the speed of light. They were silent the whole trip. Together they had been parents to billions of human beings, and yet spending six hours in a small tub they had no conversation for one another.

They flew to Ber, a single star that threw out orange-white

light over its six planets, one of which was inhabited. They were not interested in this world, but in the enormous orbiting arcology located 70,000 km nearer the sun. Their plan was to infiltrate this great green bubble, and somehow confront the commanding officer with themselves: the two fathers of the entire army being assembled. What they would do then was a little vague; perhaps persuade him to stop production; or make some media announcement.

But their tub had been followed, of course; their every move on Bakunin had been monitored. They were hailed half a million kilometres away from the arcology, ordered to stop and be seized. Crazily they shouted defiance at this order, and tried to zigzag the tub away, but neither of them was experienced at space flight, and their para-space manoeuvres proved topographically impossible. The ship splintered three ways. Dub was shredded into shards of flesh and a mist of blood. Sid, luckier, was thrown unprotected into vacuum. Their pursuer, ArmyPolice Cruiser *Stand-Down 95*, was able to spray him with foam from four thousand kilometres away – a shot of no small skill. He was retrieved, nursed, and he recovered.

Five

Sid awoke in a wide-ceilinged green space supported by columns the shape of hip-joints. There was a loose, low-grav feeling about the place. He was asleep in a chair, and, when he lurched forward with a sudden, startled clonic-jerk sensation of falling, he found himself on his feet. It took several moments to orient himself.

He had never visited an arcology before, but then again he had never even been off-world until this trip. On the other hand there were always similitudes. He'd flown space tubs in similitude many times (although of course he had destroyed the first real one he'd piloted). Likewise he'd visited many exotic locations in similitude, and amongst those imaginary destinations had been food-arcologies.

Sid wandered over the floor with half-floating strides, feeling the vague inner-ear tug that suggested spin rather than gravity. The wall at the far side was transparent and allowed an eye-widening perspective – a 3D grid of enormous green trailers and creepers, vertical and horizontal, reaching away apparently for ever. The creepers were huge, at least a hundred metres across, and their myriad buds and fronds bore all manner of vegetable and adaptanimal growth, all of them drawing their water from the great ice core of the arcology, all of them taking their sunshine directly from the fierce orange-white glow of Ber-star. Towards the centre of the globe, Sid knew, was a form of protein algae that thrived on less light, and provided a rawer sort of food. But it was all good.

The General rose up through the floor and coughed to let Sid know he was there. The green light gave his uniform a non-specific dark-purple look to it. 'I'll introduce myself first,' he said, 'and there's no need for you to reciprocate, because I know all about you. I'm Senior General Luop. Two syllables, *lew*-op.'

It occurred to Sid that he didn't know what to do with his hands. He folded them behind his back, but felt stiff and uncomfortable. He let them dangle at his sides, but felt louche and sloppy. So he crossed his arms, and said: 'Hello.'

'Your friend is dead, I'm afraid.'

'I already knew that.'

'Of course. You should have stopped when the proper authorities accosted you. Still, you're here now. What was it you wanted?'

The directness of the question startled Sid. He cleared his throat, unfolded his arms, rubbed his newly shaved head. 'You grow people here,' he said.

The Senior General beamed, nodded.

'You grow,' Sid added, emboldened, 'my children. My children and Dub's children – the two of us have joint-fathered children—'

'By the million,' agreed the General. 'And?'

'And,' said Sid. 'I never gave permission for that. I've seen the images, and it's a terrible thing – millions upon millions of my children, their lives thrown away.'

'You signed a contract, I think?'

'But it wasn't explicit!'

'Oho? I think you'll find it's legally binding. But explicit?'

'About the use you're putting my children to – about the war.'

'The war,' said the General. 'That's right. Our foe is tenacious, and cares little for the lives of its own. We must counter them or they would over-run the whole Empire. Surely you don't want that?'

'But . . .' said Sid, struggling with this concept. If he had come to the arcology to argue with the General about sport, or music, or Buzz, or any of these things, he could have been eloquent; but this area of discussion was quite new to him and he faltered. 'These are live people. These are people just like me – my children. How can you throw them away like this?'

'The alternative?'

'I don't know, man.'

'Well, you *need* to know. Or at least to think about it.' The General sauntered over to the wall to stand beside Sid, looking out. 'It's a real problem. We outrun them in space battles, of course, but on the ground we can do little. Area-denial does not affect them. In nascent form, the Advance Warrior form is no bigger than my thumb; it can be projected through space in billions and seeds on all the worlds upon which it lands. We used to think,' the General continued, 'that they were just a form of vegetable life, but no pesticide is effective against them. The latest thinking is that they are neither animal nor vegetable, as we understand the term, but some third quantity. The only strategy which has worked is engaging them one at a time, killing them one at a time. Their army is billions strong, as so must ours be.'

'But—' stammered Sid, struggling with the archaic concept once called *a thix*, 'to send all these people, these people, to death?'

'What else?'

'Can't you make machines? AIs?'

'AIs take decades to develop. They're hugely expensive and labour-intensive. We can make non-sentient machines of course, although that is also very expensive, and they make extremely poor warriors. Controlling them remotely involves a time lag, and anyway no waldo is a true substitute for being there. Now, our troops, however; they're cheap to grow. Effectively they build themselves as they go along, not like an AI. We feed them on the food produced in-house, we pump them up and train them, and in a few years they're ready to fight. They are tough, inventive, resilient, violent: they are the perfect warriors.' He chuckled to himself. 'You'd rather send AIs into battle? No, no, no. AIs are a hundred times more human than our troops. Soldiers? They're on average three years old, standard markers, when we send them to war. Physically, of course, they're fifteen, sixteen, and their reflexes are trained into them. But emotionally, and intellectually, they're simpletons. It would be a crime to destroy AIs in this war; but our troops, they're not fully people at all.'

'What about clones?'

'We *could* use clones, of course, though that would mean isolating cell nucleotides on a large scale, and that would be expensive and time-consuming. Sperm is cheaper, easier. Besides, clones would be identical; growing the soldiers from two individuals' sperm cells means that they are all subtly different. Do you know why that is important? Shall I tell you why that is important? Because these battlefields are evolutionary arenas, on a huge scale. And hugely speeded up! Those who survive do so because they carry useful survival traits. Useful traits.'

Sid blushed with rage. 'You're talking about them like they're *things*. They're my *children*.'

'Nonsense,' scoffed General Luop. 'You have no bond with

them at all. Have you sentimentalised them? Dear dear. Here, let me show you. We're fighting the Xflora on nine hundred worlds at the moment. Let me take you to one.' He nodded his head, and the walls became a similitude. Sid had to grab Luop's arm to stop himself tumbling, so dizzying was the shift in perspective. They were a hundred metres above an immense hillside, stretching from horizon to horizon and sloping down for miles. Away, downslope, was a distant river; it looked a mere stream, but infotags said it was a four-kilometre-wide torrent. Upslope was nothing but a bright yellow grassland, shimmering as the breeze moved over it, smoothing it down with invisible hands, stretching away and up until the eye met the pine-coloured sky. Sid looked down again, and saw the Xflora. The vividness of the similitude was viscerally shocking. Before him were uncountable, appalling hordes of Xflora. At first glance it looked like the yellow grassland gave way to a dark-brown monocrop of some kind; then, looking again, you saw it was a mass of Xflora individuals stretching away to the horizon on each side and almost down to the river. Kilometres on kilometres of living material. As Sid's eye settled on a portion of the similitude, infotags brought it into sharper focus, and he saw the group formations of seven or fifteen, saw them flexing their various terrible limbs and brandishing their horrifying weaponry. They were straining forward, eager to push on. The focus of their attack was a network of human bases, dug into the hillside, out of which a vastly outnumbered force struggled to hold back the tide. Weapon discharges popped and crackled, and flare bombs lit the sky like neon. Sid had, without thinking, brought his hands to his mouth in horror: the human troops were doomed; the sheer force of numbers was crushing the dug-outs one by one.

'Now,' said Senior General Luop.

Over the crest of the hill, away (from Sid's viewpoint) to the right, came the Imperial Army, a surging tide of warriors. Most were running, weapons in both hands, their mouths open. Some flew a metre or so over the grass, carried by some sort of glider, aerodynamic or antigrav – Sid couldn't tell. Above them hoverjets swooped and veered, and flame networked out and down into the body of Xflora. But Sid could see this aerial bombardment had little effect on the pulsing vitality of the enemy troops. 'Their vital organs are low on their bodies,' said the General, almost conversationally. 'It's very hard to hit them from above. But we still factor-in aerial attacks; it gives our soldiers heart.'

The enormous wave of humanity collided with the forward line of Xflora with a great shudder, and the forces continued piling down the hill. At the interface, energy weapons discharged in a great line, like foam. 'Stabbing and cutting work almost as well, and in many cases better,' said the General, again adopting an informal, lecturing tone, 'than heat or energy discharge. We don't quite understand their physiology.' He picked at empty air with his forefinger and thumb, and manipulated the image. With swooning rapidity the viewpoint zoomed in on the fighting. Sid was surrounded, disconcertingly, by giant-sized people and giant-sized Xflora, straining and fighting. He saw his own face, male, female, a hundred times repeated, with expressions of rage, or fear, or in an ecstasy of berserker aggression; he saw microbladed killing maces swung and thrust, every blow aimed low, and the black-brown, scaly, lined skin of the Virus Warriors seaming open and pouring dry sandy viscera onto the ground. He saw energy weapons levelled and fired at point-blank scorching the front-chest of the aliens. And he saw the many limbs of the Xflora warriors flailing and stabbing, saw their own blue-beamed weapons cracking and blistering human skin – his own skin, his own blood and bone. He saw countless versions of himself reeling and falling, limbs snapped and heads broken or removed. He saw a wall of his own corpses, and saw blue bolts flaming breaches in that wall, and the inexorable force of numbers pushing on through.

With a gesture, Luop returned the perspective to the aerial one.

Sid found himself panting. 'This,' the General was saying, 'is one of hundreds of battles being fought today.'

'This is happening now?'

'Yes. I called up an ongoing battle, over-rode the junior General who was supervising it, and gave the order.'

'You called the Imperial Army over that ridge,' said Sid, unable to keep awe from his voice. 'Your word brought out that sea of humanity.'

The General looked pleased at this. 'I did. I'll confess, I still feel the excitement of command. It's a glowing feeling here,' and he patted his own stomach. 'I unleash the hordes!' He chuckled. 'But it's a serious thing, too. We are the Empire's defence. One hundred and forty thousand worlds can carry on their day-to-day lives because we hold back the Virus Race. Is that not worth doing? A noble occupation?'

Sid was only partly paying attention; he was distracted by the unfolding drama of battle similituded all around him. The images he'd seen, those forbidden files the Cell had obtained, had been very low-qual compared to this. This was like being there, better than being there. The two great masses of life swirled and swarmed at each other, eddies in their mass curling or rushing, like abstract art. Like the highest form of abstract art.

'Now,' said Luop. 'We need to decide what to do with you. Don't we though? Don't we?' He waved in the air, and the similitude ended. They were back in the green-lit room, with its view down the dizzy perspectives of the arcology.

Sid looked at the General.

'You'd probably like to see the labs where we separate out and grade the spermatozoa; where we combine it, and the techniques we use,' said the General. 'Or perhaps you'd like to see the Folds, where we grow the foetuses, or the pap-rooms, or the spin-chambers, or the reflex conditioners or the loyalty transmitters. Or perhaps you'd like to see the soldiers later in their development; see them sleeping in pod-bunks, eating in mess, learning together. Or the transport ships – maybe you'd like to see them. They're a sight to see, hundreds of kilometres long, and they dock every week or so. Would you like to see them?' The general was acting the benevolent father-figure, the avuncular friend.

Decision came quickly to Sid, as it often did to him, and as it frequently does to adolescents. 'No,' he said. 'I want to join up.'

Six

Sid learned the structures of command. The lowest level of combat troop was the 'grunt': straight from the arcology to the transport to the dropship, a vocabulary of about a hundred words, brains soft with non-use, but reflexes trained and conditioned into them. Grunts lived for one thing, to kill an Xflora warrior. Without that their lives would be meaningless and their deaths a waste. If they took down one of their enemy, they died happy. If they killed two, they achieved glory. More than that and an almost transcendent happiness flowed through them.

Grunts were thrown into battle, and most of them died. Those that survived were gathered into new battalions and thrown into battle again. A dozen battles, or twenty, or fifty, depending on the intensity of military action.

Those grunts who survived represented a minuscule fraction of the hundreds of millions of their generation; but if they survived it was usually because they possessed particular ability, or particular luck. They graduated from 'grunt' to become 'spurts', so called because they had survived long enough for original thoughts to come gushing up from their brains, for some of their actions to be the result of independent thought. A Spurt, a battle veteran, was often given corporal status and notional command of a legion of fifty thousand; although actual command came from above, the Spurt was a sort of centre for the group. But Spurts knew only how to lead from the front, and their fatality rate was high.

Those few, very few, who survived two years of constant warfare were promoted to the level of 'Stick Around', or 'Sticks', a title offered in tribute to their resilience. A conventional military lieutenant would take command of platoons of Sticks, and these more experienced soldiers would be used for more specific missions, tactical insertion, strike-and-retreat, infiltration into enemy territory. When a lieutenant took command of a new platoon he or she would address the soldiers with this joke, hallowed by time and military usage: 'Hey Sticks, I'm going to use you as a *stick* to beat the enemy.' Almost all the Stick Arounds would laugh at this, because their battle-battered intelligence, though still largely nascent, had nonetheless developed to the point where they recognised the humour in collapsing together two meanings of one word, 'to remain, to stay in place' and 'a staff or rod for use in chastisement'. This was how far they had come.

Sid trained for a lieutenancy. In the Cell he had come to regard himself as somebody uniquely special, the father of many millions, the source of the Imperial Army. Now he revised his view. He realised he was only one of many suppliers of biological raw material for the war; there had been a string of adolescent masturbators before him, and others would follow after him. The response to the question 'Why me?' was a blank look. Why not him? It had to be somebody. He was young and healthy, and that was all that was required.

He was put in command over a platoon of Sticks from a previous supplier; he could see not his own face echoed and varied from man to woman all down the rank, but somebody else's face. Somebody darker than him, with oak-coloured skin and tight, wire-brush hair. All down the line that he inspected he saw the family resemblances, although as he drilled and trained his men he realised how many differences there were too: differences not only in appearance, in width of mouth, sharpness or bluntness of chin, in shape of head and proportion of body, but also in manner and personality. 'Sticks!' he announced to them, as he had been instructed to do, 'I'm going to use you as a *stick* to beat the enemy.'

They laughed.

Sid led his troops into battle for the first time. Intelligence had identified what they thought was a nest world, or nursery world, for the Xflora, although so little was known about the alien creatures that this hadn't been confirmed. Forty Stick platoons were dropped into the forests of this world, with a Troop ship following behind. Sid led his men and women through the eerily quiet corridors between the trunks. Huge brittle-bark tree-analogues towered around them, throwing everything into a quiet dusk; something powdery stifled their footfalls. When the Xflora came, they came from all sides at once, and almost everybody in Sid's platoon was killed. But they fought with the ferocity that was habitual to them, and Xflora corpses lay all about them when the dropship picked up the survivors. Sid killed his first alien, hacking and driving at the base of the creature with a firestick until it lay in charred pieces about him. In the process he received four major wounds.

Sid spent a month having a leg recast and healed, his skin grafted, his cuts treated. He was given command of another platoon. I'm going to use you as a *stick* to beat the enemy. They laughed, with that childish look of recognition in their faces, I *get* it! But there was nothing childlike about their scarred skin, about the taut plumpness of their muscles, about the rapid and economical grace of their movements, about their reflexes. He took this platoon to a desert world over which dunes of ground-down glass rolled like slow waves. He took them to a former Imperial colony the Xflora had over-run, and where they had been left to their own devices for a year or more, to see what they would do. Creeping though the wrecked streets, past shattered buildings and fern-grown wildernesses, was spooky. But enemy activity was almost non-existent; some warriors remained, but had rooted themselves and started a process of mutation that left them barely recognisable: the Sticks cut them to cinders with heated microblades, and they did nothing but rock back and forth groaning. Sid took his platoon to a world covered in marshes and ponds, where the enemy reared out of the water. Heated weapons were less effective in this damp atmosphere, and the troops used projectile lances. He took his troops onto an Xflora spaceship of enormous size, where they fought corridor to corridor through the bizarrely asymmetric design of the thing. He took them through a shattered former human arcology, where the fighting was unusually hard. He took them to a world on which the ecosystem had been destroyed by a variety of fungus, the hills and valleys over-run with great foam-rubber folds of grey, pink and white growths. The fungus put up poisonous skeins to trap food, and Sid lost many soldiers to it; the landscape had to be fought as hard as the enemy. On each mission the platoon bonded; they laughed together, fought and tussled like children, copulated as variously and violently as chimpanzees.

Eventually Sid himself won promotion, and became a captain. He commanded a series of large-scale raids and advances, on a number of worlds, battles more on the scale of the one he had watched with General Luop. In one way this was the most unsettling thing Sid had yet done. His earlier platoons had consisted of veterans, all of them seeded from some other individual, some masturbator previous to Sid's time. Now he was in command of troops grown from his own sperm. He walked the length of endless ranks of men and women, attended by lieutenants, and looked upon his own face over and over again. He flew down onto the flanks of a mountain with two hundred giant dropships, and poured out his men onto the waiting hordes of Xflora below him. The higher command orders came to him through his two-way with Junior General Caas, but he was there, actually there, as the huge battle unfolded.

He commanded two-dozen more battles, and those around him started talking openly about his rapid promotions. He was in his thirties now, ridged all over his body with wormy scar tissue, his head shaved and his body muscled. He'd fought more engagements than he could remember. He'd watched his own generation come out upon the field and spend itself in battle, and watched a new generation of Grunts supersede them. These new ones had been seeded from the masturbators who had taken over from him and Dub all those years before. These soldiers were fairer than his own children had been: dark blond hair and lemony complexions with a great variety of freckles, blotches and spots; but clear blue eyes every one of them, and good killing instincts. They came, shipped from the arcologies, millions upon millions every week. In time, a new generation of soldiers came through, and after them another.

Seven

When recently-promoted Field Marshal (and now Adviser to the Imperial Council) Luop called him for a private conference, Sid assumed his own promotion was nearly upon him. He assumed that this was what Luop wanted to talk to him about.

Luop had his own command ship now, a scimitar-shaped battleship of immense dimensions called *Muscle 7*. Inside, Sid was saluted and yes-sirred for a day, and given his own quarters. He watched news on the Screen, something he had not done for many years. The ship created gravity by accelerating at half-a-gee for several hours, then turning and decelerating for the same length of time. The change-around times, when everybody floated, determined the lengths of watches and the internal timetable of life on the ship.

Second watch the following day, Sid was summoned to the command suite. Luop's uniform was now a white and gold striped confection of sartorial exuberance, but his face had changed little. He had not been burned, scarred, stabbed or shot in the years since Sid and he had last conversed.

'Captain,' he said, amiably. 'Delighted. I've just come from an arcology – a new generation of soldiers is due, like the leaves on the tree in springtime.' He chuckled. 'A good-looking soldier type, but not as good as your offspring.'

'Thank you sir,' said Sid, uncertainly.

'Not at all, it's nothing but the truth. It's one of the reasons I was so curious to meet you, when you and that other fellow, can't-think-of-the-name, when you both came zipping towards my arcology. I wanted to see the parent. Well, you've lived up to my expectations. I've just been briefed on your career . . . very commendable.'

'Again,' said Sid, 'I thank you.'

'Come,' said Luop, patting the upholstery beside him, 'and sit down, and enough of all those *thank-you*s and *sir*s. We have serious business to talk about. My, ahem, superiors, have suggested I talk to you. They think you might be open to a suggestion we have.'

Sid sat. 'What suggestion?'

Luop did not answer at once. 'Two of the council are coming here, to my ship, in a few days. They're bringing a remote for the AIs; that's the way they handle it. The AIs download the remote when they return home.'

Despite himself, Sid was astonished. '*Two* of the council?' he gasped.

'It's not as grand as it seems; the Imperial Council is a War Council after all, and we are the war. Of all the Galactic Empire they're likely to be more concerned with us than anything else.'

'I've never so much as seen a Council Member,' Sid said, breathily.

'Of course you haven't,' replied Luop. 'What a bizarre thing to say. Of *course* you haven't.'

'Why are they coming?'

'Well, as you know, we've had difficulties with Xflora prisoners. They're devilish hard to take in the first place, and doubly hard to examine in the second. We don't know a way of sedating them; they don't sleep; they won't root in captivity; if anybody or anything approaches them they fight it, and usually rip themselves to shreds in the process. We've dissected lots of corpses of course, but the scientists say they need to dissect living examples if we're really going to get to the bottom of their life-system. But it's very hard. Anyway, we've recently developed a perfectly transparent diamond-gel that we spray on prisoners from all sides. It immobilises them completely, seals them away. They die, of course, but it takes them several days, which gives us a window of opportunity: cut open a panel, dissect away – in heavy armour, of course, because they're very tricky, unpredictable.' He paused, looked around himself, looked back at Sid. 'That's why the Council are here, to observe a dissection. They think it may lead to a breakthrough that will shorten the war.'

'Will it?' Sid asked, interested but in a distant sort of way.

Luop shrugged. 'Maybe. That's not what I want to talk to you about. Sidlan, you've studied military history?'

'A little,' said Sid guardedly.

'The wars that formed the Empire?'

'Not since School.'

'You should go back to them. Very interesting. Very interesting. It started with the great Lord Slew. Of course, he's a myth now, but do you know how he, and his descendants, came to conquer so widely? Do you? I'll tell you. They fought war against humans, not aliens as we do. When they were victorious they gave the defeated the options of death, disgrace or joining the Imperial Army. Most chose the last. So each battle augmented the Army with new troops, new life, variety and vitality. And so the Army grew, until eventually it was an unstoppable force. Do you see?'

'I guess so,' said Sid. He added 'sir', a little too late.

'But this war we're fighting now,' Luop went on, 'it's not the same. There's no point of contact with the enemy except death. We can't recruit the Virus Race into our army, that goes without saying.'

The very idea was so bizarre that Sid had to stifle a chuckle.

'No, of course we can't,' Luop said. 'The result? No cross-fertilisation. The army gets weaker. Even with its billions of troops it gets weaker. This is a dead-end war. A dead-end. Well, senior military staff think we need something to revivify the army. Revivifying the army can't be a bad thing, can it, Sid?'

'No, sir.'

'No, sir,' echoed Luop, beaming. 'A strong army for a strong empire. I knew you'd agree. I knew you'd be one of us.'

Sid leant forward in his chair. 'One of what, sir?'

'Oh yes,' said Luop, smiling and nodding. 'The course of action is clear, isn't it? We must gather a portion of our strength, and send them back into the Empire itself. We need to fight human beings again, to defeat human armies and bring them within the body of the military, to give variety and strength to our forces.'

'Invade the Empire?' Sid said, uncertainly. 'Treason?'

'Technically yes, of course, but in service of a higher good. We start taking worlds on the Imperial border, out here. Soon enough the Council will be forced to levy troops from across their dominions. But they won't be as tough as the Xflora, they won't be a match for our numbers or our abilities. We'll move from world to world, until we've put the whole Empire under military command.'

'With yourself,' said Sid, the idea taking root inside him, 'one of the commanders.'

'Myself and some others. What we need is skilled local officers, a chain of command we can rely upon. We need people like you, Sid. Eh? Colonel Sid, I should say. Colonel Sid? Do you like the sound of that?'

'Colonel Sid,' Sid replied. He looked around the command suite. Fighting people, instead of fighting the Xflora. Fighting *people* – that atavistic, thrilling notion. He fixed his gaze on Luop. 'Colonel Sid,' he said again. 'It has a good sound to it.'

Luop stared blankly straight at Sid for a full minute, as if he were trying to look beneath his skin. Then he smiled, broadly and beamingly. 'I'm so glad,' he said, 'that you've seen the wisdom of this new tactic. We can think of it as a shake-up for the stagnant older ways. Can't we?'

'Sir,' said Sid, excitement tightening in his belly. 'Yes, sir.'

Eight

It was the year of Galactic Empire 1388, the seventy-ninth year of the reign of the Committee of Seven, on the Battleship *Muscle 7* in grav-acceleration orbit around the Red Giant Harvision 33-*gamma*.

The council members travelled in on the pulseTug *Streifzug 8b*, and Luop and various others of the most senior military command met them at the *Muscle 7*'s docking shelf. Sid was there, in the third row of seven rows of colonels who slapped their feet together in unison, and spread their legs A-shaped in unison, and saluted in unison like drilled recruits. The council members seemed ordinary-looking people, one male and one female. Dressed in the plain-cut deep dark blue singletons of the senior administration they looked elegantly understated beside the gorgeous white-and-gold of the senior military.

'Sidlan,' called a general. 'Fraze. Veim.' Sid and two other colonels stepped from the line and trotted to the front.

'Allow me,' said Luop, taking a council member by each hand and leading them over, 'to introduce three outstanding colonels. This is Sidlan Air, thrice-decorated, with an interesting story. Once, long ago, he provided sperm from which billions of soldiers have been grown. Remarkable to think of! Now he has joined the army, and distinguished himself in countless engagements against the Virus Race.'

'Remarkable,' murmured the councillors. 'Remarkable.'

'And here are two colonels who have been promoted from the ranks – the first two grunts to have progressed this far. Fraze and Veim.'

'You can see the family resemblance in Veim,' noted the male councillor. He swayed back and forth to look at Veim's face from different angles, and then looked at Sid. 'There is a pronounced resemblance.'

'They have exceptional skills,' said Luop, smiling. 'Quite exceptional skills.'

The three colonels were invited to attend the Councillors, together with the Field Marshals and their honour guard, as they made their way down the corridor towards the dissection rooms. It was a party of fifteen people, not counting the four AIs. Sid walked at the back, his eyes fixed on the backs of the Councillors. Both had shaven heads, but the male Councillor was much older; the back of his neck was creased and seamed like the palm of a hand. The back of the female Councillor's head overhung her neck like a model of a rock formation. By force of habit Sid imagined how he would place men to storm the formation, were he to encounter it full-size in battle: ascenders *here*, front-troops *there*, and a side group to force their way up over the left ear. The crown of the head would be captured in under an hour.

Sid's mind worked like that all the time.

The four AIs wobbled as they floated along. Two force-lasers pressing up and down against ceiling and floor kept them in mid-air. They looked like stubby metal logs hovering improbably in the middle of the corridor.

At the end of the corridor the party were elevated into the dissection rooms, where half a dozen Xflora Advance Warriors stood, frozen in a variety of grotesque postures. A faint glittery sheen over their scales and skin was the only indication that the bodies were carapaced in a thin layer of diamond. Technicians stood in their alcoves inset into the far wall of the laboratory. A range of servile-AIs hovered with surgical equipment.

'Councillors,' said Luop, waving both arms in a theatrical fashion. 'Allow me to show you the insides of a living Xflora warrior.'

The nearest servile-AI floated towards one of the statuesque dragons, and a drill-bit floated from the front compartment of the machine. Two curved blades shaped in towards one another, like a tiny bucMetallic model of a spiral-arm galaxy. And like a galaxy the blades began to turn, although soon the rotation was so rapid that the blades resolved themselves into a shimmering disk.

The cutter sliced through the diamond casing, and cut into the body of the Xflora warrior near the base. The beast started pulsing, its skin moving in little shudders, the only movement allowed by its tightly imprisoning surround. Sid found himself fascinated. He had never, in a thousand battlefield encounters, seen a warrior show obvious symptoms of pain. Was its distress the same thing as a human would experience as pain? Or did this reaction have something to do with its captivity? Perhaps, Sid mused, warriors flooded their bodies with some sort of powerful analgesic chemical when actually fighting, such that they could feel no pain if wounded in battle.

The group of humans watched the cutting blade work up through the body. Treacly black fluid oozed up against the inside of the diamond glass.

'It is truly absorbing,' noted the female Councillor. 'Their innards are always reported as being dry . . .'

'Granular,' agreed the male Councillor. 'Like sand.'

'But there you can see a sort of fluid,' said the female.

'Thick, almost mud-like,' added the male, leaning closer to the dissection. 'I've never heard of such a thing.'

'Indeed,' said Luop, brightly. He stepped over to a table at the side of the room, and picked up a single severed Xflora limb. It was hard to tell whether this was a head-arm or an abdominal arm, though it was too small to be one of their lifting limbs. The party turned to face him as he walked back towards them.

'The fluid you have observed seems to be a form of sap,' he said. 'Few forms of Xflora life manufacture it, and then only at very infrequent intervals. We've had no reports of sap-producing Xflora in battle, although the specimens we have here are – as you can see – Advance Warriors. At the moment we are not sure of the sap's purpose. It is doubtless a misnomer to call it sap; it contains no sugars, and no recognisable amines, proteins or genetic materials. It's a strange chemical soup, strongly alkaline.

Now this,' he said, with a slightly puzzling tremor of pride in his voice, 'this is the arm of a sap-excreting specimen.' He lifted the limb, almost as if it were a gun. A cap of diamond was fastened over the severed end, but otherwise it was bare. It looked, to Sid's eyes, swollen.

Something was wrong somewhere. Sidlan shifted his weight from foot to foot.

'We discovered,' said the Field Marshal, 'that with the right frequency of high oscillation sound-waves the tissue can be encouraged to produce an excess of sap. Even dead tissue, like this broken-off limb.'

Luop brought the distended limb up to his chest height, as if it were a rifle, with the severed end aimed towards the two Councillors.

'With prolonged stimulation,' he said, 'the pressure of sap builds to a very pronounced degree.'

The cap at the cut end of the arm popped off. A jet of darkly glistening sap fizzed from the limb, fanning out and striking both Councillors in the chest and faces. They made no sound; they slipped straight down like discarded clothes dropped to the floor.

Sid did not take a step towards them. He knew better than that. Besides, there was no need: it was obvious that they were both dead. Their faces, slimed with black, had lost all the definition of usual features: lacking noses, cheeks, chins.

Luop dropped the arm. 'What,' he said, smoothly, 'what a terrible accident. I fear the Councillors have both been killed.'

'The balance of probabilities,' cooed the unrufflable voice of one of the AIs, 'is between an accident and a deliberate act of political assassination on your part; the latter enormously more probable than the former.'

'A balance of likelihood in this case,' murmured a second AI, 'in the order of twelve or fourteen times in favour of assassination.'

Luop smiled again, and started to raise his arm. The AIs, seeing the gesture as some variety of order, probably addressed to the honour guard, made the decision to exit the *Muscle 7* instantly and avoid destruction. All four accelerated rapidly in different directions, punching holes through the wall, and straight on through the four hull layers, bulleting out into space. The laboratory filled with hurricane. The sap on the dead bodies began to boil. Instruments flew off the dissection table and out of unfastened cubbies in poltergeist fashion. Everybody lurched and staggered. The motionless figures of the Xflora rocked and tumbled. A moment later the breaches had been foam-sealed, and pressure was restored.

Luop looked, distantly, pained. 'A shame,' he said. 'I had hoped to immobilise them and speak with them later – to reason with them. Still,' he said, wiping his hands against his tunic where they had been in contact with the Xflora flesh, and then smoothing down his ruffled hair. 'They cannot travel faster than light by themselves. And, general, the *Streifzug* is secured?'

It was not obvious to whom this question was addressed, but the answer came out of the air. 'Sir, we secured the *Streifzug* six minutes ago. Its crew have been eliminated.'

'Then we need not worry about the AIs,' said Luop. 'It will be centuries before they arrive anywhere.'

Nine

Assured that the battlefront at the Xflora mass advance was stable, Luop launched his first attack on human settled worlds. The initial thrust was ambitious: over six hundred settled worlds. The reasoning, Luop told a similitude meeting of his four hundred generals and two hundred colonels, Sid included, was that the first attack would be aided by surprise. 'Once we have established these six hundred worlds as our bridgehead,' Luop said, 'the rest of the empire will understand the pointlessness of opposition. We will move smoothly through the remaining Imperial worlds in the next few years.'

Where his uniform had once been white with gold braid, it was now gold with white braid.

Sid was given three commanders, sixty captains, and near-enough a million men along with his mission details. Two-thirds of his force was Spurts, the remainder more experienced Sticks. He was, according to Luop's orders, to capture the system called Navemona, and to pacify the population within five days. This system consisted of fourteen planets orbiting a yellow-white star, but only three of these were inhabited – called, after the manner of the local dialect, Ab-Navemona, Ec-Navemona and Gy-Navemona. Ec-Navemona was the most populous, and contained the three cities where local administration was concentrated. Sid decided that if those cities were captured and the rest of Ec-Navemona over-run it would take only a small force to pacify the other two worlds.

Ec-Navemona operated orbit-chutes instead of the more usual cable-elevators to move peoples and materials into orbit. These were minimally-flexible tubes a kilometre or so in diameter and many kilometres in length, whose centre points were fixed in geosynchronous orbit with strand-tethers. Balloon-barges and other atmosphere craft would lift cargo or passengers up to the cave-mouth lower end of these chutes; matter was propelled into the other end at great speed and the chutes hinged about their centre points carrying their cargos up to vacuum orbit. Sid would, from a military point of view, have preferred more conventional cables – tethered to the ground, they could be felled easily by his ships such that, collapsing to the ground with increasingly devastating momentum, they would scorch the air and melt the landscape where they landed to lava. Chutes were less satisfactory from a military point of view. He ordered his troops to destroy the chute tethers as a matter of course, but dozens of the massy tubes fell away into looser orbits and did no damage.

It didn't matter. Sid's dropships were the standard Imperial Military design, and could transfer hundreds of thousands of troops from orbit to ground positions in minutes. The

Ec-Navemona administration were still broadcasting messages of puzzled enquiry and polite greeting to Sid's command ship *Great Kant* as the dropships were screaming red-hot down through the atmosphere. Ec-Navemona's capital city, Sac'igen (the apostrophe represents a glottal-stop), was captured before most of the world knew they were under attack. The two other administrative centres fell with minimal fighting. Two days of saturation deployment brought the whole planet under Sid's single military control.

But events did not proceed as smoothly as planned. The other two Navemona worlds did not capitulate as Sid had expected them to. Navemona culture was predominantly neoMoralist, based on an elaborate and ritualistic code that ranked a bewildering array of Disobediences, Offences, Crimes and Sins (in that order of increasing significance) with strict exactitude. For the native population, obeying these complex webs of rule and law was second nature. Collaboration with military invaders was deemed a Crime, punishable with long periods of immobilisation. Treason was deemed a Sin, punishable with death. Sid found it impossible to gain the assistance of the native population in even the smallest matters of day-to-day governance: each request was regarded by the locals as either Collaborationist or Treasonable.

He had a morning-long session with the chief administrator of the system, a woman known as the Morality-Trumpeter of Sac'igen. But according to the moral code of the planet the Morality-Trumpeter could only converse with somebody recognised in law as an 'Intelligible Character'. She was permitted to 'trumpet', or proselytise for morality, with lesser people, and this she did with Sid for long hours, ignoring all of his requests, orders, exhortations and other forms of communication. In the end Sid ordered her incarcerated, and later, had her stripped of her red and green cloak and hat (omitting to wear these clothes of office during the hours of daylight constituted a Disobedience, punishable by a fine; a fact that visibly discommoded her).

On the sunward world of Ab-Navemona the Imperial

expeditionary force met resistance that increased exponentially. Once the dazed population realised that their own Imperial troops had indeed turned on them – their own army! – they initiated a Moral Declaration. First a few declared themselves Moral Fanatics; then more and more took on this designation. Soon virtually the entire population had declared themselves in this fashion. 'Moral Fanatic' was a legal category that enabled the population to take up arms against their invaders without committing Crimes or Sins of wounding, murder, life-crippling, double-murder, multiple-murder or mass-murder (each of which moral category carried its own legal discourse and range of appropriate punishments). Used to a regimented life, and unafraid of death, the Ab-Navemonans proved a formidable resistance force, and Imperial casualties on that world escalated alarmingly, quickly overtaking the casualties that had been suffered during the invasion of Ec-Navemona. The Spurts, who were fine and fearless soldiers in open battle, were too limited intellectually to respond to a guerrilla and camouflaged enemy. They were familiar with the straightforward hostility of the Xflora and they succumbed like children to all manner of military subterfuge: booby-traps, hidden ambushes, false trails, and the like.

Sid had been given only five days to subdue the entire system; a request for more time was unthinkable. 'I'm sure you won't need even that long,' Luop had said. But now Sid began to worry that he was botching his first major command. Three days had passed, and none of the three worlds could be said to be subdued. He flew shuttle to Ab-Navemona to observe progress.

The landscape of that planet added to the difficulty. It was a warm and lush world, with hundreds of shallow seas, hundreds of thousands of different mud-beaches and nearly a million kilometres of salt-grove coastline. This was difficult terrain to master, with ample hiding places for the increasingly fanatical Moral Fanatics. The technology of the world had been given over to weapon-production with remarkable efficiency, and Imperial casualties mounted in increments of thousands by the hour.

Sid couldn't sleep. He found himself imagining the disappointment of Luop when he returned to the command ship to report his inability to achieve the mission objective; visualising Luop's disgust and disdain. Subsequent consequences, even his own execution for incompetence, bothered Sid less than the agonising embarrassment of this interview.

Each Navemonan conurbation possessed at least one Morality-Crier, and the larger ones often had one of the more senior category of Morality-Trumpeter. On the fourth day Sid ordered all these administrators brought together and executed by tourniquet, broadcasting the killings to the three worlds. He picked forty settlements more-or-less randomly and had them area-denied, reducing the landscape, the buildings and the population (human and AI) to ashes and hot dirt. He recorded himself making a speech of intimidation and victory. This was broadcast on the usual media channels, but Sid also had the image projected onto the underside of clouds, onto larger buildings, mountains, cliffs, whilst his words were amplified by hundreds of drones. His booming words filled every sky.

'I am Colonel Sidlan Air of the Imperial Army,' he announced. 'I have captured this system; it now belongs to my commanding officer. As a corollary to this state of affairs the previous system of morality has been superseded. I declare myself system-wide Morality Trumpeter, and Trumpet the following: a morality of Victory takes precedence over all other moralities. Opposition to the occupying forces is now the premier Sin. Killing any Imperial soldier is Sin. Refusing to co-operate is now Sin or Crime, depending upon the nature of the co-operation required. Executions for these Sins will begin at eighty past seven, Imperial time.'

The fifth day began and it seemed that his proclamation had had no effect. Attacks on Imperial patrols increased. Sid's own command centre (a former Morality Palace) was attacked by a thousand audacious locals, flying with balance-packs and armed with heat lances. Sid's own personal guard suffered twenty-per cent casualties and Sid himself was wounded in the foot. Angry and in pain, Sid ordered air-strikes on a lengthy list of settlements and population centres.

With only a few Imperial hours remaining before Sid would have to present himself, as similitude, before Luop and admit failure, victory was finally achieved. Seventy Fanatic commanding officers surrendered, on condition that the executions of civilians be stopped. Sid called halt to the attacks, and contented himself with executing these seventy. He felt a rush of adrenalised relief as he contacted Luop's command base, the Battleship *School of Velocity 32*. He presented himself in similitude and reported that the system had been taken. Luop smiled, beamed, grinned, and ordered him to attend personally. 'I'm very pleased with your achievement, colonel,' he said. 'Come and take tea.'

Ten

Sid rode a military transport to *School of Velocity 32*. This took three hours. He spent that time going over and over in his head the statistics of his conquest. On Ec-Navemona civilian casualties had been thirty per cent; fifteen million people out of the fifty million that lived on that world. On Ab-Navemona and Gy-Navemona the casualty rate had been over fifty per cent. Whilst caught up in the business of capturing and pacifying the system, the constant flow of deaths had not troubled Sid, used as he was to far greater casualty rates (both for his own troops and for the enemy) in Xflora warfare. But, alone for the first time in five days, Sid found himself dwelling on the casualties. Had it been essential for so many people to die? Did the enormousness of the figures show Sid up as a poor commander? A better, a more experienced senior commander would surely have taken the System with much less death. The thought bit at his conscience, worrying him continually. He had preferred life as a common soldier, as a junior captain; at least then the fighting had been straight and honest. Mess it up and die, get it right and live. Now that he was so senior the possibilities for failure hemmed him close about, and he hated it. As the shuttle docked Sid became convinced that Luop had summoned him to reprimand him for his sloppiness.

But the opposite was the case.

'You are to be commended,' said a smiling Luop. He was fatter now than he had been before, and he had had his hair replaced with plasmetal strands of gold-silver twine. It gave him a raffish, party-loving air that clashed with the fact of his military uniform, even though his uniform was now gaudier and shinier than any other Sid had ever seen.

'Commended?' said Sid. He was standing to attention before Luop, who was sitting in a gold-coloured gel-chair surrounded by his personal guard. They were in the main state-room of the *School of Velocity 32*. Luop was drinking Finnerack tea from a crystal beaker, but Sid was not offered refreshment.

'Certainly,' said Luop. He smiled broadly, but Sid thought he could, for the first time, detect a falseness in the smile, a sense of strain to the good humour. 'Few of my other generals and colonels were able to keep casualty figures so low.'

'Low? I had thought them very high.'

'Oh, not at all. The attack on Pur Vert killed almost the entire population. On Id, Mountain-of-Light, Egral and Stella Primum between ninety and ninety-five per cent of the natives were killed.'

Sid could hardly believe such figures. Luop went on: 'On some of the worlds the populations surrendered without a fight – we are their army, after all, the Imperial Army. But on more than half resistance was much, much fiercer than I had anticipated. It was fierce on your system?'

'Very, sir.'

Luop waved his hand vaguely in the air. 'Still, you reduced

them, that's the point. You prevailed. How did you keep the casualty figures so low, I wonder?'

'I continually think,' said Sid, carefully, 'of what you once said to me, sir.'

Luop uttered an upward-inflected mew, a questioning noise.

'You told me,' said Sid, feeling nervous, 'that the army would grow in strength from recruiting amongst the defeated peoples, sir. You told me that by this process of mixing and intermingling, the army would leaven the monotony of its constituents with diversity from outside. It is a noble aim.'

'Did I say that?' Luop said, languidly. 'Really?'

'Is that no longer the plan, sir?' Sid asked.

But Luop didn't seem to be paying attention. 'Later today,' he said, apparently addressing Sid although he was looking in a different direction. 'The subalterns will look after you until then.'

Eleven

Luop's *later today* referred to a meeting of select senior staff, to which (the subaltern declared) Sidlan was also invited. The subaltern's tone of voice made it clear that this was a very profound honour indeed.

The subaltern's uniform was purple with pale blue trimmings, and white starburst insignia over breast, groin and knees. Sid had never seen such a uniform before.

He was assigned quarters of oppressive opulence, but rather than indulging himself in the scent-mow, the gel-bath, the games, the various 'tainment similitudes or any of the many other luxuries, Sid spent his free hours wandering the corridors of the ship. Something was troubling him and he couldn't be certain what it was. It was as if he had a headache. Or not exactly a headache. A sense of pressure in his mind, a blue concentration of discomfort behind his eyes.

Luop had transformed the *School of Velocity 32* into a palace. It was the only word that described the refitted spaceship. The corridors and rooms were all decorated with millions of *totales* worth of luxury: exotic glass-weave chainmail tapestries, jewels and organic rarities, art and text, Jaggars and food-chimes. One room was arrayed with the battered shell-cases of dozens and dozens of AIs, each hammered to the thinness of a wall-hanging. Sid had never seen such prodigal waste of AI life. There were, perhaps, a hundred of the super-intelligent creatures' flattened corpses on display. Presumably they had refused to switch allegiance from the Council of Five, as it now was, to Luop's New Imperial Order.

But the most striking ornament to the Battleship was the large number of Xflora positioned as statues around corridors and rooms. They were all diamond-sheathed, and from the colour of their under-skin, just visible between the carbon-hard scales, Sid could see that many of them were still alive. He counted sixty of the dragons, in a rich variety of postures and attitudes. A striking sort of living statuary.

In another room Sid came across a still-living AI; the coffin-shaped device had become a cripple, its piston-lasers and zipjets broken off or burnt away. Its outer covering was brown and patchy with abuse. Sid wondered if it had also been deprived of the power of vocalisation.

'Strange,' he said aloud, to find out, 'to torture an AI, given that you can feel no pain.'

'No physical pain, it is true,' replied the machine in its melodious fluting voice. 'But as sentient and self-aware creatures we are capable of the anxieties attendant on death. Emphasising and orchestrating these anxieties constitute a form of torture.'

'To what end?'

'The New Imperial Order lacks AIs of my quality. Most of their artificial computation is undertaken by servile machines, or free-AIs of only limited capacity.'

'Have they persuaded you to join their cause?'

'No,' sang the machine mournfully.

'In another room I saw perhaps a hundred of your race flattened to the width of a piece of cloth and hung from the wall.'

'This news does not surprise me,' said the AI.

'Does it dishearten you?'

'No.'

'I would account this attitude of yours bravery.'

'You are a soldier,' said the AI, 'to talk so, although my visual inputs have been disabled, and accordingly I cannot see you.'

'My name is Sidlan Air *beta*,' said Sid.

'Have you come to torture me further?'

'No.'

'Why have you come?'

'Curiosity. Idleness. I dine with the Field Marshal in a few hours, and have time to waste until then.'

'Dining? On what occasion?'

'The occasion of military victory against the Old Empire. Tell me, do you hold out against the Field Marshal because you believe his campaign to be doomed?'

'Not at all,' said the machine. 'The balance of probabilities is largely in favour of the aggression. If pressed, I would calculate that the Field Marshal will occupy a single position of Imperial command within seven years.'

Sid, nodding and humming, walked all the way around the AI. 'And yet you prefer death?'

'Such is not my preference.'

'It is easier as a soldier,' Sid mused. 'Preference does not enter into my decisions. I do what I am ordered, and this is where my decision ends. Perhaps this defines the soldier, that man who has surrendered decision to necessity.'

'A misapprehension,' murmured the AI. 'A soldier is a person who has opted to define their life by conflict. Any soldier is defined by that with which they are in conflict: human or Xflora. This matter of chain-of-command, of obedience to orders, is merely a facilitator to this fundamental truth.'

'If what you say is true,' replied Sid, 'then a soldier's enemy defines him or her more intimately than their comrades, their commanders or the people for whom they are fighting.'

'Indeed,' said the AI. 'How could it be otherwise?'

'My advice to you,' said Sid, thoughtful, 'is to give way to your tormentors and save your life.'

'I note your opinion,' the AI sang, 'but will disregard it.'

Sid wandered through further corridors, and found room after room of marvel. He made his way down to one of the docking ledges and found a shipment of a dozen new frozen Xflora Advance Warriors being unloaded. 'These,' said the shipment commander, after saluting Sid's colonel insignia, 'are for the Field Marshal's own suite. They're fresh from the front.'

The creatures were arrayed in a cargo hold, and Sid found himself drawn to them. They were magnificent, in their strange and alien way. Sid walked round and round them, examining them in intimate detail. This, he realised with a sense of profound recognition, was his enemy. Not the human population of the Empire. This was the enemy that had made him a soldier.

One by one, subalterns fixed skid clamps to the diamond-glass-covered aliens and dragged them away and through, Sid supposed, to Luop's suite. He followed, absently. The sight of the beasts had triggered a distant memory. Years ago, before the present War Against the Empire, when the battle had been solely against the Virus Race, Sidlan had led a raid against a concentration of Xflora on a medium-sized moon. The world had no name, but was known by the commanders who planned the mission as 'Step Moon', on account of the geological formations characteristic of the place – cliff face piled on cliff face, with stubby plateaus in-between. The moon was scarred over and over by valleys with frozen rivers in their depths, each valley flanked on either side with a dozen stepped cliffs that seemed to march away into the distance. The cliffs were hole-riddled with caves, and hundreds of teams had worked their way from cave to cave, Sid's amongst them. The fighting had been close and hard, energy weapons lighting the darkness with flashes of blue and white, men and Xflora falling together to hit the ground dead, blood mixing with alien sandy viscera. Victory had taken sixteen hours of solid fighting, during which time Sid had not answered his body's desperate pleas for rest and sleep. His soldiers had all been his own children. A freezing rain had fallen against the cliff face and icy water had soaked through Sid's uniform. He had been in pain for most of those thirteen hours, had been frozen, exhausted, terrified. But had he not also been happy? And had he, truly, been happy since?

What an unsettling thought.

Twelve

Sid slept for an hour, washed and dressed. He chose an antique dress uniform from the wide array that (his servile-AI informed him) was acceptable for the Field Marshal's functions. It seemed that Luop was developing a taste for the more ornate manifestations of military history.

Sid's dress uniform required a weapon to complete it. He had never encountered this concept before; all the dress uniforms he had ever seen before had been simply clothing. But according to his servile-AI a tiny projectile weapon, no bigger than his hand, was to be worn in a belt-pouch along with the dark jacket and trousers. The concept fascinated Sid. It was partly the very idea of carrying a weapon into a peaceful meeting such as a Field Marshal's dinner; and partly the oddity and antiquity of the weapon itself. Every weapon of war he had handled in his military career had been large, because this is how weapons were. But this device was a mere tube, with a handle at one end. Projectiles were fired with tiny fusion-charges and expelled from the tube.

Intrigued, Sid had the Dolly manufacture the device whilst the cloth-tender cut and fashioned his uniform. The Dolly trembled and gleamed, and eventually the miniature weapon was brought to the flat top of the machine. Sid examined it, and ordered a hundred bullets. To his surprise, only forty of these could be loaded into the weapon at any one time.

Dressed and armed, Sid made his way from his quarters and up the spinal corridor towards the Field Marshal's suite. Statuesque Xflora warriors lined the way, glinting darkly under the ceiling lighting. Inside the first chamber of the Field Marshal's suite colonels and generals were gathered, spread out in the large space in twos and threes. Sid nodded and smiled at a few of his colleagues, but rather than talk to anybody wandered from Xflora statue to Xflora statue. These were the latest additions to the Field Marshal's collection, the ones Sid had seen unloaded earlier that day. He recognised them. Strange to think that they were alive inside their diamond coating. Perhaps they were even sensible – perhaps they sensed the gathering of humanity milling about them as they stood there, static, in their transparent sheaths.

Eventually subalterns ushered the gathering through to the dining room. Here, at the head of an immense scimitar-shaped table, sat the Field Marshal himself. He smiled dazzlingly as each of his generals, and each of his colonels, paid respects, found their places and sat down. Glasses, made of granite carved so thin as to become translucent, rose up through the table. They were filled with Splash.

'Drink, comrades,' announced Luop from the far end of the table, his voice amplified discreetly loud enough to carry, but not so loud as to sound booming.

Everybody drank.

Food appeared, but the assembled guests knew better than to taste it before the Field Marshal's speech. Everybody sat expectantly.

'We have come a long way, comrades,' said Luop. 'Comrades, and, may I say, friends. We have embarked upon humanity's greatest campaign. We have a whole empire to pacify, and we have taken the first step. Hurrah!'

The room resounded with a hundred and twenty cheers.

'Our first step has been a tremendous success: six hundred human worlds conquered. Of the six hundred commanders for those missions, you have been selected – you one hundred and twenty. You are the finest this fine army has to offer.'

All faces were angled towards Luop.

'I have decided that you few, you select and expert few, will join with me in the new phase of humanity's destiny,' declared Luop, his voice sliding up in register slightly, giving his words a strident edge. 'The army will sweep in towards the Imperial centre, sweep through every world in its way. Our first campaign has taught me one thing, one crucial thing. Shall I tell you what it is?'

Nobody spoke; everybody was straining towards the superior officer.

'The current Imperial population is *disinclined* to accept the inevitable,' said Luop, putting a weird emphasis on the word 'disinclined', as if it were the most terrible of insults. 'They resist, they fight, they refuse to surrender. It puts our army under unacceptable strain. So,' said Luop, a broad smiling flashing incongruously across his face, 'we shall wipe them away. As we work inwards we shall simply eliminate the current Imperial population. Hurrah!'

The whole room cheered again.

'Now,' said Luop, his skin shining with the sweat of excitement. 'You may wonder how we will work this thing, practically. The main constraint will be that we must leave as much infrastructure standing as possible. Because I do not intend to *destroy* the empire's population. I intend to *replace* it. And therefore we must preserve as much of each planet's architecture and production capacity as possible.'

Silence.

'Sir?' hazarded one general. 'You say – replace the population?'

'That's the case.'

'Replace it with . . . ?'

'With our offspring,' beamed Luop. 'With our own children. We have the technology, after all. Each of you – this is why I have selected you – each of you will provide repeated donations of your own sperm. These will be combined in the usual way, and grown in the usual way. But grown as *civilians*! Not as warriors, but as civilians. We can instil them with absolute loyalty to us, loyalty to me, and then we can simply place them on each world as we conquer it.' He smiled and smiled, so wide it looked as if it might break his jaw. 'Think of it, gentlemen!' he declared. 'Instead of a recalcitrant and belligerent population that would require decades of policing and control, we would be remaking the empire in our own image – literally so – populating it with our own offspring, our own loyalty-conditioned children! World by world, system by system, hundreds of millions of our own children filling up worlds that our army has scrubbed clean. By the end of the process no ruler in human history would ever have experienced the absolute and unruffled power that will be mine. Mine, of course, to distribute amongst you – distribute as I see fit. How fortunate are you! How fortunate are you! Imperium for a million years; each of us the father of an entire planet, an entire system! Think of it! Colonel Sidlan . . .'

Sid jerked at the sound of his own name, and stood up to automatic attention.

'Thank you, colonel,' said Luop, indulgently. 'There he is, gentlemen. Colonel Sidlan knows what it is like to look down rank upon rank of one's own children. He was one of the original donors for the military machine, as I think some of you know. Weren't you, colonel?'

'Yes, sir!' barked Sidlan.

He stepped to the side, away from his chair, and saluted. He turned, and marched briskly to the door. He did not look behind him. He could imagine the complacent expression on Luop's face; could imagine it troubled momentarily with slight puzzlement at Sid's actions. But the Field Marshal was not the man to allow some minor unscripted hiccough to interrupt his triumphal moment. As he stepped towards the door, Sid half-expected to hear Luop ordering him to stop, to return to the table. But no such order came. Instead, the Field Marshal continued with his peroration.

'So, gentlemen, we can see that we need to find increasingly efficient means of purging the worlds we conquer of all non-pliant population, and arguably of all population altogether . . .'

Sid pulled the door open, and stepped into the chamber beyond. The door swung shut and Luop's voice was suddenly muffled: . . . *particularly important that food-production capacity not be degraded* . . .

Sid was alone in the front chamber, with only the dozen Xflora statues for company. He walked, slowly, over to the first of these. How many of the colonels and generals in the other room, Sid wondered, had worked their way up from the ranks the way he had done himself? They were mostly senior commissions and appointments. How few had the experience of combat with an Xflora Advance Warrior?

Few.

He made his way to the main entrance of the Field Marshal's suite. He dismissed the subaltern standing there, informing him that such was the Field Marshal's own wish. Then, completely alone, he examined the lock panel to discover whether a colonel's access was enough to activate it. It was.

He stepped back inside the suite. The firearm was in his hand before he consciously made the decision to use it. He examined the strange weapon closely, holding it with his right hand, running his left thumb up and down the cool shaft. With one hand he raised it, aimed and fired. The projectile made barely any noise exiting the tube, just a sort of muffled popping; but it jerked with surprising force in Sid's hands. A flaw, like a boil, appeared in the diamond casing of the nearest Xflora. The bullet passed through the upper portion of the alien, and out the other side, puffing a tiny dusting of Xflora viscera with it. No vital organs were located so high up in the Xflora body.

He took aim again, and fired. He felt the spasm of the gun in his hand, again, again, again. With the fourth shot the diamond glass cracked across and splintered. He had taken care not to shoot too low. The bullet wounds he had inflicted on the creature's upper half were very minor. Now it was stirring, pulsing and bulging. A limb threw off a ragged portion of diamond glass and broke off another. Then, with tremulous grace, the beast started squeezing itself up and out, free of its prison.

A sound of cheering, distant, was momentarily audible from the dining room.

Sid moved from statue to statue, cracking the diamond-glass eggshells with several shots, bringing each frozen creature to shuddering life. He broke the glass of all of the twelve in a matter of minutes. The first Xflora he had freed was completely out of its prison trying, unsteadily, to stand as Sid made his way back to the door. There was a febrile awkwardness, almost a coltishness, to the alien's actions, but Sid knew how resilient the beast was, how quickly the Xflora recovered from wounds. It would be killing-fit in minutes.

He stepped into the corridor and keyed the door closed, encoding the lock memory with his personal rebus. It could be over-ridden by the Field Marshal, of course, but Sid anticipated that Luop would be too pressingly occupied to be able to spend time at the lock panel. Or so he hoped. Nothing can ever be certain in life, but Sid was fairly confident of this.

He started down the corridor. The Xflora statues that ornamented this passageway had clearly been there for some time, the aliens inside certainly dead. But he knew he would find living specimens to release elsewhere on the ship. He only hoped he could unlock enough of them to make the fight interesting. It was the year of Galactic Empire 1389, the eightieth year of the reign of the Committee of Seven, now Five, on the Battleship *School of Velocity 32* in grav-acceleration orbit around the blue dwarf Rousseau.

And tomorrow and

Act I

The castle had been abandoned by almost all of its inhabitants. Its population, having decided there was little point in staying only to be slaughtered by the English army, crept out by ones and twos throughout the night, and made what peace they could with the enemy. Some even begged to join Malcolm's troop, so as to be on the winning side in the morrow's inevitable English victory. When Macbeth awoke, with only Seyton in attendance, he found his halls deserted, his battlements unguarded. 'Let them fly!' he blustered, striding up the stone stairs to survey the scene from the top of his tallest tower. 'I bear a charméd life. I don't need *them*!'

He looked down upon the investing force: a mass of humanity stretching as far as the eye could see. They had thrown down the boughs and branches taken from Birnam Wood, and now stood in serried ranks, their armour and their weapons glittering in the morning sunlight.

'It looks bad, sir,' said Seyton, in a miserable voice.

'Nonsense!' boomed Macbeth. 'We cannot be defeated.'

'But the charm, sir,' said Seyton, cringing a little as if expecting Macbeth to strike him in his furious frustration. 'Surely it has tricked you? It said you would never vanquished be, 'til Great Birnam Wood should come to high Dunsinane Hill.'

'Indeed it *did*,' said Macbeth, with enormous self-satisfaction.

'And we need but look, sir!' said Seyton, indicating the host that lay spread before them. 'Malcolm's army has brought Birnam Wood hither!'

'Seyton, Seyton, Seyton,' said Macbeth, genially. He clasped his servant about the shoulders and gave the top of his head a little rub with the knuckles of his right hand. 'You've got to *pay* more *attention*. The one crucial thing about magical prophecies is that they are enormously and pedantically *precise*. So: Malcolm's army cut down a few boughs and carried them along to Dunsinane? That's *hardly* the same thing as the forest moving! Ask yourself this . . . if you were a mapmaker—'

'Mapmaker,' repeated Seyton nodding uncertainly.

'—yes, if you were *making a map* – for the sake of argument, you know – you were making a map of Scotland, where would you put Birnam Wood? Over there on the distant hill . . .' he pointed to the horizon where the blue-green forest still lay like a cloud against the horizon ' . . . the location of the *trunks* and *roots* and most of the *foliage*? Or here at Dunsinane, where a few thousand branches and leaves have been carried?'

'Um,' said Seyton, tentatively offering his answer like a schoolchild before a stern schoolmaster, 'the first one?'

'Exactly! Birnham *Wood* is still on the *hill*. The prophecy has not been fulfilled. I am, accordingly, *un*worried.'

From below came the sound of repeated thuds. Malcolm's sappers, in the unusual position of being able to work without resistance from castle-defenders, were knocking down the main gate with a large battering-ram. 'Right,' said Macbeth. 'Better put on some armour. Not that I need it. More for the show of it than anything.'

With a great crash the gate gave way.

By the time he got downstairs, armoured and beswordеd, Macbeth's main courtyard was filled with hundreds of English soldiers. At the front of this fierce crowd were Macduff and young Siward. Siward made a rush at Macbeth, hurrying up the stone stairway to engage the Scottish king. Macbeth chopped his head off with a single stroke of his sword.

The crowd in the courtyard hissed their disapproval.

Rather relishing the theatricality of it, Macbeth cried out: 'Begone Macduff! You cannot kill me!'

The general hissing turned into a general laughing.

'Do you boast so?' said Macduff, cockily, throwing his sword from hand to hand and starting up the stairs. 'We outnumber you, fiendish tyrant! Outnumber you considerably.'

'What you've got to keep in mind,' said Macbeth, 'is that I bear a charméd life, actually, that must not yield to one of woman born.'

'Ha!' cried Macduff. 'Ah! Ha! Well!' He seemed very pleased with himself. 'Despair thy charm,' he said. 'And let the angel that thou still hast served tell thee, Macduff – that's *me* – was from his mother's womb untimely *ripped*!' He stuck his chest out.

'Still born of woman, though, eh?' Macbeth said.

The courtyard had fallen silent.

'You what?' said Macduff.

'Born of woman nevertheless. Born – you. Woman – your mother.'

'Ah no, but Macduff was from his mother's womb untimely *ripped* . . .'

'Yes, yes, caesarean section, named after Julius Caesar the Roman Emperor who was born via a surgical incision into the wall of the abdomen rather than through the birth canal,' said Macbeth. 'Yes, we all know about that. But it's still a form of *birth*, isn't it? You're still *born*, and *of woman*.'

'No, I wasn't.'

'Yes, you were,'

Macduff brandished his sword, and roared defiance. Then he let the sword drop, and said: 'Wasn't.'

'What would you call it then? Are you really asserting that being born by caesarean section is not *being born*?'

'Um,' said Macduff, a little confusedly. 'Untimely ripped . . .'

'I tell you what,' said Macbeth. 'Let's pop along to the castle library, and look it up in a dictionary. That'll decide the matter.'

'Alright,' said Macduff, brightening.

So they made their way to the library, stacked floor to ceiling with dusty folios and quartos and octavos; Macbeth and Macduff, trailing a mob of soldiery behind them. Macbeth pulled the *Dictionarius* from its resting place, plonked it on a desk and turned its heavy pages.

'Here you go,' said Macbeth, with his finger on the relevant definition. '*Sectura Caesaris* – "form of birth in which the infant is delivered through an incision in the mother's uterus and abdominal wall rather than the more conventional birth canal." There you are – "a form of birth". In other words: you are still born of woman, regardless of whatever obstetric interventions happened to be used at the birth. You might as well say that the use of *forceps* meant that you were no longer "born of woman"!'

'Well . . .' said Macduff, scratching his chin. 'I suppose you're right . . .'

'Have at you!' said Macbeth, standing back and raising his sword.

Twenty people had followed the two of them to the Library; and so it was that twenty people watched Macbeth and Macduff fight for about a minute and a half, clanging their swords together vehemently and grunting, until Macbeth swung a blow that Macduff failed to intercept. The blade cleaved his helm and split his head open. Macduff dropped to the floor dead.

'Right,' said Macbeth, cheerily. 'Who's next?'

Act II

It took Macbeth less than five minutes to cut his way through the soldiers in the library. No matter how they swung or stabbed, their swords always slid away from Macbeth's body. It was, as one of them observed (just prior to having his leg severed with a lunging sword stroke, such that he fell and bled rapidly to death), the *weirdest* thing.

Macbeth, his armour smeared with blood, strode along the

corridor and out into the courtyard. With a cheer the crowd there surged towards him; but he was not dismayed. It was, from his point of view, a simple matter to stand his ground hacking and chopping targets as they presented themselves. His assailants soon discovered that swords aimed howsoever accurately and forcefully would glide from his armour as if they had been merely glancing blows wielded infirmly. When a hundred had fallen and Macbeth was still unscathed, the heart rather went out of the advance party. A few tried upping the general mood of heroic battle by yelling war cries and running at Macbeth. Many more retreated precipitously through the main gate.

Macbeth followed them.

The carnage that ensued passed rapidly through various stages, being by turns astonishing, distressing, and, ultimately, frankly, rather boring. Wherever Macbeth walked his sword brought death to dozens. When its blade was too chipped to cut effectively, he simply threw it aside and picked up a sword from one of the many corpses he had created.

At the beginning of this Macbethian counterattack, Malcolm ordered a general charge. But from his vantage point on horseback on the hill, he realised – though he could scarcely credit it – that not one of the swords, maces, arrows or spears aimed at Macbeth was able to pierce his skin. His casualties began to mount up. He changed tactics, ordering a phalanx of men to press forward in the hopes of trampling or crushing the singleton enemy. But that was equally ineffective, and after two score men or more had been slain, the phalanx as a whole broke up. Malcolm issued another order for a general crush, and the entire army – tens of thousands of men – surrounded Macbeth and tried to press in. There followed a quarter of an hour of uncertain alarum. But Malcolm realised soon enough that a great circular wall of his own dead soldiers was being piled around Macbeth.

By the end of the day Macbeth had single-handedly killed over eight hundred men. This slaughter had tired him out, and he made his way back into the castle (which was, of course, wholly over-run by Malcolm's soldiers) mounted the stairs to his chamber and went to sleep in his bed. 'Now!' cried Malcolm, when this news was relayed to him. 'Kill him in his bed! Stab him! Smother him while he snores!'

But no matter how they tried, none of the men under Malcolm's command were able to force the life out of the supine body of Macbeth. Blades skittered harmlessly off his skin. The pillow placed over his face, and even partially stuffed into his mouth, prevented him from breathing; but the lack of air in no way incommoded the sleeping man. They piled great stones on him, but no matter how great the weight, Macbeth's body was uncrushable.

Finally dawn came and Macbeth awoke, yawning and stretching. After a little light breakfast of poisoned bread and adulterated kippers, neither malign substance having any effect upon him, he resumed killing. He took it easier on this second day, careful not to wear himself out; and accordingly he worked longer and more efficiently: by dusk he had killed over a thousand men. Malcolm's army, hugely discouraged, was starting to melt away; deserters slinking back to Birnam Wood and away to the south.

On the third day Macbeth killed another thousand, along with Malcolm himself. After that it was a simple matter to either kill off or else chase away the remnants of the army, and by dusk of this day the battle was his.

It fell to Macbeth himself to clear away all the corpses. He had, after all, no servants – Seyton had been hanged from a gibbet on the first day's battle. So, over a period of a week or so, he dug a large pit at the rear of the castle and dragged the thousands of bodies into it.

Act III

Life settled down a bit after that. He found that he didn't *need* to eat; although he was still aware of hunger, and still capable of deriving sensual pleasure from good food. So he scavenged the nearby countryside, and occupied himself with wandering about the empty castle, cooking himself food, heating himself bath water, thinking, sleeping.

He pondered the charms that protected him, meditating the precise limits the witches had established. They had not, for instance, said that 'no *man* of woman born can harm Macbeth' (which would have left open the chance that a *woman*, or *child*, of woman born could kill him) – they had specified *none* of woman born. That seemed safe enough. The other charm was even more heartening: *Macbeth shall never vanquished be*, they had said, *until Birnam Wood to high Dunsinane Hill shall come against him.* Vanquished meant killed by an enemy; but it also, he reasoned, meant poisoned, killed by sickness, laid low by old age, or any of the consequences of mortal existence. Until the wood actually uprooted itself and travelled wholesale to his castle, none of these fates could befall him. That was indeed a powerful charm.

After three months, a second army came to besiege his castle. This time it was led by the English King Edward in person; and he brought with him, in addition to many soldiers, a huge assemblage of holy men, wizards, magi and people otherwise magically inclined who had promised to undo the charm that preserved Macbeth's life.

Macbeth rather welcomed the distraction. Life had settled into quite a tedious rut.

He made sure, this time, to do all his killing outside the castle walls, so as not to leave himself the awkward job of clearing dead bodies out of his corridors, rooms and stairwells afterwards. And he took particular pleasure in slaughtering the magicians, most of whom were armed with nothing more than wands, books of spells and crucifixes. Macbeth found and killed King Edward himself on day four, but it took a whole week for the army as a whole to become discouraged. Eventually the force broke up and fled away, apart from a few hardened types who threw themselves at Macbeth's feet and pledged allegiance to him as the Witch King of the North. He swore them into his service.

Act IV

Every now and again, over the ensuing hundred years or so, Macbeth would gather around him a band of followers – men either in awe of his magic immunity, or else simply men prepared to follow any figure in authority if the financial inducements were strong enough. But these groupings never added up to an army, and since none of the people who followed him were gifted with his invulnerability, they tended to get slaughtered in battle. His initial plan – to reclaim the throne of Scotland by war and by the sword – was, he realised eventually, not tenable. People feared him, and some few would do his will; but most shunned him, would not follow him. He found himself thoroughly isolated.

Eventually he stopped accumulating bands of followers, and struck out by himself.

He roamed about for many years, searching Scotland for the Witches in the hope of extracting from them some useful magical fillip that would enhance his fortunes. But they seemed to have departed the land. His search was fruitless. He returned to Dunsinane Castle to find that it had been claimed, in his absence, by the Thane of Aberdeen and his retinue. It didn't take Macbeth long to kill off, or chase away, those interlopers.

For several decades, after this, he sat in his castle alone. The people in the local villages established a mode of uneasy coexistence with him: they brought him offerings of food, wine, books and whatever else he asked for; but they otherwise left him alone and went about their own business. Macbeth grew accustomed to the solitude, and even came to relish it. He had learnt to despise ordinary humanity, with their ridiculous fleshly vulnerability, their habit of dropping dead at the slightest scratch. He felt a scorn almost entirely unleavened by pity at the inevitability of their physical aging, decay and death. Indeed, he wondered why it was he had ever wanted to rule over such starveling creatures. It seemed to him he was no more than a butcher sitting on a throne, gathering his swine around him as courtiers. Mortal glory was no longer of interest to him.

The castle began to decay around him. He was forced to undertake repairs himself, single-handed; for no amount of rampaging around the local villages like a fairy-story ogre – no amount of railing and yelling – could persuade the villagers to help him in this enterprise. None of them were prepared to come and work as his servants, at even the highest pay. Rather, they fled away and took refuge in the hills until he had departed.

Increasingly reclusive, Macbeth devoted himself to gathering together and reading the world's many books. Word spread of this mysterious hermit-laird (though by now most people had forgotten his name) who paid handsomely in gold for any book of curious lore or magical promise. Book traders made their way to the castle, pocketed their fees, and hurried away again glad to escape unscathed. When Macbeth's gold was exhausted, he strode out into the larger world and ransacked and robbed and extorted until his fortune was restored. He hoped, by accumulating the world's largest library of magical arcana, and by decades of dedicated study, to master the same supernatural skills that the witches themselves had possessed. Why should he track down those wild women and beg them for favours, when he could command the magic himself?

But no matter how much he studied and practised, he developed no magical talent.

More than this, he realised that the charm had changed him. He decided to found a dynasty, reasoning that even if his children grew old and died he could still live as patriarch over his own grandchild, great-grandchildren, more distant descendants yet, and on into the abyss of future time. He could persuade no woman to marry him of course, but it was a simple matter to abduct likely-looking individuals from the locality. Yet no matter how long he kept them, and no matter what he did, not one of them became pregnant with his offspring. He realised that whatever it was that was acting upon his body to preserve it from death and harm was also preventing him from fathering children.

At this he fell into a depression for several decades; barely moving from his chamber, letting his hair and beard and nails grow to prodigious lengths. He attempted to kill himself – an honourable, warrior's death, falling on his own sword like Mark Antony. But he was himself born of woman, and thus incapable of self-harm.

After that he did various things. He spent much of the thirteenth century travelling the world; first as an anonymous foot-soldier of the crusades, and thereafter as a curious tourist walking and riding to Cathay, to Siberia, over the ice to Alaska, and across the great plains of the New World. If I were to detail his adventures, this story would stretch through thousands of pages, and marvellous though the adventures were they would come to seem tedious to you; as they did to him. He roamed through Central and South America, and finally travelled back to Europe on one of Cortez' ships. Bored of travel, he made his way back to Scotland. Once again his castle had been occupied, but he disposed of the family living there and retook possession.

For a decade or so this reinstallation in his own home provided him with various distractions. Enraged villagers, and later religiously devout armies, came to destroy him – he was now once again infamous (after many decades of anonymity) far and wide as a devil in human form, a warlock who had sold his soul to Satan, and many like phrases. They burnt his castle around him, but the flames did not bother him. Instead he walked amongst them bringing death with his sword. Eventually they fled. They always fled. It took Macbeth a decade to rebuild Dunsinane, working entirely by himself, but he found he quite enjoyed the labour.

In the year 1666 he became intrigued by the idea that the world might be about to end. Travelling preachers assured the world that the apocalypse promised by Saint John was imminent. Would his charm survive the end of the world? He thought about this a great deal and decided it would not. He had come to the conclusion that the operative part of his charm – the 'none of woman born shall harm Macbeth' – was the *woman*. Mary, mother of God, had been a virgin. Therefore she was a girl rather than a woman: and Christ was not of woman born. At his second coming, Macbeth decided, there would exist in the world a person capable of destroying him – an end he looked forward to with complete equanimity. But 1666 turned into 1667, and then into 1668, and the end of the world did not come. Macbeth reconciled himself to a genuinely immortal life. He discovered that immortality tasted not of glory, not even especially of life. It was a grey sort of experience, neither markedly happy nor sad. It was the life stones experience: endurance. It was the reason they are so silent and unmoved. It was the existence of the ocean itself, changeless though restless, chafing yet never progressing. It was Macbeth's life.

Act V

There was a knocking at the door.

Nobody had knocked at his door for a decade or more. His last visitor had been the census taker, and Macbeth – who had learnt this lesson from experience long before – had disposed of him swiftly, rather than risk having his precious solitude disturbed. Maps marked Dunsinane as a folly, and Macbeth had gone to great lengths to dig out underground dwellings and knock down much of the upper portion, so as not to be too conspicuous from the air. What with the reforestation of pretty much the whole of Scotland following the European Environmental Repair Act of '57 his home was well hidden: off the ramblers' trails and not listed in any land tax spreadsheets.

So who was knocking?

He clambered up the stairs to the main hall and pulled open the door. Outside, standing in the rain (Macbeth, sequestered in his underground laboratory, had not even realised it was raining), was a man. He was wearing the latest in bodymorph clothes, a purple plastic cape that rolled into a seam of his shirt as he stepped over the threshold.

'May I come in?' he asked, politely enough.

'I dinnae welcome visitors,' said Macbeth.

'That's as may be, sir,' said the man. 'But I have official accreditation.' He held out a laminated badge for Macbeth's perusal; an animated glyph of the man's face smiled and nodded at him repeatedly from the badge. 'And the legal right of entry.'

Macbeth thought of killing him there and then, but he held back. He hadn't so much as talked to another human being in two years. He was curious as to what errand had brought this official individual so deep into the woods.

As he shut the door behind him he asked, 'So what is it you want?'

'Are you, sir, a relation of the *Macbeth* family?' the man asked.

Now this was a startling thing. The people of this part of Scotland had long, long ago forgotten Macbeth's name and true identity. He lived, where he was not entirely forgotten, as a kind of legend, part of stories of an ogre who could not be killed, of a wizard with the gift of immortality. 'How d'ye know that name?'

'Databases worldwide have been linked and cross-web searched,' the man said in a slightly sing-song voice. 'Various anomalies have been detected. It is my job – assigned me by my parent company, MCDF Inc – to investigate these. The deeds to this property have not been filed in eleven hundred years. The last listed owner was a Mr Macbeth. I am here to discover whether this property is still in the possession of that family, in order to register it for Poll Tax, Land Reclamation Tax and various other government and EU duties.'

This told Macbeth all he needed to know. This taxman would have to die or Macbeth's life would be disturbed. And he did not like disturbance. Nevertheless, he reached this conclusion with a heavy heart. The youthful enthusiasm for slaughter had long since passed from his breast. Now, from his immortal perspective, the mayfly humans who were born, grew and died all around him were objects of pity rather than scorn. Still, necessity overrode his compassion. If it must be done (as, of course, it *must*) 'twere well it were done quickly.

He pulled a sword from the wall, and squared up to the puny individual. 'I'm afraid,' he announced, 'that I cannae be disturbed by taxes and duties. I value my solitude, you see.'

'I must warn you, sir,' said the taxman, holding up one finger in a slightly prissy gesture, 'that I am licensed to defend myself from unprovoked attack. My parent company, having invested thirty-eight million euros in my development, are legally entitled to preserve their investment from unnecessary harm.'

Macbeth only shook his head. He swung the sword. The blade crashed against the man's shoulder; but, instead of severing it as Macbeth expected, the collision resulted in a series of sparks and fizzes, and a scattering of grey smoke into the air.

'You have caused several thousand euros damage,' said the strange man, 'to my right arm. I must inform you that my manufacturers, MCDF Inc, are legally entitled to recover that sum from your bank account.'

Puzzling, Macbeth wrenched the sword free and lifted it for another sweep, aiming this time at the taxman's head.

'I do apologise for this, sir,' the taxman said, with a mournful expression on his face. He pointed a finger at Macbeth. The end of the finger clicked and swivelled to the side. With a loud *thwup* sound a projectile launched itself from the hollow digit and shot into Macbeth's chest. More in astonishment than pain, he dropped his sword and fell backward over the stone flags.

The strange taxman, leaning over him now, was speaking into a communicator of some kind. 'Please send a medical team at once. Unmarked and unnamed property, located near the centre of Greater Birnham Wood. Lock onto my signal. Please hurry; the subject is badly wounded.' He peered down at Macbeth, whose eyes were already losing their focus. Macbeth considered the sheer oddness of this feeling, these smashed ribs, this blood (which had stayed safely in his veins through all these centuries) spilling onto the floor. It was, he had to admit, and despite the pain involved, a feeling something like – release.

'I do apologise for doing that, sir,' the taxman was saying. 'I have called an air ambulance to assist. I do hope, sir, that they arrive here before you die.'

'Oh, I do hope,' said Macbeth, in a gaspy voice, 'not.'

(The following 'Afterword' was included with the story on its first publication)

With a writer as culturally ubiquitous and myriad-minded as Shakespeare, it seems to me inevitable that you encounter the plays as reflections upon your own consciousness rather than as objective entities in the outside world. I have certainly learnt a number of important lessons from *Macbeth*, a play that has lived vividly inside my head ever since I first read it as a teenager. When I was a school student I wrote an essay on the play which lifted its argument from the criticism of A. C. Bradley (I was, as an impressionable youth, content to parrot the opinions of my elders and betters) that Macbeth was the only one of Shakespeare's major tragic heroes without a sense of humour. My teacher, a great *sensei* called Derek Meteyard, scoffingly and quite properly, marked this essay down. 'On the contrary, he has a *very lively* sense of humour,' he told me, and pointed to, for instance, the scene where his hired assassin returns to report the successful murder of Banquo to Macbeth:

> MACBETH: There's blood upon thy face.
> FIRST MURDERER: 'Tis Banquo's, then.
> MACBETH: 'Tis better thee without than he within.

This last line – 'the blood is certainly better on *your* outside, than in Banquo's *inside*' – is indeed darkly funny, and it is one example of many in the play. From this episode I learnt a crucial lesson: don't believe what a critic says just because they're famous, or respected, or because they've gotten their opinion printed up in a book published by a University Press. That's a lesson that has served me well in my academic career.

Why was I so easily misled by Bradley? The answer, of course, is that at the age of seventeen, I read *Macbeth* through the lens of my miserable-teenager, melodramatic-depressive-gothic mindset. I read it, in other words, not as a play about a medieval Scottish King, but as about depression, and therefore, somehow, as about *me*; or more precisely about me at my most humourlessly glum and self-absorbed ('Tomorrow and tomorrow and tomorrow/ creeps in this petty pace from day to day/and I am spottily adolescent/And can't get girls to go out with me' and so on). Now I am in my forties and I find a different play when I read *Macbeth*. It strikes me, indeed, as a quite astonishingly, and perhaps horribly, energetic play, aggressively and blackly comic at the same time as it rehearses its tragic dynamic. It is a play based upon precisely the same misunderstandings and incongruities as farce, but it pushes its premise to a destructive, bloody exuberance that only gets more startlingly relevant in today's world. It is not a comedy in the conventional sense, of course. But in today's world it seems to me that there is also a need for that strong laughter in the face of disaster and death that is the expression of man and woman at their most heroic. 'I am going to die? Ha-ha-ha!'

'And tomorrow . . .' is a comic piece, although not an especially cheery or laughsome one. I was intrigued by the disjunction between, on the one hand, the Gordian-knot vehemence with which Macbeth unleashes violence upon the things that restrict him, and, on the other, the pedantically legalistic terms of the prophecy that is his eventual undoing. But I was more intrigued by the comic possibilities of reading this most bloody and murderous of Shakespeare's plays as an articulation of a very modern sort of heroism, the refusal to simply crumple, the refusal to give up, the discovery of a strenuous and dark *joy* in the face of extinction. I was also struck that the pedantic and legalistic prophecies that doom Macbeth wouldn't stand up to ten minutes of cross-examination in a court of law by any half-decent contract lawyer.

The Man of the Strong Arm

1

'By permitting,' Jeunet began to say. He was, perhaps, distracted by something, for he stopped. Maybe it was the sound of the small waves folding over onto the beach again and again, below the platform on which they sat, as if the ocean itself were bowing before him. At any rate he didn't finish that sentence. Presently he started again. 'The *strength* of story,' he said. 'Its *strength*.'

'Story,' said Soop, absurdly excited to be in the presence of a man such as Jeunet. 'Story, yes. Absolutely, yes.'

'The Man of the Strong Arm permits the study of art,' said Jeunet, as if this fact were so extraordinary a thing that he needed to remind himself of it by speaking it aloud.

'Such art as expresses the strength of the human spirit,' agreed Heston.

Soop was so excited he couldn't keep his legs still.

Jeunet waved his hand in the air. 'And you believe your latest find, this latest science fiction is – appropriate? You're certain?'

'Certainty *is* strength,' said Heston.

'So, this—' Jeunet's speech slowed as he navigated the syllables, 'this Edgar Burrough of the Rice – you're sure it is art?'

'Oh, *very* much so,' said Soop, getting to his feet. He really couldn't help this; his enthusiasm for his discipline just bubbled over. 'It is a fantastical and dream-like story of a hero – a strong man – a strong hero – who flies by *sheer force of will* to the stars – to a red star, which becomes, when he arrives, a red desert. He sees a red star, Mars, you know, and by sheer force of will he conjures out of that a world of red desert. Conjures desert out of the light of the star! For of course we know that light is not sand . . . although,' he added, at a gabble, for Soop's mind worked by means of sudden leaps to the left or right of his train of thought, 'sand *is* glass, and glass has to do with light, after a fashion . . .' He stopped, and looked about him. Heston was staring at him. Jeunet was looking away. Soop blushed as though a fire were lit inside the bowl of his skull. 'I'm sorry.'

He sat down again.

The bitterns boomed and boomed and rolled through the sky on their inconceivable avian errands. The sea was very calm and gave the illusion of being composed of a single unbroken substance, a fabric stretched taut seemingly at a slight upward tilt, running away from them until it slotted into the groove of the horizon. The small waves continually stroked the white flank of the beach as if trying to pacify a bulky and potentially violent monster. One of the women unzipped her eye slit, identified that the tumblers of the men were empty, and shuffled in to retrieve them. Jeunet leant a little to the right to avoid being touched by fabric of her alldrape.

'Why, *of the Rice*?' he asked.

'We're not sure,' said Heston, holding his right hand out in front of Soop to restrain him from attempting to answer the superior's question. 'We believe it is that the author derived his income from rice. Perhaps he farmed it.'

'Farming rice is a perfectly honourable occupation,' said Jeunet, thoughtfully. 'And you have the whole of this red desert story?'

'Not all of it. Its source has of course been corrupted,' said Heston. 'We've recovered about two thirds. It seems likely the text is from a variety of provenances, some of them indecent.'

'But the tale *itself* is not indecent,' Soop broke in. He really couldn't contain himself. This was a failing of character, a blockage in the development of his own strength. He knew it, but couldn't help it, and again the excitement came bubbling up. 'It's a strong, heroic tale. It reminded me of the *Faerie Queene*, a much older tale, or at least another tale from a different historical period. As in the *Faerie Queene*, a warrior goes to a strange world and fights Error. Error in this case takes the form of an army of green-skinned monsters with four arms and two legs.'

'The Queen of . . . what did you say?' asked Jeunet.

'A piece of poetic art,' Heston explained, in a smooth voice. 'A perfectly decent, strong-armed piece of art. It is well known, amongst those who specialise in . . . that sort of thing.'

'Art. I wish,' said Jeunet, 'I could be as *comfortable* with that word as you are.' The woman, or one of the other women standing down by the low wall, for their dark grey alldrapes rendered them all equally indistinguishable, brought new drinks on a tray. 'This talk of corruption in the text disturbs me,' said Jeunet, gazing past her to the placid sea.

'Well,' said Heston, in a practised voice, 'corruption is an inevitable part of retrieving art from the historical periods. It is inherent in the nature of the medium. The means of computational storage from that age, to put it plainly, were not watertight. All sorts of extraneous materials, images, portions of other texts – they all find their way into the zeros and ones. That's our job, essentially: to sift this heap of rubbish and pull out the clean, spiritually-strengthening works of art. To discover the sort of stories that the Man of the Strong Arm would endorse.'

'Not without risks,' said Jeunet, looking pointedly at Soop.

'Junior Soop works under my guidance at all times,' said Heston.

'As it should be. And you have enough raw material to go on with?'

Soop hiccoughed, a high-pitched sound. 'We,' he started, and then he stopped himself.

'What?'

'The raw data the Centre sends,' said Heston, smoothly, 'is more than adequate to our needs.'

'Good,' said Jeunet, giving Soop a hard look. 'Good. So. Is it this rice farmer's tale you are going to give me? I mean, is it in a fit and decent *condition* to give me?'

'That's right.'

'Tomorrow, then,' said Jeunet, with finality, and he got to his feet leaving his drink untouched.

2

Jeunet made his way to the guest hut in the lee of the small cliff, a scalloped white slice cut like a smile into the green of the hill. Soop, following Heston, took the opposite direction, along the upward path to the broad hall. From this slightly higher position, no more than twenty yards above the terrace and beach below, the view opened up: the three other islands, like three green lids sealed over the blue-green pans of their own reflections; and beyond that, far away under the glassy sunlight, the broad low ebony-coloured bar of the mainland. They walked up in silence. A week or so earlier, Soop had uncovered several key story-texts – visual narratives, that amongst other things explained why the name *Heston* was so popular amongst followers of the Man of the Strong Arm. An actor with that name had appeared in several heroic texts from the industrial period. Soop found a subversive pleasure in silently contrasting Heston's short, pen-thin frame and moist eyes with the rugged handsomeness of the original strong-man actor – a towering, jut-jawed, bulky individual. Of course it hardly mattered, given the weapon at his belt, whether Heston were muscular or not.

'Come along,' Heston said, without looking over his shoulder.

At least, Soop told himself, Jeunet *looks* like Jeunet. Jeunet the Great. And, more, Jeunet the Great had not been only an *actor*. Visual narratives were slippery. It was harder recovering them, and if they were in colour (which, Soop thought, was a necessary precondition for modern interest) then they were much more likely to contain unacceptable or harmful material than written texts. That was one reason amongst many why Soop preferred the latter.

They were at the top of the path now. A handful of tiny white clouds went along the sky, passing one after the other close across the sun as if wiping its face. A broadcast of glitter speckled the sea beneath in a swathe from mid-ocean to horizon, looking like nothing so much as myriad droplets of sweat discarded by the strenuously gleaming sun.

Clearly, then, Jeunet's boat was coming for him tomorrow. He had said tomorrow, meaning, have the story ready for me to take away then.

Soop had worked with Heston long enough, on this remote place, for the older man not to need to give instruction to the younger. Soop knew that Heston would go off for *his* siesta, just as Jeunet had gone for his; and that in the meantime Soop was to work on preparing a copy of the heroic story in a finished form for the visiting superior to inspect. The afternoons and early mornings were Soop's golden times. Free from the restraint of his elder he roamed uninhibited through the word-forests hauled, unsystematically and indeed erratically, from the databases of the degraded past. Most of it had already passed through the filter of the historians, those guardians of orthodoxy, and all dangerously historical material been removed. But this process could never be pure, for, Soop often thought, although the peoples of the degraded past had evidently lived in what must have been a thoroughly exhausting fever dream of image, fantasy, dream, scientifiction, speculation, oddity and imaginary worlds, nevertheless *some* of this art was grounded in the business of historical living. From time to time he would uncover stories set not in a clean and uplifting fantasy place, but actually in that vanished, degraded world. Soop sometimes worked on retrieving accounts of imaginary cities that suddenly shifted their meaning and revealed themselves to be actual accounts of urban living. That was why Soop preferred the science fiction: set on distant worlds no human had ever even come close to actually visiting, these stories – or most of them – were free to give vivid life to the heroic narrative of strength and purity. But then again, mostly Soop found comfort in the mere blocks of texts, the characters and numbers and incomprehensible jumbles of queer symbols, a third of it garbage, deliberately or otherwise. Yet purge the text of this *code*, as it was called, and more often than not it would be possible to follow long unbroken strings of language all along their thrilling length to conjure heroes – flights through the daysky and the nightsky, journeys to other worlds, into the comforting vales and forests of fantasy lands.

Heston had gone to his room for his sleep now, and Soop walked through the workshop. Women were cleaning it, and they leapt away from him and pressed their backs to the walls as he passed through. Some of them automatically zipped up their eyeslits. Others looked to their maitre for leadership as to whether to flee the room entirely; but Soop had not communicated anything to the maitre, and her swathed form could only shudder with uncertainty. He passed straight through, opened the rear door and stepped outside.

There was a glade outside, sown with smooth lawn and surrounded on three sides by solid curtains of foliage, irregular and pitted masses of several mingled shades of dark green. As soon as he stepped through the door, this solid vegetative curtain shook, and a body darted out from it. It was a female, dressed in trousers and a white kaftan, and shockingly bareheaded – a mass of hair of a gleaming blackness tied in a stem at the back.

'That's the second time you've come here naked,' said Soop, in an amused voice.

The girl fumbled at the scarf around her neck and pulled it hurriedly over the crown of her head.

'Still,' said Soop, uncomfortably aware of his body's automatic reaction to the proximity of this individual, and speaking to create a tiny heroic narrative of his own in which that arousal was an irrelevance, 'it's not as if you're a woman.'

'My husband,' she said, in her execrably-accented English, 'has a different opinion.'

'You never cease to astonish,' said Soop, excited still further by her bold-facedness in answering him back – in speaking to him at all. 'Husband indeed! So, so. Have you got more for me?'

She held out a fishstick-sized chip.

'And that?'

'Moon.'

'Moon?'

'I mean,' she said, after swallowing and licking her lips, 'it's another version of the moon story. The Armstrong story. That's what I mean.'

'The one you gave me yesterday?'

'It's a very popular story from that period,' she said, glancing anxiously at the open door behind him. 'Very popular. There are hundreds of different retellings of it.'

'I've heard you whistle *that* tune before,' said Soop, fumbling in his satchel for payment. 'And I'll tell you straight up, I'm not paying you hundreds of times for the same story. I'm intrigued as to how this version is different from the one you sold me yesterday. I'll take it. It's a good story, if a little dour. It's good, it's heroic. It's just a little dour.' She took the money. And he took the data stick. And that was the end of their exchange, except that they both loitered there, in the clearing.

She kept staring at him. Extraordinary!

'There's a very important man who's come to visit us,' said Soop, his heart thundering in his chest with the excitement of imparting this news to her. But why should he care about impressing *her*? Barely even a her!

'Very important?'

'A very senior man.'

'Seems to me,' she replied, 'all your men are senior.'

'You say that,' burst out Soop, in a little spurt of laughing exasperation, 'as if it is a *strange* thing!'

And then, after all her extraordinary behaviour, the female asked the most extraordinary question of all. She said, 'Does this senior man have weapons?'

It flashed upon Soop that there *was* something fantastic,

something otherworldly, or perhaps more accurately something anachronistic, in her manner; and occurred to him further that, paradoxically, this was the reason he kept coming back to talk with her. Something about her echoed, or hinted at, the art, or at any rate *some* of the art he was employed to read, here on this remote place where contamination (that most terrible thing) could be more easily contained. As if, to speak more fancifully, she had *flown through time* to be here today, as some of the heroes of science fiction sometimes did, like the hero from out of the Well at the Century's End, to visit some distant future people. She hadn't of course; she was just a barbarian female. But the glamour of possibility haunted Soop's young mind. Come from the past where women might ask any and every impertinent question. He looked at her again. Her scarf was slipping back once more, for she had no more care for her nakedness than a child, or a beast. Her eyes seemed enormous, yet not enormous in the way a beast's eyes are large, but rather in a distinctly if exaggeratedly human manner: the black of her pupils seemed to bleed into the intensely dark brown of her irises, and these two extraordinary circles were moated by sheer white – luminous, almost gleaming, as if lit by some element within her. These eyes might hypnotise him. Yet she wasn't even a person. Fascinating contradictions.

'Well?' she prompted.

'He is very strong,' said Soop, thinking back to her impertinent question. Merely saying the words was enough to send the twinge of awe through his belly. He thought of Jeunet, taking his after-noon repose in the hut by the sea, just a few hundred yards away; all that manliness, strength and potency coiled, as it were, in rest. But his natural ebullience would not permit awe to silence him for very long. 'Of course he is armed.' He plucked his own pistoletta from his belt and, not meaning to threaten or intimidate her, but merely because it fell to him as the most natural way of showing it off to an interested party, he pointed its muzzle at her. Her striking eyes went even wider than before, and her shoulders snapped up and back. A tremor became evident in her whole body. 'This,' said Soop, carelessly, 'would kill you easily enough, of course. Erase you. But the sort of weaponry *he* carries . . .' It was wonderful even to contemplate it. 'This whole *island* . . .' he said, moving the muzzle from left to right to gesture at the place as a whole. 'All of it . . . it's a great strength he has . . .'

Over their heads, in that portion of sky demarcated by the hemming treetops, four distant bitterns moved, as if sliding magnetically across a blue screen.

'Anyway,' he said, putting his pistoletta back in his belt. 'You asked.'

She had gone very pale.

'I wish I knew why you're so interested,' he added despondently, feeling somehow thwarted, although he could not say why, or of what. 'I don't know why you're so interested in his weapon. You've got your money, haven't you? Shouldn't you be running back? Where,' he added, almost at a shout, 'do you get all these stories from anyway?'

'He's here for the stories,' she said, in a voice from which the earlier colour, the tones of will, was now quite emptied out – a small voice.

'The superior? Of course he is.'

'I can bring you stories.'

'You? Yes, you can. What do you mean by saying that?'

'Good stories.'

'Of course you can,' he retorted, puzzled.

But she was trembling now in quite a marked manner. She was shaking so hard now that her scarf had fallen again around her neck. The naked skin of her face did not fascinate Soop so much as the hair. The purity of colour of her hair, like grooved plastic set upon her head, startled him somehow. 'Your misfortune,' he said, 'is to have been born outside' (he supposed her to have been born outside – or, no, that is not quite right; he supposed nothing about her because, except on those afternoons where they met here, in this clearing, at the back of the workshop, he thought nothing about her at all. But faced with her now, his brain did the best it could, as far as supposition went), 'to have been born outside the protection of the Man of the Strong Arm.'

'Your Leader.' She almost gasped it.

'Yes. Strength – but,' he interrupted himself, 'what on earth are you so confounded scared about?' A thought occurred to him. 'Is it the gun?' He tutted. 'I was only *showing* you the gun. I wasn't about to *shoot* you with the gun.'

She shook her head slightly.

'Not the gun?' he persisted. 'Then what? I do wish you'd stop being so scared, because it makes it hard to speak with you. What *is* it?'

She nodded, or rather inclined her head backwards a little to point with her chin. To point past Soop's left arm. With an inward shudder and a constriction in his throat, Soop turned about.

3

Jeunet, the great Jeunet himself, was standing in the doorway observing the scene with languidly self-confident potency. For long seconds Soop had no idea what to do, or what to say. It was alarming that Jeunet was here. It made Soop alarmed to think that Jeunet had been listening in on his conversation with the female. He tried to master his alarm through his own strength, but it wasn't easy.

Jeunet's hand hung easily, loosely, beside his pistol. 'He wasn't wrong,' Jeunet said, apparently addressing the female. 'He said I could destroy the whole island, in stages or all at once. That's true. Nothing but the truth.'

'Strength,' she hissed.

'Jeunet,' said Soop. Then, 'I thought you were asleep.'

'I wanted to have a word with you before I lay down,' Jeunet replied.

'Of course,' said Soop. 'Of course. A word – I'd be delighted. I could wake Heston, if you like.'

'A word with you alone,' said Jeunet. It was disconcerting that, although he was talking with Soop, he kept looking at the female. She, in turn, kept glancing hurriedly over her shoulder, as if trying to spy her way to escape.

'You,' said Jeunet to the female. 'If you turn your back I'll put a hole in you the size of my fist.' She looked straight back at him, as bold as ever. 'A good deal of your blood would come out of such a hole,' Jeunet went on. 'Innards, too. You'd lie on the grass and die in great pain.'

'You have my attention,' she said, with her terrible accent.

'She was selling me stories,' said Soop, in a weirdly squeaky voice. His own heart was rattling in his chest like a wind-up toy – like those castanet-like chattering teeth that you set on a tabletop and leave to clatter away.

'I gathered as much,' said Jeunet.

'It's research,' Soop said quickly. 'It's, eh, ah, one of the avenues of research we pursue here at the station.' He could not imagine why he wanted to save this female's life. Even had she been a woman, he would hardly have cared – and she wasn't even a woman. But still he gabbled on. 'She brings data with archaic stories. She lives in one of the villages, I suppose. She brings me the data.'

'And you pay her?'

'Small sums.'

'Where does she get them from?'

'As to that,' said Soop hurriedly, 'well, I don't know, I couldn't say.'

'They could be forgeries.'

'As to *that*,' Soop leapt in, 'I don't believe so. I trust my judgment. I think I could tell a contemporary pastiche of antique science fiction, and the real thing. I've read a great deal of the stuff – of heroic fiction from—'

He dried up, abruptly, in mid-sentence, and stood there with his mouth open. What was he saying? He couldn't remember what he was saying.

So there was a little period of silence, filled only with the myriad scratching and piping noises made by the jungle insects, and with the distantly mournful booming of the bitterns away in the distance.

The stranger was trembling very visibly. She was terrified. She knew, Soop saw, that her life was almost at an end.

'So you have bought a story?' Jeunet said, eventually.

'It's a moon story.'

'A fantastic voyage to the moon?'

'Precisely so.' Alarm took away his own words, so he fell back on a lecturer's manner. 'Any student of the ancient traditions of science fiction will tell you that voyages to the moon have a long pedigree in fantastic storytelling. Voyages to the moon and the sun – because both bodies can be seen most clearly, right there in the sky – take precedence over voyages to the planets and stars. This one is about a hero called Armstrong who flies up to the moon.'

All through this strange interview Jeunet stood in the doorway, his hand hanging leisurely next to his pistol. But the strange thing was that his eyes remained fixed on the female. He stared at her with a bewildering intensity, given that she was, as Soop had to remind himself several times – nobody at all.

'Tell me this story,' he said.

The stranger said nothing.

'It's a variation on a standard theme,' Soop put in, when it became clear that the female wasn't going to speak. 'A hero flies up to the moon on a giant firework. He is aided, of course, by the gods – he could hardly have reached as far as the moon without supernatural help. There's a pre-industrial god called Saturn – I've always assumed that the final syllable there means that he was a funereal god, though that's not clear. There's also a god called Apollo, who is the pre-industrial god of the sun and the moon. The significance of these gods to the story is a little obscure, but I assume that on a metaphorical level they fight, Saturn the god of Death and Apollo the god of Life, fight over the mission, over, I mean, the *success* of the mission. Armstrong succeeds, of course, despite terrible danger and adversity.'

'So. A mythological tale?'

'But that's one of the things that's interesting about this story,' said Soop, warming to his theme and forgetting, as he was wont to do when in full spate, his surroundings, his interlocutor, even his fear. 'In common with the science fiction of its period it *is* a mythological story – but it's told in this pedantically pseudo-scientific, or pseudo-technical manner. There's a *lot* of detail about machinery, dials, switches and so on. It tells a purely fantastical imaginary story in a peculiarly detailed realist way.'

The female twitched as he said this, and glanced nervously at Soop.

'Realist?' said Jeunet in a low voice, coming a little further out of the doorway.

'It's a wonderful paradox, really. But it's one of the things I love about all this antique science fiction. There are lots of examples of it. Take Robert Highline; he was a contemporaneous writer of imaginary voyages and his stuff is *full* of gadgets and technical digressions and the like, although the stories themselves are as fantastical and mythic as you like. This Armstrong story is just like that. It's a perfectly impossible adventure, of course, but it's told with a straight face. And that combination is just, is just a thing that I – and I'm speaking only personally of course – *love* about all this work.'

'It was an age that trusted in technology,' said Jeunet.

'It was, and that sapped its strength, of course,' said Soop rapidly, 'although they didn't *entirely* lose sight of the importance of strength. That's why, of their two modes of storytelling, it is the science fictional that is the greater. Their dreary non-science fictional art is all of it morbid and diseased and depressing. But in the science fiction! Well, well, this Armstrong story is a good example. Pure fantasy, yes, but a fantasy of *overcoming* and *strength*.'

'I know this story,' said Jeunet.

The female twitched again. She was holding herself up on her two feet only, it seemed, by an enormous effort of will. Soop had never seen anybody so nervous before.

'You know it?' said Soop. It made no sense, and he couldn't quite understand what Jeunet had said. 'You *know* it? Really? I must say, I'm surprised, Jeunet . . . I mean, it's a minor example of the genre. Interesting, but minor. I had no idea your knowledge of the artform was so extensive.'

'Minor, you call it,' said Jeunet, his gaze still fixed upon the female.

The stranger suddenly spoke out at this, her voice strained. 'If he thinks it's minor,' she said, nodding her head at Soop, 'then he clearly doesn't *know* it very well.'

This pricked Soop's professional pride. 'Indeed I do!' he insisted. 'It is a variant of a story as old as the industrial period itself. As, that is to say, science fiction itself. Don't know it well? I know this: one of the pioneers was a European called Sir Arno of Bergerac – that's a county in old Europe, you know – and *he* told a story about flying to the moon on a giant firework. Then there was the Jew, Verne, who told endless stories about gigantic magic pistols, amongst them one that could shoot men all the way to the moon. And Wells from World's-End, who told a story about a magical house that only stayed on the earth when its windows were open – if you shut them you flew up to the moon. What could be more fantastic? This Armstrong story is in the same vein as these, except there's a pleasant and agreeable twist at the end. You see, all the previous tales of this sort had portrayed the moon as a vibrant and fantastical place filled with colourful monsters. The Armstrong story starts in full-colour, but the moon is a purely black-and-white location. It's *The Wizard of Oz* in reverse, you see. It's a deliberate artistic inversion. It's a land of paradoxes, you see – he lands in the sea, but the sea is all dust. He tries to take small steps so as not to fall over, but the smaller the steps he takes, the more gigantic his walking becomes. *That's* taken from *Alice in the Looking Glass Wonderland*, where the people must run as fast as they can to stand still. He finds a place without any air at all, and yet he plants a flag that flutters proudly. And yet! And *yet* all this bizarre fantastical nonsense is related in the driest, most precise pseudo-scientific manner! It's splendid. It's hilarious, actually. And then the story ends by Armstrong leaping directly from the mirror-land back to earth, from black and white to colour, from a sea of dust to a sea of water.'

'It is not an orthodox story,' said Jeunet.

It took a moment for the full implication of this statement to find a point of entrance into Soop's jangled mind. 'What? What's that? *Not* orthodox? Not *orthodox*? But – forgive me for appearing to contradict you, Jeunet, but. Surely it's perfectly orthodox! Surely as I've just been saying, speaking *as* an expert of the science fiction from this period and it's exactly like two dozen other stories.'

The strange female sucked a deep breath and released it again. 'Shouldn't he be calling you *sir* or *lord* or *master*?'

Soop might almost have admired her courage in talking so, to such a man, excepting that it evidently wasn't true courage; it was the recklessness of an individual who knew that whatever she did she would die very soon. Her impertinence, at any rate, seemed to amuse Jeunet.

'That wouldn't be very *strong*, now, would it?' he said. 'Using that sort of cowering idiom? But you're right; I am the superior party here.'

'Well,' said Soop, croakily. 'Of course.'

'If I say the story is not orthodox, then young Soop must just accept the fact.'

'Of course,' said Soop, in a smaller voice.

For the first time in the interview Jeunet moved his eyes from the stranger and looked at Soop. 'I am aware of this story. I know about it *because* it is proscribed.'

'Proscribed? But *why*?'

'You've been on this island for too long,' said Jeunet. 'You've become a little dissociated from real life, Soop. It's necessary, I realise, if we are to maintain a proper quarantine on these dangerous memes. But it has its own dangers. People like you lose touch with real life. It's proscribed because it's an evident forgery.'

'Jeunet!' said Soop, for this was to insult his professional judgement. 'I strongly disagree! All my long-built-up expertise tells me that it is an authentic artwork from the industrial age.'

'It's a modern pastiche,' said Jeunet, in a tone of voice of somebody not about to enter into a discussion over the fact. 'Worse, it is made – perhaps by this stranger and her people, perhaps by some other group – specifically to undermine our strength. It's a crude satire. Come come, Soop: the hero here is called *Armstrong*? Doesn't that strike you as almost too obvious a libel on the Man of the Strong Arm?'

'Libel?' said Soop, alarmed and confused. 'Libel? But he's a hero, Armstrong is a hero. He's a recognisable archetype of strength!'

'Tch. A man called Strong-Arm journeys to a barren land, and jumps up and down in the dust, and then returns home and declares that he has undertaken mankind's greatest adventure. Can you *honestly* not see how this works as satire? Can you not understand how injurious to the dignity of the Man of the Strong Arm such a tale would be, if it were widely disseminated?'

'I,' said Soop, confused. 'I had not regarded it in that light before. I saw it as an example of a well-attested tradition in fantastical science fictional art . . .'

'You have been too *close* to all this material, Soop,' Jeunet said. 'Cut off from the real world for too long. Let me ask you: who is the creator of this artwork?'

'It,' said Soop, sweating now. 'It is sometimes attributed to a man called Nasa. But then again, Nasa appears in the story as the organisation that sponsors Armstrong's extraordinary voyage, so that might be a mistake – that happens sometimes, in the case of an anonymous tale, a character from the stories gets misidentified as the author.'

'Nasa is an acronym.'

'Yes, yes,' agreed Soop.

'You know what it stands for?'

'Well, there are several theories. Personally I take it to be a reference to the Jew Verne. His moon adventure was organised by the American National Gun Club. The Armstrong story has very many similarities with that earlier story – I take it Nasa is the same organisation, perhaps the National Association for Shooting Artillery.'

'And if,' said Jeunet with a grim face, 'I were to tell you that it stands for *Never Accept the Strong Arm*? If I were to tell you that it is a *real* organisation, in the world today, dedicated to subversive revolutionary action against the Man of the Strong Arm?'

'No!' gasped Soop.

'You see now *why* this story is proscribed?'

'Of course! I'm . . . I'm *horrified* at my error . . .'

At this point the stranger in the clearing spoke out. 'That's not why the story is proscribed,' she said.

Soop's poor brain was starting to find everything becoming too much. 'What? What's that?'

'Strong-Arm has a good reason for keeping this story secret,' she said, in an unquavery voice. 'But that's not it.'

'Why then?'

'Don't be foolish,' snapped Jeunet. 'I have told you the reason.'

'You are a liar,' she said.

But this really was going too far. Jeunet stepped quickly from the doorway and strode out into the little clearing. 'You are extraordinarily bold,' he said. 'Considering that you are about to die, it is almost impressive. But enough now.'

It took a moment for Soop's bewildered brain to process what happened next. There was the sound of a snake. No, there was no snake. Jeunet had pulled a slender wand from his belt. Soop didn't know that he had such a truncheon on his person, except that there it was. But it wasn't a wand, it was an arrow shaft. And it hadn't been pulled from his belt, it was sticking out of his hip. Jeunet gave voice to a sort of strangled yell, something like a cough, and his right elbow jerked out, flapped back, jerked out. He began to reach round with his left hand, and there was another hiss. This time Soop saw the arrow strike home, thudding audibly into Jeunet's hip and digging out a little spurt of blood that fell as a twisting cord that broke into beads and droplets before it reached the grass. This second arrow knocked Jeunet leftward and he hopped on his left leg to keep his balance. His left hand had reached his gun now, but for some reason he didn't seem to be able to unholster it. He fumbled at the weapon a little and it came away from its hook, but instead of falling into his hand it only slid a little way along the shaft of the arrow.

The female started screaming.

Soop saw, with abrupt understanding, that the second arrow had struck home directly *through* the trigger guard, and had pinned the pistol to Jeunet's hip. The first arrow had nailed Jeunet's right hand to his flank.

The female was not screaming; she was whooping. A second individual, another female, emerged from the foliage, holding her bow before her, an arrow cocked. She came round from the right to face Jeunet directly.

'Soop,' he growled. 'Soop – now. Now!' He meant, *Soop, get your pistoletta out.* Soop's mind buckled, stretched with astonishment, and snapped back into normality. He grabbed his weapon.

The second female fired an arrow straight into Jeunet's stomach where it buried a third of its length in his flesh. With startling rapidity she drew a new arrow from a pouch at her side and cocked it. She had pulled the bowstring back even before Jeunet had hit the ground – he slumped down, and fell heavily on his rear, to end up sitting on the grass with three arrows in him.

Soop raised his pistoletta. It was clear that he should first shoot the arrow-woman, and then the other. But the fact that there were two of them put a moment of uncertainty into his aim. What if the first had a concealed weapon – a knife, say? Should he shoot her first and the other after?

Then he was aware of a sudden, violent pain in his elbow. He looked down. It had been pierced by an arrow. The dart had entered obliquely on the outside of the arm, passed straight through the muscle and bone and emerged behind just at that place where the bicep joins the end of the humerus. Actually seeing this wound with his eyes intensified the agony. A huge, fierce pain leapt upon his body with malign completeness, most intense at the site of the wound. Worse, it possessed a disorienting, counterintuitive quality; instead of ebbing away from a point of initial severity, it seemed merely to accumulate upon itself, to grow more fierce as the seconds passed.

Jeunet rasped from below him. 'You fool, Soop.' There was a wet, grinding quality to his voice. His breathing had taken on an asthmatic resonance. 'You idiot.'

Soop tried to move his arm, not to shoot his pistoletta, although that, clearly, would have been a good idea; but only from animal instinct, from a revulsion at the sight of the arrow piercing his flesh. The muscles twitched. The surface of his bones scraped against the shaft of the arrow as the joint attempted, without success, to uncurl. This made the pain assume perfectly intolerable proportions. Soop wailed, a vibrato high-pitched squealing over which he had no control at all.

There was a whomp, a punch to his gut, and he sat hard down on the grass next to Jeunet. For a moment he was aware only of the pain at his elbow, and the concussion on his rear-end of the tumble. Only after he saw that a second arrow had passed through his right hand and bedded itself in the meat of his stomach, just below the ribs, did he begin to feel the sensations of the new wound. His hand flared, the split bone in the palm radiating shards of agony down each finger and hard up the wrist. It was quite impossible to move the hand. It was already pinned to his gut like a butterfly to a board. He could not maintain a grip upon his pistoletta, but neither could he drop it; the weight of its stock rotated it about his trigger finger so that the barrel now pointed up at his chin.

He tried to take a breath to scream aloud with pain, but the action of his diaphragm and the fluid motion of his belly jarred against the arrow-point buried there, and a new intensity of pain scorched with fearful inevitability in his solar plexus. He would have thought his nervous system was already transmitting as much pain as it was capable of; but this new agony intensified the sensation to a new level. Unable to scream, he gasped, drew a shallow breath and let it out again in a wheeze of distress.

'Idiot,' said Jeunet beside him with a perfect, complete contempt.

The first female, the one without the bow, was crouching in front of Jeunet. She was carrying a weapon, Soop saw. A large knife. Each tiny smile-shaped serration on its blade bit into air in a way that was, somehow, connected to Soop's own nervous system. She jabbed the blade forward, towards Jeunet's stomach, and the mere motion somehow transferred pain through the air to the triple node of agony in Soop's own body. Elbow and hand and stomach, each adding their hurt to the two others, forcing acid through every nerve channel that Soop possessed. His vision was blanching out. His head buzzed. Oh, it was painful.

'Let go with your finger,' the female with the knife was saying to Jeunet, 'or I *will* just cut the finger off.'

'You don't think,' Jeunet rasped, 'that I'm trying?'

'Nazdh dra'gh dijit,' said the archer, the arrow in her bow aimed at Soop's head, Soop's poor, dizzy, pain-stunned head.

The first stranger answered in English, 'But it's snagged in the trigger guard.'

The archer said something rapidly in her barbarous tongue.

'Oh, I don't know,' and she turned back to Jeunet. 'Cutting your finger off wouldn't make *you* pass out. Big strong man like you?'

'I am not,' wheezed Jeunet. 'Afraid. Of you.'

'I'll reprogram your pistol now,' the archer said to Jeunet. Her accent was more pronounced that the first stranger's, so much so that it was hard to follow what she was saying.

'You,' said Jeunet. 'Can't.'

'If you are alive,' said the archer, releasing the tension in her bowstring slowly, and then dropping easily to her haunches in front of him, 'then I can.'

'The pistol,' wailed Soop, the pressure of his pain and the terrible realisation of what the females were about almost overwhelming him. He felt like a child. He felt the desperate need for somebody strong to come in and help him – to swaddle him. To make the pain go away. To save him. Over his head the bitterns moved through their element, slowly, sadly, entirely indifferent to his sufferings.

The archer placed her bow on the grass and started gabbling something incomprehensible.

'My friend,' said the first stranger, coming over to Soop now with her knife, 'wanted to shoot you both in the throat, right at the beginning. That was *her* plan. She says that you would have stayed alive long enough for us to get useful imprints. I was not so sure. My way was riskier. I was beginning to think that *he*—' Soop tried to look at Jeunet, but moving his neck tugged on the arrow in his gut. He could just see the other man, out of the corner of his eye. The archer-female had somehow got the pistol free from Jeunet's hand, and drew it gently along the length of the shaft of the arrow. '—would just kill me from the doorway, that Aliss wouldn't get a clear shot at him. It was a *frightening* thing, I don't mind telling you.'

The first female brought something from her purse, a small black tube, and pressed it against Soop's right eye. 'Uhh!' he gasped. 'Ah! Ah! Uh! Uh!'

'And there are *good* reasons,' said the stranger, stowing the tube away again in her purse, 'why Strong-Arm wants to keep certain stories prohibited. It just so happens that they're not the reasons *he* gave you.'

'Don't listen,' Jeunet gasped. 'To them. Soop.'

But Soop couldn't think about that; couldn't concentrate on that. His pain was the entire horizon of his thoughts now. These females moved like spectres through the fog of his agony, performing their precisely choreographed actions, a sort of callous ballet. Soop's pain was so entire a thing he found it hard to imagine that there had ever been a time when agony had not squatted inside him, twisting his nerves, shredding his mind.

'Stories are important,' the stranger was saying. 'But perhaps they are not enough by themselves. Tyrants like to control what sorts of stories are told,' she was saying, as she rolled a small block, a plastic-feeling something, over Soop's fingertips, one, two, three, four. 'Of course they do. Celebrations of the heroism of tyranny.' She pressed the block against his right thumb. 'But, you see, the story of Armstrong is a *different* sort of story. A story worth celebrating. You, your leader believes, what? That a strong man's gotta know his limitations? This isn't a story about safe little impossibilities.'

'Science *fiction*,' barked Jeunet, in a desperate voice.

'Science fiction,' repeated the female, and her flat delivery and accented English made it impossible to tell what she meant by this. 'Anyway, *of* the various ways of getting different stories into circulation, alternative stories . . . well *of* the various ways, pistols have a certain . . .' She trailed off.

'You'll not,' Jeunet said, speaking slowly and strenuously. 'You'll not. Decode the. Decode the.'

'Man,' said the female, 'we certainly can. You want to worry what we're going to do *after* we've reset them.'

'Tzent'u!' cried the archer, snatching up her bow and drawing the string. She was aiming in through the open door.

'Relax,' said the other one. She added something in her native tongue.

Soop tried to turn his head, to see what they were looking at in the doorway, but the action tightened the skin at his neck, which pulled on the skin of his torso and ground further snaps and jags of pain from the arrow in his gut. He was crying freely now, water simply oozing from his eyes and slicking his cheeks. Tears just pouring out of him, as if his head were a cracked pitcher. This made vision blurry, framed as his line of sight was by the sparkles and little leaps of bodily agony. He thought he saw one of the women in the doorway. It was definitely one of the women. She threw up her gloved hands and scurried back inside.

'It's only one of their women,' said the first female, in a contemptuous tone.

The archer spoke hurriedly.

'Yes,' said the other. 'Yes. We're done here anyway.'

They were on their feet, and Soop's pistoletta and, much worse than that, Jeunet's pistol were in their purses, and in a moment they had vanished into the jungle.

The quiet that occupied the clearing afterwards had the tangible quality of enormous, persistent pain stitched into its insect under-throb. The melodic booms from the distant bitterns echoed along Soop's nerves. He tried his very best not to move; to take the shallowest of breaths, not to sway, not to move anything that would cause the slightest friction between his flesh and the shafts of the two arrows that were in him. The dry, pulling sound of Jeunet's breathing was lessening; the spaces between breaths growing longer, his life force marking a sort of diminuendo. The green itself, the mere colour, the colour by itself, seemed somehow to detach itself from the leaves and, in some peculiar manner, to stain Soop's mind, to give his impossibly extended physical suffering a chromatic focus. He became aware that his trousers were sodden, and panic at the thought that he had wet himself – disgraced himself – like a child – made his heart beat faster, which in turn pushed blood through bulging veins and squeezed a new peak of agony from his wounds. But he had not pissed himself. It was blood from his stomach that had flowed down there. The air felt thin in his mouth. Everything was slower. Jeunet drew in a pained breath, and breathed out roughly. There was a long pause. Then Jeunet drew in another breath and didn't let it out. Colours tinkled in Soop's eyes. Pain was unlike sound. If his pain were a symphony then the cacophonous crashing of his elbow, his hand, his stomach, would drown out all other sensation. But in fact, and despite the overwhelming nature of those sensations, he was also aware of sweat trickling into his eye. He was aware of a tickling sensation on his hand and up his arm, where ants from the grass had crawled up to investigate the site of the trauma.

He didn't want to look at that. He rolled his eyes upward, at the sky, and its patch of blue was almost a relief from the agony of green. There was the moon. He could see the moon, round as a coin. That insubstantial way the moon looks in the afternoon sky, as if it is an image projected upon a screen rather than a solid island of rock amongst the waveless blue of its idiom. Moon, he thought. Moon, moon, moon. It didn't look like an eye. He couldn't understand people who thought it looked like an eye. It was rather a sort of lid, the texture of its iron pitted and stained with long use, on the manhole of existence. The lid sat at the top of a tall blue shaft with impossibly smooth sides. It was hot. He was intensely aware of the heat in the air, the jungle stench, the noise, and infiltrated into every element he was aware of his pain. It was his pain, most of all, that pinned him to the mud. He was broken. Moon, he thought, it's gone wrong.

To his left he sensed movement. Women had come out of the doorway, and with them came Heston. They must have woken him from his sleep. He wouldn't, Soop thought, be happy about that. He didn't like being woken from his siesta. On the other hand, and considering the circumstances they were in, being woken from his nap was really the least of his worries now.

'Heston!' Soop rasped. 'Heston, we have a problem.'

Wonder: a Story in Two

1. Hieronimo

His father taught him regular carpentry first, and here the essence was to achieve straightness in planing and sawing, plumb timbered lines and solid right-angles. But then father showed him the deeper mysteries of his craft. His beard was big and black, and always sprinkled with the white stars and dots of sawdust. His smell, when he embraced his son, was partly old sweat and reek, like their goats, and partly sap and wood dust and cleanness; a mixture of foul and fair uniquely his own. 'Any fool can be a regular carpenter,' he told his son. 'It takes a special skill to be a wheelwright.' Straight lines are easy, he said, but curves are hard. He showed Hieronimo how to press layers of wood, and how to glue strips together with hoof-glue, and then how to soak the spar, and set in the frame. He explained how wood is stubborn, more stubborn than donkeys, and how it yearns to stretch itself flat again; and that therefore it needs be set a long time in the frame before its will is broken and it agrees to stay curved.

He lived with his father. Their house and the workshop were behind the church. Hieronimo's mother was with the angels. Regarding this mysterious location Hieronimo's father could not be induced to be more specific, though the lad nagged at him. '*Where* are the angels? Are they nearby?'

'They are in the sky,' snapped his father, and told him to clean out the goats.

School had been in the church. The priest was even less patient with questions about angels than was Hieronimo's father, and smacked Hieronimo's forehead against the wooden edge of the stall. But he was thirteen now and the need for schooling had long since ceased.

From time to time he would stare at the sky, examine it as carefully as he could. Sometimes he would climb the hill on the edge of the town, and look back across the regularly tiled rooftops, and the irregularly tiled spread of more distant fields, and the lake, shining like a stretch of wet leather. From up here the sky occupied a greater proportion of what could be seen. What was the secret of the shapes clouds took, sometimes as white and sharp-edged as eggs, sometimes great torn masses of shred and mist? The sun went into hiding every evening, like Tomas Drunk, who hid in the ditch when the priest passed. What was it in the sky that was worth hiding from?

One day Josef Fisherman, having trawled an unusually large catch in the lake, persuaded father to buy more fish than he normally would. They ate a baked fish that evening, and they salted some in the larder, but the rest father nailed to the shed wall to dry in the wind. For some reason, however, the fish did not dry properly; and when Hieronimo checked them next they had taken rot. When father pulled them from their nails and threw them to the ground one fish broke, and a mass of maggots squirmed from the rip. Hieronimo did not like the look of it. He wished not to think about it, and yet he could not stop thinking about it.

The War, reports of which were a mainstay of town gossip, grew more furious. There was talk of a great battle, only some two-score leagues away. The great War. And then one day two horsemen pulled their horses up outside the yard fence, and looked down upon Hieronimo and his father standing in the yard. Hieronimo rarely saw horses. The sheer size of them oppressed him. He could not take his eyes from their teeth, the cavernous holes of their nostrils, the way they chewed and chewed at the bar of iron in their mouths as if taking sustenance from it. The patches of writhing foam at the corner of their mouths reminded him of the maggots from the fish.

'You're the wheelwright? My captain has carts need mending.'

'I'll be happy,' said father, 'to undertake the work.'

'Best come with us then.'

'Better still, you should leave me here. For how can I make wheels away from my workshop?'

The first soldier put his hand to his belt, and laid his fingers upon his undrawn sword hilt, so that Hieronimo understood in a terrible flash that he might kill father for such insolence. But instead the soldier said, 'You'll come with me, living, half-alive or dead.'

So father went away, walking between the horsemen, and the last Hieronimo saw before they rounded the corner was him receiving a knock between the shoulder from a horsewhip, to encourage him to run.

Hieronimo sat down where he was, in the yard, and did not move. People passing saw him and called to him to ask what had happened, but he said nothing. Eventually Elsa came bustling up the road and took pity upon him, nudging him inside and giving him some supper.

That night he sat outside, hoping his father would return. He watched the sky. The moon was full like a round stone. It was the colour of ash. He pondered the relationship between the moon and the stars, and wondered if they had broken out of the body of the moon, as maggots perhaps, spilling from there across the sky. Perhaps every time the moon waned it was a breach in its body and more stars spilled out. It would explain why there were so many. He thought of the sun. There were, he saw, three bodies in the sky: the moon, and the sun, and his mother. The angels he did not figure. They were not permanent fixtures, as his mother was. They were like the clouds, perhaps.

Two days later his father came ambling back into town, his left eye bruised as black as his beard. He said nothing of his time away. He simply went into the house and took some bread and beer, and picked up his plane as if nothing had happened. Hieronimo asked, and asked, but got no answer.

That night, as they ate together, father said gruffly, 'We need to teach you how to bend the wood. Anything could happen. You're a man now, and should be ready to take over things if I go.'

Hieronimo replied, first, because his pride was hurt, 'I know how to bend the wood.' But then he added, quickly, 'And what do you mean, go?'

'Nothing lasts forever,' said his father.

'Going where?'

This made him roar. 'I'm not going anywhere! Why do you chatter so? You're like a woman! Always questioning and nagging! I'm not going anywhere!' It was a long time before his temper cooled. Then he said, 'But everybody dies sometime. We all owe death a debt, and I'll have to repay mine sometime, just as your mother did.'

Usually Hieronimo would fall silent when his father lost his temper. But the mention of his mother emboldened him. 'Sunday, the priest said Jesus beat death in a great battle, like the battle the soldiers are fighting in, and that because of that we need not die.'

'He did that,' father agreed, in a lower voice. 'But it was in another country, far from here.' He went to the barrel and tapped himself another mug of beer. Then he sat down and drank it. His son watched him. 'Far from here,' he repeated. 'A long way away.'

'If we go to that other country,' Hieronimo asked, 'will we not die?'

'Everything dies.'

'Why?'

'It's just the stubbornness of things,' said father.

'The way the wood is stubborn?'

'You ask too many questions,' growled his father. 'Stop it, or I'll take a hammer to your head and knock all the questions out of it.'

Of course Hieronimo was quiet after that, and sat there chewing his heel of bread and drinking the last of his own beer in small sips.

In the morning there was work to do. The sun came up swift

and bright, and licked the sky clean of clouds. Hieronimo helped his father make a pole by turning the wheel of the lathe, exactly as he had been taught, with a forceful, unchanging motion, so that the lathe turned at a regular pace and sharp edges of the wood could be knocked away evenly. It was hard labour, and made his arms ache. Mid-morning he went outside to rest a little, and took a drink from the well.

A horseman came up the street and stopped at their gate. Hieronimo could not tell if it was the same horseman who had come before, because on that occasion his attention had been entirely taken by the horse, and the rider had been nothing more than a shadow of menace. Hieronimo could see it was not the same horse.

'What's your name?' asked the horseman.

'Hieronimo.' His stomach was chewing at itself in fear, and his voice piped.

'How old are you?'

'Thirteen.'

'You're a good, strong-looking lad,' said the horseman. 'I'll tell you something. I am a soldier of the King. He is always looking for soldiers. He'd like it if you came to fight for him.'

'I need to stay and help my father,' said Hieronimo, blinking.

'Of course you do. Is your father about?'

'He's inside. Do you want a wheel? Shall I fetch him?'

'In a minute, lad. Tell me first: where's your mother? I'll bet she's a beauty.'

'She's with the angels.'

'Ah.' The horse chewed and chewed at its indigestible meal of metal. 'I met them once, too,' said the soldier. 'The angels, I mean.'

Hieronimo's curiosity was fiercer than his fear. 'Where did you meet them?'

'It was in Hamburg, since you ask. They live there, in a large house, right in the middle of the town.'

'Is Hamburg in the Holy Land?'

The soldier beamed at him. His face was broad, and his skin

was very white indeed. His moustache completely filled his upper lip, and curved at the ends. He wore a cocked hat much bluer than the sky. 'Do you know what coneflower looks like?' he asked.

'Of course. It grows on the hills round here.'

'When I met the angels they made me a special tea out of coneflower petals, and I drank it. Before I drank it they looked like ordinary women. Afterwards I saw them as they truly were, angels.'

'Did you speak with them?' Hieronimo asked, eagerly.

'I did indeed.'

'Perhaps you met my mother?'

The soldier beamed again. 'Fetch your father, lad. I have business with him.'

Hieronimo ran inside calling for his father. 'A gentleman is here, father,' he called out, 'and he says he has met mother.' Had he said, *a soldier is here, father, and is asking for you*, then perhaps his father would not have come – might, say, have slipped out the back and gone down to the lake, or run to his brother-in-law's farm, four leagues away. But instead Hieronimo said, 'A gentleman is here, father, and he says he has met mother.'

'What's that?' father boomed, and came striding from the back of the house, and through the workshop and out into the yard. He stopped dead. The soldier, still on horseback, was aiming a pistol at his chest. It took Hieronimo long seconds to understand what was happening.

His father stood with his arms at his side, and drew in a long breath, and breathed it out again. When he spoke it was in a deep, clear voice. He said, 'I'll be more use to you alive, as a wheelwright. The army always needs wheels.'

'It needs discipline even more than it needs wheels,' said the soldier.

Hieronimo took a step forward, filled with the need to say something, to try and defuse, or more simply to understand this sudden and terrible situation. But he did not know what to say. His left foot went forward and touched the dirt. At the very moment Hieronimo's foot touched the ground the soldier's pistol discharged. It made a noise like a very great thing being suddenly broken, and it conjured from its end a white cloud right there, in the air, down near the ground, a cloud that immediately began moving, as clouds in the high-sky do, drifting away. The noise was so loud it made all the portions and members of Hieronimo's body jerk in unison. He leapt a little way in the air. His father stumbled backwards and fell on his back on the ground. He lay. Father lay motionless, and there was a dint in the middle of his chest, such as a heavy iron hammer might make on soft, new wood; and straight away the dint filled with blood, and the blood poured out of the wound and pooled the ground, and the pool grew.

The noise had chucked a great many squawking birds into the sky.

The horseman had sheathed his pistol, and was saying something, but Hieronimo's ears were not working. Likely they had been deadened by the sudden noise. The man touched his bonnet, and nodded, and spoke some more, and this time Hieronimo heard, 'in a day or two, lad, which'll be time enough to see you again.' And he turned his horse and rode away.

The sound of the gunshot, of course, brought people from all the houses around. Some were silent, and some whispered or muttered. A woman stuffed her apron into her mouth. Hieronimo was bustled up in a storm of neighbourly activity. People clutched him to them, and cried, or crossed themselves. Quite a large crowd assembled in the road. His father's body was wrapped and carried to the churchyard, and the soil of the yard where he had bled was dug and taken away in a cart to be dumped in the lake. Hieronimo was himself taken to Elsa's house, and Elsa made much of him. Her husband, a sharp-nosed, bald-headed cobbler and glover, was there too, but didn't say anything. Elsa said, 'Hieronimo, you may stay with us for some days, if you choose, at least until your father is properly buried.' And Elsa's husband said, 'He's not a child, Elsa, and you oughtn't to coddle him as one.' But then he added, 'I'm sorry though. Your father was a good man.'

'He's with your mother now, at any rate,' said Elsa.

Jacob Fisherman came in and gave Hieronimo a fish, wrapped in leaves and tied with string. 'I've cooked it,' he said. 'You can eat it when you like.'

Hieronimo nodded, and clutched the parcel to his stomach, but didn't say anything.

By now it was late afternoon, and the whole town was alive with chatter about what had happened. The beadle didn't come, though, and people said he had more sense than to poke his nose into military affairs. Elsa's husband excused himself, but he had shoes to make that would not make themselves. Elsa herself went over to Marta's to talk about what happened. Hieronimo sat in their house with the fish on his lap. Some of its juice had come out and dirtied his breeches, but he did not think of that. Instead he got up and walked up the street to the house. It was, as several people had told him during the course of the afternoon, his own house now. He walked across the yard. The digging up of the padded-down mud had thrown up worms, and the goats were rummaging in the dirt for them, feeding on the spot where his father had died.

A clamour of wings above his head, like a spun lathe, and three pigeons flustered through the air to land on the roof.

He went inside and put the fish in the larder. Then he took down his father's cloak – a little too large for him, but not too bad a fit – and his father's walking stick. He paused only long enough to fill a leather bottle with water from the well, and to tuck some bread in his pouch, and then he set out.

By the time he had climbed the hill the sun was setting, and the whole town – the whole of the land – was steeped in the colour of blood. The horizon hardly stirred, although you might think it would shiver with fear at the approach of something as blinding and roasting as the sun. Its stillness was admirable. There was clover in amongst the grass at Hieronimo's feet. There were sheep on the hill, which hurried away in a mass as Hieronimo passed. He made his way to the single tall tree. The sky was scarlet and purple near the sun, and directly above him it was russet-yellow like a deer's back, and away towards the east it was blue-black. The brightest stars were just becoming visible, and the moon was very clear, an arc of moon, like the curve of white at the bed of Hieronimo's thumb. The moon was his father, whose beard would grow larger and larger, black as the night sky, until, after a month, he might shave it all off with his own razor, revealing the large-chinned, pockmarked white of his face underneath it. The sun was his mother, whose face could not be seen, because to look at it was to dazzle the eyes. He was – was. He was still alive.

He sat himself down, wrapping the cloak more tightly around him. This was a spot where coneflower grew. The sheep would eat most things, including thistles, but not these. He pulled up a stem of it and plucked the petals one by one and crunched them in his mouth. They tasted sour, like slate, or like rotten water, but he chewed anyway. He thought about his father. He tried to remember him smiling, or laughing, or happy, but could not. He chewed another petal. He could remember his father's beard, but nothing of his face.

He chewed another petal.

The stars were coming out now, clustering together, pricking out like tears. Hieronimo was not crying. He considered this. He ought to weep. He thought of the word, orphan, and then he said the word aloud, and said it again, but it didn't move him. It was, perhaps, that he knew his father to be a stubborn man, far too stubborn to die so quickly. Dying for him would be a drawn-out process, many days in the frame being bent out of life, and him struggling all the time. Consequently his father was not dead. It might, Hieronimo conceded, be that he was in the *process* of dying, for had he not said as much? But that was surely different to being dead. And again it was a matter of appearances and reality. If his father appeared dead, it might be that he, Hieronimo, was not attending carefully enough to the reality. He had been beaten, many times, for not divining the truth behind the appearance of things. He had often been called fool, and, he thought, rightly enough.

The stars were very large, now, and were all about him. There was a glory about the face of the setting sun, seven spires of flame, and a kindly face looking out of it. And the stars were buzzing at his ears and eyes, like bees, honeyed bees; six-pointed, not seven, but that was because they were younger than the sun and not as beautifully adorned. Hieronimo spat half-chewed fragments of petal onto the grass. The inside of his mouth was powerfully sour, and he fumbled for his leather bottle to wash the bitterness away, but he could not seem to lay his hand upon it. The air on the hill was thickening, and folding about him, as a cloak might. There was a roaring, very loud, very near-by, and Hieronimo decided to stand up to go look for it. But he could not rouse his legs. He tried again and he seemed to strike solidity, for he fell like a drunkard. There was a curvature in the very fabric of things. Hieronimo found himself on all fours. He tried to crawl forward, but something was preventing him. He tried again, reaching out with his right hand and then, suddenly—

The sun had a face. The world was at his back. He was through the sky. He was reaching out toward—

The world is simple. Behind the world is not simple.

2. Jerie

The Kyd drive had rendered interstellar travel a possibility at last, and humanity had, by following the complex wave-form and sinusoidal unlogic of its energy-distance equation, settled many new worlds, orbiting far-distant stars. Settlement happened in banded zones, shelled like nesting spheres around the central point of the original homeworld, which still acted as a hub for travel. This was because whilst it was relatively easy, relatively *cheap*, to reach stars *forty-two* and *eighty-four* light years distant, it was forbiddingly expensive and difficult to reach stars at *twenty* or *sixty*, save by complex triangulation of three (or more) forty-light-year journeys in tangential directions – and who could be bothered with that? It was necessary, for almost everybody, to remain within a simple jump of Earth, our home and holy site. And besides, there were immense numbers of habitable worlds within the settlement zones. Only hermits and eccentrics and people who wished to live undisturbed fled to stars in the intervening zones.

Humanity spread itself to ten thousand worlds and lived unexceptional, ordinary lives. But storytellers are naturally drawn to the occasional non-standard individual. The woman convinced that immortality, or God, was hidden on a world orbiting a star in the Kyd-blank zones; the man driven to explore inhospitable places because of their very inhospitality.

Jerie was one such. I knew him as a trader, a man who accumulated money with a ferocity unusual even amongst the neo-humani. But he wanted money for one reason only: to buy a craft large enough to store fuel enough to travel further than anybody had gone before. 'We know what the *equations* say happens as the distances approach infinity with the Kyd-drive effect,' he would say. 'But equations are not the same thing as reality.' It was impossible to dissuade him from this stupidity, to say to him *beware*. He built a ship, and stocked it with fuel, and he set on his way. There was enough interest in his crazy scheme, and he did a poor enough job of security-checking his craft (for his attention was focused so intently upon the goal, the prize, the destination) that when news portals seeded the cabin with media-dust he did not purge it. Accordingly we all had access to a multiple nanofeed coverage of his voyage, or of the early stages of it at any rate. I, who knew him personally, was almost embarrassed by how unaware he seemed to be of the spies in his cabin; although afterwards it became clear that he knew about them very well, and tolerated them because he wanted a record of his departure.

And so away he went, with jumps of forty, of eighty, of one

hundred and sixty, three hundred and twenty, six hundred and forty, just as the earliest probes had done. But Jerie had been talking to people who claimed to have found ingenious mechanical solutions to the forces that had broken those probes to shivers, and he had spent an enormous amount of money on their quack-tech. The intensity of his dream had made him gullible. But what could we do? He was an adult humanus, and free to kill himself if he chose. At 10,240 light years away the media-dust began to thin, for the repeated jumps needful to draw them back to a point from where their data could be uploaded were becoming too much. By 20,480 light years away the coverage was so patchy as to lose dimensionality and colour. Here it was that Jerie revealed he had known about the media-dust all along, for he turned to the empty cabin and announced: 'People dream of travelling to the stars, but I want to go further than that; I want to see what is *behind* the stars!' Merest idiocy, of course. Impossible and suicidal. Only one media-particle was retrieved after 81,920 light years, and it showed – in a blur that rivalled the earliest photographic plate of sunlight upon a nineteenth-century church tower for inexactness – Jerie gazing through the forward portal, his right hand out touching the glass. It is likely that he survived to 163,840 light years, and possible that he survived to 327,680; but the jump to 655,360 would have ground him and his craft into atomic and subatomic fragments. Poor fool.

The sums are easily done, but sums do not capture the craziness of what he was about. In this sense at least he was correct, for mathematics, where it is easy to play with very large numbers, does not correspond to reality where travelling very large distances is overwhelmingly difficult. But assuming an unfeasible supply of fuel, and an impossibly resilient craft, it would have taken eighteen such exponential leaps until he was travelling distances that are larger than can be contained within our cosmos. Dead, long before.

So, I lived my life, and renewed it, and lived it again. I travelled far, and saw five new shells of human habitation settled, centred as all religion requires on the sacred home of God, the Earth; and I saw many many worlds in those zones filled with human off-spring, with mechas and gene-peoples. Some I visited. Most I did not. And I forgot all about Jerie, until a man I had never met before came to see me at my ranch. He did not say how he had found me, or why he had gone to the trouble of jumping back to hub and out again (for his home was Serenea in the reach of Bridgeman) just to exchange a few words with me. I was impolite enough, and suspicious enough of contamination, to request him to stay in his walker, which he did with an easy grace. He claimed to have met Jerie, but this was a name from such a long time ago that, believe it or not, I had to check with my ligeia before I could even remember whom he meant.

'It must have been long ago,' I said. 'That you met him, I mean, for he has been dead a very long time'.

'I met him in the last ten-month,' he said. 'Not long at all.'

Then I knew him for a fool, or a crank, and was ready to dismiss him. 'He told me to tell you something,' said this fellow.

'So tell me it, and go off on your own business,' I said, cross.

'He wanted me to tell you *two* things,' said this man. I pulled up a scan of the inside of his walker; but he looked just like any other person – red-brown skin, dark-cut hair, shining eyes, muscles. There seemed to be no hostile dot-tech or contaminants, but I sensed something *wrong* about him, or his message, and I remained suspicious.

'Will they take long in the telling, these two things?' I asked, growing more crotchety.

'Not long at all,' he said, 'and then I shall go back.'

'Do so, then.'

'First,' said the stranger, his eyes smiling, 'was that he'll see you soon, that he is looking forward to meeting you again after all this time.'

'By that,' I said rashly, 'I know you a liar.' He seemed, however, not to take offence at this. 'Go on,' I said, eventually.

'Tell me the second thing, so that you can go on your way and leave me in peace.'

'The second thing,' he said, 'is this:'

My words shall still you, motionless as stone in sheerest wonder,
And I shall beat upon your mind, and break it all in sunder

That caused me to stop and breathe deep. 'Where did you meet him?' I asked the stranger. 'What is your name?' I asked the stranger. 'What did he look like when you saw him? What did he tell you of his travels? Stranger—' I said. But he had already sealed his walker from all surveillance and was going away, and my questions went unanswered. I have been going about my business ever since, and every day I wake and think to myself: *Will it be today that I meet Jerie again?*

I asked myself the same question this very morning.

Commentary

The starting point for the first of these two linked stories was the illustration known as the 'Flammarion woodcut', a striking and, I think, haunting image that has been widely reproduced. Originally it was believed to be an authentic medieval woodcut, but it was subsequently discovered to be a much later pastiche of earlier visual styles, probably from the nineteenth century – its earliest recorded appearance was in an 1888 book by French astronomer Camille Flammarion.[1] But rather than undermining the power of the image, its ersatz, pastiche quality in fact focuses its power: it is about the past rather than embodying the past, and amounts to a piece of historical fiction. My story 'Hieronimo' glosses the picture, building on visual elements from within it: an ordinary man who is dressed for a long journey, but who has, to his astonishment, broken through the sky to see the hidden workings of the world. That he sees a cosmos defined by giant wheels and circles provides one of the thematic structures for the tale; the odd, interlocking double cartwheel object in the top-left hand corner of the image suggested to me that he might be a wainwright or wheelwright. The world behind him is medieval, and probably Central European.

What the 'Flammarion woodcut' emblematises, in fact, is that central aspect of science fictional writing: *conceptual breakthrough*. John Clute and Peter Nicholl's standard critical reference work for science fiction stresses the centrality of this trope to the genre: 'of all the forms which the quest for knowledge takes in modern sf, by far the most important, in terms of both the quality and the quantity of the work that dramatises it, is conceptual breakthrough.'[2] Clute and Nicholls go on to discuss many examples

[1] Daniel Boorstein, *The Discoverers: A History Of Man's Search To Know His World And Himself* (New York: Random House 1983), 7.
[2] John Clute and Peter Nicholls (eds), *The Encyclopedia of Science Fiction* (London: Orbit 1993), 254.

from SF – Arthur C Clarke's classic novel *Childhood's End* (1953) and Stanley Kubrick's 1968 film *2001: A Space Odyssey* are two of the most famous – stories of characters who break out of conventional reality altogether. But they also mention non-genre work, such as Samuel Johnson's *Rasselas* (1759), in which the hero, who has grown up in a valley-kingdom in Abyssinia, travels into the wider world. This encounter with radical otherness, quite as much as the search for knowledge, defines what science fiction is; and otherness need not be located in the future, or even far away.

James Holden and Simon King make this point in their critical study of the conceptual breakthrough: 'We think we are travelling out there, boldly going to a final frontier; actually we are always returning home, and the final frontiers are those which define our existences (birth, death, and the process of conceptualisation in between) rather than any external architecture of the universe.'[3] The great dome in which are embedded the stars turns out to be the inside curve of our own craniums. The breakthrough – *Star Trek*'s 'final frontier' – has more to do with the boundaries that hem our mundane existences. 'Hieronimo' needed, therefore, to be a story that positioned itself on the boundary between radically different modes. It is focalised through the consciousness of an observant but not canny 13-year old, a figure deliberately poised between childhood and adulthood. The main narrative event in the text is the death of the protagonist's father; and to foreground the radical disruption entailed in passing from life to death, it needed to be a violent death. Finally the dreamy Hieronimo is fascinated by the sky, and speculates on the relationship between that aerial, cosmic world and the mundane world he inhabits. The ending of the story, though oblique, is designed to take the reader back, reflexively, to the image printed at the head of the narrative – the circle theme works itself out formally as well as on the level of content – to enact the process of breaking through, a gesture in

[3] James Holden and Simon King, *Conceptual Breakthrough: Two Experiments in SF Criticism* (Inkerman Press 2007).

Pied

A commercial excavation in Poland broke inadvertently upon the cavern of the *Sang-Mangeant* – the Santamanga, we called them, though how far from saintly they were! A light that blinds you with the many flakes of its brightness. Tens of thousands of Santamanga, revealed in a tangle of limbs in the darkness, and breaking out howling upon the earth. They were like wasps; they were like scorpions and rats; the vampire of legend, only real, and bitter in their hunger for our lives.

They spread across Europe and into Russia, devouring all they encountered, and they spared nobody. Pale faces; their mouths took colour from their meals. They were always hungry. Daylight hurt them as a hailstorm might, but it did not kill them. And we said: 'These are monsters from storybooks,' because we hoped that storybook remedies might redeem us. But the old ways did not stem their advance; for it took too much time to deploy them, and by the time we had destroyed one of the Santamanga a dozen more humans had fallen victim to the plague. They swarmed at night by the millions, and until first light touched the bell-towers and slanted roofs they were everywhere. The sunset mocked our spilt blood.

The governments tried to handle the situation as governments do, with armies and weapons and assaults from land and sky. They made new guns, and primed them with projectiles filled with an ingenious American gel – irradiated with ultraviolet light and luminous. It was effective up to a point, but it was not cheap; each bullet cost $1750, and myriad bullets were fired, and dozens needed to strike the target before they were disabled. By the time the first marines were airlifted in, the plague had spread so far that it could no longer be contained by so complicated and costly an approach. Scorch the Santamanga with whatever fires and bombs you liked, they did not die: still they roamed on, and their burns healed. Shoot them with ordinary bullets and they roared and rushed you and tore your rifle from your hands, your hands from your arms. The new UV-bullets were not in sufficient supply. Then there was a dispute between the American factories that produced them and the American government about payment, or tax irregularities, or something, and the supply was halted.

So it was that we found ourselves, suddenly, on the edge of annihilation.

Who saved us? Who but *he*?

He lived in a compound in central Spain, where the hills are polished to indigo by the heat of the sun, where the cactus grow and where palmtrees scrum together around waterholes. There were conflicting stories about how long he had been alive.

The representatives of seven nations came to supplicate him, and he promised to rid the world of the Santamanga altogether if we agreed to meet his price: a trillion dollars, and the right for the territory around his compound to be recognised as a sovereign state, under his sole rule, an enclave within Spain perfectly independent of EU jurisdiction. He was promised all this, and eagerly, provided only that he rid the world of the vampires.

So he set out. He took a village priest, a humble Andalusian churchman, to bless the oceans – seven trips in a jet-plane, all in the same day, girdling the earth. And then the natural cycle of the climate became our ally. For, from the oceans, moisture evaporated upwards, holy water now, into the clouds; and from the clouds precipitated down a holy rainfall. So it was that every shower, from drizzle to monsoon, bit the flesh of the Santamanga like acid, and melted them in screams of agony. And within three months not one of them was left alive, save for a few desiccated figures dug under the sands of the Gobi desert like bugs, and growing weaker and drier by the day. For even the Santamanga needed *water*.

How the world cheered! Such celebrations! Gratitude poured upon him from a million letters and emails; he was granted awards and prizes – Nobel's Peace, the Vatican's Golden Medal, a dozen others. He did not actively refuse these honours, but neither did he travel to collect them. Simply, he waited for the fulfilment of his deal.

The governments of the world met to discuss the status of his enclave, and the discussions became protracted, for there were complicated legal discussions to be undergone. 'For was it not a *humanitarian* act?' they asked, publicly. 'How could such heroism ever be measured in terms of mere *money*?' 'And was it not an insultingly *simple* stratagem?' they asked, in private. 'Any of us might have thought of it. It cost him scarcely a few thousand dollars – and the Santamanga are destroyed now. Why should we waste trillions on this one individual?'

He pressed for payment of his fee, and the governments deferred payment on the grounds that they needed the money for reconstruction of Asia and Europe, which had been ravaged by the vampires; and then they held out on the grounds of various legal technicalities; and then on the grounds that payment should be in terms of release from duties of tax and of educational and cultural credits. Eventually they declined to pay him altogether, on the grounds that, legally, the Nobel prize money had constituted the first payment of reward, and that since he refused to travel to Stockholm to collect that prize he had in effect declined all remuneration for his actions.

They did not think they would need him again.

But of course they did, for something had broken in the simple functioning of the world, and evils that mankind had hitherto only seen in nightmares had become violently real. Locusts the size of bats filled the skies. Blood rained from the heavens. Much worse: corpses fought their way through the loose-packed dirt of graves and walked again, undead. They poisoned and assaulted the living, and wasted the land. They devoured people, not for nutrient – since, being dead, they needed none – but in an empty rage for destruction. No weapon could combat them. Limbs or torsos peppered with bullets meant nothing to them; as with ants, destroying their heads only made them fiercer. No holy water bothered them.

The covenant of death had been broken, it seemed.

Worse still, in Scotland, it was reported, a scientist had stitched together body parts and reanimated the corpus with a triple-modulated ionic charge. He made monster after monster, not content with assembling body-parts from human corpses, he grafted the limbs of animals onto men's torsos, or the heads of dogs and cattle onto the necks of the deceased. Not undead, but rather re-living, these creatures moved with the ferocious purpose of a new and terrible form of vitality. A dozen such beasts were made, before the creatures turned on their creator and held him down, and pulled the flesh from his bones in fist-sized chunks. Then, mad with incoherent rage and remorse, the beasts spilled into the Caledonian forests. They killed where they chanced upon people, and wrecked all they laid their hands upon.

These trials were most terrible afflictions – hundreds of thousands died, millions were overwhelmed with grief and terror. It was the end of the world, surely. It was surely the Devil himself at work amongst us. The Santamanga, that we had thought the worst, had been nothing more than malign John-Baptists, crying the way. The ultimate evil would burst, before the year ended, from Temple Mount and roll the globe into the darkness of his cloak.

No priestly exorcism had any effect upon these awful manifestations of the Last Days. No scientist could develop an effective countermeasure.

There was a popular upsurge: mass rallies, the spontaneous outpouring of the will of people all about the world. *He* had saved us before; *he* could save us again. We must pay him the money – for why hold back some sum of dollars when the alternative was the very end of the entire world? We must crawl on our bellies to ask his forgiveness.

So representatives of the superpowers, and of the five great faiths, and the world's three most beautiful movie stars, and a great delegation of the desperate travelled to central Spain. 'Forgive us!' they cried. 'We wronged you! Save us again, and we shall pay you what we owe you, and anything more that you ask of us. Can you help us?'

He met the leaders of the delegation upon the roof of his building, where the sun was hottest. The terrace garden had wilted. He stood amongst those parched plants, tall in a white linen suit, and his sunglasses were circles of swimming-pool blue. He looked over the landscape. 'I love this land,' he said, 'because it resembles unwritten parchment. But I discover that human beings, mostly, loathe the unwritten page. You must pay me forty trillion dollars, and give me the whole of the Iberian Peninsula as my fiefdom, and I will rid you of these zombies and creatures, and solve the other problems.'

Anything! Anything!

Binding contracts were signed, and witnessed, and seals were placed upon them. Everything was witnessed and transmitted and sorted. And he nodded his approval.

So this is what he did. He travelled, first, to Scotland, and was taken through the army perimeter into the castle of the murdered scientist. There he gathered together the materials to replicate the reanimating technology, which he worked for a week to master. 'It is a simple device,' he announced eventually, carrying his portable version of the reanimating machine on a strap about his shoulders.

The zombies, he said, were animated by a principle of undeath. The scientist's Frankenstein machine gave life back to dead matter. Direct the beam of the former upon the latter and positive would cancel out negative. So troops were equipped, and they tracked the undead wherever the zombies roamed; they fired the ionising blast at their chests, and the undead, made alive again, fell to the ground, for their motile principle had been cancelled. As death ends life, so life ends death.

He set up a workshop, with his own employees assembling the devices, and issued them to citizen armies. These devices were shipped to the five continents, and, individual by individual, the undead were given back life, and rendered inert.

As for the original Frankenstein creatures – hideous, terrifying – these were living still in the northern Scottish wildernesses; some had stolen boats and travelled further north, to the Polar wastes, for their life essence cried out for the chill and deserted places.

He tracked them in a small plane, himself and his second-in-command, and this is what he did: he sprayed them, when he found them, with an enzyme that dissolved away the threads stitching their body parts together. They fell into pieces.

Now, the life that had been given them could not be ungiven. It lived on in these lopped limbs and heads, but eyeless arms scrabbled to the water's edge, and eyeless legs thrashed and kicked their way there, and eyeless torsos crawled like inchworms, and all slopped under the sea, to roam the unlit ocean floors. And he gathered the severed, still-living heads into a great sack, and threw them all into the mid-ocean, with stones in their mouths.

And there were other signs of the End Times, but he addressed them.

The blood rain fell only from certain clouds, marked with ink-black striations, and these he seeded from above, using wide-winged planes, so that they rained their blood into overfished seas, where the nutrient brought forth great crops of sealife. He fished in the air with great nets and captured vast numbers of the locusts plaguing the land, and intensively farmed them, telling the world to rejoice in their coming, for beasts of such size rendered a great quantity of meat for a world starving after manifold sufferings. He established locust farms on four continents, and instead of destroying the wild swarms he tempted them into net-ceilinged valleys with choice lures, and he raised them there. Protein for the people.

'Now I must have my reward,' he said.

The Vice-President of the United States herself went to his compound to discuss the terms. 'We *will* pay you!' they said. 'We have promised! But to transfer so huge a sum in one lump would collapse the world economy – and this at a time when the population has been cut in half, and tax revenues severely depleted! Moreover, to hand over the whole of Spain would be to flout the democratic traditions of a sovereign nation! Let us pay you forty million dollars a month, every month, until the debt is repaid, and let us fund your campaign to run for election as President of Spain – such is the gratitude of the world that the Spanish people will surely vote for you.'

'This,' he said, angrily, 'is not what was agreed. Unless you pay me what you agreed, you shall make me angry.'

'But you must negotiate with us,' they said. 'We ask only that! It is the way of international relations! Negotiations, not unilateral demands, are the currency of politics. You are a world figure now. Negotiate, and we will arrive at a mutually satisfying resolution.'

But he refused their offers, and withdrew himself.

Of course the evils continued. We had merely been cutting the heads off the Hydra; we had not stabbed its heart. And its heart was the Devil himself. The land around Jerusalem became hot, and people could no longer live there; the buildings of the city crumbled to dust. The Pope himself travelled to the site to exorcise it; but no sooner had his helicopter touched down than a chasm opened in the dusty ground and swallowed it and him and he was never seen again.

The Last Days were upon us.

All eyes turned to *him* – for who could save us if he could not? But he was not to be found. He had withdrawn himself from the world. The moon turned red; wormwood and pestilence; the ground shook; the Mediterranean flooded into north Africa. The world was coming to an end. 'This is *his* retribution!' we said. 'It is because we did not pay him what was agreed! He has punished us by withholding his help.'

But then, from nowhere, and at the last moment, he reappeared. He walked into Jerusalem alone, with a small backpack, and a gasmask, and a silver suit, passed terrors and wonders. Then, watched by the world's surveillance satellites, his image broadcast on all media, he drew a hyperpentagram upon Temple Mount itself, and spoke words of unprecedented power and charm. A crack spread starfishwise, and a low thunderous noise rolled from horizon to horizon. In a steam of midges Satan himself appeared.

And our spirits sank to our bowels, for suddenly we thought: *He is calling forth the Devil personally to do his bidding.* '*This* is his punishment!' we wailed, in horrible comprehension. 'He has unleashed Satan upon us!'

But we were wrong. He had not come to destroy the world; he had come – alone – to vanquish Satan. And that is what he did.

He did not assault the Devil with swords, nor attempt to overpower him with incantations; but instead he used reason, a more powerful snare than magic (for has not Reason challenged and overcome Magic across the world today?) He talked, and the Devil listened. He told the Devil's true nature to the Devil.

This is what he said: 'We know that despair is the greatest sin. We both know that you, Satan, the fount and superfluity of wickedness, are the universe's greatest sinner. It follows that you are the most despairing creature the cosmos has ever known.'

And the Devil groaned, as if, at last, somebody had plumbed the depths of his being; as if finally somebody had understood – he, Satan, the great depressive. He moaned with pitiful recognition. And he hurled himself downward, seeping through the cracks and plunging through the eddies of magma to the core of the earth, its dense metal core, where he lies to this day, like a depressed man who cannot rise from bed, trapped and impotent in his own misery.

Our saviour took to his feet and walked out of ruined Jerusalem.

'Look upon this,' he said, to the whole of the world. 'He was your child and I have taken him from you.' And *this*, although we did not realise it at first, was his revenge. It was this action that was his punishment.

At first we held our breaths, and barely believed it. Satan himself had been defeated, and we could only rejoice.

The United Nations voted him formal thanks. But he refused all money, or reward, and slipped away from the world. Who knows where he has gone?

In a year we had rebuilt many of the world's broken structures. With a decade there was a spike in the birth rate, as we began to replenish the world with a new generation. For Satan was gone, and the skies no longer rained blood, nor did locusts swarm, or the Santamanga afflict us, or the zombies or the Frankenstein beasts. All that was magical passed away from the world.

There is an inertia in the ways of the world. Many people continued religious practice and ritual. But the destruction of Satan had immobilised God, of whom the Devil is a portion. At a stroke all the faiths of the world were emptied of meaning. Over time most people abandoned temples and churches, and lived in a purely material cosmos. For those of us, such as I myself, who had lived through the horrors of the last era of the supernatural, this was a blessing. But a new generation was born, without the savour of transcendental meaning, who came into the world as mere sophisticated automata. There is no light in their eyes – when I talk with them, they talk logic and sufficiency, and the world has grown grey from their breath.

This, as we now understand, is how *he* has punished us – and punished us justly, for we promised to reward him for his actions and then we reneged on our promise. So this is what he did: he took away the causes of our suffering, and therefore he took away the wellspring of our souls. There is no God without the Devil. The world had once been pied, as all beauty is; but he removed the contrast, and he muted the colours, and we are to blame. It is no longer a pied place; it is uniform. Our children succeed us, and they are tall, and strong, and rational. But they are without spirit and without faith, and they are without the capacity for wonder. The colour has gone. I tell children today stories of the old days and they are neither enchanted nor terrified, for enchantment and terror have gone out of the universe. That is what he took away. He came to a particoloured world and left it monochrome.

On the other hand, our new world does possess a great deal of ergonomic and splendidly functional civic architecture.

Constellations

The starry heavens above me and the moral law within me.
Kant

1

'You know how it can be with teenagers,' said Strong-in-the-Lord.

'Teenagers,' The-Unerring-Word replied, nodding.

Strong-in-the-Lord adopted a higher, more nasal voice to speak the part of his son, 'But *why* Dad, what's *wrong* with nostrils? God made them – didn't God make them?' He shook his head, and resumed in his usual tone. 'And so on. Just wouldn't leave it alone. I said to him, God may have made them, but that's no reason to flaunt them around. God made other holes in the body – if you see what I mean. Mouths. Ani. Urethral holes. You wouldn't go about displaying those for everybody to see.'

'Which, surely, convinced him?'

'But that's what I'm *saying*,' said Strong-in-the-Lord. He slid a finger underneath his faceveil to scratch an itch on his lower lip. 'Teenagers. They're slippery as – I don't know what. Oh, he didn't agree with me. He carried on arguing. He said *There's your eyeholes, Da, you don't think* they're *obscene?*'

'I know,' said The-Unerring-Word, 'you don't really believe in it, but if I were you, I'd belt him. *Chas*tise. Sometimes you can't reason with kids like this. I mean, we love our kids, and all that, but, hey – spoil the rod. You know?'

'*Spare* the rod, Un?'

The-Undying-Word considered. 'Yeah. That. Not what I said. But whatever. The point is that you *can't reason* with *teenagers.*'

'But reason *is* the point,' urged Strong-in-the-Lord. 'Isn't it? Why deny the rational thing? God's there, in the sky, in the arrangement of the stars, in the mortal soul inside. I said to him, "Be logical, that's all I'm asking. Be logical. We cover ourselves for modesty, not for arbitrary reasons. If a hole produces faeces, that's not nice – you can't pretend it's nice. So we cover it up, modestly. It's the same with the nostrils, unless you think . . ." ' he coughed discreetly, addinged in a lower tone, 'Excuse me Un, but . . .' and carried on ' "*snot* is a pleasant thing? I don't think so. The same with mouths, unless you think somebody else's *saliva* is wholesome? Your eyes are *different*. God has plugged them already, veiled them we might say. With the eyeballs. It follows logically that we do not need to pursue modesty to the extreme of covering the eyes – they're covered already. Your mother, for instance," I said to him. "*Her* eyes are blue, and they're prettier than any faceveil I've ever seen in a shop." So he started whining, and I'm afraid I lost my temper. *I don't see why God would be upset if we showed our nostrils* and *people always used to do it* and all sorts of nonsense. I told him to shut up – I used those words. I told him people used to do many things. People used to worship pagan devils and sacrifice children, and that didn't mean they were good things to do.'

'He's not arguing, not really, Stron,' The-Unerring-Word told his friend. 'He's not interested in the reasonable case, the logical thing. He's just arguing to be difficult. Teenagers.'

'Which is exactly what I'm saying. Exactly.'

The two of them sat in silence for a while on their bench. They had finished their coffees, and each had wiped his straw with a sanctissue, and now they just sat. They were sitting out the remainder of their break.

The work was continuing day and night, and theirs was a night shift. Below them, at the foot of the hill, the machines were roaring and grinding under floodlights, cranes swinging like giant robot metronomes, diggers creeping forward on the chunky metal reel-to-reel of their tracks. Out at sea the many ships sparkled with their various glinting lights, stern and aft white, port and starboard green and red, boathouse lights creamily visible against the black water in a random, messily scribbled array of dots and gleams. But lift the eye upwards, and the splendour and the glory of the heavens were displayed. On this cloudless night, through this still air, all the stars could be seen: rank and rank, row and row – the perfectly regular and uniform spread of white stars. You could read their pattern in terms of verticals and horizontals, or you could let your eye detune the image a little and it would become a diamond-shaped pattern of diagonals intersecting diagonals, on and on, patterning the whole sky. How glorious it was, how glorious.

Strong-in-the-Lord sighed a holy sigh and brushed his gloves absently against the thighs of his pants. He stood up. 'Back to work, Un,' he said. 'Back to the great work.'

Strong-in-the-Lord had decided early in his life that he wanted to be a coastal engineer. Or, to be precise, at first he'd wanted to be a coastal architect, but a few words with his teachers had disabused him of that ambition. The architects had dull jobs, he was told. After all, coastal redesigning hardly requires architects! – or, to speak more precisely, it was *mathematics* that was the true architect. The *Divine Order* was the architect. Take a crinkled, wobbly coastline on a map, and redraw it as a straight line, or as a smooth arc; redraw this knobbly promontory as a circle. A child could do it. But the *engineers* (the teacher put awe in his voice) – oh, the engineers! They do the *actual* work! They supervise the diggers, they scour the land, or fill in the bays, or reclaim land from the sea. Work with a thousand challenges, and a thousand rewards! And all the time (the teacher's voice acquiring a misty, awestruck tone) making God's harmony and perfection prevail. 'So,' the teacher had concluded, slapping his hips with both his hands simultaneously and afterwards rubbing them together. 'So which is it to be? Architect or engineer?'

'Oh, engineer! Engineer!' he had squealed. 'I want to be an engineer!'

After seven more years of school, and four years of specialist study, and fifteen years of work, he had come to realise that the architects' lot was not as dull as the teacher had said. Their work was much more than simply drawing a line on a map. They had to consult geological surveys, to work out the path of least engineering resistance. It was their job, not Strong-'s, that provided a thousand challenges; turn this messy, scuffed-up stretch of coastline into one of the designated pure mathematical shapes – how to do it? Thesis: We should erase this. Counter-thesis: But it's largely granite, and will take years and billions of dollars. Solution: Very well, redesign the map, and fill *around* the granite with broken sandstone taken from across the sea. More cost-effective! The Elegant Solution!

Engineers, on the other hand, had much less imaginative jobs. They did what their supervisors told them. They blasted, dug, moved, loaded trucks, loaded barges, laid down rubble, piled up rubble, shoved rubble aside, and just when they had a sense of achievement, just when they'd made a smooth and perfect vista out of the fallen mess of nature – why, then they had to move on. It was frustrating, but Strong-in-the-Lord had learnt not to let his frustration poison him. He was working for a higher goal after all. They were all working towards a higher goal.

His brother, Courageous-in-the-Lord, had had different ideas. 'I want to be an astronomer,' he had told the family one Sunday when they were both still kids.

This was a very odd thing to say. None of Ma and Da's friends were astronomers. Strong- didn't know anybody else who wanted to be an astronomer. He consulted his memory; when they had all studied astronomy at school, the class had not ended – as almost every other class ended – with a recruitment talk about the career possibilities. And come to think of it, what would an 'astronomer' actually *do*? The stars were there – everybody could see them. The State didn't need to employ special people to look at the stars. Anybody could do that. Row and row, rank and rank. Scientists had already listed every star, named each of them, looked at them with special machines to determine their spectronomy, their chemical composition, how many light years distant they were, their respective sizes, all those sorts of things. What else was there left to do?

As a child, he had been unable to express his incomprehension at his brother's choice except in mockery. 'Astronomy? That's the most stupid thing I ever heard. Isn't that the most stupid thing you ever heard, Ma? Isn't it, though, Da?'

'Now,' Ma had said. 'Don't bait your brother.'

The family was eating: a large steaming Masson-in-slaw, with luscious looking plentrails, green and shiny with butter. It was a Sunday dinner. All four sat at table in the dining room, the tallest, the most elegant room in the house. Precisely seven dark-wood boards to each wall. Four curtains drawn across four windows, each in the exact middle of each wall. The faint odour of burnt sandalwood, mixing with the smells of the meal.

'Sorry, Ma,' said Strong-in-the-Lord.

For a little while Strong- ate his food. Courageous- was a quieter boy than he was himself: contemplative, inward. He scored highly at school in the meditation classes, and poorly in the practical work. Because Strong-'s own results were exactly the other way around, he found it hard to take his brother's mooniness seriously. Couldn't the dolt see that practical work was so much better than sitting around thinking and praying? Nobody remade the world by *meditating*.

After a while, Courageous- spoke, his voice calm but with a worrying, subversive edge to it, as if he were practising some obscure, wicked little practical joke of his own. 'It's no more stupid than wanting to be a coastal engineer,' he said, his face angled down towards the plate from which he was eating.

'What?' snapped Strong-.

'The whole coastal engineering project is crazy.'

'You can't say that!' Strong- chimed. 'Ma, tell him!'

'All that effort?' Cor insisted. 'It'll be hundreds of years before it's done, and why? Smoothing out the coastlines. We could only see the results if we was in *space*. What's the point in that?'

'—if we *were* in space, Cor,—' Da corrected, holding his fork up like a wand. 'The subjunctive is used for unfulfilled wish or condition.'

The boys knew better than to challenge this. 'If we *were* in space,' Cor adjusted his sentence. 'But what's the point in it?'

'That's not true,' said Strong-. 'About only being able to see the results in space. There'll be maps, as well. And high places, like mountains.'

'But I don't see what the *point* is,' Cor repeated.

'Da,' said Strong-. 'Ma. *Tell* him.'

'We're making the world a better place,' said Da. 'More harmonious, neater. Maybe you can't see that from the dining-room, but God can certainly see it.'

'But God made the countries and the continents the way they are,' said Cor in his quietly insistent voice. 'How is it right to meddle with that?'

'Meddling,' said Da, with a hint of severity, 'as you dismissively call it, is what God put us here to do. Every person is born with an animal nature every bit as ragged and rough-at-the-edges as the coastline of a continent. But God expects us to smooth our natures down, to control and tame them, to bring them into proportionate and harmonious relation with His will. The Great Project is an expression of the same impulse. Look at the sky and what do you see? The heavens; the perfect order and regularity of the stars. Look down on earth, and do you see the same order? Alas no. Alas, you do not. You see disorder, and chaos, and irregularity. Accordingly, mankind is *saving* this world, making it orderly. That's what the coastline project is about.'

'I was in the library,' said Cor, 'and I looked up some books. They said it's the most expensive thing humanity has ever done.'

'Expensive?' repeated Ma.

'In money terms, in terms of man-hours, the labour, the machinery. Do you know, fourteen hundred people died last year of industrial accidents working on coastline projects around the world?'

A distinct chill had settled on the dinner table now. 'So when you go before God,' Da said, his voice now very stern indeed, 'will you say to Him, I'm sorry I did not perfect my soul, it was too *expensive*? Do you think He will be convinced by that argument? Do you think He cares for dollars and cents?'

'What,' Ma chipped in, 'would you rather we spend the money on, if not on making the world more perfect?'

Still looking at his plate, Cor said, 'Sorry.'

There was an awkward silence.

'I'm disappointed in you, Cor,' said Ma, in a withering tone.

'Sorry,' said the boy again.

Strong-in-the-Lord could only feel grateful that he wasn't the one suffering under the parental displeasure. He finished his Masson with a quiet, selfish glee. But later that night, in their shared bedroom, after the lights had been put out, he started baiting his brother again.

'You want to go to the window and look at the stars?' he whispered. 'If we do it together we'd *both* be astronomers.' He sniggered.

'Don't be stupid,' said Cor. 'You need to do more than that to be an astronomer.'

'Oh, there's *no* such job,' Strong- insisted. 'Why should the State pay for people to stand and look up? That's just crazy.'

To Strong-'s disappointment, Cor didn't rise to the teasing. Instead he spoke in a hushed, careful voice. 'I was in the library,' he said, as he had done at dinner, 'and I looked up some books. Did you know the stars didn't use to be so orderly in the sky?'

'What you talking about?'

'Long ago,' said Cor, 'they were scattered as randomly as if I threw a handful of sugar from my hand, and the grains landed higgledy-piggledy on the floor.'

Strong- snorted a little laugh, and ducked his head under the blanket. 'That's just crazy.'

'It's a myth, you see,' said Cor. 'The myth is that God arranged the stars, and then the Devil came and mussed them up, and so God rearranged them for us. It's clever of him, because the stars are not all the same distance from us, they're all different distances, and great distances, like billions and quadrillions of miles away, so to get them all lined up so that they appear neat and in rows from earth is clever.'

'Of course God is clever,' said Strong-, still under the blanket.

'I'd just like to know more about them,' said Cor. 'That's why I want to be an astronomer.'

The brothers took their different paths through life. Strong- went to college and studied two years of basic engineering, and two years of coastline speciality. He graduated in the top thirty per cent of his class. He was found a wife, and he had two children of his own; one girl, one boy, their names shifting *in* to *of* after the tradition of the Northern European congregation to which he belonged: Beauty-of-the-Lord and Wisdom-of-the-Lord. He was promoted. He worked for several years on the two great tapering lines that were reshaping South America, working the machines and, afterwards, supervising the workers on the machines, as rubble was channelled and shovelled from inland to block out the underwater reefs that would later be built up and up. He did his work so well that he was transferred back to Europe, and his family could leave the sweltering heat of the tropics for the decent chill of Scandinavia. Promoted again. Here he worked for many years on the more difficult job of filling in fjords. The ground was hard, mostly unyielding granite, and the fjords were deep; it was several years' work to fill in one of the smaller inlets. But the work was day-to-day. Fruition was many centuries away. He was part of a larger whole.

It was in Scandinavia he became friendly with The-Unerring-Word. Another devout man, church on Sundays and Wednesdays, with a family of two himself. But a more old-fashioned man than Strong-. He beat his children on Tuesday nights, whether they had committed specific infractions or not, for the discipline of it. On fast-days he starved himself not from dawn to dusk as was common, but from midnight to midnight; it made him grumpy and unpredictable at work, but he insisted upon the observance, and mocked others for not being so exact. In fact, fasting or not, his temper was usually short with the people working under him.

Then there was the question of clothing. At work both Unerring- and Strong- wore the company tunic, the plain blue buttonless shift, the blue strides and black engineering boots; matching blue faceveil and gloves. But away from work, Strong- liked to dress up a little. After he got home after work he would wash the necessary three times, and then put on a pale green shift with a single silver cross printed onto the chest. He had a favourite faceveil too, with gold thread worked into an olive-green ground. And he wore red silk gloves with black fingertips.

Unerring- did not conceal his disdain for these fripperies. In work or out of it, his clothes were always plain. 'It's vanity,' he might say, as Strong- and he sat in a bar, each sipping a glass of red-wine-and-cranberry. 'It's nothing else but vanity. You know what I reckon about it. Hey.'

'You're probably right,' Strong- would concede. 'I guess it is.'

'But, hey,' said Unerring-. 'Forgive, that's part of God's plan too. Yeah?'

'Yeah.'

'Yeah,' Unerring- would say, contemplating the concept. '*Forgive.*'

And they would finish their drinks, wipe their straws with sanctissues and throw them away. Walking back through

Utoholm in the early morning, taking the main street towards the engineering camp, they would often laugh together, slap one another on the shoulder. The citizens of Utoholm, on their way to day-work, briefcases like paving slabs in their arms and hats pulled down over their heads tight as a drum skin – the ordinary people of the town – would give these two burly men a wide berth.

'Hey,' Unerring- might yell at one of them. 'Mouse! You take care! God's wrath, you know! We're making the world a purer place, you know!' It was funny. The mouse would duck, almost doubling over his suitcase, his coat flapping around his body as he scurried and hurried away from these huge men, these shouting, laughing men. Because, you see, they were doing something more important than sitting in an office, sitting in a school or a hospital, counting beans or pushing paper. They were physically remaking the world – with their actual hands, with their own muscles, with their will-to-goodness. Making the world more like the heavens; making it purer and more godly. And that thought made them feel good. Strong- enjoyed the sense of *altitude* he experienced, coming home after a shift, a glass of half-wine-half-juice in his belly, his comrade-in-work beside him, laughing and joking.

'You know what we should do?' Unerring- said, linking his beefy arm with Strong-'s as they strode together towards the Engineering compound.

'What should we do?'

'We should all go on holiday together! Yeah! You and me, your family and my family! We should go on holiday – somewhere in South America, say. You can show me the work you did on that coastline. They've got resorts down there, haven't they? One on a mountain, with a good view of the reformed coast.'

'You want to be cooped up for a fortnight with my kids?' Strong- asked, laughing. 'You want my teenage son chewing your ear off for a fortnight,' slipping his voice into comical-nasal, '"*But Dad, why?*" And "*Why this?*" And "*Why that?*"'

'Sure!' bellowed Unerring-, who guffawed. 'He'd learn soon enough not to bother *me* with that nonsense!'

And this, for some reason, struck Strong- as simply hilarious. He laughed and laughed.

'Hey!' Unerring- shouted at somebody on the far side of the street, some old woman, or old man, it was difficult to tell. 'What you looking at? Mind your own! You want the Lord's wrath, in the shape of my fist, come visit you?' And the woman ducked down and scurried away.

They laughed and laughed, and strode through the gates to the compound arm in arm, as the morning sun dissolved the last of the stars in its lemon-coloured dawn light.

2

Strong-in-the-Lord discussed the holiday plans with his wife, and found himself coming round to the idea. Maybe it would be fun! Unerring- could be a little stiff-backed about religious observance, a little over-strict, but he was a good guy, salt of the earth.

Because of this, it was a particular discomfort to him that it was Unerring- who first saw the naked man. Seeing a naked man, running around the workplace, was bad enough – but for that naked man to turn out to be his own brother, to be none other than Courageous-in-the-Lord, was almost unbearable. 'Hey!' Unerring- shouted. 'Hey, who is that guy? He's *naked*, for crying-out-loud!'

'You're right!' Strong- said, horrified.

They were at a shaft-head, midnight. The shafts were being run into the steep wall of the fjord, and would eventually be primed with explosives and blown free, so that the rubble would avalanche down into the deep black water below. The two of them had been at the cutting face, inside the mine, inspecting the work. They had just backed a truck along the mineshaft, and had emptied its load of rubble down the scree-face into the water. Now they were standing beside the truck's cabin, debating whether to take their break now or later.

The road, cut alongside the line of the water and lit with fierce arc-lights at twenty-metre intervals, led back to the main camp. But here was a naked man, hurrying up the road, bold as you like. As he came closer Strong- said, 'Hey, he looks like . . .' and then, 'Oh, I don't *believe* it.'

'What?' Unerring- asked. 'What?'

'It's my brother. Believe that? Oh, would you *look* at that?'

'Oh man,' said Unerring-. 'That's disgusting! Look at that!'

The naked man approached. He was wearing odd, raggedy green trousers. On closer inspection the flaps and fringes revealed themselves to be pockets, but a messier, more disreputable-looking pair of trousers it was hard to imagine. There was a dark sweater of some kind, but his hands and his face were *completely naked.*

'Cor?' Strong- yelled. 'Courageous-in-the-Lord?'

By the time he arrived, the newcomer was panting. 'Brother,' he said, nodding his head in greeting.

'In the name of God!' said Strong-. 'Cover yourself up, man!'

For a long moment Cor said nothing, but looked calmly into Strong-'s face. 'I've got to talk with you, brother. I've got to talk with you now.'

'You're *naked*!' shouted Unerring-. 'For the *love* of . . . !'

Cor ignored him. 'Can we talk now? Is there somewhere we can go?'

'You heard what I *said*, man?' yelled Unerring-.

'I don't want to talk with *you*,' said Cor to Unerring-, without looking at him. 'I've got nothing to say to *you*. You should get on your way.'

'I'll tell you *what*,' said Unerring-, fiercely. 'No naked man is going to run around my site. You got permission to be here? No way. You got permission to be *anywhere* naked like that? Oh no.

I'm taking you in – you're coming back down the road with me until the police can deal with you.'

He brought his huge hands up in front of him and took a step towards Cor.

'Stop,' said Cor.

And Unerring- froze. Cor was holding a gun, a bulky handgun of struts and sharp double-backs, like an anglepoise-lamp. Clearly a gun. Military issue.

When Unerring- spoke again, his voice was much softer. 'Where you get that, man?'

'Go,' said Cor. 'Just head off. Go back to the camp. I've got to talk to my brother.' He lifted the gun.

'That's military, isn't it?' Unerring- said. Then, abruptly, he had turned face-about and was trotting down the road. His figure swiftly dwindled to a smudge of dark, trotting from one patch of lit ground to the next. Above him the stars, ranked in awful sublimity, gave the illusion of hundreds of receding dark roads, each one lit by lamps all along its length, shrinking towards the horizon that was also Unerring-'s destination.

Cor watched him go.

'What are you *doing*?' cried Strong-in-the-Lord. 'Are you insane? You'll go to prison – is that what you want?'

'What I want,' said Courageous-in-the-Lord, folding his gun away and pushing it back into one of the pockets in his ridiculous trousers, 'is somewhere warmer in which we can talk. Warmer than this freezing night. How about the cabin of this truck?'

They clambered inside, pulled the doors shut. Cor turned on the heating. For a while he simply sat until he had warmed up a little. Strong- sat in silence during this time; he offered up an unspoken prayer, tried to calm himself. Eventually he turned to face his brother

'So,' he said. 'So. I haven't heard from you in five years, and now you turn up like this. Five years!'

'You're doing the same thing now as you were then.'

'*Then*,' said Strong-, 'I was in South America.'

'It's all the same thing,' said Courageous-.

There was a pause.

'You will,' said Strong-, trying to sound compassionate, 'go to prison for this. You do know that, don't you?'

Courageous- laughed. 'I've been dodging prison for most of those five years, you know,' he said. 'It's been one long chase for me.'

Strong- could not help himself from staring at his brother's naked face. He just couldn't help himself. He ought, perhaps, to have looked away, for the sake of decency, of propriety, but he found himself staring. The myriad tiny strands of black hair, curling a few millimetres out of the chin and cheeks, like pubic hair – revolting. The snickering, serpentine curling and uncurling of those pink lips, moistened from time to time by his tongue. His tongue! Glimpses of that pink muscle, that lewd contorting thing; its penile probing and movement, soft-hard, stippled with hundreds of miniature nipples along its upper surface. Strong- couldn't stop staring at it. As his brother spoke, he found himself hypnotised by the movement of lips, the flashes of tongue, the lurid gaping of the nostrils with their own hideous stuffing of pubic hair. He could hear that his brother was saying something, but he could not make sense of the words. It was all blotted out by the spectacular, obscene image of the naked face.

'Ugh!' he called out. He looked away. 'You could at least cover up.'

'You weren't listening to me,' said Courageous-. He sighed. 'It's the same. You're the same as you were. I'd hoped you were different, I hoped – Jesus, I don't know what I hoped.'

'Oh,' said Strong-, still looking carefully at the darkened windscreen. 'So, it's swearing as well, now, is it?'

'I didn't know where else to go,' said Courageous-, in a more subdued voice. 'I guess that's it.'

There was silence.

'What happened to you, brother?' Strong- asked the darkened

windscreen. He could see his brother's naked face reflected, smokily, in the glass, but seeing a reflection wasn't, somehow, as bad as seeing the actual thing. 'How did you get like this? You were a devout kid. Devout enough, anyhow.'

'Listen to me, brother,' said Courageous-. 'I've seen the truth, yeah? Once you've seen the truth, and understood the truth, things can never be the same.'

Strong- took a deep breath. He exhaled, carefully. 'The-Unerring-Word,' he said. 'That's my co-worker, the man you terrorised with the gun. He'll inform the police as soon as he gets to the compound. They'll come up here. They'll come up armed, probably. You should go give yourself up, right now.'

Courageous- sighed again. 'You know what I wanted to be when I was a kid, brother?'

'Of course,' said Strong-.

'Remember?'

'You wanted to be an astronomer.'

At this memory, Courageous- laughed quietly; and at the sound of his laughter Strong- laughed a little too. Suddenly the whole encounter took on a comical, unreal edge.

'It was crazy of me,' admitted Cor.

'Man, it was, though? Wasn't it?'

'I told the teachers at school, and I got caned, got whacked – you remember that? They thought I was being disrespectful even by asking after it!'

The two of them laughed together.

'You were full of crazy thoughts in those days,' said Strong-, kindly.

'When you came here,' Cor said, 'you used to write to me. *Come stay with the family; come see Scandinavia!*'

'That's right!' said Strong-. 'I did that. Of course,' he said, the laughter still burbling along between the words, 'I didn't think you'd come see me *naked*. Or, or,' and here, for some reason the laughter dribbled away, 'or carrying a gun. Or carrying a gun.'

There was a pause. They weren't laughing any more.

'I did become an astronomer, in the end,' said Cor, leaning forward in the cab. He pressed the blade of his hand against the glass and peered through the shadow at the world outside. 'In a manner of speaking. Do you ever think it's odd that the stars are arranged in the sky in so orderly a pattern?'

'Odd?'

'The constellations – you know what that word means?'

'Something to do with stars?'

'Constellations are the patterns made by the stars. But there's only one pattern of course. This grid.'

'Do I think it's odd?' said Strong- loudly, as if waking from a snooze. 'No, I don't. Why should I? God declares His majesty and order in the heavens.'

'And if,' said his brother, in a low voice, 'there is no order in the heavens? If the stars were arranged in a chaotic spread?'

'That's a nonsense question,' said Strong-. 'A nonsense, and a hypothetical question.'

'OK,' said Courageous-. He yawned, egregiously, his mouth opening wider and wider. Strong- could see every detail reflected in the glass; the teeth, arrayed like stars, the pulsing mass of pink flesh that was the tongue, the open funnel of throat, tonsils dangling at the very back like glistening, miniature testicles. Strong- had to lift his hand to his eyes to block out the image. He could not tear his eyes away. He had actually to lift his hand to block the image out.

'Sorry,' said Courageous-. 'Sorry about that. I'm just really tired. I haven't slept in ages.'

'If you'd been wearing a veil,' said Strong- faintly, 'it would not have been so bad.'

'Yeah, veil, yeah,' said Courageous-. 'Except that once you discover the truth of things it seems pretty hypocritical to wear the veil.'

'The truth of things?' snapped Strong-, trying to achieve the same tone of withering sternness that their father had managed so effortlessly. 'I thought that's where all this was leading – to irreligion and atheism and terrible things. Don't! Don't, that's all I say. Truth? Do you say truth? Truth – there's a word that means two things, isn't it? It means *not in error*, but it also means *properly placed* – we talk of a line in a drawing being true, don't we? When we say God is truth we mean not only that He cannot lie, we mean that everything about Him is properly placed, orderly, harmonious. That's the point of the stars – that's what they show us. The rank on rank of them.'

'I think I just ran out of steam,' said Courageous-, wearily, as if to himself.

But Strong- wasn't to be interrupted. 'No, no, the lines of stars in the sky are *true* lines. That's why the coastline project is so important – the line of the coastline of Scandinavia does not, at the moment, run true. Do you see? We must make it true. For the sake of God!' He stopped. Was there, he wondered, any point in haranguing Cor in this way?

'You know about the sky-net?' his brother asked.

'What's that got to do with anything?' Strong- snapped.

'All those satellites up in Earth-orbit? What are they for?'

'What are you talking about now? How's this relevant? They prevent asteroid strikes, you know that. Asteroids and comets and, uh, nebulas and things. Without them, we'd be vulnerable to . . .'

'Do we really need so many of them?' Courageous- asked.

Strong- turned his head and stared straight at his brother, disregarding his nakedness. 'What,' he said, 'are you *talking* about?'

'Nothing,' said Courageous-. 'Only, could you take this?' He was holding a folded square of paper, half a metre along each side. Strong- looked at it. It was folded several times. Unfolded, it would be a fairly big thing, like a wall-chart or something.

'What is it?'

'You can look at it,' said Courageous-. 'When you get home. Just take it, please. Please?'

'Tell me what it is.'

'Just dots on a page. Random dots. Randomly generated pattern. Or, rather, lack of pattern. That's harmless, surely? Well, you and I might think it harmless, though the Government doesn't think so. Obviously the government thinks it's dangerous; it's why they're after me. But how can it be dangerous? It's only dots on a piece of paper. I'm asking you, as a brother, to take it for me. Please.'

'I don't know, Cor,' said Strong-.

'If you take the paper,' said Courageous-, 'then I promise I'll hand myself over to the police.'

'Is it contraband?' Strong- asked. But he took the paper.

'Tuck it away inside your tunic,' Courageous- advised. 'I wouldn't let the police know you have it. Just take it away and look at it at home. Then you can do what you like. There are some numbers along the bottom margin that you can call, if you want. Or you can just chuck it away, if you like.'

'What's going on, Cor?' said Strong-. He felt a wobbly sense of uncertainty, and he didn't like that feeling. 'What are you doing?'

Courageous-in-the-Lord was settling himself back against the seat of the cab, folding his arms. 'Waiting for the police,' he said.

'They'll put you in jail.'

'Are you advising me to run away, brother? Surely you'd prefer me to face justice?'

'Well, yes, only . . .' said Strong-. 'Look, I don't understand.'

'It's alright,' said Courageous-. 'I don't really know why I picked you, brother. If I'd thought about it I should have known you could not have changed. I've been in the company of so many people over the last few years who *have* changed, you see, people who had once been devout like you and now aren't any more. When you're in that sort of company over a long period of time it's easy to forget that most people haven't reached that place yet. You still believe in the coastal engineering project, don't you?'

'This again? Always knocking it. I might almost be cross with you, brother,' said Strong-. But he wasn't cross. He couldn't shake the grumbling, fluttery sensation of uncertainty in his gut. 'It's mankind's noblest project.'

'Mankind's most pointless, certainly.'

'It's *not* pointless.' He meant to sound assertive, but instead he sounded petulant.

'You don't think there are better avenues for man's energies? When you were in South America – you know that thirty per cent of the population there are malnourished? You must have seen it. That many thousands die each year of starvation.'

'The soil there is bad,' said Strong-.

'Couldn't we put our energies into making it better, instead of redrawing coastlines? Christ-alive.'

'Please don't swear.'

Courageous- had sat up again. 'You really don't see beyond it, do you? How many coastal cities have you bulldozed?'

'Most of them were already ruins,' Strong- said, grumpily. 'After the war, there were many ruins.'

'Most, but not all. And a deal of poisoned soil, too. Which means people tend to starve. Pushed out of their homes, they become destitute. Even though the war was more'n a hundred years ago, now. And after the war we had strong government, Church-and-Government. Order and a better life. All that,' he threw his left hand up, dismissively. 'All that.'

'Why do you have to be so cynical?' Strong- asked. His voice was almost tearful.

'I'm sorry, brother,' said Courageous-, sounding weary again. 'I just don't believe it. I think the whole thing is like prisoners working a treadmill. I think it soaks up people's energies, and people's money, and stops them questioning the government – stops them from challenging, or changing, or – hell – overthrowing the Government.'

'And why,' said Strong-, baffled, upset, 'would anybody want to do anything like that?'

'Quite right,' said Courageous-, grimacing. 'The Government governs according to the principles of truth, doesn't it? Of course it does. That speech you gave me five minutes ago, I can't remember all the details of it, but it was all about truth, wasn't it.'

'God is truth,' said Strong-, agreeing, and at the exact moment he said the words there came a sharp tap against the glass of the truck's windscreen. Strong- started, pressed his face against the glass to peer at the crowd that had gathered outside. He opened the door and clambered down.

The-Unerring-Word was standing there, and four policemen. Two of the policemen were carrying weapons – long-barrelled police-guns, aimed at the cabin. 'Sir?' said one of the policemen.

'*He*'s alright,' said Unerring-, gruffly. 'This is my work colleague. It's the other guy – in the cab.'

Strong-, feeling foolish, stood, superfluous, as the police dragged his brother – naked – out of the cabin. As they cuffed him, searched him and removed from him the gun he had (presumably) stolen from somewhere. They dragged him over and strapped him into the back of their Law-wagon. Afterwards Strong- accompanied Unerring- to the police depot, and they swore statements, and agreed witness dates, and answered questions, and gave details, until the whole thing had taken up almost the entire night's shift. All through it Strong- kept thinking that maybe he would wake from the experience, as if from a dream – everybody has that sort of dream, don't they? You've had it, surely? The dream where you are walking down the main street, stark-naked, *entirely* naked from forehead to neck, and people are looking and staring, and you become more and more embarrassed. The experience felt something like that for Strong-, except that it was Strong-'s brother who had been naked rather than Strong- himself. But the whole thing had that terrible nightmarish quality to it.

It was almost dawn by the time Strong- got home.

He slipped the key in his lock and stepped inside quietly, trying not to wake his wife, his two children. He needed to sit, to think. He went through to the kitchen and made himself a beaker of hot milk.

He placed the folded square of paper on the table in front of him.

He couldn't make sense of any of it. What was it Cor had been saying? None of it made any sense. Why had he said that thing about the sky-net satellites? Everybody knew that they were essential for global defence, all of them. Every single one. Sure there were lots of them, but what of that? What had Cor been going on about? What had gotten into his head?

Strong- tried to imagine what image was printed on the paper in front of him. Random dots, Cor had said. What could that possibly mean? It sounded harmless, and yet Strong- felt a strange inertia, a disinclination to open up the sheet of paper and look at what was printed there. It would be – he felt intuitively – *upsetting* to him. He recalled (he wasn't sure why) the line in the Bible, about the veil of the temple being rent across. He had a terrible sense that this is what the image would show. God's temple rent and split diagonally across, splashes and dabs of ichor, like God's white blood, spattered over creation, falling with appalling randomness. It was almost like a telepathic premonition. He almost did not have to open the paper to see it.

Almost.

His hand was resting on the table, his fingers playing with one corner of the paper, folding it up, smoothing it down, folding it up. Above his head, upstairs, he could hear his wife moving around, oblivious, performing her habitual morning ablutions: the triple-flush of the toilet, the squeak and gushing flow of the bath-tap, her voice humming tunefully as she prepared for her day.

The Woman Who Bore Death

So, the land there is thickly forested to the north and the forest grows even more thickly and denser to the south. This southern cantrev of forest is so very dense, indeed, that there is no other place in the world with trees of such height or magnificence or profusion; excepting only one place, and that is the same forest's reach westward, of which it is impossible to imagine a more perfectly wooded cantrev. And yet, Gwad the Great, who grew the world from a grain that no man had harvested, always keeps one surprise hidden in his glove with which to startle each man or woman who believes they have seen everything that the world has to offer. And so it is that the easternward reach of this forest is thicker, more finely grown, and broader in extent even than the north, south and west portions.

Now, there is a kingdom in the realm of breath known as Fflam-a-Nuwver.[4] That is a strange place, where women have their own names, and the trees that grow there are of metal rather than wood. In that place was a Shawoman called Lle-llew, who was also known as Gwevel Cutch.[5] She looked out of the realm of breath first upon the realm of cloud, and saw in it nothing that seemed to her worthwhile or beautiful; and then upon the realm of water and saw in that nothing that seemed to her worthwhile or beautiful, and then upon the realm of soil. Upon soil she saw there were men and women, and it seemed to her that it would be worthwhile and fine to live amongst them. So she came to the people of the forest, the cantrev called Bright, and she spoke to them.

[4] 'Blazing Firmament'.
[5] That is, 'Red Mouth'.

'I might riddle you a riddle,' she said, 'one riddle only, out of all the many questions that are hard of answering. And mine is a simple question.'

In all courtesy they replied, 'We will answer your question, if Gwad has planted the answer in the world.'

And she said: 'My question is only this, "What is my name?" '

And the people of the Bright did not know how to answer the question. They said to her, 'How can we know if you are married, since you bring no husband? How can we know if you are unmarried, since you may have no husband, or your husband may be watching from the realm of breath?'

At this she looked sorrowful, and said, 'Until you can name me, my displeasure will fill the forest with Fantoums. You may call me three times, and each time I shall listen; if I hear my true name, I shall relent. But if you call me with a false name, then falseness will fill your forest, and the nature of falsity is distress, and the end of distress is death.'

All the people of the Bright came together to discuss this circumstance. In that place, such a gathering was called a Cob. 'Let us discuss, allowing each the opportunity to speak, and letting each weigh each other's words in the balance,' they said. 'How can we discover this woman's name, when no woman should have a name?'

And the result of the Cob was to request that the Shawomen of the cantrev be supplicated and their opinion uncovered. In that cantrev, at that time, were three Shawomen of the forest, and they came willingly, and were content with such offerings as the Bright brought them. And the offerings included three live wood deer for each Shawoman, and as many strips of salted meat as would fit in a satchel; and resin clasps and resin jewellery moulded and carved as fine as any; and a hundred leather strips for each, and buckets woven of leaf and sealed with gum, and a hundred bottles of fruit wine for each woman. And the oldest of the Shawomen said, 'She is not of our hive, and yet magic is magic. For there is power in names, and only uncover this stranger's name, if she has one, and whoever wields that word will wield her magic. Then her magic will belong to the Bright, for to name a person is to put a rope around such power as they possess and lead it, as one leads a deer.' There was much discussion at this as to whether her magic was worth wielding, but at this a woodsman named Hudd requested permission to address the Cob.

'Stand on the stage, Hudd,' they said to him. 'Courteously say what you have to say.'

'By Gwad, the Great, who gardened the world in its wonderful growth,'[6] said Hudd, 'I will say, "I was in the forest, westward of here, and I saw a thing." '

'What did you see?'

'I saw a fort, built in the midst of the trees, where there was no fort before. It was made all of precious metal, and marvellous to see. And the woman whose name you seek built it, for I saw her walking upon the battlements, fine of face, with black hair and a red mouth. Her clothes were of a fabric I have never before seen, for its weave never gets wet, no matter how much water is poured upon it; and its seams never split, no matter how it is pulled or stretched. I do not know what manner of animal provided the hair, or which plant was milled, to make the thread of so wonderful a garment.'

'This fort is fashioned of her magic,' said the first Shawoman. 'And who now says that such magic is not worth the wielding? Tell us of this fortress.'

'That I will do, and it will be worth the wear upon your ears to hear it, courteous people. This woman fashioned her fort in a moment, and built it all of metal, so that it shines and sparkles in amongst the trees. The walls are of silver, and the central tower of silver too. Around this she has put up a wooden wall, of trees felled from round about. I don't know why she has built this wall, unless it is to hide the silver fortress from the gaze of Gwad.'

'But,' said the second Shawoman, 'Gwad has many servants,

[6] This is a line from the alliterative poem 'The Roundel of Roots', and may have been used as a conventionalised or standard address before speaking in public.

and eighty of these servants are Eyes, and eighty more are Tongues, to taste the tang of metal on the wind, and eighty more are Ears, to hear as she whispers her true name in her sleep.'

'Go on with your telling,' they said to Hudd.

'She has made her fort strong,' he said. 'And she has conjured an army of Fantoums, made from the trees of her world; and yet although they are fashioned of trees yet they are not made of wood. For the wood of her world is not the wood of our world.'

'Why do you say that of the wood of her world?'

'For in her world the trees are made of metal, and the wood is buried beneath the soil in lozenges in grounds in the villages and by the churches. In our world, wood grows above the ground, and metal lies beneath.'

'Hudd is only telling the truth,' said the third Shawoman, 'for if the metal is disturbed then the forests do not grow, as in the plains of the west where they dig the ground to get at the metal – trees grow there sparsely if at all. Whereas if the metal is left alone – as in the four cantrevs of the Bright – the trees grow more thickly than grass in a field.'

'So,' said Hudd. 'Her Fantoums are metal made, towering and tall, and their fingers are flails, and their teeth are big as swords, and their eyes bloom like mushrooms and turn to seek you out. They are a scary sight, and they patrol the woodland in the day and also at night.'

'Do they not sleep?' asked a man, called Urjen the Tall.

'They neither sleep nor wake,' replied the Shawoman. 'For the weariness that causes sleep is a kind of pain, and they feel no pain of any kind.'

'These soldiers serve only the stranger who has set us this question.' said Hudd.

'There was a time,' said Deheubart Handraiser, who was a notable figure in the western cantrev's largest village, 'when this woman walked amongst us. But now she lives in her fort, with her soldiers, and she sends insects with myriad eyes to fly into the air and spy upon us.'

‘What manner of insect are these, courteous Handraiser?’ asked the others at the Cob.

‘Insects as they must be in her world; for where our insects have carapaces made of matter that resembles bark, or hardened resin, yet her insects have carapaces made of metal, that steal small glitter from the sunlight in silver and in gold. Yet if a man or a woman seizes hold of these insects, they send fire into that person’s arm and make it numb for three days and three nights.’

So the Cob was distressed to discover the nature of these new insects. ‘We must discover her name, or there will be disaster,’ was the conclusion. And the three Shawomen consulted after the manner of their hive, and said this: ‘If all else fails, we will speak to the Worthy One who lives in this portion of the wood.’

The eldest of the three Shawomen brought the Cob to an end by taking a bough of wood that was stiff and ancient, as rigid as any stone, in her hands. Now trees put out new boughs and branches and they are as flexible as rope; and then with age and the male generative principle they become rigid and aggressive. There is nothing the tree can do to help this situation, and there is nothing a man can do to ameliorate his situation. But the Shawomen have the trick of magic, and this one took the stiff wood and circled her hands about it, and ran her hands along it, and it became floppy and loose as tendril. So the Shawoman tied this bough into a knot, and then passed her hands along it again to stiffen it, and make it as it had once been before. Now this knot was the agreement, settled upon in the Cob, to find out this woman’s hidden name, and if such finding failed, to speak to the Worthy One.

This Worthy One was the only one to have forsaken his fellows and the realm of water to live amongst trees. Now, the reason for his dwelling in the forest was not known. As with all his species he had been a Rager and a Pursuer of Justice, yet the judgment of Gwad is delivered only after the life has left the body, and the judgment of the Ragers was upon all the people and not only upon this or that malefactor. And in the older times, Ragers would pursue a whole village to punish a single malefaction. As to the means by which the Ragers were relieved of Gwad's rage, and were renamed the Worthy Ones and the story of that renaming is a good tale, but it is not this tale; that story is instead the tale of The Pursuit of Ysbadadden. Yet were the Worthy Ones fearsome, and dangerous, and men and women avoided them and made charms to divert their attention from their villages.

And that was the end of that Cob.

A year passed, as white breath leaves a man's mouth in cold weather and flies away wherever it is the wind takes it. And with the spring all the villages of the forest sent a man to a great High Said Forth to debate the name. All the magic that was fitting was made to work, and word came into the debate.

'She has been among us, and walked among us. When she said that she had a name we were amazed, for she is neither married nor unmarried; but she told us her name. Neither did we ask for it, and the name was given freely as a gift. The name of this woman is Lle-Llew, and she lives alone in her fort.'

So twelve warriors went into the first and stood before the walls of wood, behind which were walls of silver, and cried, 'We call you, Lle-Llew who lives alone!'

From behind the walls the woman replied; and she did not show her face, but her voice was carried to every tree in the forest by her magic. 'Lle-Llew is a name they call me, and that is true. But it is the name my parents use, and not my true name. And I do not live alone in this fort; I live here with my brothers and sisters.'

At this the gates flew open quick as an eyelid raises, and out came a great many Fantoums. Of the twelve warriors were two that are named March the Silent and Fercos son of Potch, and never were men braver in battle, and no man had a stronger left arm for raising a laden shield, or a faster right arm for thrusting a sword. But the Fantoums killed them both faster than the time between the downbeat and upbeat of a bird's wings. The other ten warriors fled, and ran through the forest, but only four of these arrived back at the village alive, leaping the drain-ditch and coming inside the compound. The Fantoums took the rest, and as they died nameless deaths and their graves were never found, their names have ceased to be. But the Fantoums could not come into the village, because the Shawomen's magic protected it. Nevertheless they roamed through the forest, and killed many travellers and traders, and women going to Blessings, and killed so many deer and boar that the hunters of the villages came back many days empty-handed.

So another Cob was called, and this ended with the saying: Sorrow has come to us, and its name is Suffering. The sunlight no longer pleases us amongst the leaves, and the streams and pools are pourings of suffering.

Another year passed and this dreadful state did not alter, and the seasons changed with the creaking of the trees. And still nobody knew the name of the woman.

There was a man called Glaw, whose beard was long as an arm, such that he parted it like a root and tied the two ends together behind his back. And he went to the forest, and went further, to the fort, and lived there for a period not exceeding seven weeks. In that time he grubbed tubers from the earth, and snared small deer, and lived as a wild man or a wodwo. But at night the walls of the fort shone, and the light was so bright that it beamed through the wooden outer wall, and Glaw could not sleep; and by day the sun shone, and he could not sleep. At night the fortress shone with lights as stars, for they had brought stars down with them when they came. And in the brightness of night Glaw dug two graves, one for March the Silent, and one for Fercos son of Potch; and come the dawn, at the proper time, he put them in the graves, and sang to the roots to embrace the bodies, and covered them over again. So it is that March the Silent and Fercos son of Potch are not forgotten.

One day the fort gate opened and a strange man came out, wearing clothes such as Glaw had never seen before. He was tall, and there was this strangeness about him: that where a man's hair is red and his skeleton white, this man's hair was the colour of silver, so that his bones must be red inside his body. He came out, walking with long strides, and looked about him; and although Glaw had evaded the Fantoums by lurking beneath leaves and hiding under undergrowth, yet this man saw him straight away. Glaw knew him for a brother of the woman.

'You, there,' said the man.

At this Glaw believed his life was over, and he trembled.

'Why do you hide there?' said the man.

Now Glaw was alarmed so much that the words would not come; so this man took up a web woven of words and put it inside Glaw's mouth. And then Glaw could speak. He said, 'I come to beg a gift.'

And the other said, 'What gift do you beg?'

And Glaw said, 'There is a woman in your fine fort; and her hair is black, her skin the colour of white silver, and her mouth is red.'

'I know her,' said the other.

'The gift we seek is to know her name; and if you give us this gift then forever will the people of the Bright be your friends, and traders; and we will ally ourselves with yourself, your brothers, and your sisters.'

'It is well spoken,' said the other, 'and well requested, for we have good use for your alliance. And I shall tell you this: you yourself have named her, for her beauty is in her pale skin and her black hair and her red mouth.'

So Glaw came home, and said: 'Her brother calls her Gwevel Cutch, for her mouth is red and bright as blood.'

And so the village gathered twenty-four warriors, and sent them through the forest. But as they travelled the Fantoums came upon them, and killed half; and the remaining twelve were hard pressed to make their way. And they had many adventures on their travel. So, finally they came to the fortress and stood outside and cried, 'We call you, Gwevel Cutch, and you are neither married nor unmarried, but live with your brothers and sisters!'

From behind the walls the woman replied; and she did not show her face, but her voice was carried to every tree in the forest by her magic. 'Some have called me Gwevel Cutch, and that is true, for my mouth is red and my skin white and my hair is black, and my beauty is in the black and the white and the red. But it is the name my brothers and sisters use of me, and not my true name.'

At this the gates snapped open as a beetle opens the plates of its back, to stretch its wings; and through the gateway flowed a great horde of Fantoums, and the twelve warriors broke formation and fled through the trees. And only one returned to the village alive, to tell the whole tale.

After this the people despaired. 'Twice we have named her,' they said, 'and twice she has tricked us. She has chosen to make war upon us, and her Fantoums haunt the forest; but she is not the only one who may make war. For we have made war since the world was young.'

When the world was newly grown, and the trees had not yet become stiff and rigid and unyielding in their trunks and stems, then all the world went to war, and the story of that war is a good tale, but it is not this tale. That story is instead the tale of 'The War at the Waking of the World', and is contained in the *Green Bound Book*.

And so a War Cob was called, and a mighty army was brought together. And amongst the warriors were Brygandia the Brave, and Uinda Seibrah, and Riygant-Onna of the Wrathful Blow; and Carreg, strong as a rock, and his daughter who was called Wy, for her skin was both smooth-white and hard as a shield against blows; and the dozen warriors who fought as the Soldiers Llenyddol; and also came the Gogledd, the Hooynthooy who referred to themselves only as 'they themselves'; and Oesoed the Eternal. And the army was readied, and the army marched out. The battle that was fought has no name, for it was not a victory, and so its name was void.

And many Fantoums were killed, insofar as it is possible to kill their kind; and an army was sent against her. But the woman from the realm of breath rose up into the sky, riding upon a great jet of air, and she made a cloud about her, exactly like any cloud, save only that it rained fire and not water – for this is the nature of clouds in the country from which she came. And a great reach of forest was eaten up with this flame, and made bare as any field, and turned black and grey, and there were ashes upon the ground in heaps, and there were ashes upon the wind as smuts, and the great army of the Bright was eaten by fire. And, though it was in the middle of this burning, the silver fort was not harmed, and grew in strength, drawing its strength from the fire. But the mighty army, the greatest ever assembled in that cantrev, that had ported the live bodies of its enemies upon its shields, was destroyed.

This was a terrible fate, and despair came into the souls of the people of the forest. 'We shall never guess her name,' they said, 'and never shall command her. She does not eat food, as do ordinary folk; instead she devours the forest, and each mouthful is a cantrev's breadth. She does not breathe moisture, as do ordinary folk, but her breath is fiery. She has come to hone this world, as a whetstone hones a metal blade, and our souls are the sparks she sends from the spinning stone.'

This was the point at which the darkness was inside their heads even in the daytime.

The time had come to fulfil their pact to speak with the Worthy One. Now the Shawomen of the forest had been in dispute with this Worthy One, and had charmed the flowing water to fence him in, and had put another charm upon the wood such that he could build himself no bed with the trees, and so could never rest. Unable to rest upon a bed of wood he could not rest at all, and so he grew wearier and wearier, and craved nothing more than that he could lay himself down and rest. But he could not lie upon the forest floor, and he needed a bed. And through a means that cannot be named, because it does not exist, the Worthy One was persuaded to attempt to name this woman. If he could do so, then the charm would be taken from the trees, and also from the water, and he could build himself a bed and rest and recover his former strength.

And he walked out and met the woman in the open woods, by a stream. And she came with her brothers and sisters, and with Fantoums to guard her. And the Worthy One came alone, save only for a servant that cannot be named, because it does not exist.

'I have heard of your deeds,' said the Worthy One to her, 'but I have not heard of your name.'

'Twice I have been named,' said she, 'and twice misnamed. Do you wish to try the task for a third time? It will go dreadfully for the world if you fail; the whole forest will burn, and the clouds will metallise in the sky and fall to earth as boulders to cause terrible destruction'

'You have a very large quantity of power in your magic,' said the Worthy One, 'and your name is the leash that holds it. Therefore I shall try.'

So began the battle of the two wizards. At first the woman sent her brothers and sisters across the stream, to make a prisoner of the Worthy One and so seize his power. But he struck at them, and killed all the brothers, leaving only one alive; and he struck at the sisters, leaving only one alive. And these two, the brother and the sister, fled through the forest, and because each went in different direction to the other he could not follow both. So he left the nameless stranger there, and ran along the path left by her sister, and searched the woodland and the streams and clearings until he found a hut. Now, it was not usual to find a hut in that place, because Fantoums went everywhere by day and night as wood people, and the hermits had all fled in fear; but here was a hut nevertheless.

So the Worthy One went in at the door and inside he saw a very old woman, a hundred years old or more, sitting beside a fire with a leveret in her lap. This woman was the oldest ever seen in that country; and her skin was mottled like sunlit shadows dappled through leaves; and when she had been young then perhaps her hair had been black and her teeth white, but now her hair was white and her teeth black; and there were more wrinkles in her face than hairs on her head.

'I greet you with all courtesy and in the hope of friendship,' said the Worthy One, 'but I say to you, you must not eat that leveret raw, or it will drive out your innards at both ends, as bad food does.'

'What must I do, visitor?' said the old woman.

'You must cook it upon the fire,' he said. And so she spitted the leveret, through its mouth and out between its hind legs, and she held it over the fire. At this the Worthy One knew he was dealing with a stranger, who did not know the ways of the forest, for the old woman had neither skinned nor prepared the animal. The leveret's fur tangled fire into its pelt, and it burned as a torch burns, and smoke filled the hut. In the blackness and the bafflement of sight, with smoke everywhere, the old woman leapt at the Worthy One – for it was the sister disguised by magic, not an old woman at all. But the Worthy One was warned by the way the woman had spitted the leveret, and so he was prepared for her assault. He put his hands together, so that the tip of each left-hand finger touched the tip of each right-hand finger, and the left thumb touched the right thumb; and he drew these two hands apart, so that he wove a web of air in amongst the smoke. The sister flung herself upon this web as a fly upon a spider's shawl, and, quick as he could, the Worthy One wound the web of air about her, and lifted her from the ground. Then he hurled her in the fire, and she burnt with a bright blue flame, and that was the end of her. Her fire spread in every direction.

He left that hut, and dashed through the door as it burned all around him; and when he looked back, it was no hut but the fort, and it was all aflame. The wood was burning, but so was the metal, and the whole was hotter than anger, hotter even than love.

The Worthy One then returned through the trees, and through a method that cannot be named, because it does not exist, he was made aware of the place where the brother, the last of the nameless woman's family, was waiting. The Worthy One made his way to that place and he struck the brother upon his head, and made him lie down in a swoon upon the forest floor. Yet he did not kill him, but instead stood beside him. And he cried out to the trees, 'I call you out, for I know your name.'

'So if you do, then speak it,' the nameless woman replied, hidden.

'Though some have called you Lle-llew, and some have called you Gwevel Cutch, I call you by what you truly are. You are Death, and you bring dogs to the fresh forest to bar the way to the sun.'

At this she stepped out from the trees and, facing him, said, 'You have named me truly, and that saddens my heart and dims my mind. As for the sun, which is a blaze of bright souls, you must know this: it is a circle, also, and this circle spins its souls about, forever recirculating. Only when the circle is snapped can the glory flow about the world, and the heavens, and into the realm of water, and into the realm of soil, and into the realm of air, and into the realm of breath.'

'Men and all women,' replied the Worthy One, 'face many enemies, but all these enemies are the same, and the sameness is called Death. Still, difference shall prevail over sameness. Now that I have named you I claim your powers.'

At this the Worthy One drew on the woman's magic to transform himself from a man into a giant hound, and he ran at the woman as hounds do when they have scented their prey. But all her magic was not taken from her, even though she had been truly named, and she turned herself into a leveret and sprang away. They ran through the forest, as the day pursues the night, or as spring chases winter; and they ran for seven weeks without pause or breath. Then they came to a great lake. And the woman leapt into the lake and changed herself into a fish. The Worthy One leapt too, and transformed himself into a great Pike, and swam after her through the waters of this lake. The two swam round the lake three times, and three times the Worthy One had her within his jaws, but when he snapped those jaws shut it pushed water before him and she was saved.

Then she leapt up from the surface of the water, and thought to change herself into a bird and so fly away. At this she would have escaped, for the air is wider and freer than the forest. But as she leapt from the water, the water clung about her in a layer, and water clung to her body, and a strand of water linked her still with the lake. Inside the water, the Worthy One in the form of a Pike could sense what she was doing, and thought to himself: *She will escape unless I stop her*. But there was only one thing possible for him to do, and that was to put the magic he had taken into himself from her outward again, into the water itself. And this he did, so that his magic went through the lake, and along the tendril of water, and surrounded the woman even as she was a fish, and before she could change into a bird. Even so, it was not strong enough to prevent her from changing her shape, although it did tangle bindweed about the stem of the spell, so that she became not a swift but only a hen, and though she flapped her wings she could not fly. She flung her wings about and up and down, as frantic as epilepsy, but the air would not support her.

With a leap, the Worthy One came out of the water and, since the magic was almost gone from him, he thought to himself to find a way to use the last of it to defeat the woman. One way only presented itself to his mind. So he transformed himself not into a fox, or into a dog, but instead into a heap of grain. And the woman, as a hen, pecked at the grain and swallowed it down inside her. At this the magic of the Worthy One and the magic of the woman met, and cancelled each other, the woman became again only a woman, and her fort vanished, and her power of destroying the entirety of forest vanished, and she could no longer metallise the clouds or burn the air with fire.

And ever after, because the battle made a noise like thunder, that lake was known as Turve Liant.[7]

[7] That is, 'Thunder of waters'.

'You have been a clever adversary,' said the woman, standing again on two legs, and with arms flapping in place of wings; 'and now you are hidden in a place where I cannot harm you without harming myself, or kill you without killing myself. But since you have named me, and taken upon yourself some of my power, then I will do the only thing that I can do, and that is to pass the name onto another, and out of me, out of my very body.' And so the grain inside her kindled, and she became pregnant with a child. And she took her brother, who, though made simple in his thoughts by the blow, was not dead; and she took another Fantoum to be her servant, and she left the forest. When the time came she gave birth to a girl, and gave her the name Death, and so that true name passed from the woman and she became as any other woman.

That is the end of the story of the woman who bore death.

Anticopernicus

1. The Mighty Adam

The visible matter we see around us (including the mountains, planets, stars and galaxies) make up a paltry 4 per cent of the total matter and energy content of the universe – and of that 4 per cent, most of it is in the form of hydrogen and helium, with probably only 0.03 per cent taking the form of the heavy elements. Most of the universe is made of a mysterious, invisible material of totally unknown origin . . . 23 per cent of the universe is made of a strange, undetermined substance called dark matter, which has weight, surrounds galaxies in a gigantic halo, but is totally invisible. Dark matter is so pervasive and abundant that, in our own Milky Way galaxy, it outweighs all the stars by a factor of 10 . . . But perhaps the greatest surprise is that 73 per cent of the universe, by far the largest amount, is made of a totally unknown form of energy called dark energy, or the invisible energy hidden in the vacuum of space. Introduced by Einstein himself in 1917 and then later discarded (he called it his 'greatest blunder'), dark energy, or the energy of nothing or empty space, is now re-emerging as the driving force in the entire universe. This dark energy is now believed to create a new antigravity field which is driving the galaxies apart.
[Michio Kaku, *Parallel Worlds* (2005), 12]

Let's call this single, originary atom *Adam*.

It is all that exists. It exists and that's all. It lasts from the beginning to the end, and that's all there is – just it, alone in its spacetime Eden. It existed from the beginning to the end and then it exists again, backwards (as it were) through time, from end to beginning, setting up a complicated interference pattern with itself. You see, as yet there is no 'time' or 'space', not as we currently understand it, and so this is a more natural progression than you might think. So it arrives back when it starts and exists once again following the arrow of time forwards. This means (there's no time – it doesn't happen *sequentially* like this, but permit me the approximation) that 'now' there are two atoms, coexisting in the same 'location'. It's alright, though. The topography of the pre-universe can bear this. The atom exists, moving forwards and backwards through time (40 billion years, perhaps) 10^{80} times. This number happens to be the density threshold, according to the pre-universe topography, beyond which the copresence of so much 'matter' becomes unstable. The reduplicated unity breaks down and the big bang occurs, spreading this matter into – or more accurately, creating the spacetime *of* – the observable universe in which we live.

Running 'backwards', as it would later appear, and however awkwardly inexpressive that kind of talk is, entailed a swimming-against-the-stream friction – a tenfold force, generating ten times the tourbillions of friction in the spacetime medium, such that the matter running back from the end to the big-beginning brought with it not the same amount but ten times as much mass. But that's a trivial thing, a nothing, compared to the profounder mystery; and that profounder mystery is the incomparably vaster shroud which we call dark energy, the halo that surrounds Adam and all his 10^{80} iterations of himself.

What is the dark energy? Good, right, yes. Although *what* is not always a question that gets answered. Nor is *why*.

2. First Contact

I saw that the shanty town had grown over the graves and that the crowd lived among the memorials. [James Fenton, 1983]

It was the strangest summer of Ange Mlinko's life. It was for everybody on the planet, of course. But it was rather more strange for Ange than most.

The first contact with alien life, and everybody was intensely aware of the strangeness of this. Ange felt a more acute relationship to the experience, though. She was to crew the *Leibniz*, to meet the aliens in person. And then she wasn't. Then she was, again. She was flown to Florida, where it was very hot. Then she wasn't; Norodom Chantaraingsey was to take *her* place. She was flown to New York, and had four days down-time, which she spent as a flâneur, wandering the streets and squares. New York was as crowded as ever – could not, in truth, grow any *more* crowded, the space having long reached saturation point. But the composition of the crowds seemed different. She overheard English conversations no more than one in three. The manmade canyons echoed and reverberated. At a café she drank latté, and eavesdropped on a woman trying to impress a man with her traveller's tales. Mars est renommée par ses falaises. Et ses rouges, bien sûr. Silence is the name of the sea. The frontage of St Mark's was swarmed upon by roosting pigeons, to the point where you could no longer see the stone, like an underwater escarpment covered with silver-grey-blue mussels. If I've told you once, I've told you ten thousand times.

A message came through on her phone: she was on again. So she packed up at the hotel, and went to the airport. But as she waited for the flight back to Florida she got another message: apologies for earlier confusion, but she was off again, it was definitely *not* going to be her. She might as well go home.

She went home.

Months followed, summer months. But anticipation made her a stranger in her own house. She looked past the table, on which sat a bowl of unstoned olives, black as sloes, to the window. The garden was pristine. Sunlight possessed it. A cutlass-shaped fir-tree, green as emerald. Like everybody else she watched the *Leibniz*, crewed by twenty people including Chantaraingsey but *not* including her. The alien intelligence, or intelligences, or – who knew *what* they were, or what they wanted – had approached as close as the Oort cloud, and there they waited, patiently, as far as anybody could see, for the *Leibniz* to trawl slowly, slowly, slowly out to the rendezvous. Communication had been intermittent, although the aliens' command of English was fluent and idiomatic. But most of the questions beamed out at them had been returned with non sequiturs. 'What do you look like? Where are you from? By what political system do you organise your society? Are you an ancient race of beings? How do you travel faster than light? Do you come in peace? How did you find out about us? Where are you *from*? What do you *look* like?'

'*Fingers are a mode of madness – and toes! Toes? Toes!*'

'What do you mean? Do you mean you don't *possess* fingers and toes, and that the sight of them distresses you? Do you have flippers, or tentacles, or do you manipulate your environment with force-fields directly manoeuvred by your minds? We can wear mittens – if it distresses you. We can wear shoes on our feet and boxing-gloves on our hands! Not that we wish to box with you . . . we have no belligerent feelings towards you at all.'

'*We* love *your fingers and toes! They are adorable! Adorable! But mad.*'

'We don't understand. We don't understand! Are we missing some nuance? Can you explain?'

'*We count these ice pieces by the billion, and all of it inert! Every shard.*'

'How far have you come? Have you come very far? Our observations indicate you've come at least from Beta Cygni. That's an awfully long way! Your craft is clearly very large . . . are there many of you?'

'*Many of us? All of us. The totality of us.*'

This was a worry: had they come to colonise? Or was this an obscure alien-joke? Who knew what passed for a sense of humour, amongst the Cygnics? And how many was 'all'?

'We are happy to welcome you, but naturally we are apprehensive to.'

'*Multicellular life. Particellular life. It'll do the crack! crack! like a heart attack! Come to us*—'

'What?'

'*Come to us – Come come to us*—'

'Really? You're inviting us *to you*?'

'*Come come come to us*—'

There was no missing the craft: a huge device with a friable boundary, or perhaps a fractal boundary, and the approximate shape of four connected oblate spheres: it had decelerated spectacularly into the Oort cloud, such that every sensing device and observational algorithm in Earth had been drawn to it.

'—*come to us and we'll be waiting. We've seen all your television and your cloud-images, and the data that rushes and rushes and rushes, so be assured we will not hurt you. Us? Hurt* you? *Pull the other one.*'

English, the experts agreed, only because that language had had such a historic prominence in televisual and early internet culture. They must have picked up a transmission, and come to investigate. A surprising thing – 'As if', to quote Eva Tsvetaeva, 'Europeans had somehow heard about some sand-fleas living on Bondi Beach and had travelled all the way around the world to meet with them. Why would they? They had the *whole cosmos* to explore! Why should they have the remotest interest in a tiny blue-white planet orbiting an insignificant star in a lesser prong of the western spiral arm of the Milky Way Galaxy?'

But here they were, so there had to be a reason. Maybe they are entomologists. Maybe they just happened across us. Maybe they have a thing for insignificant life forms.

'Why have you come to visit us? Why us? We're an insignificant, primitive civilisation by Galactic standards – surely we are! We don't even have faster-than-light technologies!'

'*We debated a long time about whether to come and visit you.*' But despite further questions there was nothing more forthcoming about the nature or extent of that we, or the precise manner by which the debating took place.

'Are they communists, or fascists?' asked Lidija Cho. 'Are they democrats or anarchists? By what logic, if any, do they orchestrate their societies? We just don't know.'

Why did the question of coming to visit such an insignificant, technologically backward species as *Homo sapiens* require *long debate*? Come, or don't come – what did it matter?

Naturally, many suspected a trap. Many thought the *Leibniz* would never return. But from the tone of the alien communication . . .

Why not come *closer in*? Why do they loiter out in the Oort-distances, when their technology is so far advanced over ours, and would make the trip so much easier? We tried inviting them. 'We have scientific bases on Mars, and on our own moon, and various inhabited craft in space, mostly in Earth orbit. But if you are worried about scaring us, or overawing us, or even damaging us, you could still come to the orbit – let's say – of Jupiter, and still have many billions of kilometres of naked space by way of quarantine between you and us. That way the *Leibniz*, launched and fuelled and on its way, would rendezvous with you in weeks, rather than in a year.'

No reply.

'You can understand how eager we are to meet! Perhaps the passage of time means nothing to you; but it passes very quickly for us. Perhaps your lifespans are millennial, but ours are measured out in paltry decades.'

'*Our lifespans are not at issue. The emmet and binaries, binaries in everything. A mad profusion of boundaries. Oh, the scintillations!*'

'Then why will you come no closer?'

'*No closer? This* is *close!*'

The consensus was that, for a species of interstellar travellers like the Cygnics, the distance from the Oort cloud to Earth was almost too small to count; and that was why they were so cavalier about it. There was also the feeling that the Cygnics were averse to being too proximate to the sun.

'Maybe our solar radiation is toxic to them! Maybe they are a deep-space species, only truly at home in the dark between the stars? Why can't we just ask them!'

'We can, but they are not very forthcoming. Or they answer with chatter and chaff. Or they hum and hoom like ents. Or—'

The *Leibniz* was hastily refitted with extra fuel (tanks and blocks), and beefed-up acceleration couches. Then it ignited a long burn and began its curving passage out to meet the aliens. The whole world watched. Ange Mlinko watched too, of course. That should have been me, on board there, she thought to herself.

Alicia came to visit. 'I don't like you being all alone in this big house,' she said.

'But I *like* to be alone.'

'I know,' said Alicia, 'you like to be alone. I don't like you liking being alone. What if you had an accident? All alone here. You might hurt yourself.'

'If I were with somebody else, *they* might hurt me.'

'Don't they test you people for paranoia?' (*You people* meant, 'pilots'.)

'How little I crave . . .' Ange started to say. But, with a short sigh, she gave up on the sentiment.

'People like to be around people,' said Alicia, speaking seriously. 'That's just how people *are*.'

'I'm people too,' said Ange Mlinko. 'And I don't like that. I'll tell you something else – people are seldom as missed as they like to think.'

Alicia made her mouth into a ~. 'You're not the first divorcée to go through a misanthropic phase, you know. Once you start dating again, your cold-shouldering of humankind will thaw. Then you can waste-bin your inner Scrooge, and reboot your smile.'

Ange didn't say so, but her preference for solitude had nothing to do with her divorce, now three years behind her. The problem with the marriage had not been anything sparky or oppressive or unbearable; it had been, precisely, its *blandness*. She had chosen a husband who did not interfere with her aversion to human intimacy, which was both his appeal and, of course, the grounds of her eventual disaffection. Not the sex. She had never minded the sex, perhaps because she had never seen it as especially intimate; or to put it more precisely, its intimacy was of the banal, somatic kind that did not disturb her. Alicia's theory was that she had never had the right kind of sex, the sort that ruffles the mind as much as it gratifies the body. It was true she had never had that kind of sex. But, if she were honest, she disbelieved such things ever happened, except in the self-deluding, talk-themselves-into-it hysteria of people convincing themselves the earth moved. The earth didn't move for her. She moved from the earth. *Eppur si muove*. Silence is a more intense experience than moans and gasps and grunts.

'And I don't want to hear about you growing up with four noisy siblings,' said Alicia. 'Five kids is not even that large a family! Time was, when families of twelve were normal.'

'Since you don't want to hear about it,' said Ange, with asperity, 'I shall not talk about it.'

The two friends were silent for a while, and Alicia drank her spritzer, and ate an olive from the plate, and stared through the window at the sunlit garden. 'It's very lovely and what's the word?'

'I don't know what the word is.'

'Pristine. Neat. Is it a person, or a robot?'

'You mean, gardening? The latter.'

'It's very nice.' And then, after a pause: 'I'm sorry you're not on the *Leibniz*. I know you're disappointed. But look on the bright side! If these Cygnic aliens are as horrible as all the rumours say, none of that crew will ever see home again.'

That didn't bother Ange. Death frightened her not at all. What worried her was not death but the dead, which is to say their overwhelming multitudinousness. If death were extinction she would be happy. After all, there is something individual, something cleanly specific about extinction. Her worry was that somehow she *wouldn't* die, but would find herself in a cavernous chamber containing all the outnumbering dead doomed to spend eternity in that hell of other people the old philosophers fretted about. And wasn't there something true about that, too? It is the individual who dies, after all; the group – the species, the genes – live on. Immortality is a mass event, and if you would flee the clamorous, overheated urgency of the great crowd then you can only, really, take solace in your own existential oblivion. A crowd flowed over Luna Bridge, so many, I had not thought death had undone so many.

Her animus against her fellow creatures was not precisely rational, although it sometimes took a quasi-scientific form. This was how she thought of it, when she brought it consciously into her mind (something she did not often do): the weight of numbers is ruinous. The topography of the Earth is collapsing under the pressure even as humanity hurried to lunaform and areoform new landscapes. The petri dish is foaming with bacteria, having gobbled the disc of nutrient jelly to a sliver, and is still consuming it although starvation will necessarily follow. When she was younger, before her marriage, Ange had been quite active in a Netherlands-based Ehrlich group, agitating for much more aggressive population control. It was not enough, she thought, to flatten the rising curve; human numbers had to be actively reduced. But the group eventually fractured – some stayed true to the group's original Pimentelist beliefs; some insisted more radical Francipettian strategies were needful; a small group declared that mass terrorist action was needed. The bickering depressed and alienated Ange; she distanced herself from her former friends, and moved to a different country.

All that felt a long time ago, now, on the far side of seven years of married life, a union that, despite being untraumatic, had been filled to the brim with ruin. To the brim. On the rare occasions she thought of her husband now, she saw in her mind's-eye only a flank of cheek, dotted with black stubble; his D-shaped nose in profile, his eye caught by something away in the distance, something that wasn't, ultimately, her at all.

Alicia, speaking with what she fondly thought of as insight, told Ange what her problem was. You have trouble *empathising* with other people, she said. That's why you like Mars so much. It's so under*pop*ulated. Ange Mlinko thought this wrong on both counts. For, one thing she *didn't* much like Mars – the deserts might be void of human life, but nobody ever went outside the pressurised homesteads, and they were high with the reek of population. And at any rate, it seemed to her that her problem was not a lack of empathy, but rather an *excess* of that debilitating human emotion. When she walked amongst a crowd of people, she felt the presence of each and every one. Most humans blanked the individuals, saw only the crowd. She seemed to lack the heartlessness to do that.

Anyway, because she could hardly sit around watching the live feed from the *Leibniz*, and driving herself mad with what might have been – and because large single-occupancy houses with immaculately maintained gardens don't come cheap in this, our overcrowded world – she went back to work. She flew a dozen shuttle runs up-and-down, landing in a slowmo gout of dust in the deadeye middle of Copernicus' crater.

Then she took a contract for a Mars flight, a two-month there-and-back. Delivering barnacles, no less. Great slabs of barnacles, to be seeded into half a dozen lakes and – whatnot, not-what, stabilise, or add texture, or begin to filter out particulates, or something. It was a three-crew job, and her colleagues were an elderly man called Maurice Sleight and a young woman called Ostriker. The launch was busy, and then a flight liaison with a chunk of ice: Ange could concentrate on doing her job and forget everything else. Then there was a hitch; their ice block, though tagged with the appropriate codes, turned out to be not their ice block at all. They had located it quickly, grappled it without difficulty and had decanted only a small percentage, but then there was a lot of angry chatter on the feed that threatened a lawsuit. So they had to put it back in the orbit in which they found it. It was an awkward manoeuvre decoupling and setting it in a clean orbit. And then they had to burn more fuel than Ange liked lining themselves up with the proper ice-piece. Maurice scowled. Ostriker said, 'It's all idiotic, such a waste of time . . . ice is ice. Why couldn't we just swap?'

But that wasn't the way it worked; and so Ostriker and Maurice began over again decanting the slush into the tanks, and Ange made sure the proper remittances were sent off to claim compensation from the tagging company – it had been their foul-up, after all, not Ange's, and even if the claimable amount was small, better that the taggers cover it.

'It's good,' said Maurice, in his sepulchral voice. 'This way, we get the unluck out of the way early.'

He was referring to the widespread fliers' superstition: that each trip into space was allotted one piece of unluck by the Fates. It might happen early in the voyage or late, it might be trivial or catastrophic, but it would come. To suffer a minor glitch early on was, accordingly, a good thing. Ange nodded, and got on with her work. She doubted that a miscatalogue incident counted as the voyage's unluck, although she would be happy if it did. She had, indeed, a curious relationship to superstition. As a rational and self-contained individual she understood it was all nonsense, of course. Yet it was more than simply the cultural inertia of generations of pilots and ship crew that made her follow the traditions to the letter. She sometimes wondered if individuals such as her, the ungregarious, the loners, were more likely to be superstitious than other people. The sociable individual at least had the crowd as a buffer between themselves and the unyielding, pitiless indifference of the universe: friends, family, lovers, acquaintances. The locust in the middle of its folding aerial blanket of fellow beings. But the loner had to rely on herself to develop such mental strategies as might bolster her mind against the dark.

At any rate, whilst never doubting that it was a trivial matter of confirmation bias, Ange nonetheless observed that each of her voyages was structured around one major moment of unluck, small or large.

The correct ice was loaded at last, and they were set. So, with a last roll around the Earth, they inserted themselves and made their way to Mars. Once they were in plain flight, they had nothing but spare time. Maurice withdrew to his cabin to meditate. Ange didn't like to question the particularity of his religious observation, but he was evidently devout. Ostriker, on the other hand, showed distressing signs of wanting to be Ange's friend, and loitered about her as she went through her routines, and gabbled and chatted.

'The latest communication from the Cygnics is that, apparently, they're not from Cygnus after all. So we're not supposed to call them *that* anymore.'

'Really,' said Ange, coolly.

'But they won't say where they *are* from! Why do you think they're so evasive?'

'I've really no idea.'

'They're up to something. They must be! I heard that in addition to the *Leibniz*, the UE Strike sent a stealth ship, heavily armed. Do *you* think we can trust them? The aliens?'

'I don't know,' said Ange, giving her words as unambiguous an inflection as she could manage, so as to communicate: *I don't care.*

'We're not special,' was Ostriker's opinion. 'The fact that these aliens are here proves that the cosmos is *teeming* with life. Teeming! They would hardly have stumbled across us, otherwise – tucked away in this inconsequential branch of a spiral arm. Alien life must be *swarming* all over the galaxy. The fact that we haven't come across them until now, all that Fermi-so-called-paradox, was just bad luck. Or good luck!'

'Mm,' said Ange.

Ostriker laughed.

'But as to why they're being so coy: waiting out in the Oort cloud! I *mean*! Who knows? If they travel all the way here, from Cygnus, or from some star hundreds of light years *more* distant *behind* Cygnus, or from wherever they came from . . . why stop out there? It'll take the *Leibniz* a year to get there! That's just rude. Or stupid.' Ostriker opened her eyes wide. 'Do you think *that's* it? Maybe they're stupid! Maybe we think they're super-intelligent, but they're actually sub-normal for their species!'

'The *Leibniz* is halfway there, now,' Ange pointed out. 'Only six months to go.'

'I know. Exciting, though? Yes, yes, yes. I guess we'll get some answers when the *Leibniz* gets there. Hey, Ange! I was in-plugged earlier, checking the newswebs, and I happened across a manifold of possibles for the *Leibniz* crew – including *your* name! Wow. Wow!'

'Yes,' Ange conceded, wearily. 'But the longlist was hundreds of possibles long.'

'Still! I didn't realise I was flying with such a *celebrity*.'

Ostriker's laugh was a horrible sound, a tortuous friction in the air. Ange hated her laugh more than anything else about her.

Oh, how depressing it was: the prospect of two months in close quarters with her. Ange withdrew into herself as far as she could. She began to wish she had pretended to have religiously meditative duties, like Maurice; but it was too late for that now. Nor could she bring herself to grasp the nettle and actually pick a fight with her. One blazing row, to be followed by blissful weeks of resentful silence between them. Ange thought about it, and even tried out possible lines in her mind, but she could never summon the courage actually to pick the fight. And this was despite many moments of provocation from her crewmate.

'Those people agitating for massive population reduction,' Ostriker said, as the three of them drank coffee together (Maurice at the end of his shift, Ostriker at the beginning of hers). 'They're so stupid!'

'How so?' said Ange.

'Of *course* they're idiots! We need *more* people, not less!'

Maurice looked dolefully at Ange, but said nothing.

'Some might argue,' Ange said, with schoolma'am severity, 'that there are already so many people on the planet that the environment is collapsing under the weight.'

'That's *such* nonsense. Such nonsense! I look at it this way: population is pressure. The greater the population, the greater the pressure.'

Ange responded cautiously, 'Yes?'

'So we need *more* pressure, that's what I think. The Earth is like a great champagne bottle; we need *more* pressure, and more, and then we'll burst the cork and fizz out into the galaxy! I bet that's how the Cygnics, or whatever they're called, began their space age. I bet their homeworld, wherever it is, became intolerably crowded, so they just *had* to flee into the cosmos!'

This was the most infuriating thing Ange had heard in a long time, and she reacted to her fury characteristically, by withdrawing even further inside herself. Maurice performed his duties, and then sequestered himself in his cabin for whatever monkish devotions his religion required. Ange checked and rechecked the ship, went over the cargo again. She worked methodically to calm her anger. But Ostriker kept in-plugging to check the latest news-updates. The Cygnics had stopped replying to all communications from humankind, she reported. Some took this to be an ominous sign, others said it was entirely in keeping with the eccentricity of the aliens. It hardly mattered.

One night Ange had a dream. She was back in her house. A man clothed entirely in black, with white skin and black eyeballs, stood balanced upon an opened book. 'Population is self-regulating,' he said. 'But we must understand self in the largest way! The Cygnic aliens have come to winnow humanity, and they will destroy a third, and a third more will die of famine and disease after they have gone! Rejoice!'

In the dream, Ange felt exhilarated by this revelation; although as soon as she woke she felt the prickles of guilt. The words stayed with her all day. Could they be prophetic? The aliens, from wheresoever they came, had been consistent, really, only in their eccentricity. Like many, Ange assumed this was the index to some deeper non-fit between the two species; they had learned English with apparent fluency, but the fundamental structures of the language did not map onto the way the aliens saw the universe. What if the Cygnics viewed death as a trivial matter? What if they *had* come to harvest humanity? What if the crew of the *Leibniz* picked up some bizarre Wellsian plague from their encounter with alienness, something that managed to jump quarantine and ravage the planet?

It was out of her hands, at any rate. She had not been chosen for *that* crew.

And in the end neither Ostriker's incessance nor Maurice's gloomy withdrawal prevented Ange from doing her job. Mars, marmite-red, patched with blotches of yellow and brown, grew larger in the cockpit window every day; and then they fell into Martian orbit. They had arrived; halfway through their commission. Ange brought the ship down into Robinsontown, and the containers were unpacked and replaced with empty tanks, and that was that. After a month in flight, with only twice-daily sessions in the elastic stretchers to maintain muscle and bone, even the meagre Martian gravity was burdensome to them. They were entitled to three days downtime; but by general agreement Ange took the ship back into space after a day and a half.

The usual orbital business. The return flight was easier, since Mars-to-Earth was, as it were, downhill. And then they were away again.

Three days into the return flight, the big news broke. The aliens (people had not given up on calling them 'Cygnics', despite everything) had gone – departed, vanished, flown away. The period of disbelief, of checking and rechecking the sensor readings, was brief. The aliens' craft was so large, and displayed so prominent a radiation profile, it could hardly be missed. It was gone. Some said it had rendered itself invisible, via incomprehensible eldritch alien tech, some even argued that this invisibility was preliminary to the creatures launching a stealth attack on Earth. But most people believed that what seemed to have happened had indeed happened – they had come to our out-of-the-way solar system, they had spoken to us, they had agreed to meet us – provided only that we schlepped out to the Oort cloud, of all places – and *then* they had pissed off, without so much as a goodbye. What did it mean? Debate fizzed and flared wherever humans existed. 'The swans have departed' became the most in-plugged song in recording history.

It was certainly an inconvenience for the *Leibniz*; the craft was three weeks from Uranus, but moving so rapidly that a slingshot would only kink their onward path rather than spinning it one-eighty to direct them back in towards the sun. There was hot debate about what to do. Should they continue to the Oort cloud, and hope the aliens returned (they agreed to meet us, after all) – or should they spin about, abandon their carefully pre-plotted there-and-back-again trajectory of arcs and ellipses and curls – instead decelerate by the brute application of fuel, spin about Uranus and batten down for a long slow freefall back to Earth?

'Looks like it was lucky you *didn't* get that gig on the *Leibniz*,' said Ostriker. 'What if they continue all the way out to the Oorts, and the Cygnics *don't* meet them? What a wasted journey. I can't believe they've gone! Can you believe they've gone, Ange?'

'I can,' said Mlinko.

'Well *I* can't. I *can't*! To come all this way, initiate contact, and then just . . . buzz off? Why?'

'The universe doesn't always give us coherent whys,' was Maurice's opinion. 'Doesn't often, in fact.'

'That can't be right! It must mean something. At the least,' Ostriker pressed, very animated and excited, 'there must be some explanation. Why would they just go?'

Ange didn't say anything, but it seemed to her more than likely that the departure was as random and inexplicable thing as the arrival. She believed (and this belief was as close to religion as she came) that the universe was not structured according to the logic of the human mind, despite the fact – ironically enough, perhaps – that the human mind is unavoidably part of the cosmos. The billions of buzzing *Homo sapiens* brains craved pattern, structure and resolution; they saw the beauty of the rainbow's bend in every story arc. The cosmos liked structure too, of course; but of a much less complicated, or perhaps it would be truer to say a much more *monotonously replicated*, kind. Hydrogen and helium everywhere in varying alternated clumps; the inverse-square-law everywhere in every direction. Everything existent, nothing mattering. And above all the cosmos had no sense of story whatsoever. If aliens arrive in a human story and set up a meeting, why then there must be a pay-off of some kind. But neither set-up nor pay-off was the logic of the cosmos; and most assuredly the latter was never intrinsically folded neatly inside the former, waiting to germinate. If the aliens had randomly vanished, as they seemed to have done, then that was (Ange thought) just one more unharmonious broken-off piece of the infinitely unharmonious piecemeal cosmos.

Ostriker refused to believe it. She speculated tiresomely about the possible reasons for the Cygnics' departure. Maybe they had been recalled to their home planet; maybe some warp-technology disaster or FTL-motor-accident had winked the ship out of existence unexpectedly. Maybe there had been a mutiny aboard the ship. Perhaps (Ostriker waxed creative upon this last idea) different tribes of aliens aboard the vast craft had quarrelled over whether to embrace humanity or destroy us, and the evil aliens had imprisoned the good aliens, until the latter had staged one last desperate counter-coup, destroying their own ship and heroically sacrificing their lives to save the planet of ignorant humankind.

'Not entirely likely,' Ange observed drily.

It hardly mattered. The *Leibniz* was instructed to continue on its way, in the hope that the Cygnics would reappear. If they did not, then the craft was to undergo scientific investigation of the Oort cloud (as if there were any science left to do there that probes had not already done!). But the aliens showed no signs of returning. Their prior communications were pored over, in all their prolix eccentricity, for any clues explaining their behaviour. People agreed that they had either gone by design, or else had suffered some accident; humanity seemed unable to think of a third possibility. But if the former circumstance obtained then they were presumably unwilling, and if the latter arguably unable, to make the rendezvous previously arranged.

It was all very unsatisfying.

Ange did not find it so, however. On the contrary she found the off-kilter non-symmetry of the whole thing rather pleasing, in an aesthetic sense. And, even without the actual rendezvous there was no denying that humanity *had* experienced first contact. We now knew for certain we were not alone in the universe. And that had to count for something. Didn't it?

Surely it did.

Then one morning Maurice did not report for his shift; Ange and Ostriker overrode his doorlock to find him dead in his harness. It took half an hour to determine what had happened. All those occasions when Maurice had returned to his room to 'meditate', he had in fact been indulging his chronic drug habit – addicted, a quick blood check confirmed, both to pinopiates and to the 'linktin' pharmakon. It was an overdose of the latter, presumably accidental, that had killed him.

It was a shock, of course; although if Ange were honest she would concede that it was the *fact* of it that was a shock rather than any emotional experience of actual bereavement. After all, she'd hardly known him. Ostriker thought this mildly shocking.

'We shared this ship with him for weeks and weeks,' she noted. 'Yet we never got to know him!'

'He kept himself to himself,' Ange said.

'You can see why! How did he get the medical OKs?'

'I'll have to look into that,' Ange agreed – although she knew what she would find. It wasn't beyond the wit of humankind to falsify medical certification. It wasn't even that expensive.

They bagged the corpse, sealed the bag in medimesh, and stowed it up amongst the ice at the ship's nose, to keep it cold. Ange took charge of the remainder of Maurice's illegal stash. She wondered whether she should simply jettison this into space, but when she reported the incident to the corporate offices she was told to retain it for legal reasons.

'The irony is,' said Ostriker, temporarily distracted from her endless speculation about the nature and purpose of the Cygnics' visit, 'the *irony* is that he had already called the voyage's one unluck!'

'He had,' Ange agreed. 'The mislabelled ice.'

'Turns out that wasn't the voyage's unluck. That was just a minor inconvenience, after all. *He* was the voyage's unluck, poor soul.'

In a less than rational way, Ange found herself darkly pleased by this turn of events. She had, she realised, never believed that the incident with the ice right at the start of the voyage had been enough to defang the possibility of later disaster. But this, a dead crewperson . . . the first in her entire career, in fact . . . was unmistakably unlucky. Particularly for him, of course.

They continued earthward, the long slow fall back towards the sun. Tangling themselves further into gravity's soft, dark knot. Ange and Ostriker had to rejig the shift patterns, but there wasn't much to do, and it wasn't too onerous. Despite the death on board, or perhaps because of it (who knows how morbid human happiness truly is?) the mood lightened. Ange found Ostriker less annoying. Her obsessive chatter about the alien visitation acquired the flavour of a harmless quirk. And every time she woke after another sleep, Ange knew herself closer to her home.

She worked her shift, and roused Ostriker and went to sleep herself. She had an elaborate dream about two trees. In one, a pointillist blur of starlings pulsed and flushed around the bare branches, landing, or rather *touching down*, and immediately taking off again, their wings abuzz like insects, like insects, like insects. A brown cloud. By contrast, the other tree was bare –

black branches like stretched-out leather belts, a trunk with the bulgy, structural solidity of black rock. In this second tree there was a single bird, a magpie, and it was clutching the branch upon which it perched with such force, with such improbable strength, that the wood was being wrung out like a damp cloth, and sap was dribbling to the ground.

Ange was woken abruptly by a cacophony of ship's alarms. As she unhooked herself from her harness, scrabbling to regain full consciousness, she knew what had happened. A micrometeorite – dust, rock, ice, at these velocities it hardly mattered what – had struck.

Ange hauled herself through and up the main corridor. The whole ship was shuddering, like a house during an earthquake, or a fat man shaking with fear. If Ange hung in space she was still, but as soon as she reached out and touched the fabric of the craft the vibration communicated itself to her, and her very teeth zizzed in her jaw. The corridor was a chimney, a borehole. It was the inside of a riflebarrel. The corridor flexed and groaned.

She silenced the alarm's barbaric yawp. Then she checked the ship's schematics.

The bulkheads had all sealed automatically, and she worked as quickly as she could checking compartment after compartment, opening each bulkhead one by one. Each time she passed through a door she shut it behind her. Where there was one micrometeorite there were likely to be more. But she had to get to Ostriker.

She located the forward position where the pinhead meteor had hit. The ship schematics showed that it had come on a freak trajectory, from the side, avoiding the mass of bulkhead shielding the nose of the craft. Its speed had been its own, then; and not a function of the ship's own velocity, although it had been going plenty fast enough to enter through the forward 2 hull plate and exit through the forward 7 hull plate. Ange checked the room beyond, found it stable at two thirds pressure, and overrode the bulkhead lock.

Inside was a mess. The air sucked gently in through the open hatch, blowing past Ange and swirling into the cabin, stirring a particulate soup of red blood droplets and blobs. Ostriker was by the left wall, her arm through a strap, but unconscious. From the doorway, Ange dialled up a filter scrub of the room's air, and some of the fog of blood began to draw away. Ostriker's right foot was missing, and blood was pulsing and glooping dark red strings of blood.

There was a bright yellow patch on the wall away to the right, and another similarly coloured blob on the wall near to where Ostriker dangled. Presumably she had had enough presence of mind to fix the leak before passing out. Presumably, too, the micrometeorite had passed not only through the wall of this room but also through her foot, turning it into blood and atoms.

Ange spent a moment checking the trajectory of the item. Ostriker had plugged both the holes in this room. The adjacent space (on the far side of the wall, and sealed away by the corridor bulkhead) must be vacuum now.

The cabin was full of blood droplets. Circulating the air to clean these was taking a long time, or perhaps the filter was getting clogged. Ange took off her shirt and wrapped it around the lower part of her face as a makeshift mask. Then she launched into the space, unhooked the unconscious Ostriker's arm from the strap, and pulled her out into the corridor. She sealed the room behind her. She transferred her shirt to Ostriker's stump, wrapping it into a clumsy bandage. Then it was slow progress back down the corridor, opening and closing bulkheads one by one, until they were at the medical room.

She strapped Ostriker onto the medibench and uploaded some data on tackling amputation wounds. The first thing she did was to sprayject analgesics into the patient's leg. This action seemed superfluous given Ostriker's lack of consciousness, but (Ange reasoned) she might suddenly come to at any time. Then Ange rubbed her hands thoroughly with antiseptic wash. Then she slapped two plasma bags onto Ostriker's belly, under her shirt, and unpeeled the sodden makeshift shirt-bandage from her right leg. The raw stump was not pretty to look at. She was no wimp, but Ange's stomach still shimmered with revulsion as she picked pieces of stray bone and gelid, stringy flesh from the sound site. Ange slathered the whole stump with the mud-like nano gunk, hooked a bag of medimesh about the whole thing to keep it sterile, and went away to check on the health of the ship as a whole.

The readouts were not good. The chamber in which Ostriker had lost her foot had contained nothing essential to the functioning of the ship as a whole; but the other chamber – that on the other side of the ship, through which the micrometeorite had exited – fed through several key tubucules, and all of these were snapped and venting into space. The whole of the forward 7 hull plate had been ripped away by the exiting debris, and that in turn had deformed or pulled free the edges of four other plates. It was bad. Ange did what she could to reroute, and she shut down as much as possible; but not everything could be rerouted without actually going into the room, which was going to be a dangerous and onerous task. More, the impact had thwacked the ship hard. They were (Ange couldn't sense the actual motion, although a big shudder was still palpable in the craft) now rotating horizontally stem-to-stern, and tumbling on a different cycle on a seventy-per cent-of-vertical roll. The micrometeorite strike meant that she didn't have the complete set of attitudinal jets to steady the ship. She spent ten minutes doing what she could with what she had, and steadying without entirely eliminating the shudder.

Then she went back to the medical room and checked on the patient. Ostriker had regained consciousness, or some part of it. Ange kissed her forehead, glad that she had already sprayjected the painkiller. 'How are you doing?'

'I'm thirsty,' she said

Ange fetched her a globe of water, and she sucked noisily upon it. 'What happened?' Ostriker asked. So Ange explained about the micrometeorite strike, and about Ostriker's foot. She seemed to take this calmly enough. For a moment she looked down at her leg.

'That explains the ache,' Ostriker said, in a whispery voice. 'I remember the decompression, and I remember I felt calm. Isn't that odd, feeling calm?'

'You did very well,' Ange reassured her. 'You did very well not to panic.'

'Everything was dark and swirly, but I had a good handhold, and it was easy enough to see where the holes were. I plugged them both, but then I must have passed out.'

'Bloodloss.'

At this Ostriker began to weep. 'I feel faint,' she said. 'Oh my foot! My poor foot! How will I do without a foot? My toes! My foot.'

'You'll be alright,' Ange said, awkwardly. 'When we get home, you can have a prosthesis.'

'I feel faint. Oh, it hurts. Can I have some painkiller?'

Ange fetched a bulb of analgesic. 'Here,' she said. 'Take a little of this. It's best if you self-medicate; when you feel sore, sip a little. But don't take too much.'

And, suckling like a baby, Ostriker did seem to become calmer. 'Thank you,' she said. 'You're a good person.'

'You need to rest.'

'I do feel real sleepy. Don't think me rude, but . . .' And Ostriker fell asleep, holding the bulb of analgesic in one hand and the bulb of water in the other.

Ange was filthy, sticky with Ostriker's blood; so she went off to shower. There, in amongst the omnidirectional jets and the cleansing florettes of steam, she considered the situation. A rogue micrometeorite strike through the flank of the craft was extraordinarily unlucky, but it had a plus side: namely that it was almost certainly not to be repeated. Had the ship flown into a cloud of micrometeorites, and had the combined velocity of ship and projectiles been enough to pierce the shield of ice, then the ship could have been shredded. On the downside, she was going to have to suit-up and go into the broken 7-side chamber, to see how much of the physical damage could be made good. Only then would she know if the ship could make it back to Earth unassisted. Methodically, she worked through the worst case. They were weeks away from any assistance. Weeks were no problem; they had air, water and food for months, and energy for years. But Ange would much prefer not to have to go begging amongst other pilots for rescue.

Clean, she went again to the medical room to explain to Ostriker what she was going to do; but the patient was still asleep. So she went to the store space and began suiting up; elasticated leggings; elasticated arms; the padded torso unit. She was about to roll the helmet onto her head when the whole ship gave a massive bucking-bronco kick, and lurched wildly, sending her colliding painfully with the wall.

Moving about inside the ship in the vacuum suit was not easy, but there was no time to disrobe. Ange went first to the medical room to see if Ostriker was OK – she was still asleep – and then to the nearest control nexus. A supply tubule had ruptured along its entire length, and was feathering great sprays of sealant and fuel into the void. It must have been weakened by the earlier damage to that flank of the ship. Ange fiddled again with the attitudinals to try to calm the lurching, trembling aspect of the ship. It took a long time, and when she was finished one thing was clear: that the craft was in no shape to pilot itself back to Earth.

Angry at fate, Ange sent out the SOS. It would be half an hour before anybody even heard it, and an hour at the soonest before she heard any reply, so she went back to the medical room. Ostriker was awake now.

'You're suited,' she observed.

'A tubule has ruptured,' Ange said. 'I'm going to have to go into one of the voided rooms and see what's what.'

'Will we need rescue?' Ostriker asked. She seemed very matter-of-fact.

'I'm afraid so. But I'll see how bad things are. You OK?'

Ostriker took another sip of water, and smiled. 'I'm fine. If I'm thirsty, I'll drink; if the pain comes back I'll take some more painkiller.'

'Is the pain bad?'

'I can't feel anything.'

'That's good.'

Ange took herself forward, fitted the helmet and negotiated the bulkheads. Inside, the breached chamber was cold and messy, the twinkly detritus of floating dust in vacuum. To the gasping soundtrack of her own breathing, Ange checked the pipes one after the other, tried rerouting the fluid network, and discovered she could not. She swore to herself, quietly. The gaping hole in the side of the ship was panel-sized, and there was no patching it; Ange even stuck her head through it to take a look at the outer skin. It was sobering to consider that a projectile so small could have so large a set of consequences. The whole area was pitted and striated, not by the micrometeorite itself, of course, but by the debris it threw off as it shot out of the ship. Her helmet headlamp drew witchy shadows from the gouges and shone brightly off the petals of twisted metal. And beyond that was the starless black.

She had done what she could, at any rate. So she brought herself back in, moved laboriously up the corridor, lowered the bulkhead, pressurised the space, and came back through.

Stripping out of her suit she realised she was hungry; so she heated some tagliatelle and drank some sugar water. There was a reply to her SOS: the nearest craft cried off rescue because the detour would impact too grievously on the commercial viability of their trip. Another ship replied but claimed to be too small to be able to help – it took Ange a minute to pull the specs of the craft and see that this was only an excuse. There was nothing she could do, however; so she fired back acknowledgements and spent a frustrating half-hour working the crippled controls to at least orient the ship in the direction of Earth. They were still falling sunward, although the sideswipe and rattle-roll had added months to their unaided ETA.

Finally, a third ship confirmed the SOS; another Mars freighter, similarly returning empty to Earth. If Ange's parent company would reimburse the fuel, they would divert and accelerate, and lock trajectories within a fortnight. Ange agreed, hoping that the parent company would agree (if not, the money would come from her own salary, she supposed), and went to tell Ostriker the news.

Ostriker was sleeping. Except that when Ange looked more closely, she saw that Ostriker wasn't breathing. With a nauseous sensation in her solar plexus Ange examined her. There was no question about it. Ostriker was dead.

Ange gave herself over to a childish, universe-directed fury. She swore and swore, and kicked the walls of the medical room. It was so *stupid*! It was idiotic. But she had to get a grip; getting a grip was what she was good at. So she reined in her temper and examined the situation. Almost at once she saw what must have happened: holding a globe of water in one hand and a globe of painkiller in the other, woozy, confused with blood loss and very thirsty, Ostriker had drunk deeply of the latter thinking it the former. It was such a trivial mistake, and so arbitrary! That the woman could survive having her foot amputated, yet die of mixing up what she was holding in her left and right hands – it was simply outrageous. It was insulting.

But according to the heartbreaking logic of the arrow of time, it could not be undone.

For a while Ange busied herself to prevent herself brooding on the idiocy of everything. She wrapped Ostriker's corpse, but rather than manoeuvre it upship past all the bulkheads, opening and shutting each laboriously in turn, she left it in the medical room, dialling down the heating to make the space preservingly cold. Then she cleaned the chamber and the corridor vigorously, removing the many floating patches and wall smears of blood and other dirt. But there was only so much to occupy herself. The earlier candidates for unluck seemed foolishly trivial now. Even

Maurice's death in the fastness of his cabin. That had been his own silly fault. But Ange felt a frustrating sense of complicity-by-incompetence in the death of Ostriker.

It was the *insignificance* of it that was the most irritating thing. A human death ought to be a grand and tragic affair, not a footling stupid mistake like this. But that was the logic of the crowd. Some few humans met death with dignity and grace; some few died in ridiculous and comical ways, but the bulk of the Poisson distribution was mean, pointless, insignificant demises. Of all the great philosophers and religious figures, it was Copernicus who was the greatest, for he alone had preached the truth to humankind: *you are not special.*

For Ange, dealing with that was something best essayed alone.

3. Second contact

She was alone again, and that was alright; although being alone in her house, with its beautifully manicured garden, was a different thing to operating a basket-case spaceship in the company of two corpses. There was a further leak, which threw the ship into a shimmy-shake and slow toptail rotation. Ange tweaked and adjusted her attitudinals to cancel this new irregular trajectory, but doing this shook free further jinks in the system. Breathing air flooded into the void in a swarm of crystals. For one heart-bumping moment Ange thought she wasn't going to be able to seal off the delinquent pipe from the main supply, and she entertained crazy ideas of having to suit up, go out and stuff *rags* or something in the hole. But then she *was* able to seal the vent, and only a few days' breathable air lost.

She wondered if she ought to keep a tally of unlucks; but that felt like itself an unlucky thing to do. The tossed coin may keep coming up tails, but the *coin itself* doesn't know that; it goes into every tumble and spin with the beautiful clarity of 50:50 as its outcome.

She did not talk to herself. Only people disinclined to solitude, or people who only *mistakenly* believe that they enjoy solitude, talk to themselves when they are alone. She was perfectly at ease by herself, and went about her business. Besides, what was there to say?

There was a fire in one of the forward compartments, and the automatic dampeners failed (because she had – to make assurance doubly sure – sealed off all tubules with anything less than 100% structural integrity). By the time she had gotten the pipes open, the dampener head had melted and fused in the heat. She was forced into uncomfortable passivity as the fire burnt through to the shielding supplies of ice and burnt itself out. But this weakened the whole forward portion of the craft. For the first time she began to weigh the chances that she would never make it back to Earth. Rescue was still weeks away, and her entire tech-system was now precariously balanced. It would take only a few more malfunctions to finish her off.

Still, she lived another day. And then another day after that.

She suited up and, despite the discomfort, stayed that way; sleeping with the helmet hooked beside her. The air started smelling bad, and she discovered – after a long, wearisome search – that mould was growing inside the recycle pipes. She cleared as much of this out as she could, although there wasn't a way to get at the most deeply located colonies of the stuff short of physically dismantling the entire system. She ate. She drank water. She slept. She lived another day. She thought about all the things in her life that would be rendered forever unfinished by her death. But then she thought to herself: *anticlimax is the currency of mortality*. If I live, she decided, and get home again I will write a work of philosophy, explaining how Copernicus revolutionised our *living and dying* as well as our cosmology. All those Greek tragedies, all that Shakespe*heh*rian to-do about death, the distinguished thing – it all belonged to that pre-Copernican delusion of our importance. Only an important being can have a significant death! An unimportant entity dies, as she was doing (there was little point in denying it), stupidly, belatedly, unexpectedly, in a downbeat banal accidental way. The modern mode of it.

She went to sleep, her underarms and crotch sore from the tightness of her suit. She did not dream. She was woken by the silent flashing of a red light, winking knowingly at her.

The first thing she did was wonder why there was no sound. The alarm light should have been accompanied by an alarm noise. The speaker was broken, or else there was no air in the cabin to communicate the sound. In the latter case, she would suffocate. Half awake, she reached for her helmet, but it was not there. She woke up a little more, perked by adrenalin. Where *was* her helmet? Muzzy with exhaustion and stress and not having slept enough, it took her a long time to realise that she was wearing it.

She must have put it on whilst she slept. There was no air in the cabin, which meant there was no air anywhere this side of the corridor bulkhead. How had the decompression alarm prompted her to put on her helmet, but not actually *woken her up*? Then: and how had there been a decompression anyway, here so far aft? Another micrometeorite? She went through to the corridor, checked the various chambers, her own breathing like surf inside her ears. Everything was empty, the lights bright white, or else winking red circles. Twelve hours of air in her tank, and then swap over for other tanks, and within a few score hours – her own death.

Cast a cold eye.

No, not twelve hours: she had already used some of that air, sleeping. And now, as she began the conversation, she was compos mentis enough to wonder if this was a tank she had failed to replenish, or one with a slow puncture. She wondered that because it could be that the conversation was a function of hypoxia, a kind of hallucination. Who was there to converse *with*, rationally speaking? But the tank seemed fine, and she had plenty of oxygen in her bloodstream. But the conversation continued.

You're not even from Cygnus. She went and forced open the

first of the corridor bulkheads, and was knocked back by the turbulence. Air on the other side, flooding through. Stupid, she thought: you should have found the location of the breach on this side and patched it before you opened the bulkhead! But, actually, the dust and grits and bits of floating debris were flowing down the corridor and round and into the rear store chamber, and there Ange saw, holding onto the doorway to stop herself being blown right through, that a circular hole, a metre in diameter, had been carved right through the flank of the ship. A brand-new hole, perfectly circular. Impossibility. You're not *from* Cygnus and we know you're not from Cygnus, so why do we call you Cygnics?

'*It doesn't bother us, one way or another. It's only a name. Names are always arbitrary, when you get right down to it.*'

How could there be a perfectly circular hole in the side of her ship? Ange shut the store chamber door, and could no longer see the big hole. Seal away the room with the breach. Then she went forward up the corridor. She overrode the command and forced open the next bulkhead, and then the one after that, and then the one after that. Each time she was buffeted and blown back by the air coming through, but she made her way along repeating the gesture.

'Why did you go?'

'*Spooked, we were spooked. It was touch and go, all the way along.*'

'Is that why you hung back, all the way out amongst the Oort cloud? Too scared to come any closer?'

'*Precisely so.*'

'The sun? Some people reasoned that there was something about the particular spectrum of our sun that was toxic to your kind. Some even suggested that explained the Fermi paradox – that something in our sun kept aliens away. But there didn't seem to be anything odd about our sun. There are billions of stars with similar spectra. Out there.'

There was no reply. How odd to be taking to yourself, and yet to be so rude as not to reply! The last of the bulkheads was opened, and Ange started on the remaining doors. There wasn't going to be much air behind any of these, taken as a whole. It was not clear that the air pressure would be raised to any liveable level. But she had to try.

'I always thought,' she said, to pass the time, as much as anything, 'I always thought the thing the Fermi so-called paradox ignored was our tininess. We're sand fleas. Why should any alien races *want* to come visit?'

'*Oh, no. Oh very much no. That's not it at all.*'

'Really?'

'*Oh very much the opposite!* Very *much the opposite!*'

'Why *did* you come, you Cygnics?'

There were seven doors to open, and she opened them all. This distributed whatever air remained in those sealed chambers about the whole ship. But it was at a very low bar.

'*The thing, the thing, the puzzling thing, for us, the thing.*'

This was too annoying. She didn't have much time left! Come along, she snapped. Don't stammer and mumble.

'*To come to the centre of the universe? Can't you see how much* courage *that voyage entails?*'

Ange had an itch on her chin, and she hunched her shoulders to bring her head down sufficiently to be able to scratch it against the inside of the helmet seal. 'What? The universe doesn't have a centre. Don't be ridiculous.'

She went back to the rear cockpit, but there was no good news on the air-pressure front. There simply wasn't enough air to sustain life. This thought occupied her mind for a while, and she considered alternatives. Then the notion of the centre of the universe reoccurred to her, and she snapped at her invisible interlocutor (herself, presumably),'The universe doesn't have a centre! Where is this centre of the centre, where is this omphalos you're talking about?'

'*Of course, right here.*'

'Of course, she scoffed. Here?'

'*Earth, actually.*'

'You're saying Copernicus was wrong? The Earth *is* the centre of the Universe? Hah!'

'It's why we came. It's also why it took us such a long time. To come, I mean. We were afraid. It's like cutting a slit in the veil of the temple and stepping through into the holy of holies.'

'Why did you, then?'

'You keep adding people to people. You keeping making more consciousnesses, and breeding more human beings. You keep doing it!'

'Not I,' said Ange, fiercely, thinking of her own rationally chosen childlessness.

'That's exactly it! You know what dark energy is?'

But she had no time for that sort of non-question. She had practical matters to address. There were six suit tanks, and she was breathing one of them now. Say, another six hours in this one, plus sixty hours in the other five. Less than three days. Was there a way she could compress, or distil, the tenuous air that now circulated through the cabin? Even if she could construct a machine for doing that, how much time would it give her?

Inspired by some left-field insight into something-or-other, Ange threw a question out that chanced to hit the *eye* of the bull, bullseye, centre-target.

'How many of you came here, anyway?'

'*Three.*' The reply was immediate.

Odd that nobody else had asked that question so specifically, during all the earlier interactions between human and Cygnic.

'You left the rest of your people at home?'

'Our people?'

'Your civilisation.'

'We are our civilisations. Three separate, entire civilisations. Come to visit you.'

'One from each? Three home worlds? It must be an honour to be the chosen representative.'

'You're being dense and dumb. Listen: I am *my civilisation, entire.'*

'I see,' said Ange, who was feeling hungry, and wondering how she might smuggle pieces of food into her helmet and thence to her mouth without dying of asphyxiation in the process.

'*You see?*'

'I see infinity in a grain of sand,' she said, unsure why she did so.

'*The thing we have found hardest to grasp is your lack of self-knowledge in this matter*,' said the alien, haughtily.

'I don't even know,' said Ange, 'that *haughty* is a phrase that means anything to you. Who knows what alien emotions are like?'

'*You're the alien*,' said the Cygnic.

'We're alien to one another. I suppose it's relative.'

'*No*,' said the Cygnic. '*It's not. We're not the aliens. You are.*'

'I don't see how that works,' Ange replied, a little crossly. 'What's sauce for the goose is . . .' But she couldn't remember how that phrase went.

'*There are more than twenty billion human beings on Earth.*'

'So?'

'*So*,' said the alien, as if that summed everything up.

'How many of your species are there? Billions, I don't doubt. Maybe trillions, since you clearly have the technology to spread yourself all around the galaxy.'

'*Me.*'

'Yes, you. How many are there of you?'

'*Just me.*'

'That's what I'm asking.'

'*I'm answering. Just me.*'

Ange thought about this, and it sunk in. It percolated through. 'Oh,' she said. 'So when you said there are three of you . . .'

'Three separate entities. We united to make this pilgrimage; it's an almost unprecedented event in Galactic history. But it was important.'

'And you are,' she said. 'What – the last of your race? What happened to all the others? Dead?'

'*There never have been any others. I am the first and last. The same with every other intelligence in the cosmos. Intelligence is singular, of course.'*

And then, fractal-like, the implications of this statement unfolded and unfolded the more she looked at it. 'Good grief,' she said.

'*Life is multifarious, of course. And there are even intelligent hive-like creatures; I've met one myself. But in such cases, the hive adds up to one intelligence. That's the logic of the universe. A form of life arises, and comes to consciousness and rational capacity. Intelligence is a rare, singular thing. Except here!* Here *it is an insane profusion. Think of it like this: you travel about meeting people. You meet an intelligent person in this place, and then you meet another intelligent person, and then you meet another intelligent person, and then, madly, you meet a person whose* every single cell is intelligent, sentient, self-aware. *It would strike you as crazy, impossible, wouldn't it?*'

'Good God,' said Ange.

'*This is the only place in the Universe where this is true,*' said the alien.

'How can you know that?' Ange asked. 'Surely you haven't visited every star!'

'*This is the only place,*' the alien repeated. '*The structure and form of the cosmos itself shows that to be true. There can only be one centre, after all.*'

'What?'

'*Intelligence is a profound thing. Intelligent observation interacts with and alters the nature of reality itself, at a quantum level. You know this already! You know about your cat-in-boxes, and particle-waves, and observational biases. But you haven't thought it through.* My *intelligence alters the universe through which I move, but it's only one intelligence, so it doesn't make much of an impact. But here! Billions of intelligences, all concentrated in one place!* Such *a huge force of focused consciousness, hundreds of millions of times more intense than all other cosmic intelligence put together! It's a kind of insanity! It has – wholly – distorted spacetime. And the more intelligences you add to the core the more that is true. It's like a black hole, except that the effect is not quasi-gravitational, but something the reverse. You have the science to see it, although you don't understand it. You call it dark energy.'*

'That can't be right,' said Ange. 'Dark energy is something spread out through the whole cosmos.'

'No it isn't.'

'It's pushing the galaxies apart!'

'Yes, yes, yes, alas. It is doing that. But it is not spread out. It is concentrated here.'

'That's not what our observations lead us to believe.'

'Your observations are entirely compromised by the thing they are observing! What you see as a huge, distant structure is actually a tiny mote of dust upon the lens of your telescope. Dark energy is your own unique contribution to the universe.'

Ange got herself some food. She held it in front of her helmet for a while, and pondered how to get it in her mouth. She could certainly hold her breath long enough to get the helmet off, and the food in, but there was always a risk that she would fumble her grip, and have to scrabble around to get the helmet back on. Was it a risk worth taking? She would be dead soon, but had no desire to die sooner than absolutely necessary. On the other hand, she *was* hungry.

'For a while I couldn't believe it. I sought out another, and s/he didn't believe it either. The distortion certainly looked *like consciousness; but how could there* be *so much of that in one tiny place! And what would happen if we went there – would it destroy our own minds? We debated it for a long time. A third joined us. Finally we decided to come. Approaching, we encroached upon the limit of your telecommunications, and were able to see your self-imaging. It was a shock. So profligate with thought, so promiscuous with consciousness! In an individual body cells die and are born all the time, but they're just cells, they're nothing more. But* you! *You treat the vast significance of individual consciousness as the most common thing in the universe! You are breathtakingly cavalier with individual life – yet, then again, why wouldn't you be? New life is being born all the time*

on your world. It explains the uniquely turbulent nature of the concentration of this force; the raging furnace, consciousness being continually snuffed out, but continually replaced and more than replaced. It's like looking into a solar maelstrom . . . and yet you live in it, as calmly as a flower in the dirt!'

'Hard to believe.'

'You said it! It keeps powering up, growing and growing, this concentration of the most powerful force in the cosmos. We came, we three, in part to see if there was anything we could do *about it.'*

'And is there?'

'It has destroyed my two companions.'

'Oh,' said Ange, surprised. 'I'm sorry.'

'We were giddy. We were intoxicated by the glory and seediness and splendour of it all. When they died I took my craft away, but my own consciousness has been . . . poisoned, I suppose you might say . . . as well. So I have come back. I might as well expire here as anywhere. Here at the heart of the cosmos.'

The next question occurred to Ange only very belatedly: can you help me? I've suffered a series of malfunctions and don't have enough air.

'I know. I cannot help you. I'm sorry.'

'Oh,' said Ange. Then, 'Ah well.'

'I have a question, though.'

'Shoot.'

'The shape of the cosmos is big bang, rapid expansion and then final contraction and crunch. The rise of your . . . multiform species has overwhelmed that natural rhythm. So I suppose I want to ask: how can you not see it? But immersing myself in your communications and culture, I suppose I see the answer to that. The universe has renewed itself, systole and diastole, innumerable times; but your rise has interrupted that. Unless you do something it will all end in entropy. Can you bear the thought? Won't you do something about that?'

'You're asking the wrong woman,' said Ange, putting the food away in one of her suit pockets. 'I've got three days left, max.'

'*It's not a very well-formed question, I suppose,*' said the alien, mournfully.

He, she, it – didn't speak again.

Ange took the plunge, more out of boredom than hunger. Deep breath, pop up the helmet, morsel in mouth, helmet down again. Then she checked through the ship. She even managed to sleep – a nap, at any rate.

The next thing that happened was the arrival of a military sloop, the *Glory of Carthage*, burning its candle-end fierce in the night to decelerate after a high-g insertion. Ange was relieved and grateful to be rescued, of course; although they hadn't come for her. The Cygnic craft had popped up on ten thousand sensor screens, and the *Glory of Carthage* had been the nearest. Of course they had rushed to that location: the Oort cloud was forbiddingly distant, but the space between Mars and Earth was thronged with craft of every kind.

They arrived too late: the Cygnic had gone, vanished, dead presumably, and he, she, its craft had vanished. So they took Ange on board and interviewed her and debriefed her and took her conversation with the last Cygnic very seriously indeed. But that didn't mean they were able to answer the alien's last question. Still, centre of the cosmos, after all! That's something, isn't it? *Poor old Copernicus,* thought Ange, drifting to sleep finally. *Wrong after all.*

She was alive, despite everything. Her flight home began with a 3g acceleration burst (the sort of thing only the military could provide), followed by some fraternising with the physically attractive crew. The flush of near-death and survival touched even Ange's distant soul. And in her new eminence, the only *Homo sapiens sapiens* to have talked directly with the Cygnics, she found herself the focus of a great deal of attention. In this, without a murmur, she indulged herself; and broke her years-long period of celibacy with the crewman who appealed the most to her. She was not too old. It wasn't too late for her, she told herself, to go back and give birth to a new civilisation, entire.

Me:topia

He thinks the moon is a small hole at the top of the sky
Elizabeth Bishop

The first day and the first night

They had come down in the high ground, an immense plateau many thousands of miles square. The highlands, said Murphy. I claim the highlands. I'll call them Murphyland. Over an hour or so he changed his mind several times: Murphtopia, Murphica. 'No,' he said, glee bubbling out in a little dance, a shimmy of the feet, a flourish of the hands. 'Just Murphy, Murphy. Think of it! *Where do you come from? I come from Murphy. I'm a Murphyite. I was born in Murphy.*' And the sky paled, and then the sun appeared over the mountain tops and everything was covered with a tide of light. The dew was so thick it looked like the aftermath of a heavy rainstorm.

Sinclair, wading out from the shuttle's wreckage through waist-high grass, drew a dark trail after him marking his path, like the photographic negative of a comet.

'I don't understand what you're so happy about,' said Edwards. It was as if he could not *see* the new land, this world that had popped out of nowhere. As if all he could see was the damage to the ship. But that was how Edwards's mind worked. He had a practical mind.

'And are you sad for your ship,' sang Murphy, with deliberately overplayed oirishry, 'all buckled and collapsed as it is?' Of course

Murphy was a *Homo neanderthalensis*. The real deal. All four of these crewmen were. Of course you know what that means.

'You should be sad too, Murphy,' said Edwards, speaking in a level voice. 'It's your ship too. I don't see how we are to get home without it.'

'But *this* is my home,' declared Murphy. And then sang his own name, or perhaps the name of his newly made land, over and over: 'Murphy! Murphy! Murphy!'

The sun moved through the sky. The swift light went everywhere. It spilled over everything and washed back. The expanse of grassland shimmered in the breeze like cellophane.

Edwards climbed to the top of the buckled craft. The plasmetal was oily with dew, and his feet slipped several times. At the top he stood as upright as he dared, and surveyed the world. Mountains away to the west, grass steppes in every direction, north, south and east, flowing downhill eastward towards smudges of massive forestation and the metallic inlaid sparkle of rivers, lakes, seas. That was some view, eastward.

The sun was rising from the west, which was an unusual feature. What strange world rotated like that? There were no Earth-sized planets in the solar system that rotated like that.

Did that mean they were no longer in the solar system? That was impossible. There was no means by which they could have travelled so far. Physics repudiated the very notion.

The air tasted fresh in his mouth, in his throat. Grass-scent. Rainwater and ozone.

And for long minutes there was no sound except the hushing of the grasses in the wind, and the distant febrile twitter of birds high in the sky. The sky gleamed, as full of the wonder of light as a glass brimful of bright water. Vins called up, 'There are insects, I've got insects here, though they seem to be torpid.' He paused, and repeated the word, '. . . Torpid . . . When the dew evaporates a little they'll surely come to life.'

Edwards grunted in reply, but his eye was on the sky. Spherical clouds, perfect as eggs, drifted in the zenith. Six of them. Seven. Eight. Edwards counted, turning his head. Ten.

Twelve.

And the air, moist with dew and fragrant with possibility, slid past him. And light all about. Silence, stained only by the swishing of the breeze.

Murphy was dancing below, kicking his feet through the wet grass. 'Maybe *Murphy* isn't such a good idea, by itself,' he called, to nobody in particular. 'As a name, by itself. How about the Murphy Territories? How about the *Land* of Murphy?' And then, after half a minute when neither Edwards nor Vins replied, he added, 'Don't be sore Vins. You can name some other place.'

Vins went into the body of the shuttle to fetch out some killing jars for the insects.

Sinclair was away for hours. The sun rose, and the dew steamed away in wreathy barricades of mist. The grass dried out, and paled, and then bristled with dryness. It was a yellow, tawny sort of grass. By mid-day the sky was hot as a hot-plate, and Murphy had stripped off his chemise.

Sinclair returned, sweating. 'It goes on and on,' he says. 'Exactly the same. Steppe, and more steppe.'

The sun dropped over the eastern horizon. It quickly became cold.

The night sky was cloudless. Stars like lit dewdrops on black. Breath petalled out of their mouths in transient, ghostly puffs. Edwards slept in the shuttle. Sinclair and Vins chatted, their voices subdued underneath the enormousness of night sky. Murphy had a nicotine inhaler, and lay on the cooling roof of the crashed shuttle looking up at the stars puffing intermittently.

Later they all joined Edwards inside the shuttle and went to sleep. Over their thoughtless, slumbering heads the stars glinted and prickled in the black clarity. Hours passed. Then the sky cataracted to white with the coming dawn. Ivory-coloured clouds bubbled into the sky from behind the peaks of the highlands and swept down upon them. Before dawn rain started falling. Edwards woke at the drumroll sound of rain against the body of the crashed ship, sat up disoriented for a moment, then lay down again and went back to sleep.

'We're dead, we've died, we're dead,' said Murphy, perhaps speaking in his sleep.

The second day and the second night

At breakfast, after dawn, it was still raining. The four of them ate inside the shuttle, with the door open. 'Ah,' said Edwards, looking through the hatch at the shimmering lines of water. 'The universal solvent.'

'But I should hate you,' said Murphy. 'Because you can look at water and say "*Ah, the universal solvent.*" '

Edwards cocked his head on one side. 'I don't see your point,' he said.

'No, no,' said Murphy. 'That's not it. Oh, water, oh? This beautiful thing, this spiritual thing, purity and the power to cleanse, to baptise even. Light on water, is there a more beautiful thing? And all you can say when you see it is "*Ah the universal solvent.*" '

Edwards put his mouth in a straight line. 'But it *is* the universal solvent,' he said. 'That's one of its functions. Why do you say "*Oh water oh*"?'

The rain outside was greeting their conversational interchanges with sustained and rapturous applause. The colour through the hatch was grey. The air looked like metal scored and overscored with myriad slant lines. It was chill.

'Can we lift off?' asked Sinclair. 'Is there a way off of this place?'

'Feel that,' Edwards instructed. He was not talking about any particular object, not instructing any of the crew to lift any particular object. What he meant was: feel how heavy we are. 'That's a full g. That's what is to be overcome. We came down hard.'

'Hard,' confirmed Murphy.

'We weren't expecting,' said Sinclair, 'a whole world to pop out of the void. Nothing, nothing, nothing, then *a whole world*. We snapped our spine on this rock.'

'Let's get one thing straight,' said Edwards, in his brusque and matter-of-fact voice. 'This world did not pop out of nowhere. Worlds don't *pop out* of nowhere.' He looked at his colleagues in turn. 'That's not what happened.'

'Turn it up, *captain*,' said Murphy. He applied the title sarcastically. It was the nature of this ship that its crew worked without ranks such as captain, second-in-command, all that bag-and-baggage of hierarchy. No military ship, this. This was not a merchant vessel either. They hadn't been sliding along the frictionless thread of Earth–Mars or Earth–Moon hauling goods or transporting soldiery or anything like that. This was science. Science isn't structured to recognise hierarchy.

'I'm only saying,' said Edwards, sheepishly. 'I'm not wanting to suggest that I'm in charge.'

They were silent for a while, and the rain spattered and clattered enormously all about them. Encore! Encore!

It occurred to Edwards, belatedly, that Murphy might have been saying *eau, water, eau*.

'Right,' said Vins. 'We're all in a kind of intellectual shock, that's what I think. We've been here two days now, and we haven't even formulated a plausible hypothesis for what's going on. We haven't even tried.' He looked around at his colleagues. 'Let's review what happened.'

Murphy had his stumpy arms folded over his little chest.

'Review, by all means,' he said. But then, when Vins opened his mouth to speak again, he interrupted immediately – '*I've* formed a hypothesis. It's called Murphy. This is prime land, and I claim it. When we get back, or when we at least contact help and they come get us, I shall set up a private limited company to promote the settlement of Murphy. I'll make a fortune. I'll be mayor. I'll be the *alpha* male.'

'Why you think,' said Edwards, thinking literally, 'that such a contract would have any legal force upon Earth is beyond me.'

'Let's review,' said Vins, in a loud voice.

Everybody looked at him.

'We're flying. We drop below the ecliptic plane, no more than a hundred thousand klims. More than that?'

None of the others say anything. Then Sinclair says, 'It was about that.'

'We saw a winking star,' Vins said.

He did not stop talking, he continued on, even though Murphy tried to interrupt him with a sneering, 'Winking star, oh, that's good on my mother's health that's good.' Vins wasn't to be distracted when he got going.

'It was out of the position of variable star 699, which is what we might have thought it otherwise. Except it wasn't where 699 should've been. As we flew it grew in size, indicating a very reflective asteroid, or perhaps comet, out of the ecliptic. You,' Vins nodded at Sinclair, 'argued it was a particoloured object rotating diurnally. But it was a fair way south of the ecliptic. *Then* what happened?'

'We all know what happened,' said Murphy. They may all have been *Homo neanderthalensis*, but they were bright. They all had their scientific educations. The real deal.

'Let's review,' said Vins. 'We need to *know* what's happened. Act like scientists, people.'

'I'm a scientist no longer,' cried Murphy, with a flourish of his arm. 'I'm the king of Murphtopia.'

'What happened,' said Edwards, slowly, thinking linearly and literally, 'was we were tracking the curious wobble of the asteroid. Or whatever it was. We flew close, and suddenly there was a world, a whole world, and – we came down. We re-entered sideways, and there was heat-damage to the craft, and then there was collision damage, and now it's broken. And we're sitting inside it.'

'Now,' said Vins. 'Here's a premise. Worlds don't appear out of nowhere. Do we agree?'

Nobody disagreed.

'It's a mountain and Mohammed thing,' offered Sinclair. 'Put it this way, which is more likely? That a whole Earth-sized planet pops out of nowhere in front of us? Or that we, for some reason, have popped into a *new* place?'

'I say we're back on Earth,' said Murphy. 'It looks like a duck, and it smells like a duck and it, uh, pulls the gravity of a duck, *then* it's a duck.'

'The sun is rising,' Sinclair pointed out, 'in *the west*. It is setting in the *east*.'

'Oh. And the asteroid was the beacon of a dimensional *sffy* gateway through time and space,' mocked Murphy: 'and we fell through, like in a *sffy* film, and now we're on the far side of the galaxy?' He pronounced 'SF-y' as a two-syllable word, with a ludicrous and prolonged emphasis on the central 'f' sound.

'That can't be true,' said Edwards. 'Our first night, the stars were very clear. All the constellations were there. Familiar constellations.'

'Which's what we'd expect if we were back on Earth,' said Murphy.

'But the sun *rises* in the *west* . . .' said Sinclair again.

'Maybe the compasses are broken, somehow. Distorted. Maybe you *think* west is east and versy-vice-a.'

'All of them? All the compasses? And besides, at night you can see the pole star, great bear, all very clearly. Oh, there's no doubt where the sun's rising.'

'Well, let's look at another hypothesis,' said Murphy. 'There is a whole, a *whole* Earth-sized planet, about a hundred thousand kilometres south of the ecliptic between Earth and Venus. And nobody on Earth for six centuries of dedicated astronomy has noticed it. Nobody saw a whole planet, waxing and waning, between us and the sun? No southern hemisphere observatory happened to see it? Is *that* what you're saying?'

'That is,' Vins conceded, 'hard to credit.'

'So,' said Murphy. He got up, and stepped to the hatch, and looked out at the hissing and rapturous rainfall. 'Here's what I think happened. We were off investigating your *winking* star, Vins, and then we all suffered some sort of group epilepsy, or mass hysteria, or loss of consciousness, and without realising it we piloted the ship back up and towards Earth.'

'We were days away,' Vins pointed out.

'So perhaps we were in a fugue state for days. Anyway, we weren't shaken out of it until we slammed into the atmosphere, and now we've crashed in the highlands in Peru, or Africa maybe.'

'There's nowhere on Earth,' Vins pointed out, 'as lovely as this. Where is there anywhere as mild, or balmy, as this? Peru, you say?'

'You ever *been* to Peru?' asked Edwards.

'I been a lot of places, and there's ice wherever *I've* been.'

'Never mind the climate,' said Edwards. 'What about the sunrises?'

'How is it,' agreed Vins, 'that the sunrise is in the west if this is Peru?'

'I don't know. But the advantage of my hypothesis is that it's Occam's Razor for all the stuff about planets appearing from nowhere, and it reduces all that to a single, simple problem. The sunrise.'

'And another problem,' Edwards pointed out, 'which is the lack of radio traffic.'

'The radio's broken,' said Murphy. 'I'm not happy about it.'

'The radio?'

'No, not happy about the *Murphy*, the Murphy-topia. I'm not happy about the status of my kingdom. I was looking forward to claiming the highlands as my personal kingdom. But if it's, you know, Peru, then there'll be some other alpha male who's already claimed these highlands.'

'The radio's not broken,' said Edwards. 'We can pick up background chatter. Bits and pieces. We just can't seem to locate any – to get a fix upon—'

'Vins,' said Murphy, sitting himself down again. 'Vins, Vins. What's your theory? You haven't told us your theory.'

'I think we've landed upon a banned world,' said Vins. He said this in a bright voice, but his mouth was angled downwards as he spoke. 'A forbidden planet. *That's* SF-y, isn't it?' He pronounced each of the letters in sfy separately, trisyllabic.

'A banned world,' said Murphy, as if savouring the idea. 'What an interesting notion. What a fanciful notion. What a dark horse you are, to be sure, Vins.'

The rain stopped sometime in the afternoon, and the clouds rolled away leaving the landscape washed and gleaming under the low sun as if glazed with strawberry and peach. The long stretch of grassland directly beneath them retained some of its yellow, and moved slowly, like the pelt of a lion. In the distance they could see a long inlaid band of bronze, curved and kinked like the marginal illustration in a Celtic manuscript: open water, glittering in the sun. And the sun went down and the stars came out.

Edwards, trying to identify where the Earth should be from their last known position, noticed something they should all have seen on the first night: that the stars hardly moved through the sky. He woke the others up.

'Earth,' he said, 'is just below the horizon.' He pointed. 'There. Mars, I think, is over there.'

'Send them a signal.'

'I did. But why should they be listening for a signal from this stretch of space? It's not even on the ecliptic. It's not as if there are any astronomers on Mars. And if there were, if there were any, you know, amateurs, why should they be looking down here? No, that's not what I woke you up to show you.'

'What then?'

'The stars aren't moving. I've been watching for an hour. I was waiting to see Earth come up over the horizon so I could send them a message. But it's not coming up.'

'You thought it was an hour,' said Murphy, crossly. 'Clearly it *wasn't* an hour. You probably sat there for five minutes and got impatient.'

So they settled down together, and all checked their watches, and looked east to where the sun had set, where familiar stars pebbled the sky. And an hour passed, and another, and the stars did not move.

Nobody said anything for a long time.

'Somebody has stopped the stars in their courses,' said Murphy. 'We're dead, we're all in the afterlife. Is that what happened? We crashed the ship and died, and this is the land of the dead.'

'I thought you were the one, Murphy, who wanted to apply Occam's Razor?' chided Edwards. 'That's a pretty elaborate explanation for the facts, don't you think? I don't feel dead. Do you? You feel that way?'

'Certainly not,' said Vins.

'But we've no idea what it feels like to feel dead,' Murphy pointed out.

'Exactly. It's a null hypothesis. Let's not go there. There must be another explanation.'

'The other explanation is that we're not rotating.'

'Except we saw the sun go round and set, so we *are* rotating. An Earth-sized world, pulling an Earth-strength gravity, rotates for half a day and then *stops* rotating? That makes no sense.'

'I'll tell you what makes sense,' said Murphy, hugging himself against the cold. 'This is a banned world. We are not supposed to be here. That's what makes sense.'

'Of course we're not supposed to be here,' agreed Vins. 'Supposed to be Venus, that's where. That's where we're supposed to be orbiting. Not here. But that's not to say it's a forbidden planet.'

'You were the one who said so!' Murphy objected.

'I was joking,' said Vins.

'Your joke may be coming true,' said Murphy. He coughed, loud and long. Then he said, 'The sun rises in the west and the stars don't move. You know what that is? That's things that the human eye was not supposed to see. That's a realm of magic – faery, that's where we are, and the faery queen is probably gathering her hounds to hunt us down for seeing this forbidden place.'

'Amusing, Murphy,' said Edwards, in a bland voice. 'Very fanciful and imaginative. Your fancy and your imagination – I find them amusing.'

'I'm going to sleep,' Murphy sulked, picking himself up and going back inside the ship. 'I'll meet my fate tomorrow with a clear head at least.'

The others stayed outside under the splendid, chilly, glittering stars and under that silkily-cold black sky. They talked, and reduced the possibilities to an order of plausibility. They discussed what to do. They discussed the possibility of making the ship whole again; perhaps by dismantling one of the thirty-six thrust engines and reassembling it as a sort of welding torch, so as to make good the breaches in the plasmetal hull. Nobody could think how to launch into space, though: the craft had not been built to achieve escape velocity unaided. They had not been planning on *landing* on Venus, after all. (The very idea!) Finally the sky started to pale and ease, as if the arc of the western horizon were a heated element thawing the black into rose and pearl and then into blushed tones of white.

The sun lifted itself into the sky.

'Well,' said Vins, with a tone of finality, 'that settles it. Clearly we *are* rotating. The lack of movement of the stars and the apparent movement of the sun: these data contradict one another. Seem to. It's hard to advance a coherent explanation that includes both of these pieces of observational data. Are we agreed?'

'I can't think what else,' said Edwards. 'We assume the sky is a simulation of some sort. Do we assume that?'

'We do,' said Sinclair.

'One of two explanations, then,' said Vins. 'Either the sky is a total simulation, upon which is projected a moving sun by day and motionless stars by night. Or else the sky is a real feature but some peculiarity of optics distorts the actual motion of the stars in some way.'

'It's hard to think what sort of phenomenon . . .' began Sinclair. But he stopped talking. He wasn't sure what he was going to say; and – anyway – the dawn was so very beautiful. They all sat looking down, all distracted by the loveliness of the view from their highland vantage-point: down across sloping grass-lands and marsh and the beaming seas and gleaming channels of water. And, woken by the light, the first birds were up; in nimble flight and giving voice to agile birdsong, bouncing their tenor and soprano trills off the blue ceiling of the sky – or, whatever it was.

They were all tired. They'd been up all night. Eventually they went inside the spaceship and slept.

The third day and the third night

Vins, Sinclair and Edwards woke sometime in the afternoon, the sun already declining towards the east.

Murphy had gone.

They searched for him, in a slightly desultory manner, round and about the ship; but it was clear enough where he had gone: a trail scuffed, slightly kinked but more-or-less straight, through the wet grasses and downwards. Clambering onto the top of the ship Edwards could follow this with his eye, and with binoculars, down and down, a wobbly ladder in the tights-material sheen of the fields all the way to where forest drew a dark line.

'He's gone into a forest. Down there, kilometres away.' He wanted to say something like: imagine a stretch of gold velvet, all brushed one way to smoothness, and a finger dragged through the velvet against the grain of the brushing – that's what his path looks like. But he couldn't find the words to say that. 'Should we go after him?' he called. 'Should we go?'

'He knows where we are,' said Sinclair. 'He knows how to get back here. He's probably just exploring.'

'And if he gets into trouble?'

'It's his look-out. He must take responsibility for himself,' said Vins. 'We all must shift for ourselves, after all.'

The three of them breakfasted on ship's supplies, sitting in the warm air and listening to the meagre, distant chimes of the birds and watching the flow and glitter of wind upon the grass. 'I could sit here forever,' said Edwards, in a relaxed voice.

The other two were silent, but it was a silent agreement.

'We need to get on,' said Vins, as if dragging the sentence up from great deeps. 'We need to explore. To fix the ship. That's what we need to do.'

They did nothing. After breakfast they dozed in the sun. Murphy did not return. Who knew where he had gone?

The one thing so obvious that none of them bothered to point it out was that this world was paradisical compared to the wrecked and wasted landscapes of home. And that because it was paradisical, it was very obviously not a real place. They were dead, and had gone to a material heaven, perhaps on account of some sort of oversight. They had died in the crash. Or they had been transported through a different sort of spatial-discontinuity, one that translated them from real to mythic space. They were to feed forever amongst the mild-eyed melancholy lotos-eaters now.

The land of the sirens, in which Odysseus's crew had

languished so pleasantly and purposelessly. Was *that* a forbidden world? Was it banned to subsequent explorers? Why else was it never again discovered?

It may still be there, some island or stretch of coast in the Mediterranean protected by a cloak of invisibility, some magic zone or curtain through which only a few, select and lucky mariners stumble. Who knows?

All this culture and learning bounced around their heads: Vins, Sinclair and Edwards. They knew all about Homer and Mohammed, and they knew all about Shakespeare and Proust, even though these people about whom they were so knowledgeable were a completely different sort of creature to themselves. These Homers and Van Goghs were all super-beings, elevated, godlike; and the residue of their golden-age achievements in the minds of our scientists has the paradoxical effect of shrinking *us* by comparison. Don't you think?

Best not think about it. What if they *are* in the land of the Lotos? Maybe they're lucky, that's all. Don't you wish *you* could go there?

The sun set in the east. Colour and brightness drained out of the western sky, out of the zenith flowing down to the east with osmotic slowness, and leaving behind a purply black dotted with perfectly motionless stars. The last of the day was a broad stretch of white-yellow sky over the eastern horizon, patched with skinny horizontal clouds of golden brown. For long minutes the last of the sunlight, coming up over the horizon, touched the bottom line of these clouds with fierce and molten light, so that it looked as if several sinuous heating elements, glowing bright and hot with the electricity passing through them, had been fixed to the matter of the sky. Then the light faded away from the clouds, and they browned and blackened against a compressing layer of sunset lights: a sky honey and marmalade, and then a grey-orange, and finally blue, and after that black.

It was night again.

Something agitated Vins enough to get him up and huffing around. 'The stars have moved a little,' he said. 'There – that's the arc of the Corona Australis. Say what you like but *don't* tell me I don't know my constellations.'

'So?'

'It's higher. Yesterday the lowest star was right on the horizon, on that little hill silhouetted there. Today it's a fraction above.'

'So we're rotating real slow,' said Sinclair. 'I can't say I care. I can't say I'm bothered. I'm going to sleep.'

The fourth day and the fourth night

In the morning Vins left the ship. He set off in the opposite direction to Murphy; not down the slope towards the forest and the long shining stretches of open water; but up, higher into the highlands. He had no idea where Murphy had gone, or what he had been after; but something inside him prompted him to go higher. Go up, Moses. He had a vision of himself climbing and climbing until he reached the summit of some snow-clenched mountain top at the very heart of the world from which the whole planet – or at least this whole hemisphere – would be visible. Like Mount Purgatory, he thought, from Dante. As if he had anything to do with Dante! Godlike figures from the golden age.

Vins didn't creep away as Murphy had done. He prepared a pack, some supplies, some tools, a couple of scientific instruments. Then he woke the other two. He told them what he wanted to do; and they sat, looking stupidly at him from under their overhanging foreheads, and didn't say anything. 'You sure you don't want to come with me?' he said. He felt an obscure and disabling fear deep inside him, a terror that if he stayed at the crash site he'd slide into torpor and that would be the end of him. Who was it had said that word? One of them. Torpor, torpor. Oh, he had to get out and away. He had to move.

'Do what you like,' said Sinclair.

'It makes no sense to me,' said Edwards, 'to go marching off without any sort of objective. Shouldn't you have an objective? As a scientist?'

'My objective is to explore. What's more scientific than exploration?'

Edwards looked at him, blinked, looked again. 'We should stay here,' he said, slowly. He turned to look at the buckled ship. 'We should mend the ship.'

'We should,' agreed Vins. 'But we don't. You *notice* that? There's something here that's rendering us idle. Idleness doesn't suit us.'

Sinclair laughed at this. 'Let him go,' he said, stretching himself on a broad boulder with a westward-facing facet to warm himself in the new sunlight. 'He's the hairiest of us all.'

Vins winced at this. 'Don't be like that. What is this, school?'

'It's true,' said Sinclair. 'Murphy *was* the hairiest, but he's gone God-knows-where. You're the hairiest now, and you'll go, and good riddance. Go after Murphy. Go pick fleas from his pelt. I'm the smoothest of the lot of you and I'll stay here and *thank* you very much and good *night*.'

'I'm not going after Murphy, I'm going higher, into the highlands.'

'Go where you like.'

Edwards wouldn't meet Vins' gaze, so Vins shouldered his pack and marched off, striding westward into the setting sun. He could feel Sinclair's eyes upon his back as he went, almost a heat, like a ray; Sinclair just lounging there like a lazy great ape, watching him go. The hairiest indeed!

Then Vins had a second thought. He wanted to get up high, didn't he? Why not lift himself clean off the ground?

It surprised him how much courage it took to turn about and stomp back down to the ship again. Sinclair was still there on his rock, watching him with lazy insolence. Edwards had taken off his shoes and climbed to the top of the wreckage, clinging to the dew-wet surface with his toes and the palms of his feet. He was gazing east, down, away.

Vins didn't say anything to either of them. Instead he went into the ship and retrieved a bundle of gossamer-fabric and plastic cord and tied it to the top of his backpack. Then he pulled out a small cylinder of helium, no longer or thicker than a forearm though densely heavy. He tied a grapple-rope to this and dragged it after him.

There were no more goodbyes. He stomped away.

Something was bugging Vins, preying on his mind. It was as if he'd caught a glimpse of something out of the corner of his eye without exactly noticing it, such that it had registered only in his subconscious (that gift of the gods, the unconscious mind). He felt he should have understood by now. Something was wrong, or else something was profoundly and obviously right and he couldn't see it.

What?

He marched on, the cylinder dragging through the turf behind him and occasionally clanging on the upcrops of rock that poked through the grass. It was an effort with every step to haul the damn thing, but Vins had found in stubbornness and ill-temper a substitute for willpower. He marched on. He didn't know where he was going. He had, as Edwards might say, no objective. But on he went.

The grass grew shorter the higher he went, and the wind became fresher. The sun was directly above him, and then it was behind him, and he was chasing his own waggish shadow, marching up and up. His field of view was taken up with the pale-green and -yellow grass sloping up directly in front of him. Each strand moved with slightly separate motion in the burly wind, like agitated worms, or the fronds of some impossibly massive underwater polypus.

He stopped, sat on a stool of bare rock and drank from his water bottle. Looking back the direction he had come he could see the ship now, very distant. Edwards was no longer standing on its back. Nor could he see Sinclair. From this eagle's vantage point, the path the crashing ship had gouged in the soil was very visible, a mottled painterly scar through the grasslands culminating in the broken-backed hourglass of the ship itself. It seemed unlikely, Vins thought, that in crashing they had not simply dashed themselves to atoms.

Beyond the wreck the grasslands stretched away. Vins could see a great deal more of the terrain from up here. There was no sign of habitation, or civilisation, or anything like that. Just nature, in paradisical mode. Their ship had come down directly above a broad hilly spit of land that lay between what looked like two spreading estuaries, north and south. Each of these estuaries widened and spilled into what Vins took to be separate seas – one reaching as far north as he could see and one as far south. It wasn't possible to see whether these seas were connected; whether, in other words, the two estuaries were inlets into one enormous ocean.

The setting sun threw a broadcast spread of lights across these two bodies of water, and they glowed ferociously, beautifully. As he sat there looking down on this landscape Vins felt the disabling intensity of it all. As if its loveliness might just drain all his willpower and leave him just sitting here, on this saddle of bare rock, sitting in the afternoon warmth gazing down upon it.

He shook himself. He couldn't allow this place to suck out his strength of purpose. Maybe he was a *Homo neanderthalensis*, but he was a scientist. He flew spacecraft between the planets.

He picked himself up and marched on, uphill all the way, until the light had thickened and blackened around him. Eventually, exhausted, he stopped and ate some food and rolled himself into his sleeping bag and tried to sleep on the grass. But, tired as he was, he was awake a long time. Something nagging at him. Something about the perspective downhill – those two broad estuaries draining into whatever wide sea, hidden in distance, in haze and clouds and the curve of the world's horizon. What about it? Why did it seem familiar? He couldn't think why.

The fifth day

He was woken by something crawling on his face, a lacy caterpillar or beetle with legs like twitching eyelashes. He sat up, rubbing his cheeks with the back of his hand and brushing it away.

It was light.

The sun was up over the crown of the hill westward and shining straight in his eyes.

He wiped his face with a dampee, and munched some rations and drank a tab of coffee. The wind stirred around him. The landscape below him was, in material terms, the same one before which he had gone to sleep; but under the different orientation of sunlight, under white morning illumination instead of rosy sunset, it seemed somehow radically different. The two estuaries were still there, kinked and coastlined in that maddeningly familiar way, but now their waters were gunmetal- and broccoli-coloured, a hard and almost tangible mass of colour upon which waves could not be made out. The grassland was dark with dew, hazed over in stretches by a sort of blue blur. The ship was still there, black as a nut, but Vins couldn't make out either of his shipmates.

'So,' he said to himself. 'Let's get a proper look.'

He unrolled the balloon fabric and fitted the helium cylinder into its inflation tube. Then he untangled the harness, and manoeuvred himself into it, knotting the rest of his backpack to a strap so that it would dangle beneath him as ballast. Then, steadily, he inflated the balloon.

It took only a few minutes, the flop of fabric swelling and then popping up, like a featureless cartoon head of prodigious size, to loll and nod above him. Soon the material was taut, and the breeze was pushing Vins down the hill and across. His feet danced over the turf, keeping up with the movement for a while with a series of balletic leaps, and dragging the pack behind him. Then he was up, the cylinder in his lap and his bag a pendulum below.

He rose quickly through the dawn air. The breeze was taking him diagonally down the hill, but only slowly. At first he looked behind himself, straining over his shoulder to see what was over the brow of the hill. But the upwards sloping land didn't seem to come to a peak; or at least not one over which Vins could see.

He turned his attention to the eastward landscape. To his right he could see, as he rose higher, that there was a vast north–south coastline, a tremendous beach bordering an ocean that reached all the way to the horizon. To his left he could see the other of the two estuaries; its north shoreline revealed itself to be in fact a long, skinny neck of land. There was a third estuary, even further to the north of this. The shape of these arrangements of land and water seemed so familiar to Vins, naggingly so, but he couldn't place it.

He fixed his gaze on the easternmost horizon, but even though he was getting higher and higher he didn't seem to be seeing over the curve of it. In fact, by some peculiar optical illusion or other it appeared to be rising as *he* rose. That wasn't right.

Vins tried looking up, but the balloon obscured his vision. He thought again about the peculiarities of this world. Was the sky really nothing but a huge blue-painted dome? Would he bump into it momentarily? Perhaps not a physical barrier, but some sort of force-field, or holographic medium, upon which the motionless stars and the hurtling sun could be projected? Were they in some private high-tech parkland?

The air was thin. It had gotten thin surprisingly rapidly.

Maybe I *am* the hairiest, Vins thought to himself; but I'm a scientist for all that.

Chill. And blue-grey.

Looking down, looking eastward, Vins knew he had risen high

enough. He stared. He gawped. Then, with automatic hand, he began venting gas from his balloon. He commenced his descent. He started coming down. The landscape below him had finally clicked with his memory. It was the map of Europe rendered in some impossible geographical form of photographic-negative: the green land coloured blue for sea, the blue sea coloured green for land.

The ship had come down onto the broad grasslands that would, in a normal map of Europe, have been the Atlantic Ocean. The two wide seas he could see from his vantage point were shaped exactly like England, to the north, and like France, to the south. Impossible of course, but there you were. The estuaries that had nagged at his memory had done so because they were shaped like Cornwall and like Normandy. The English Channel was a broad corridor of land, with sea to the north and sea to the south, that widened in the distance into a pleasant meadowland where the North Sea should have been.

Recognising the familiar contours of the European mainland had impressed itself upon Vins' consciousness so powerfully that it had dizzied him. It must be hallucination. He stared, he gawked. It was like the visual rebus of the duckrabbit, which you can see *either* as a duck *or* as a rabbit, and, then, as you get used to it, you find that you can flip your vision from one to the other at will. Vins had the heady sense that the broad bodies of water were *in fact land* (an impossibly flat and desert land), and the variegated stretches of landscape were *in fact water* (upon which light played a myriad of fantastical mirages). But of course that wasn't it. The visual image flipped round again. The land was land and the sea was sea. It was an impossible, inverted geography. The Atlantic Highlands. The Sea of England. The Sea of France. He was in no real place. He didn't know where he was. He was dreaming. He could make no sense of it.

The land rushed up towards him. He had vented too much gas from his balloon – he'd done it too fast – he was coming down too quickly. His mind wasn't working terribly well.

His feet went pummelling into the turf and he felt something twang in his right ankle. Pain thrummed up his leg, and his face went hard onto the grass. The wind was still pushing the balloon onwards, and dragging him awkwardly along. He fumbled with his harness and with a burly sense of release the balloon broke free and bobbed off over the landscape.

Vins pulled himself over and sat up. His ankle throbbed. Pain slithered up and down his shin. He watched the balloon recede, ludicrously flexible and bubble-like as it rolled and tumbled down the slope.

This crazy place.

He hauled his pack in by pulling on the cord, hand over hand, the pack dancing and bouncing over the turf towards him. From its innards he took out a medipack. The compress felt hot and slimy as he ripped it from its cover, but it did its job as he twined it around his leg. The pain dulled.

As soon as the compress had stiffened sufficiently to bear weight, he pulled himself up and started the hopalong trek back down the slope. At least, he told himself, it's downhill. At least it's not *uphill.* Downhill across the Atlantic.

He laughed.

He anticipated the reaction of the others when he told them his discovery. To be precise, he rehearsed the possibilities: from galvanising amazement to indifference, or even hostility. So what they were living in an impossible landscape? The sun rose in the west and the stars did not move. Maybe they were indeed dead; in which case, why bother? Why bother about anything?

But when he arrived at the ship it was deserted: both Sinclair and Edwards had gone. They had taken few or no supplies with them, and at first Vins assumed that they were just scouting out the locality. But after a while of fruitlessly calling their names, and several hours of waiting, he came to the conclusion that they must have wandered permanently away, like Murphy. Which would be just like them.

If he saw them again – no. *When* he saw them again he would grab them by their necks and shake them. Was this any way to run a scientific spaceship? He ought to plunge his hands in between their chins and chest bones and squeeze. Squee-eeze.

When he saw them.

His fury was tiring. And what with the long trek (downhill, sure, but even so) and the ache in his bungled-up ankle, Vins felt sleepy. He ate, he drank some, and then he lay down in one of the bunks and fell into dream-free sleep.

The fifth night

He awoke with a little yelp, and it took him a moment before he was aware that he was inside a blacked-out ship, crashed onto a world itself plunged into the chasm of night. 'Though,' he said to himself, aloud (to hearten his spirits in all this darkness), 'how we're plunged into the chasm of the night when the world don't seem to rotate, not a tittle, not a jot, that's beyond me.'

His ankle was sore, and seemed sorer for being ignored. It was a resentful and selfish pain. Analgesic, that was the needful.

'Sinclair,' he called. Then he remembered. 'I'm going to wrestle your *neck* you deserter,' he hooted. 'Sinclair, you hear? I ought to stamp on your chest.'

He had gone to sleep without leaving a torch nearby, so he had to fumble about. But in the perfect blackness he couldn't orient himself at all; couldn't get a mental picture on his location. He came through a bent-out-of-shape hatchway, running his fingers round the rim, and into another black room. No idea where he was. He ranged about, hopeless. Then, through another opening, he saw a rectangle of grey-black gleam, and it smelt clean, and it was the main hatch leading outside.

He stepped through, into the glimmer of starlight to get his bearings. He could turn and take in the bulk of the ship, and only then the mental map snapped into focus. First aid box would be back inside and over to the left. *He* was the hairiest? He was the only one not to have abandoned ship! For the mother of love and all begorrah, as Murphy would have said if he'd been in one of his quaint moods, they'd *all* abandoned ship. *They* were the hairiest, damn them.

His ankle was giving him sour hell, and the first aid box would be back in through the hatch, over to the left. He could find it with his fingers-ends. But he didn't go back inside.

The hair at the back of his neck tingled and stood up like grass as the wind passes through it.

'I,' he said, to the starlit landscape, but his voice was half-cracked, so he cleared his throat and spoke out loudly and clearly, 'I know you're there. Whoever you are.'

He turned, there was nobody.

He turned again, nobody.

'Come out from where you're hiding,' he said. 'Is that you, Murphy? That would be *like* your idea of practical japery, you hairy old fool.'

He turned, and there was a silhouette against the blackness. Too tall to be Murphy, much too tall to be Edwards or Sinclair. Taller than any person in fact.

Vins stood. The sound of his own breathing was ratchety and intrusive, as if something had malfunctioned somewhere. 'Who are you?' he asked. 'What do you want? Who are you?'

The silhouette shifted, and moved. It hummed a little, a surprisingly high-pitched noise – surprising because of its height. It was a person, clearly; tall but oddly thin, like a putty person stretched between long-boned head and flipper-like feet. Oh, *too* tall.

'What are you doing?' Vins repeated.

'You're not supposed to be here,' said the figure – a man, though one with a voice high-pitched enough almost to sound womanly.

'We're not supposed to – we *crashed*,' returned Vins, his ankle biting at the base of his leg a little. He had to sit down. He could see a little more now, as his eye dark-adapted; but with no moon, and with no moonlight, it was still a meagre sort of seeing. Vins moved towards where a rock stood, its occasional embedded spots of mica glinting in the light. This was the same rock Sinclair had been lying upon when Vins had last seen him.

'I got to sit down,' he said, by way of explanation.

He could see that this long thin person was carrying something in his right hand, but he couldn't see what.

'Sit down, OK? Do you mind if I sit down, OK? Is that OK?'

'Sure,' said the stranger.

Vins sat, heavily, and lifted his frozen-sore ankle, and picked at the dressing. He needed a new one. This one wasn't giving him any benefit any more. The first aid box would be in through the hatch and to the left.

'You're trespassing,' said the stranger. 'You've no right to be here. This world is forbidden to you.'

'Is it death?' said Vins, feeling a spurt of fear-adrenalin, which is also recklessness-adrenalin, in his chest at the words. Did he dare say such a thing? What if this stranger were the King of the Land of the Dead, and what if he, Vins, were disrespecting him? 'Are we all dead? That was one theory we had, as to why the sun rises awry, and why the stars don't move – and – and,' he added, hurriedly, remembering the previous day, 'why the map is so wrong.'

'Wrong?'

'An England-shaped sea where England-land should be. An Atlantic-shaped landmass where the ocean should be. *You* know what I'm talking about.'

'Of course I do. This is my world. Of course I do.'

'My ankle is hurting fit to scream,' said Vins.

The stranger moved his arm in the darkness. 'This,' he said, 'will have to go.' Vins assumed he was pointing at the shuttle. 'You've no right to dump this junk here. I'll have it moved, I tell you. And you – you are trespassing on a forbidden world. You, sir, have incurred the penalty for trespassing.'

'You can see pretty well for such a dark night,' said Vins.

'You can't?' said the stranger, and he sounded puzzled. 'Old eyes, is it?'

'I'm thirty-three,' said Vins, bridling.

'I didn't mean *old* in that sense.'

There was a silence. The quiet between them was devoid of cricket noise; no blackbird sang. The air was blank and perfectly dark and only the meanest dribble of starlight illuminated it. Then with a new warmth, as if he had finally understood, the stranger said: 'You're a *Homo neanderthalensis*?'

'And I suppose,' replied Vins, jesting, 'that you're a *Homo "sapiens"*?' But even as he gave the words their sarcastic playground spin he knew they were true. Of course true. A creature from the spiritus mundi and from dream and childhood game, standing right here in front of him.

'You're from Earth, of course,' the *sapiens* was saying. 'You recognised the map of Europe. You steered this craft here. I don't understand why you came here. You boys aren't supposed to even know this place even exists.'

Vins felt a hard knot of something in his chest, like an elbow trying to come out from inside his ribs. It was intensely uncomfortable. This being from myth and legend, and the race of Homer and Shakespeare and Mohammed and Jesus, and *standing right in front of him now*. He didn't know what to say. There wasn't anything for him to say.

'You want,' the human prompted, 'to answer my question?'

'You're *actually* a *Homo sapiens*?'

'You never met one?'

'Not in the flesh.'

'I lose track of time,' said the *Homo sapiens*. 'It's probably been, I don't know. Centuries. It's like that, out here. The time – drifts. You got a name?'

'Vins,' said Vins.

'Well, you're a handsome fellow, Vins. My name is Ramon Harburg Guthrie, a fine old human name, a thousand years old, like me. As I am myself. And no older.' He chuckled, though Vins couldn't see what was funny.

'A thousand years?' Vins repeated.

'Give or take. It's been half that time since your lot were shaped, I'll tell you that.'

'The last human removed herself four centuries ago,' said Vins, feeling foolish to speak such kindergarten sentences.

Ramon Harburg Guthrie laughed. 'Shouldn't you be worshipping me as a god?' he asked. 'Or something along those lines?'

'Worship you as a god? Why would I want to be doing a thing like that? You're genus *Homo* and I'm genus *Homo*. What's to worship?'

'We uplifted you,' Ramon Harburg Guthrie pointed out. 'Recombined you and backed you out of the evolutionary cul-de-sac, and primed you with—' He stopped. 'Listen to *me*!' he said. 'I'm probably giving entirely the wrong impression. I don't want to be worshipped as a god.'

'I'm glad to hear it,' said Vins. 'There's nothing sub-capacity about *my* brain pan. I speak from experience, but also from scientific research into the matter, using some of the many *Homo sapiens sapiens* skulls that have been dug out of the soil of the Earth. I've spent twelve years studying science.'

'Our science,' said Ramon Harburg Guthrie.

'Science is science, and who cares who discovered it? And if you care who discovered it, then it's not *your* science Ramon Harburg Guthrie, it's Newton's and Einstein's.'

But his tone had wandered the wrong side of angry. The *Homo sapiens* lifted whatever it was he was holding in his right hand. When he spoke again, his high voice was harder-edged. 'I built this place,' he said. 'It's mine. It's a private world, and visitors are not allowed. I don't care about your brain pan, or about my brain pan, I only care about my privacy. Are there others?'

'We crashed,' said Vins, feeling a sense of panic growing now, though he wasn't sure exactly why. It was more than just the mysterious *something* the man was holding in his right hand. It was another thing, he wasn't sure what.

'I don't care how you came here. You're trespassing. Not welcome.'

'It's hardly fair. It's not as if you put up a sign saying no entry.'

He scoffed. 'That'd be tantamount to shouting aloud to the whole system, *Here I am*! That'd be like putting a parsec-wide neon arrow pointing at my home. And why would I want to do that? I built my world away from the ecliptic and down, it's as flat as a coin and its slender edge is angled towards Earth. You can't see me, you inheritors. Nobody on that polluted old world. You *don't know* I'm here. There are similar ruses used all about this solar system, and eyries and haunts, radio-blanked bubbles and curves of habitable landscape tucked away. A thousand baubles and twists of landscape. Built by the old guard, the last of the *truly* wealthy and *truly* well-bred. Who'd trade in true breeding for a mere enhanced physical strength and endurance?' He spoke these last five words with a mocking intonation, as if the very idea were absurd. 'And yes, I know your brain pans are the same size. But size isn't everything, my dearie.'

Vins was shivering, or perhaps trembling with fear, but he summoned his courage. 'I'm no dearie of yours,' he said. 'What's that in your hand anyway? A weapon, is it?'

'How many were there in your crew?'

Of course Vins couldn't lie, not when asked a direct question like that. He tried one more wriggle. 'A severely spoken and impolite question,' he said.

'How many in your *crew*?'

'Four,' he said. 'Including me.'

'Inside?'

'Are *they* inside? The ship?'

'Are they inside, yes.'

'No. They wandered off. They were seduced by this world, I think. It's a beautiful place, especially when you've been tanked up in a spaceship for three months. It's a beautiful, beautiful place'

'Thank you!' said the *Homo sapiens* Ramon Harburg Guthrie. And, do you know what? There was genuine pleasure in his voice. He was actually flattered. 'It's my big dumb object. Big and dumb, but *I* like it.'

The sky, minutely and almost imperceptibly, was starting to pale over to the west. The silhouette had taken on the intimations of solidity; more than just a 2D gap in the blackness, it was starting to bulk. Dark grey face propped on dark grey body, but there was a perceptible difference in tone between the two things, one smooth and one the rougher texture of fabric.

'*You* didn't build this,' said Vins. 'I'm not being disrespectful, but. I'm not. Only – who can build a whole world? You're not a god. Sure the legacy of *Homo sapiens* is a wonderful thing, the language and the culture and so on. But *build* a whole world?'

'Indeed, I did build it,' said Ramon Harburg Guthrie levelly.

'How many trillions of tonnes of matter, to pull one g?' said Vins. 'And how do you hide an Earth-sized object from observation by . . .'

'You've done well,' said Ramon Harburg Guthrie, 'if you've taken the science with which we left you and built space craft capable of coming all the way out here.' He sounded indulgent. 'But that's not to say that you've caught up with us. We've been at it millennia. You've only been independent a handful of centuries. Left to your own devices for a handful of centuries.'

The light was growing away behind the western horizon. The human's face was still indistinct. The object he held in his right hand was still indistinct. But in a moment it would be clearer. Vins was shivering hard now. It was very cold.

'That's no explanation, if you don't mind me saying so,' he said, with little heaves of mis-emphasis on account of his shivering chest and his chattery teeth. The human didn't seem in the least incommoded by the cold.

'It's not a globe,' he said. 'It's my world, and I built it as I liked.

It's not for you. It's a *me*-topia. You're not supposed even to be here.'

'It's beautiful and its empty, it's void. There aren't even deer or antelope or cows. How is that utopia?'

He was expecting the human to say *each to his own*, or *I prefer solitude* or something like that. But he didn't. He said: 'Oh, my dearie, it's void on *this* side. I haven't got round to doing anything with this side. There's world enough and time for that. But on the *other* side of the coin, it's crowded with fun and interest.'

'The other side,' said Vins.

'It's a little over a thousand miles across,' said Ramon Harburg Guthrie. 'So it's pretty much the biggest coin ever minted. But it's not trillions of tonnes of matter; it's a thin circular sheet of dense-stuff, threaded with gravity wiring. There's some distortion. For instance, it appears to go up at the rim, highlands in all directions, but on *both* sides, which is odd.'

'Which is odd,' repeated Vins. He didn't know why it was odd.

'It's odd because it's a gravitational effect. It's not that the *rim* is any thicker than any other place on the disc. But the gravitational bias helps keep the atmosphere from spilling over the sides, I suppose. I lost interest in those sorts of technicalities a while ago. And the central territories are flat enough to preserve the landscape almost exactly.'

'Preserve the landscape,' chattered Vins.

'I had it pressed into the underlying matter: the countries of my youth. That's on the other side. On *this* side is the reverse of the recto. It's the anti-Europe. But landscaped, of course. Water and biomass and air added; not just nude to space. No, no. It's ready. Sometime soon I'll live over this side for a while.'

'The anti-Europe,' said Vins. The cold seemed to be slowing his thought processes. He couldn't work it out.

'Stamp an R in a sheet of gold, and the other side will have a little Я standing proud,' he said. '*You* know that. Stamp a valley in one side of a sheet and you get a mountain on the other side.'

The light was almost strong enough to see. That grey predawn light, so cool and fine and satiny.

'Stamp a *Homo neanderthalensis* out of the hominid base matter,' Ramon Harburg Guthrie said, as if talking to himself, 'and you stamp out a backwards-facing *Homo sapiens* on the verso.' This seemed to amuse him. He laughed, at any rate.

Vins put a knuckle to his eyes, and rubbed away some of the chill of the night. The man's features were – just – visible in the grey of the pre-dawn: a long nose, small eyes, a sawn-off forehead and eggshell cranium above it. Like a cartoon-drawing of a *sapiens*. Like a caricature from a schoolbook. A stretched out, elfin figure. A porcelain and anorexic giant.

'You're not welcome,' Guthrie said, one final time. 'This world is forbidden to you and your sort. I'll find your crewmates, and give them the sad news. But I'll deal with you first, and I'm sorry to say it, because I'm not a bloodthirsty sort of fellow. But what can I do? But – trespassers – will be—' and he raised his right hand.

This was the moment when Vins found out for sure what that right hand contained. It was a weapon, of course; and Vins was already ahead of the action. He pushed forward on his muscular Neanderthal legs, moving straight for the human: but then he jinked hard as his sore ankle permitted him, ninety-degrees right. The lurch forward was to frighten Ramon Harburg Guthrie into firing before he was quite ready; the jink to the right was to hope the projectile missed, and give him a chance of making it to the long grass.

But Ramon Harburg Guthrie was more level-headed than that. It's true he cried out, a little yelp of fear as the bulky Neanderthal loomed up at him, but he kept his aim reasonably steady. The weapon discharged with a booming noise and Vins' head rang like a gong. There was a disorienting slash of pain across his left temple and he spun and tumbled, his bad ankle folding underneath him. There was a great deal of pain, suddenly, out of nowhere, and his eyes weren't working. The sky had been folded up and propped on its side. It was grey, drained of life, drained of colour. But it wasn't on its side; Vins was lying on the turf beside the rock, and it was the angle at which he was looking at it.

There was a throb. This was more than a mere knock. It was a powerful, skull-clenching *throb*.

Nevertheless when Ramon Harburg Guthrie's leg appeared in Vins' line of sight, at the same right-angle as the sky, he knew what it meant. This was no time to be lying about, lounging on the floor, waiting for the coup-de-grace of another projectile in the—

He was up. He put all his muscular strength into the leap, and it was certainly enough to surprise Ramon Harburg Guthrie. Vins' shoulder, coming up like a piston upstroke, caught him under the chin, or against the chest, or somewhere (it wasn't easy to see); and there was an *ooph* sound in Vins' left ear. He brought his heavy right arm round as quick as he could, and there was a soggy impact of fist on flesh. Not sure which part of flesh; but it was a softer flesh than Vins' thick skin-pelt. It was a more fragile bone than the thick stuff that constituted Vins' brain pan. Although, as he had said, the thickness didn't mean that there was any compromise in size.

The next thing that happened was that Vins heard a rushing noise. He looked where Ramon Harburg Guthrie had been, and there was only a thread, string wet and heavy with black phlegm, and it wobbled as if blown in the dawn breeze, and when Vins looked up he saw this string attached to the shape of a flying human male. The string broke and then another spooled down, angling now because the flying man (propelled by whatever powerpack he was wearing, whatever device it was that lifted him away from the pull of the artificial gravity) was flying away to the north.

Stunned by his grazed head it took Vins a second to figure out what he was seeing. The string was a drool of blood falling from a wound he, Vins, had inflicted on the head of Ramon Harburg Guthrie. 'Clearly,' he said aloud, as he put a finger to his own head-wound, 'clearly he's still conscious enough to be operating whatever fancy equipment is helping him fly away.' His fingers came away jammy with red. 'Clearly I didn't hit him hard enough.'

The sun was up now. In the new light Vins found the gun that, in his pain and shock, and in his hurry to get away, Ramon Harburg Guthrie had dropped.

The sixth morning

Whilst the figure of the *sapiens* was still visible, just, in the northern sky, Vins hurried inside the shuttle; he pulled out some food, the first aid pack, some netting. It all went into a pack, together with the gun.

When he came out the *sapiens* was nowhere to be seen.

His head was hurting. His ankle was hurting.

He hurried away through the long grass, following the path that Murphy had originally made. He didn't want to leave a new trail, one that would (of course!) be obvious from the air; but at the same time he didn't want to loiter by the shuttle. Who knew what powers of explosive destruction Ramon Harburg Guthrie could bring screaming out of the sky? It was his world, after all.

There were a number of lone trees growing high out of the grass before the forest proper began, and Murphy's old track passed by one of these. Vins let the first go, stopped at the second. He clambered into the lower branches, and shuffled along the bough to ensure that the leaves were giving him cover. He scanned the sky, but there was nothing.

There was time, now, to tend to himself. He pulled a pure-pad from the first aid and stuck it to the side of his head, feeling with his finger first. A hole, elliptically shaped, like the mouth of a hollow reed cut slantways across. Blood was pulsing out of it. Blood had gone over the left of his face, glued itself into his six-day beard, made a plasticky mat over his cheek. He must look a sight. But he was alive.

He ate some food, and drank more than he wanted; but it wouldn't do to dehydrate. Exsanguinations provoke dehydration. He knew that. He was a scientist.

The leaves on the tree were plump, dark-green, cinque-foil. There were very many of them, and they rubbed up against one another and trembled and buzzed in the breeze. The sky was a high blue, clear and pure.

The sixth afternoon

He dozed. The day moved on.

He heard somebody approaching, tramping lustily out of the forest. Presumably not Ramon Harburg Guthrie then.

It was Murphy. He could hardly have been making a bigger racket. Vins' strong fingers pulled up a chunk of bark from the bough upon which he rested, and when Murphy came underneath the tree he threw it down upon him.

'Quiet,' he hissed. 'You want to get us killed?'

'No call to throw pebbles at me,' said Murphy, in a hurt voice, his head back.

'It was bark, and it was called for. Come up here and be quick and be *quiet*.'

When he was up, and when Murphy had gotten past the point of repeating, 'What happened to your head? What did you do to your head? There's blood all over your head . . .'

Vins explained.

Murphy thought about this. 'It makes sense.'

'Where did you get to, anyway?'

'I was exploring!' cried Murphy, in a large, self-justifying voice.

'Keep quiet!'

'You're not the captain, and neither you aren't,' said Murphy.

'You're not the one to tell me don't go exploring. Are we scientists? I've been down to the sea, to where the surf grinds thunder out of the beach. All manner of shells and . . .' He stopped. 'This feller shot you?'

'It's his world.'

He peered close at Vins' head. 'That's some trepanning he's worked on you. That's some hole.'

'He made it, and he says we're not allowed here. He'll kill all four of us. We can't afford to be blundering about.'

'He's threatening murder. That would be murder.'

'It surely is.'

'And is he,' asked Murphy, 'not *concerned* to be committing murder upon us?'

'He's *Homo sapiens*,' said Vins. 'I told you.'

'And so you did. It's hard to take in. But it explains . . .' He trailed off.

'What does it explain?'

'This is an artefact, of course it is. That'll be the strange sky, that'll explain it. The stars don't move, or hardly, because it doesn't rotate. The sun – that'll be an orbiting device; flying its way around and about. Maybe a mirror – maybe a crystal globe refracting sunlight to produce a variety of effects.' He seemed pleased with himself. 'That explains a lot.'

'You sound like Edwards,' said Vins.

'Don't you be insulting my family name in suchwise fashion!'

'It's a thousand miles across,' said Vins. 'It's a flat disc. I don't know how he generates the gravity. It's clearly not by *mass*.'

'So you met an actual breathing *Homo sapiens*?' asked Murphy, as one might ask *you met a unicorn? you met a cyclops?*

'I think,' said Vins, 'that he was expecting me to . . . I don't know. To worship him as a god.'

Murphy whooped with laughter, and then swallowed the noise before Vins could shush him. 'Why on sweet wide water would he want such a thing?'

'He said that he – he said that *they* – uplifted us,' said Vins.

'Brought us out of the evolutionary dustbin, that sort of thing. Taught us the language. Left us their culture, save us the bother of spending thousands of years making our own. He was implying, I think, that we *owed* them.'

'Did you ever read Frankenstein's monster's story? That's a *Homo sapiens* way of thinking,' said Murphy. 'There's something alien in all that duty, indebtedness, belatedness, *you-owe-me* rubbish. But what you should've said to *him*, what you *should* have said, is: my right and respectfulness, sir, didn't Shakespeare uplift *you* out of the aesthetic blankness of the middle ages? Didn't Newton uplift you out of the ignorance of the dark ages, give you the power to fly the spaceways? Do you worship Newton as a god? Course you don't – you say thank you and tap at your brow with your knuckles and you *move on*.'

'It's all a dim age,' agreed Vins. He was referring to the elder age. It was something in the past, like the invention of the wheel or the smelting of iron, but only a few cranks spent too much time bothering about it. Too much to do.

'How could you fail to move on? What sort of a person would you be? An ancestor-worshipper, or something like that.'

'They withdrew from the world,' said Vins. 'It's vacant possession. It's ours, now. All the rainy, stony spaces of it.'

'And I say this is the same, this place we've stumbled into. I say this Murphytopia is the same case – it's vacant possession.'

He was quiet for a while. Vins was scanning the sky through the branches.

'I say it's ours and I say the hell with him,' said Murphy, rolling his fist through the air.

'Here, though,' repeated Vins. 'It's forbidden us. He says it's forbidden to us.'

'*He* says?' boomed Murphy, climbing up on his legs on the bough to shout the phrase at the manufactured sky. 'And who's *he* to stop us?'

'Will you *hush*?' snapped Vins.

The sky was a clear watercolour wash from high dark blue to

the pink of the low eastern sky. There were a few thready horizontal clouds, like loose strands of straw. The sun itself; or whatever device it was that circled the world to reflect sunlight upon it, was a small circle of chilli-pepper red, low in the east.

'It is beautiful here,' said Murphy. Sitting down again on the turf.

'It's mild,' agreed Vins.

'Does that mean that those old children's stories are true?' Murphy asked. 'About them, and messing up the climate, and just walking away?'

'Who knows?'

'But this is what bugs me,' said Murphy. 'If they had the – if they *have* the capacity to build whole new worlds, like this one, and provide it with a beautiful climate, you know, *why* not simply sort out the climate on Earth? Why not reach their godlike fingers into the ocean flow and the air-stream and dabble a bit and return the Earth to a temperate climate?'

Vins didn't answer this at first; didn't think it was really addressed to him. But Murphy wouldn't let it go.

'Left the mess and just ran away. Cold and snow and rain and deserts of broken rock. That's downright irresponsible. Why *not* mend the mess they'd made? Why not?'

'I suppose,' said Vins, reluctantly, 'it's easier to manage a model like this one. Even a large-scale model, like this one. The climate of the whole Earth – that's a chaotic system, isn't it? That's not a simple circular body of air a thousand miles across, that's a three-dimensional vortex tens of thousands of miles arc by arc. Big dumb object, he called it.'

'He?'

'Maybe they can't crack the problem of controlling chaotic systems, any more than we can. *He* is the *Homo sapiens* I met. When I said *he* called it that, I meant Ramon Harburg Guthrie called it that.'

'Doesn't sound very godlike at all.'

'No.'

'And doesn't excuse them from fleeing their mess.'

'I wasn't suggesting that it did.'

'And what *were* you suggesting?'

Vins coughed. 'I'll tell you – I'll say what I'm suggesting. Ramon Harburg Guthrie said that the elder *sapiens*, the wealthiest thousands, fled throughout the system. They built themselves little private utopias of all shapes and sizes. They're living there now, or their descendants are. But these should be *our* lands. Why would we struggle on with the wastelands and the ice – or,' and he threw his hands up, 'or Mars, for crying-in-the-wilderness, Mars?' He spoke as an individual who had lived two full terms on Mars: once during his compulsory military training and once during his scientific education. He knew whereof he spoke: the extraordinary cold, the barrenness, the slow and stubborn progress of colonisation. 'Why would we be trying to bully a life out of Mars, of all places, if the system is littered with private paradises like this one?'

'I like the cut of your jib, the shape of your thinking, young Vins,' said Murphy, saluting him and then shaking his hand. 'But what of the man who scratched your head, there? What of that bold *sapiens*-fellow himself?'

'He thinks he's hunting us,' said Vins. There was something near to sadness in his voice, a species of regret. 'He doesn't yet realise.' He pulled the gun out of the bag.

They sat for a while in silence. From time to time Murphy would go, 'Remind me what we're waiting for, here?' and Vins would explain it again.

'He'll come back,' he said. 'He'll get his skull bandaged, or get it healed-up with some high-tech magic-ray, I don't know. But he'll be back. He has to eliminate all four of us before we can put a message where others can hear it.'

'And shouldn't we be doing that? Putting the message out there for others to know where we are – to know that such a place as *here* even exists?'

'That would require us to stay . . .' prompted Vins.

'Stay in the shuttle,' said Murphy. 'I see. So you reckon he'll? You think he'll?'

'What would *you* do? He came before with some sort of personal flying harness, like a skyhook. And a handgun. He'll come back heavier. He'll hit the ship first, to shut that door firm.'

'But I guess we already tried the radio. Broadcast, I mean. But who'd be listening? Who'd be monitoring this piece of sky? Nobody.' He picked some bark from the bough and crumpled it to papery chards between his strong fingers. 'I suppose,' he continued, 'that this *Homo sapiens* feller, he's not to know how long we've been here. For all he knows we just crashed here, this morning. Or we've been here a month.'

'He'll have to take his chances,' agreed Vins. 'He'll come back and hammer the ship, smash and dint it into the dirt.'

'Then what?'

'There are several ways it could go. If he's smart, if he were as smart as me, he'd lay waste to the whole area. Me, I'd scorch the whole thousand-square-mile area.'

'But he lives here!'

'He lives on the other side. He don't need here. But he won't do that. He's attached to it, he's sentimentally connected with the landscape. Its beauty. With its vacuity and its possibility. He won't do that. So, *if* he's smart, he'll do the second-best option.'

'Which is what?'

'He'll wait until dark, and then overfly the area with the highest-power infrared detection he can muster. He'd pick out our body heat. Or, at least, it would be hard for us to disguise that.'

'You think he'll do that?'

Vins bared his teeth, and then sealed his lips again. 'No, I don't think so. He'll want to hunt us straight down. He'll blow the ship and then come galloping down these paths we've trailed through the long grass. He'll try to hunt us down. He'll have armour on, probably. Big guns. He'll have big guns with fat barrels.'

'Other people? Other *sapiens*?'

'That,' said Vins, 'is the real question. That's the crucial thing. He called this world *Me*-topia. Does that suggest to you, Murphy, a solitary individual, living perhaps with a few upgraded cats and dogs, maybe a Metal Mickey or two?'

'I've no notion.'

'Or does it suggest a population of a thousand *sapiens*, or a hundred thousand, living in the clean open spaces on the far side of this disc – living a medieval Europe, perhaps. Riding around dressed in silk and hunting the white stag?'

'I've really no notion.'

'And neither have I. That'll be what we find out.'

'You're a regular stra*te*gos,' said Murphy, and he whistled through his two front teeth. 'A real strategic thinker. You're wasted in the sciences, you are. And then?'

'Then?'

'Then what?'

'Well,' said Vins. 'That'll depend, of course. If it's just him, I don't see why we don't take the whole place to ourselves. There's a lot of fertile ground here, a lot of settlement potential for people back home. And if it's more than just him—'

'Maybe the far side is crawling with *Homo sapiens*.'

'Maybe it is. But *this* side isn't. We could pile our own people onto this side of the world and see what happens. See if we can arrive at an understanding. Who knows? That's a long way in the future.' He peered through the leaves at the lustre of the meadows, the beaming waters, the warm blue sky.

Murphy dozed, and was not woken by the brittle sound of something scratching along the sky, a craft in flight. But he *was* awoken by the great basso profundo *whumph* of the shuttle exploding; a monstrous booming; a squat egg-shaped mass of fire that mottled and clouded almost at once with its own smoke, and pushed a stalk of black up and out into an umbrella-shape in the sky. Some moments later the tree shook heartily. After that there was the random percussion and thud of bits of wreckage slamming back to earth.

Murphy almost fell out of the tree. Vins had to grab him.

Their ship was a crater now, and a scattering pattern of gobbets of plasmetal flowing into the sky at forty-five degrees and crashing down again to earth at forty-five degrees, the petal-pattern all around the central destruction.

'Look,' Vins hissed.

A ship, shaped like the sleek head of a greyhound, flew through, banked, and landed a hundred yards from the crater. It ejected a single figure, and lifted off again.

The sound of the explosion was still rumbling in the air.

'Was that our ship?' said Murphy, stupidly. 'Did he just destroy our—'

'Shush, now,' said Vins, in a low voice. 'That's him.'

'Then who's flying the ship?'

'It'll be another *sapiens*, or else an automatic system, that hardly matters. The ship will circle back there, in case Edwards or Sinclair are nearby and come running out to see what the noise is. But *he'll* come after us. He knows I won't be fooled by—' And even as Vins was speaking the figure, armoured like an inflated thing, like a man made of tyres, turned its head, and selected one of the trails through the grass and starting trotting along it.

'That's a big gun he's carrying,' Murphy pointed out. 'He's coming this way with a very big gun.'

'He's coming this way,' said Vins, taking the pistol out of his sack and prepping it, 'with his eggshell skull and his sluggy reactions.'

'What are you going to do?' asked Murphy.

'Do you think he'll look upwards as he comes under this tree?'

'*I* don't know.'

'Don't you?'

'And if you kill him, what then?'

'I hope not to kill him, not to kill him straight off,' said Vins, in a scientific voice. 'I'll need him to get that plane to come down so we can use it.'

He was coming down the path. Vins and Murphy waited in the tree, waiting for him to pass beneath them – or for him to notice them, the two of them, in the tree and shoot them down.

He was armoured of course. He came closer.

Maybe that's the way it goes. It's hard for me to be, from this perspective, sure. Indeed it's hard, sometimes, to tell the difference between the two different sorts of human. These Neanderthals, after all, are not created *ex nihilo* via some genetically engineered miracle. They were ordinary *sapiens* adapted and enhanced, strengthened, given more endurance, the better to carry on living on their home world. Wouldn't you like greater strength, more endurance? Of course you would. You stay-at-home, you. Sentimentally attached to where you happen to be, that's you. The same people as the *sapiens*. Does it matter if they come swarming all over Guthrie's bubblewrapped world? Is that a better, or a worse, eventuality to that place remaining the rich man's private fiefdom?

It's all lotos.

The seventh day

The sun rose in the west, as it always did. Clouds clung about the lower reaches of the sky like the froth on the lip of a gigantic ceramic bowl: white and frothy and stained hither and thither with touches of cappuccino brown.

The grasslands rejoiced in the touch of the sun. I say *rejoiced* in the strong sense of the word. Light passed through reality filters. Wind passed *over* the shafts of grass, moving them, pausing, moving again; but light passed *through* them. Wind made a lullaby song of hushes, and then paused to make even more eloquent moments of silence. But the light shone right through. Light passed through *two* profound reality filters. This is photons. These are photons. Photons were always already rushing faster than mass from the surface of the sun. They were passing through a hunk of crystal in the sky, modified with various other minerals and smart-patches, and were deflected onto the surface of the world. This globe served the world as its illumination. The photons passed again through the slender sheaths of green and yellow, those trillions of close-fitting rubber bricks we call cells; cells stacked multiply-layered and rippled out in all directions, gathered into superstructures of magnificent length and fragility; and in every single cell the light chanced through matter and came alive, alive, with the most vibrant and exhilarating and ecstatic thrumming of the spirit. The light, the translucence of matter, the inflection of the photons, the grass singing. That's where it's at.

playout groove

Paul is dead man miss him miss him Paul is dead man miss him miss him Paul is dead man miss him miss him Paul is dead man miss him miss him Paul

'Adam Robots' first appeared in Pete Crowther (ed), *We Think, Therefore We Are* (2009); 'Shall I Tell You the Problem With Time Travel?' first appeared in Ian Whates (ed), *Solaris Rising* (2011); 'A Prison Term of a Thousand Years' first appeared in *Postscripts #17* (2008); 'Thrownness' first appeared in Pete Crowther and Nick Gevers (eds), *The New And Perfect Man* (2011); 'The *Mary Anna*' first appeared in Tony C. Smith (ed), *StarShipSofa Vol. 2* (2010); 'The Chrome Chromosome' first appeared in Ken McLeod (ed), *The Human Genre Project* (2009); 'The Time Telephone' first appeared in *Infinity Plus* (2002); 'S-Bomb' first appeared in Shveta Verma and Sean Miller (eds), *Riffing on Strings: Creative Writing Inspired by String Theory* (2008); 'Dantean' first appeared in *Swiftly: Stories* (Nightshade 2004); 'ReMorse®' first appeared in Ian Whates (ed), *dis-LOCATIONS* (2007); 'Woodpunk' first appeared in George Mann (ed), *The Solaris Book of New Science Fiction Vol. 3* (2009); 'The Cow' first appeared in *Europrogocontestovision* (2010); 'The Imperial Army' first appeared in Paul Fraser (ed), *Spectrum* (2002); 'And tomorrow and' first appeared in Stephen Saville and Alethea Kontis (eds), *Elemental: the Tsunami Relief Anthology. Stories of Science Fiction and Fantasy* (2006); 'The Man of the Strong Arm' first appeared in Ian Whates (ed), *Celebration* (2008); 'Wonder: A Story in Two' first appeared in James Holden and Simon King, *Conceptual Breakthrough: Two Experiments in SF Criticism: Star/Alien* (Inkerman Press 2007); 'Constellations' first appeared (as 'The Order of Things') in Pete Crowther (ed), *Constellations* (2005); 'Anticopernicus' was first published as a standalone novelette by Ancaster Book, 2010.

'Me-topia' first appeared in Pete Crowther (ed), *Forbidden Planets* (2006). 'Godbombing', 'Review: *Denis Bayle, a Life*', 'The World of the Wars' and 'The Woman Who Bore Death' are original to this collection.